PRAIS...
WICKED WOR...

"A charming and very ro... along the way. The ending puts a perfect cap on the story. I look forward to reading more books in this series to see what happens to some of my favorite supporting characters."
—Fresh Fiction

"Ah, l'amour. I adored this story and the wonderful hero and heroine, who shed all their inhibitions and fears in order to go on the most powerful journey they ever embarked on . . . falling in love."
—Smexy Books

"An exciting and sweet historical love story. It has everything that I look for in a good fairy-tale retelling while also tying back to Bradley's earlier books. I am really excited to see more of this series, particularly because of the out-of-control but still entertaining Worthington family."
—Feminist Fairy Tale Reviews

"A laugh-out-loud-funny novel from Celeste Bradley, the third in the Wicked Worthingtons series. Lighthearted but with a few profound moments, it is filled with deception, misunderstanding, exaggeration, cross-dressing, and mistaken identity."
—Harlequin Junkie

The Wicked Worthingtons Series

WHEN SHE SAID I DO
AND THEN COMES MARRIAGE
WITH THIS RING
I THEE WED

Wedded Bliss

The Wicked Worthingtons Series

CELESTE BRADLEY

JOVE
New York

A JOVE BOOK
Published by Berkley
An imprint of Penguin Random House LLC
375 Hudson Street, New York, New York 10014

Copyright © 2017 by Celeste Bradley
Penguin Random House supports copyright. Copyright fuels creativity, encourages
diverse voices, promotes free speech, and creates a vibrant culture. Thank you for buying
an authorized edition of this book and for complying with copyright laws by not
reproducing, scanning, or distributing any part of it in any form without permission.
You are supporting writers and allowing Penguin Random House to continue to
publish books for every reader.

A JOVE BOOK and BERKLEY are registered trademarks and the B colophon is a
trademark of Penguin Random House LLC.

ISBN: 9780451475985

First Edition: May 2017

Printed in the United States of America
1   3   5   7   9   10   8   6   4   2

Cover art by Alan Ayers
Book design by Kelly Lipovich

*This book is dedicated to
my dear friend Susan Donovan.*

Acknowledgments

I am grateful to so many people, I would need pages to acknowledge them all. To my friends, family, true love, leaders, inspirers, healers . . . you keep my world turning!

Chapter 1

So far, Morgan Pryce's wedding night was going swimmingly.

The woman on his lap was so soft and sumptuous that he entirely forgot his plans for retribution.

When he felt the hellfire burning beneath the cool perfection of her skin, he forgot about the salvation of his half brother, Neville. When she dug her fingers into his shoulders, wriggled her delicious bottom against his lap, and opened her hot, sweet mouth to him, he forgot the day of the month. He forgot the year. He forgot his own name.

In that moment, the honorable part of Morgan Pryce slipped away. Only the bastard remained.

And the bastard had been at sea a very long time.

There at the breakfast table of his London row house—more of a way station for a ship's captain than a true home—Morgan could not have cared less if the woman was wife, maiden, or harlot. She was woman, and he was man. They didn't need a bed. They didn't even need the floor. The chair would do just fine.

He was achingly hard and she was so . . . damned . . . soft.

"Bloody hell!" The icy prick of a steel blade nicked the tender underside of Morgan's jaw—his own damned dagger, if he was not mistaken. He dared not move.

Morgan opened his eyes to the knife-wielding vision of loveliness on his lap. She shook her blond head with prim disapproval, narrowed her blue eyes at him, and said, "Now, sir, while you might make a perfectly serviceable husband for someone, you simply won't do for me."

The captain had heard that marriage was never easy. Perhaps it was true, for his was proving far more challenging than he had predicted only hours before.

Chapter 2

"**W**HAT about what I want? Always such a good boy. Always doing as I'm told. So bloody careful never to offend!"

Lord Neville Danton, fourteenth Duke of Camberton, tossed back his whiskey with the awkward flair of the beginning drinker. He raised his arm to throw his fine crystal glass into the hearth, but hesitated at the last second. He placed it on the mantel instead. "Perhaps it's time someone worried about offending *me*!"

Morgan Pryce did not respond to his half brother's drunken rant. He remained stretched out in the large wingback chair by the hearth, toying with his favorite dagger, watching the firelight play upon the carved blade and jeweled handle.

Morgan knew Neville was a dedicated gentleman and scholar. The young duke took dutiful care of his lands and his people. He danced well, when he could bring himself to ask someone. He rode well, although horses made him sneeze. He shot well, though he preferred not to kill anything that had big, warm eyes or graceful wings. He spoke three languages and could read several more.

Poor Neville. He was quite right to itch beneath the burden of his responsibilities. Ever the good lad. Ever the good student.

Look at him now.

The thought of defying their uncle's wishes had driven Neville to seek courage in a bottle of whiskey. He'd found bitterness instead—a well of it, it seemed. It had accumulated over a lifetime of trying to perform beyond the expectations of others.

Morgan knew that if his half brother wasn't careful, the resentment would force his hand. It would push him into making a mistake. That, Morgan could not allow.

Ever since he'd been introduced to four-year-old Neville by their father, Morgan had felt achingly protective of his good-hearted, sensitive half brother. Their father, the duke, was a distant man with little interest in his sons. Morgan had needed Neville as much as Neville had needed him. Since the day he'd held that chubby hand as little Neville took him to the stables to show off some fat little birthday pony, the mantle of "big brother" had settled firmly upon Morgan's larger shoulders.

Half brother, their father had insisted, when he noticed their bond. "It's important you remember that, Morgan. He will be duke. You must never presume."

Morgan had understood that, had accepted it as only an idealistic youth could have. His role was that of protector, of loyal helper. He was his brother's keeper, there to help Neville, not the other way around.

Now Neville pounded his fist upon the mantel, unflinching when his flesh struck the stone. He whirled on his audience of one with fury in his eyes. "Well? Are you going to help me with this Bliss Worthington situation or not?"

Turning too quickly while drunk was never a good notion. Neville's face turned white. He staggered, as if he didn't know whether to stand or sit. The whiskey made the decision for him, and his legs collapsed.

Morgan put away his dangerous toy, slipping the dagger into a hidden sheath within his right boot. He stood and studied the duke, now sprawled on the carpet.

Neville blinked up at him. "Your boots are shiny. Did you know that? Shiny and black, with the turned-down top. I wish I were a ship captain and could wear those boots! Or a pirate! I would make a legendary one. Pirates have shiny boots, too, do they not?"

Although Neville was of matching height, Morgan had little trouble lifting him to his feet. He let the duke fall with somewhat more dignity into the chair by the fire.

"You came home just in time, you know." From his somewhat upright position, Neville nodded with satisfaction. "I knew I could count on you, my brother. I knew you would intervene if you understood the situation. You'll talk to Uncle Oliver, won't you? You'll help me with Bliss?"

Morgan did not answer. He'd already spoken with Oliver. He'd already made plans to intervene, and on this very night. Yes, he would help with Bliss. Yes, he would fix everything. Morgan would do what was best for his half brother in the long run.

"I can't do it," Neville murmured. "I cannot set Bliss Worthington aside just because Uncle Oliver doesn't approve." He blinked at the fire, his gaze fixed on the blue and gold flames dancing over the coals. "After all, it isn't as though there is anything wrong with the Worthington name. I know the family is a little odd. But I cannot help it. Ever since I was introduced to her at her cousin Elektra's wedding, I think of no one but her. She's so . . ." Neville trailed off, but then continued, waving his hand. "That golden hair, those eyes of sky, those—"

Neville's hands rose to map a figure in the air. His gaze lost focus.

Morgan lifted a skeptical brow. If those proportions were

accurate, Miss Bliss Worthington must indeed be the stuff of a lonely man's dream.

Neville, now clearly lost in the feminine hills and valleys contained in the imaginary cartography of his beloved, passed out.

Morgan observed the unconscious Duke of Camberton for a long moment. His half brother's limp body slithered down the fine leather, flopping over the chair arm like an unfettered marionette.

Morgan had been a young man once, too. He had dreamed of unlikely and unattainable things, just as Neville did. But when a man was a bastard instead of an heir, the unlikely remained just that, and the unattainable swung forever just out of reach.

Until he was needed. Until someone had a mission only a bastard could carry out. Suddenly, he became indispensable.

THE RAIN STRUCK sideways at the rickety Worthington carriage like a wet hand slapping at a pest.

Bliss Worthington was aware of the vibration of the storm against the elderly lacquered wood surrounding her. A bit of water dripped from the seams of the vehicle. The damp made the horsehair-stuffed cushions smell more mildewed than usual.

None of these things dug a single furrow into her determination. Not the midnight storm, not the plight of the poor carriage horses, not even concern for the driver up on his seat with only a slicker for protection.

"'Wishing clocks more swift,' dear?"

Bliss focused her gaze upon her aunt Iris, who sat across from her. Iris Worthington seemed as unperturbed by the horrid London weather as was Bliss. In fact, she seemed to be enjoying it. Iris always did like a bit of theater, even that of a natural variety.

"That's from *Winter's Tale*, pet. Act one, scene two."

"Yes, Aunt Iris. I know." Dear Iris. Bliss loved her, but if ever there was a more useless woman than Iris Worthington, Bliss had yet to meet her. Iris lived in a world filled with fantasy and drama and foggy perception. William Shakespeare was her constant companion.

Reality was not.

Which was precisely why Bliss had selected her dotty auntie as her coconspirator in this little plot.

To keep their vows hidden from Neville's uncle, Lord Oliver Danton, they had to keep the nuptials a secret. Aunt Iris did not count, for no one listened to her anymore. Flights of fancy poured from her lips on a daily basis.

If Lord Oliver learned of Bliss and Neville's plan to circumvent his silly objections to Bliss's suitability, he might do something drastic. Neville believed his uncle was only a bit of a snob. Bliss was not so sure. He seemed to be a very obstinate sort of man—one with his own notions of Neville's future. That future did not include Bliss. Therefore, it was best that they take matters into their own hands and present Lord Oliver with a firmly legal marriage he could do nothing about.

Hence, the late hour, the remote chapel, the fat bribe to the priest, and the easily influenced witness in Aunt Iris. Bliss had been a very busy bee for the last several weeks. Of course, she had made sure that Neville was fully informed of her plan—their plan!—by means of secret notes passed through a channel of trusted servants. It was a great deal of trouble arranging matters so furtively, but Bliss had always been good at making things just so.

The old carriage struck a pothole, jarring both ladies. Bliss clasped her gloved hands in her lap. She remained undeterred by the weather, or the time of night, or any other single thing. If the narrow London streets flooded, she would hop from the carriage and swim herself to the chapel.

After all, she was about to marry the man of her dreams! She smiled to herself. Darling Neville. He was handsome, in a youthful, bookish way. He was rich, which would be more pleasant than being poor. He was titled, although Bliss could honestly plead no interest in that.

No, it was Neville himself she preferred over all other men. At her cousin Elektra's wedding to Lord Aaron Arbogast, Bliss had picked Neville from the crowd of young, titled gentlemen guests at first look. His clean-cut, handsome appearance had caught her eye, but it was his temperament that had fixed her attention completely. His manner had been so congenial, so eager to please.

Further acquaintance had proven Bliss's first impression to be correct. Neville was gentle, and kind, and good-natured, and thoughtful. He was a good and fair master to his dependents and a most diligent landholder of his estates. As the Duke of Camberton, despite his mere twenty-seven years, he was beyond reproach.

Neville's scholarly bent did not dismay Bliss. She was quite accustomed to people who studied and read and piled books here, there, and everywhere. Worthington House was a riot of books and brilliance and the occasional accidental explosion. It was an exciting existence.

However, Bliss was through with excitement. Neville's propensity toward quiet reading would be positively refreshing.

Bliss knew that Neville adored her right back. As well he should. Her appearance was quite fetching, she'd been told, and her figure registered on the riveting side of generous. She was fashionable without being intimidating, and her taste was impeccable. She was patient and even-tempered, yet intelligent. She would make an outstanding duchess and an exemplary wife. These were the simple facts.

She'd never been terribly romantic, another way she differed from her Worthington cousins. That didn't mean she minded the notion of pursuing the upcoming pleasures of marriage with her handsome husband.

With a slight easing of her perfect posture, she leaned back into the musty cushions with a delicate sigh. The storm was slowing her progress toward her future, which was unacceptable. Yet she refused to become frustrated. With each grudging clop of the horses' hooves, she grew closer to the moment that would change everything.

Neville had become duke at the age of twelve. The great responsibility had made him dedicated and painstaking, and best of all, predictable.

In contrast, Bliss grew up in the sheep-infested county of Shropshire in the care of a foster mother. Her parents continued their exciting, separate lives in London. All her life, she had lived day to day, never knowing when her father or mother might come. Weeks or months or years passed before a fine carriage would jingle down the country lane to Mrs. Dalyrymple's cottage. A footman would leap from the top seat and flip out a small folding step and hand down either a veiled and silk-clad woman or a stout and silk-clad man.

Mama and Papa were darlings, and of course their lives were busy and important, but to wait, and wait, and everloving wait! Then of course, they would arrive while she was elbow-deep in stove black, or disheveled and sticky from berrying, or worse, in the middle of a good book! Very early on, Bliss learned that the best thing was to remain "just so" at all times, always perfectly presentable, just in case.

In short, she had spent her entire life waiting for someone to come home.

Now she was in London at last, and had been residing for months with the dear Worthington clan. The family had accepted her easily, had absorbed her into their numbers with careless generosity, then proceeded to go about their business, flowing around her like a river around a stone. Bliss was welcome, but not really necessary to anyone's happiness.

Neville made her feel that she was wanted at last. Better still, Neville didn't care for travel. Long carriage rides made him ill. Neville wanted to stay home and study his butterfly collection and sit in his study to write long letters to naturalists around the world.

For the rest of her life, Bliss would always know precisely where Neville was. Like a beetle stuck to her board with the pin of matrimony, he would never leave her all alone.

No more lonely waiting. Ever again.

Chapter 3

B LISS and Iris entered the small Anglican chapel on the outskirts of London. It was an unimportant, unfashionable area, far from Camberton House and Neville's interfering uncle. The priest was already standing before the cloth-draped altar with his Bible in his hands.

For some reason, the priest did not seem as familiar to Bliss as she thought he would be. True, she'd spoken to him only once, a month ago, when she secured his silence with a purseful of gold and a demure flutter of her lashes. But in the light of a single candelabra set near the door, he looked older and smaller than she recalled. At some point during the past weeks, it seemed he had somehow lost most of his teeth as well. Still, he stood attired in his satin surplice and only slightly dingy robe. He did look a bit dull and sleepy, the poor man.

Bliss supposed one should expect that with a secret midnight wedding. There were no other guests, no other witnesses. Bliss's walk down the aisle would go unseen by anyone but stained-glass saints and shadows. That was a price she would gladly pay to prevent Lord Oliver from keeping her from her destiny!

Bliss lifted her chin. No matter if the occasion was not perfect. The ceremony was but a moment. Afterward, she and Neville would be free to celebrate for the rest of their lives.

A hush had descended upon the dim chapel, a hush that had nothing to do with the muffling effect of the pouring rain outside. Secrets, it seemed, were best told in whispers. Bliss found herself treading softly, as if she could keep Lord Oliver from hearing her hesitant step miles away.

At her side, Aunt Iris began to hum the wedding march beneath her breath. When Bliss shot her a startled glance, Aunt Iris only smiled and patted the hand tucked into her elbow.

"Dum-dum-de-dum . . ."

When Bliss and Iris had progressed halfway down the aisle, a tall, dark form stepped from the shadows behind the priest. Bliss felt something relax in her shoulders.

Neville.

Didn't he seem dashing and mysterious, with the hood of his rain cloak covering his head? The flickering candlelight made him seem quite looming. Even the silence lent the entire proceedings a sinister tone.

Which was rubbish. She was overreacting. After all, she herself had retained her cloak, for the chapel was damp and chill. And while she would have liked a few more candles, it seemed a petty thing to complain about. Dim and damp was merely dim and damp. There was no reason to wax theatrical!

Aunt Iris gave a delicious shiver. "My, it's a dungeon in here. You are like a traitorous princess, walking to the guillotine!" Her stage whisper would be quite audible to the men standing before the altar, even over the hiss and rumble of the storm.

Bliss sighed. Trust Iris to dramatize a dreary room and

a musty draft. And seeing dear inoffensive Neville as an executioner? Flagrant silliness! Although he was quite tall, Neville's guileless blue eyes and diffident manner made him most congenial.

She could barely see his face as he half turned to watch her walk down the aisle toward him. Though shadowed by his hood and only dimly lit by the candles, she knew him by the silhouetted planes of his dear face and the tilt of his head.

So why did her belly flip like a fearful fish in a too-small pool of water? Perhaps Aunt Iris's overactive imagination was contagious.

Then Neville turned his back once more to await her at the altar. With a squeeze of her hand, Bliss signaled Aunt Iris to hurry them along. Tradition was all well and good, but this slow ceremonial walk was of little use without an audience!

When Iris swept her up to the altar and deposited her there with a sigh of a job well done, Bliss found herself a bit breathless. When Iris stepped back, Bliss felt colder than before.

You adore Neville. Neville adores you. You will be most happy together.

And you will never be alone again.

With a brisk twitch of her skirts and a pat to her dampened hair, she lifted the bouquet of dahlias to her bosom and smiled at the priest.

"Erm . . . Dress . . . Bread Eye?" The priest yawned.

No, not a single tooth remained. It seemed his diction had suffered as a result.

Neville stepped closer to stand with Bliss. His damp cloak carried a trace of faraway places and salt water, wafting past her senses like a distant memory. She shook the curious notion from her mind, ready to focus upon the priest who would bind their two separate souls into one. This was a sacred occasion. Bliss refused to allow a storm, a dotty

auntie, or an interfering uncle to delay this ceremony for
one more instant!

"I am ready." More than ready. She fixed her gaze upon
the priest. Her most ardent desire was about to become her
reality!

"Beer Blood, see Goatherd Togger . . ." The priest began
to drone, his weary mumble barely audible over the storm.
Bliss found herself distracted.

There was a leak in the chapel roof. Upon the pulpit
directly behind the priest, rain dripped down from the high
arched ceiling into a dented pewter chalice. Each drop
struck the chalice with the force of a hammer, sending an
annoying *clang* through the mostly empty chapel.

The cold night air made Bliss tug her cloak tighter. She
could hardly feel the hand that held the trembling bouquet,
despite the perfect fit of her fine kid gloves. Perhaps she
ought to have traded her dainty undergarments for woolen
ones—but one had such hopes for one's wedding night!

Apparently, the priest had just dispensed with the pre-
liminaries and began the vows. Bliss tried to pay attention,
she truly did, but the old man garbled and yawned so. She
could scarcely attend him over the roar of the rain, the rumble of thunder, and the incessant pinging of water-to-chalice.
Instead, her senses fixed upon Neville at her side. Which
was odd, because as dear as Neville was, one would never
consider him fascinating. Sweet, charming, pleasant . . .
comfortable, yes.

Riveting, no.

Yet at the moment, Bliss found herself decidedly uncom-
fortable. The thick shoulder that brushed her own provided
the only warm spot on her body. Heat seemed to radiate
from his big male presence like a pile of glowing coals.
Again, the scent of wild air teased at her senses, bringing
to mind exotic spices or perhaps stormy seas . . .

Neville became seasick in a rowboat on a pond. It had to
be the rain. Perhaps the dampness had brought out the tang

of old incense from the ancient stones. Or perhaps Iris had switched out her customary rosewater for something more unusual.

"Blister China Worrisome—"

Bliss blinked at the priest. He was speaking to her, apparently, though he mangled her name so that she barely recognized it. He raised his bleary eyes at her, waiting.

"Bliss Regina Worthington," she corrected politely. "I will." She didn't think the vows required much else.

Neville shifted at her voice. Had she not sounded thrilled enough? It was late and she was cold and the storm was worsening outside, the rain drowning out the priest's next words.

A great crack of thunder rattled the chapel. Bliss wasn't one to fear a storm, but she found herself startled into reaching for Neville's arm. Her fingers dug into a muscular biceps.

Oh my.

Neville must have been taking exercise! Poor dear, did he imagine that she didn't find him pleasing? His lanky form was just fine with her. Besides, she had great confidence that he would fill out someday. Then she recalled her own decision on the lacy underthings. Everyone wanted to please their newlywed spouse, did they not?

She gave his arm a comforting pat as she released it.

The chalice had filled and now overflowed onto the embroidered parament beneath it. Bliss twitched away the compulsion to clean up the water pooling at the base of the altar.

"More Than Rice. Duty Big Swimming Table . . ."

Bliss was swept with an entirely inappropriate desire to laugh. Iris was already giggling away behind her.

"I will." Neville's voice was deep and husky.

What a pity! Her inattention had caused her to miss the priest reading Neville his vows. It seemed all memories of her wedding ceremony would be categorized as "dim," "dripping," or "garbled"! But again, this was a mere moment of her life, one that hereafter would provide her with a lifetime of Neville's gentle companionship. She pasted a pleasant smile upon her lips.

Almost there.

"Gumption and Strife!" the priest intoned with enough energy to be heard over the rain, then shut his book.

Husband and wife.

Suddenly, it was done.

From her place in the front pew, Iris clapped her hands together in delight. Bliss allowed herself to relax at last. The priest gestured to the table where the marriage contract lay awaiting their signatures. Bliss hurried to delicately inscribe her full name, Bliss Regina Worthington.

As she stepped back to allow Neville his turn, Bliss felt the warmth of accomplishment infuse her. She no longer cared one little bit about the cold and wet. She had achieved the impossible. All her secret notes to Neville, all her detailed arrangements and generous bribes to servants, everything she had done had borne fruit.

She was now Lady Danton, Duchess of Camberton. She leaned forward with a smile to watch Neville sign his name below hers in a broad, scrawling hand: *Morgan Pryce*.

What?

She blinked against the dimness and peered at the contract.

Her eyes had not deceived her. Thoroughly confused, she turned to look up into Neville's hooded features.

She saw Neville's jaw and cheekbone. She saw Neville's dark hair and dark blue eyes. Yet the man who glared back at her was a complete and total stranger. Older. Harder.

Morgan Pryce.

More Than Rice.

"Who are *you*?" she breathed, her voice a horrified whisper.

The handsome not-Neville glared down at her. "I am your husband, Mrs. Pryce. Neville is now safe from your grasping ways. Happy day to us both!"

Chapter 4

OUTSIDE, the storm clouds had blown away, and the chapel was illuminated by the moon's pale glow. The last dark wisps sped past the waxing moon. Morgan helped his new aunt-in-law into the rickety Worthington carriage. The woman gave a cheerful wave as he shut the carriage door. She seemed unaware that anything untoward had occurred. Morgan decided the carriage itself was a rolling act of neglect, and took care not to pound too hard on its side as he signaled the driver. His fist made a strange slushy sound against the waterlogged wood.

Iris Worthington leaned out of her window to blow her niece a kiss. "Have a lovely wedding night, dearest! Remember, it's perfectly fine to say naughty words in the marriage bed! *Bon nuit!*"

Then she was gone, rattling away down the cobbles. There remained nothing visible but a voluminous lacy handkerchief waving good-bye. In his mind, Morgan calculated that the carriage would last another twenty minutes before disintegrating from wood rot. It would not be Neville's coffers that would pay for a new one, thanks to Uncle Oliver's well-plotted rescue.

Although Morgan had never met the Worthingtons, he had heard of them. Mostly it was the Worthington men who made the gossip sheets—and by association, their ladyloves. Even in far-flung ports, the local British transplants delighted in rumors about their homeland, and the Worthingtons seemed to be a very juicy source of tittle-tattle.

Surely the feminine apples didn't fall far from the wicked tree. Lord Oliver certainly seemed to believe that.

Morgan turned to examine his new bride. He hadn't managed a good look at her in the dim candlelight of the chapel. She now stood in the light of the moon, an enigmatic figure in her white wool cloak and hood. Then she raised two delicate, gloved hands and pushed her hood back.

Bloody hell.

Bliss Worthington was beautiful. In the moonlight, her fair hair shimmered white. Those "eyes of sky" that Neville had carried on about had gone silver and otherworldly. She turned that eerie gaze upon Morgan, causing an inexplicable shiver to run up his spine.

Morgan turned his grunt of surprise into a menacing clearing of his throat. Of course she was attractive. Neville might be young, but he had excellent taste. It seemed that while liberating his half brother from the clutches of a fortune hunter, Morgan had netted himself a truly stunning wife.

She parted her entrancing lips. "I appreciate your seeing Aunt Iris safely home, but may I inquire where I am going, if not with her?"

Morgan let his lip curl. "We are well and truly married, Mrs. Pryce. You will accompany your husband wherever he sees fit."

She tilted her head. "I see. May I assume that Neville is well and that he is not bound and gagged in some cellar?"

Her calm demeanor surprised him. He reminded himself to believe nothing this manipulative creature did or said.

She had seduced a naive young man into believing himself in love. She had then tried to bully him into a secret marriage, despite the concerns of his family.

Morgan had read the notes Uncle Oliver had intercepted from Miss Bliss Worthington and kept from Neville. Neville, although he pined for this wayward creature, knew nothing of this overwrought plan. Morgan was aware that every bit of this night was her idea and hers alone. If he hadn't arrived home in time to commandeer her plot, she might have eventually succeeded!

Morgan had nothing to be ashamed of. His trickery bordered on heroic, in his mind. Saving Neville from a disastrous marriage was reward enough. No one needed to know that Lord Oliver had sweetened the deal considerably.

It was not gold that Morgan desired. There was only one lure that could have tempted him to dismiss his satisfactory bachelorhood without rancor. His own ship. Captain-owner of the *Selkie Maid*, free and clear. Such a prize was well worth the burden of a grasping wife! He had saved Neville and his own loyal crew in one simple act of subterfuge.

So why did he feel a twist of guilt in his belly and a flush of shame rise up the back of his neck? At best this woman was a social-climbing fraud. At worst, she qualified as a confidence trickster of the highest order.

Liar. Scheming little tart. Yet despite his scorn, he found himself reacting to her as if she were the lady she purported to be. He answered her question.

"Neville is at home, quietly passed out from drink. I bribed your priest to go on his way and brought in a man guaranteed to follow orders."

"As incomprehensibly as possible, yes?"

"A fortunate arrangement."

She shook her head. "'Gumption and Strife,' indeed."

Morgan lifted his chin and straightened. "I could not allow my brother to throw his future away upon a common fortune hunter!"

She blinked her wide, strange eyes at him. "What fortune hunter is that?"

Her tone was breathless and sincere, as if she truly had no idea. Morgan restrained an outright sneer. "That miscreant is you, Miss Worthington!"

"I thought my name was Mrs. Pryce." She looked down while she tugged at her gloves and he thought he saw a slight smile form upon her lips. "I can see how one might think—"

Her smile infuriated him. "I think you have been entirely defeated this night," he reminded her. "You can never have a place at Neville's side now."

Morgan knew his temper caused large, barbaric sailors to cringe before him. Yet this female remained unaffected. She only frowned at him with a quizzical wrinkle between her eyebrows. Her gaze held the cool flavor of a disapproving governess. Boyhood conditioning almost prompted Morgan to apologize on the spot. Then his anger swelled once more to the fore. He stepped in closer, menacing her with intent. "So, Mrs. Pryce, you will hoist your greedy arse into that carriage and go home with your husband, where you belong!"

MR. PRYCE HAD a hired carriage that was waiting outside the chapel, presumably the carriage in which he had arrived. Bliss took his hand to ascend the steps but kept the contact brief.

He disturbed her. What was it about him? Was it that he looked rather like Neville, but a brawnier, more dangerous version? Or was it that he was a stranger who had intentionally foiled her plans for happiness? Either way, it would be highly impractical to stand on the street in the middle of the night to discuss it. Thus, she agreed when he suggested they retire to his home.

She wasn't afraid of him. For all his swagger, he did not have the air of someone who preyed on others. Neville spoke of him often and always with glowing admiration. In fact,

Neville idolized Morgan and always referred to him as "brother." The words "bastard" or "by-blow" were never uttered. Furthermore, Neville seemed to believe that Morgan returned his esteem.

At any rate, Mr. Pryce's illegitimate birth did not concern Bliss. She was confident she could sort out this entire mess in short order, and did not intend to stay wedded to him one second longer than required to secure an annulment. If he wished, he could prevent that. She must make sure that he would not. Getting the Church to agree was another matter. Still, she felt confident she could manage it once she had Mr. Pryce's agreement.

The carriage began moving as soon as Mr. Pryce had settled in his seat across from her. She had not managed to hear the address he had given the driver, but it didn't matter. She would find out soon enough.

How odd to think she had been so looking forward to meeting the man whom Neville so admired! And here she was, wedded to him, alone with him, and going toward his—their!—domicile. It occurred to Bliss that perhaps she ought to have left with Aunt Iris. But her sole focus was to learn what could have driven Mr. Pryce into sabotaging her nuptials, and to undo it.

She gazed at him as he sat across from her in the dark carriage. The moon's emergence in the rain-washed sky gave them some light. Yet Mr. Pryce, perhaps suitably, sat in shadow.

Bliss folded her hands in her lap and cleared her throat. "Sir, I—"

"I am no sir, so if you must address me, you may address me as 'Captain.'"

"Very well. Captain Pryce, I would like to know how you came to be standing in the chapel tonight instead of your brother."

"Half brother. The Duke of Camberton and I share only a father."

He called Neville his half brother? Bliss filed that fact away under Useful Knowledge. "Do you plan to continue to correct me, or is it possible you might soon answer my question?"

She could not see him, but she heard him shift in his seat. Excellent.

Bliss was well aware that the world saw her as mild-mannered. In fact, she cultivated that air of placid composure. It served as a useful cover for her ruthless patience. In all her life, no one had yet managed to outwait her, outlast her, or outplot her. She doubted that this Captain Pryce would provide any challenge whatsoever.

She knew Neville's half brother was a sea captain. It followed, then, that he was adventurous and fond of acts of daring. After all, what could be more audacious than sailing the vast seas in a fragile wooden vessel? In her experience, those who sought danger attended poorly to the arts of patience and planning.

He had already ruined one plan of hers. Yet a Worthington remained agile in thought and purpose at all times. She needed a new plan.

He let out a breath. "Your letters were intercepted. Neville has neither received nor answered any of your manipulative notes."

To hide her reaction, Bliss looked down at her hands in her lap. Neville had never agreed to wed her?

She resolutely decided to believe that he would eagerly do so, given the chance. "I see. Yet I adore Neville. Neville adores me. How do you think he will react when he learns of your trickery?"

The man across from her shifted once again, straightening in his seat. His movement disturbed the air and brought the warm scent of India spices and the tang of salt water to her senses once more. At the same moment, she realized that although Mr. Pryce sat in shadow, she herself was entirely illumined in moonlight. Ah. Confusion to the enemy. Men did tend to become somewhat more simpleminded when bosoms entered the arena. She began to tug at the knotted ties of her cloak.

"I'm sure he will come to understand . . . eventually." The way he cleared his throat belied that assurance. "The Duke of Camberton is no longer your concern, Mrs. Pryce. He is now your half brother as well."

That would not do at all. Perhaps it was time to attack. "Do you always answer a question with an unrelated statement of fact?"

He didn't hesitate. "Do you always propose to marry men you don't know in the middle of the night in secret?"

"Neville and I have been acquainted for several months. He is a dear friend to my cousin Elektra's husband. They went to school together." She continued to tug at her cloak ties, as if fretted. "I would say it is you who does not know him, for you to shatter his dreams of happiness with lies and subterfuge."

He snarled at that. "Such accusations from a confidence trickster such as yourself! After all, you schemed to advance from a country nobody to a duchess in a single Season. I could almost applaud your ambition if not for the fact that you turned your avarice toward a member of my family. You are nothing but a—"

Bliss gave her cloak ties a last stealthy yank. The heavy damp wool fell away with a sodden rustle.

Captain Pryce stopped speaking.

MORGAN WAS TRYING valiantly not to swallow his tongue. Good God, she was breathtaking.

Over the past half hour, Morgan had forced himself to become accustomed to the lovely face and the shimmering hair. He ought to have been ready for the rest of her.

And yet he found himself most unprepared.

She had the figure of a goddess—and no trifling, insipid marble goddess one might place in one's foyer. No, this woman was a goddess of some primitive culture inclined to the worship of generous bosoms.

Morgan had to admit to a personal preference of his own in that area, and the vision of her luscious breasts, captured most demurely in a shimmering lace bodice, rising and falling in the moonlight, was most disconcerting.

Oh, that figure! Over his pounding pulse, Morgan recalled how a drunken Neville had outlined an overly curvaceous female shape in the air.

The boy had been spot-on.

Morgan looked away from the temptress who sat no more than an arm's length from him.

His *wife.*

Beautiful, delectable wife, at that.

Lying, manipulative wife.

It was possible that he had taken on more than he was prepared for. Then again, he intended to remain in port for only a matter of days. Now, with his mission accomplished and the imminent transfer of title to the *Selkie Maid* to his name, a fortnight at the most.

At the moment, his brooding silence seemed to make no impact on her. She perched on the cushions as if she sat upon a throne.

Morgan felt a childish urge to order the driver to gallop to disrupt her poise. But although he had no sympathy or concern for her comfort, he did try not to be a complete arse most of the time.

Besides, her figure would no doubt jiggle enticingly in the moonlight. It would not do to arrive at his house aroused.

He'd been far too long at sea. He ought to get himself to Mrs. Blythe's House of Pleasure forthwith!

You are a married man. Married. Forever. With vows and all.

Morgan smiled sourly to himself. Vows meant a great deal to him, unfortunately.

He had made a few dubious decisions in his career as a

ship's captain for the White Rose shipping fleet. Necessary, sometimes, but traveling on the knife edge of underhanded. After years of shading both sides of the fine line of honor, a moment had struck when he had to make a decision to either cross that line, and become a different sort of man, or step away from it forever.

At that moment, Morgan had decided enough was enough.

A bastard might be many things, and Morgan was most of them, but while he had breath in his body, he could still choose to be a man of his word.

And he had just given his word to cleave to this woman only, now and forever. Well, if that wasn't just perfect. His choices were this faithless vixen, or an eternity of monkish celibacy.

He closed his eyes against his new bride's spectacular beauty and let this morning's conversation roll through his mind.

"It is for his own good," Lord Oliver had insisted. "That criminal female has dazzled him to blindness! If Neville knew of this secret wedding, I don't doubt that he would agree at once!"

Fresh off his ship, Morgan had run a hand through his overlong hair, and considered his half brother's predicament. "Why do you not simply expose her efforts?"

"I believe she would only try again in some other manner, one which I might not discover in time. The only way to remove her permanently from Neville's ardor is to, in effect, turn her into his sister."

Morgan had to admit that his uncle had conceived a clever solution. The Worthington woman would be as forbidden to Neville as a sibling. Even if Morgan died and left her a widow, English law prohibited a widow from wedding her late husband's brother.

And it wasn't as though he, Morgan, cared about marriage one way or the other. His life was at sea. If he had a wife, she would remain in England where he would scarcely ever see her.

Morgan had hesitated as he mulled over his uncle's words. Then Oliver offered the one thing Morgan desired in all the world.

"If you do your brother this kindness, I will reward your commitment to the good of the family by granting you full owner's status on the *Selkie Maid*."

Morgan had been thunderstruck. To be sure, he was the most successful captain in the fleet and had made enormous profit for the concern. Yet Lord Oliver had always withheld the reward of ownership.

Morgan knew that in truth, the Duke of Camberton owned the fleet, and that was now Neville. The former duke, Morgan and Neville's father, had begun the White Rose fleet with a single ship won in a card game. According to family legend, he had handed over the ship to his younger brother with a laugh and an offer. "Make a profit in a year's time, and I'll buy you another one."

Young Oliver had taken his ship, and his next ship, and the one after that. He had turned the White Rose into the most profitable concern in the vast network of the Camberton wealth.

Morgan could understand why Lord Oliver felt himself to be the sole proprietor of the fleet. But the fact remained that the ships were gained with the duke's gold, and they belonged to Neville.

Morgan had often considered making his case to Neville himself. He was sure his younger half brother would have granted him a ship. But it would have led to a confrontation between Neville and Lord Oliver.

And Neville had never been one for confrontation.

So there it was. Morgan had saved Neville and now would have his own ship. And, apparently, his own bride as well.

It was worth it.

He only wished he knew what to do with her.

Chapter 5

At Worthington House, candlelight warmed the book-littered drawing room, giving the worn, shabby furnishings a homey charm they never managed to achieve in full daylight. Iris entered with her usual dramatic style. "Hello, my darlings! Oh, what a *night*! The wedding was *so* exciting!"

Atalanta Worthington bit down upon her lip in anticipation. If her mother's flamboyant gestures were any indication, her tale should be wildly entertaining.

As usual, the entire Worthington clan had gathered together after a late dinner, scattered about on sofas, hassocks, and armchairs, sipping tea or brandy into the wee small hours. Even Attie, the youngest, was never told to go to bed and often read until dawn.

Daedalus, Attie's eldest brother, did not bother to look up from his evening newssheet. "Yes, Iris. I'm sure it was." Dade turned a page, scanning the print.

"Oh, indeed! The *secret* wedding included a *secret*

groom!" Iris sighed dreamily. "Shakespeare himself would have found it riveting!"

Castor shot an exasperated look at his eldest brother, then rose to greet his mother with a kiss on the cheek. "And what secret wedding would that be, Iris?"

Castor's wife, Miranda, smiled wearily from her chair where she engaged in the eternal jiggling of little eight-week-old Aurora, who had been born a true Worthington and never slept a night through.

Attie didn't much pity her sister-in-law, however, as all the Worthingtons did their fair share of baby jiggling.

"Was the wedding from a play?" That was Attie's father, Archie, looking up from his book and perking up his ears. "I don't recall any of Shakespeare's plays with both a secret wedding and a secret groom!"

"Oh, it was vastly better than a play!" Iris fairly swooned onto the sofa next to her husband. "The *drama* of it all! A shadowy chapel, a stormy night, a leaky roof, and a mysterious, cloaked stranger waiting at the altar!"

Attie looked askance at her mother. "Neville couldn't be mysterious if he tried," she stated flatly.

That got Dade's attention. "Neville? As in 'the Duke of Camberton' Neville?" He laid his newssheet down on a table. "Neville was in a play about a secret wedding? In a storm? Under a leaky roof?"

Attie snuggled her bottom deeper into the hassock on which she perched. This was going to be most diverting. And here she'd worried she would have to set fire to something in order to dispel her boredom.

"Bliss eloped with Neville tonight," Iris sang out.

"What?"

"Oh my heavens!"

"But how?"

Amid the general outcry of disbelief and confusion—which Aurora exacerbated by wailing loudly at the noise—Iris only smiled mysteriously.

She beamed down at Attie. "You knew, didn't you?"

Attie nodded. She might have been the youngest Worthington, but she was no slacker when it came to the gathering of information.

Iris pinched gently at the tip of Attie's nose. "Aren't you a clever little pickle!"

Attie leaned upon her mother's knee. "I know everything." How bothersome to have repeatedly explain that to everyone. As if a thirteen-year-old girl couldn't be a genius!

Iris waggled one finger at Attie. "But did you know it wasn't Neville at all up there at the altar? When the vows were done, he pushed back the hood of his cloak to reveal"—Iris paused for dramatic effect—"the Bastard of Camberton!"

Attie's jaw dropped. Castor's jaw dropped. Dade went completely ashen, then gradually began to turn a bit purple.

In contrast, the Worthington patriarch blinked vaguely. "Neville portrayed a bastard?" He pondered the ceiling for a moment. "That wholesome lad? Sounds like a bit of poor casting, if you ask me."

Iris patted Archie on his wrinkled hand. "I agree completely, darling. So true." She turned back to her children, bathing them all in the glow of her blissful smile. "Isn't it wonderful?"

Then came what was usually Attie's favorite part of any venture. The Worthingtons were at their best when the family circled round, ready to form a plan. This time, the plan centered on rescuing Bliss from her mistake.

Dade's idea was terribly boring. "We shall take it up with the bishop," he declared. "There must be a law against that sort of trickery!"

Iris clapped her hands. "Oh, wouldn't that be fun? I do adore a courtroom drama! But, dearest, Bliss did make her vows and did sign the marriage contract, even after hearing the priest say the groom's name."

"We could simply kill him," Castor suggested. Miranda held her hands over Aurora's tiny ears, but she didn't gainsay the concept. And Lysander, who had joined them post-chaos, looked vaguely supportive of the idea.

Iris, however, insisted that they wait until Bliss actually asked for help. "After all, perhaps she had this other fellow in mind all along. I liked the look of him." She hugged Archie's arm flirtatiously. "He put me in mind of a dashing pirate!"

Since Iris rarely knew what day it was, much less took a defined stance on anything other than the existence of fairies, the Worthington siblings reluctantly agreed to wait—for a brief time.

Attie, however, heard the word "pirate" and slipped quietly from the room, her face fixed in a frown of deep thought.

CAPTAIN PRYCE'S FOREBODING silence ended when the carriage stopped at last.

When he grunted briefly at her and alighted, Bliss took advantage of the moment to peer through the window at a row of terraced houses.

Hmm. It was difficult to tell much by the light of the moon and the lit streetlamps at the far corners of the block. The houses were all joined at the sides, but by the distance between the front doors, the facades could not be more than one large room wide.

There was no evident poverty, but neither was there sign of evident wealth. These were not the homes of gentry, but neither did they seem hotbeds of criminal activity. They were quite possibly the homes of bakers and butchers and tradesmen.

Her assessment was confirmed by the defiant glare Captain Pryce sent her as he helped her down to the walk. Apparently, he imagined she thought herself too grand for such a place. Was he trying to upset her? Did he think that no woman who aspired to be a duchess would willingly spend a night within such humble walls?

He clearly expected distress, aghast expressions of refusal, perhaps even a fainting spell or two.

Really, men were so obvious. It never ceased to amaze Bliss how some men preferred women to be categorized like insects and preserved in frames. This one is for marrying. That one is for bedding. Any other, being neither, was either one's mother or a nun.

Such simple creatures, men.

If Captain Pryce believed that she would be at all discommoded by his modest house and humble neighborhood, it pleased Bliss greatly to disillusion him. Worthington House, though large and rambling, was in profound disrepair. Her guardian's cottage in Shropshire had been a spare and functional place, for all its many rooms.

How Mrs. Dalrymple would snort at this fellow if she were here! "Good and plain is good enough for anyone, prince or pauper! Luxury is for the weak, and the hardworking have no need of it!"

Bliss knew from Neville's admiring tales that Morgan Pryce was hardworking, indeed. It made perfect sense to her that he kept a simple home. What need had he for ostentatious luxury when he remained at sea for a year or more at a time?

WHEN MORGAN USHERED his bride into his tiny foyer, he felt a pang of regret that he'd not thought to have the place dusted or swept in his yearlong absence. When he'd dropped his trunk upstairs this morning, he found a broken window in the second bedroom. Pigeons had taken to nesting in the furniture over the summer months, and now the chamber was quite unusable.

The fact was that he'd never much cared about the house itself. He simply preferred the quiet of his own residence over the rowdy dockside inns where most sailors passed their time off ship. And although he knew some would consider this abode to be small, it seemed a gracious plenty after the narrow captain's cabin on the *Selkie Maid*.

He'd never wanted more than that. He'd certainly never been interested in anything like Camberton House.

Although they looked very much alike, Morgan and his half brother, Neville, had very little in common. Morgan's Welsh mother had been the old duke's housekeeper, before Neville's mother had taken her place as the Duchess of Camberton. Nine-year-old Morgan and his mother had been banished to a crumbling lodge on the far edge of the vast estate Camberton Park, where the new duchess need never lay eyes upon either of them.

When Her Grace had died delivering a stillborn sister for five-year-old Neville, the old duke relented on the separation of his sons. Morgan's mother held her ground, refusing to take up residence in the manor house, but she sent Morgan off daily to benefit from the tutors and governesses brought in for Neville.

Morgan had never resented that his younger half brother was duke while he himself was no more than a ship's captain in the fleet owned by the family. In fact, he'd felt a bit sorry for him.

While he was very fond of Neville, Morgan still thought of him as an inexperienced boy. When Lord Oliver had labeled Neville's lady love a gold digger, Morgan trusted his uncle's judgment completely. Marriage to a bastard seemed a fitting punishment for such a creature, Oliver had pointed out, and Morgan need not trouble himself about her once wed. After all, he could simply sail away.

Although he'd only been home for a day now, Morgan twitched at the thought of the sea. A man could breathe at sea the way he couldn't do in filthy, congested London.

No, Neville could have the dukedom and Camberton Park, and all of England, for that matter! Morgan had what he most desired.

He wasn't the Bastard of Camberton when at sea. He was

Captain Pryce, known in harbors around the world, respected by his men. He had always loved the sea, and had worked his way up from cabin boy to captain. And now captain-owner.

He did not need, or particularly want, a wife. But if wedding this girl gained him his dream, it was worth the inconvenience.

Why, then, did Morgan feel embarrassed to show his unpretentious house to his bride, who was not even an honorable lady, but a woman of secrets and manipulations?

Stubbornly refusing to speak even now, Morgan kept his gaze averted from her unnerving eyes. He gestured indifferently up the stairs. Bliss Worthington only tilted her head and remained right where she was. Irritated by the woman's unwavering calm and his own nagging discomfort with his actions of this night, Morgan turned away and stalked to his tiny study. He firmly shut the door on her beauty and her finery and her stoic lack of feminine theatrics.

AFTER BLISS WATCHED her alleged husband walk off and shut the door between them, she let the silent house and the moon-streaked night ease the tension from her shoulders. She let out a soft sigh as she briefly closed her eyes. At last, a moment alone to think. Unfortunately, the only thing she could think was that the grimy little foyer smelled just a bit like wet sheep.

Oh no. That was the wool of her cloak, gone too-long damp. Well, the clearly little-used house was every bit as damp as her cloak, so where ought she dry it?

First, light. There was a good amount of moonlight coming in the front windows, but that would not last. Bliss set about finding a stove, for where there was a stove, there would be a flint and steel.

Kitchens were generally to be found back and down, in any house. This one was no exception. Bliss made her way down the hall and the back stairs primarily by feel. It was slow and awkward and took her entire attention.

It was nice to think about something other than her predicament for a moment.

She found the flint and steel just where she herself would have kept it, in a tin perched on a shelf above the big old stove. In the box next to it she found cheap tallow candles. Tinder came in the form of an old bit of toweling greasy enough to light easily.

Soon, she had a small blaze going beneath the smaller oven. There wasn't enough wood in the box to fire up the entire stove, although that was what it would have taken to warm the space.

In the center of the kitchen was a large scarred worktable. Beside it sat an old chair with a woven seat, much the worse for wear. Bliss pulled it close to the stove and spread her cloak upon it to dry.

She was now quite chilly without it, but if the cloak didn't dry, the wool would be ruined forever. And Mrs. Dalrymple had always told her that if she was cold, better to warm herself with wholesome efforts than to laze about a fire.

Old Dally would not approve of the theatrical events of this night, that was for certain. She would doubtless utter pithy commentary about how none of it would have happened if Bliss had had the sense to see herself to bed at a decent hour.

Bliss allowed herself a moment to mourn the loss of the gruffly loving woman who had raised her in the absence of her true parents. Bliss still recalled every detail of that horrible night. Mrs. Dalrymple had nodded off in front of her fire, rocking in her chair, as she had every evening for years uncounted.

Bliss hadn't known anything was amiss until the old woman's knitting slipped from her hands and fell to the floor. Dally would never have been so careless with her wool.

Why am I thinking of Dally at a time like this?

Because everything was strange and new. Just as it was on the first day Mama had brought her to Shropshire, to hide her away in a farmhouse in the middle of nowhere. She'd been taken far from her home and her many cousins and left in the hands of someone her parents trusted to give Bliss a new life, a safe life.

For all the good that had done.

And here was Bliss, living in London for months now, and her own mother had not seen fit to call.

She shook herself slightly and ran her fingertips over her eyes, dashing away a bit of water no doubt caused by the wood smoke. Clearly, the flue was in need of a sweeping.

No more woolgathering. What she needed to do was prepare her case to present to Captain Pryce. Once Bliss had explained matters to him, she was certain he would do the sensible thing and assist her in gaining an annulment. Someone had made a mistake, that was all.

It disturbed her habitual calm to think that someone might well be her! After all, it had been very careless of Bliss to write Neville and then allow the letters to fall into the wrong hands. Some busybody in the ducal household had designs against Neville's happiness, it seemed. Bliss thought she might just know who that person was, but that knowledge had come a bit too late.

Now she must put the irascible captain in a more receptive mood. This was where her experience with many male cousins benefited her. She knew quite well that hungry men were not capable of reason.

It was only a few hours until dawn, close enough to be thinking of breakfast. She would cook something for the sulking captain now holed up in the study. Hearty food would tame his mood and leave him more receptive to logic. First, she would gently explain how it was impossible for her to be a fortune hunter. Then she would describe how her affection for dear Neville was entirely sincere and entirely mutual!

The annulment itself would be a pickle to arrange, it was true, but Bliss had great confidence in her power of persuasion. Once she had Captain Pryce's agreement, she would throw the entirety of her resources in the matter at the Church of England.

Neither party really stood a chance, now that she thought about it.

Reassured by her plan and newly determined, Bliss hunted down the larder. She found the barest rack of supplies. There was some hardened lard, a bit old but kept cool enough to be usable. She also discovered a bit of cured meat and a rocklike wedge of cheese. In the pantry she found some flour, only a little mealy, and a single sealed jar of summer plums.

It would have to do. It seemed that Captain Pryce wasn't much interested in the fine art of cookery.

Tying about her waist a voluminous apron that she found hanging on a nail on the back of the pantry door, she set about turning her terrible night around.

Chapter 6

MORGAN knew he had done the right thing when he saved Neville from ruin. But his heroic deed had left him saddled with a wife—an outrageously beautiful one, but a wife nonetheless. He could not help wondering whether he'd sacrificed his own freedom for that of his half brother.

There ought to be a bottle of rather good whiskey in the bottom drawer of his desk. Morgan found it and twisted the waxed cork free with a single furious motion.

The heat of the liquor sliding down his throat did nothing to diminish the lingering heat of his lust. He wished he'd slaked that thirst when he had the chance. His lack of feminine company over the past many months hadn't seemed like such a hardship at the time. The shipping season had been an unusually stormy one. It had taken all of his wit and his men's strength and perseverance to bring the *Selkie Maid* limping into the London Harbor at last.

Morgan rubbed his hands over his face. He'd not slept a full night in weeks. He couldn't even recall the last time he'd eaten. So when the scent of frying bacon teased at his senses, he worried it was a trick of the mind.

No. He did smell food. And his stomach growled in response.

Too hungry to ignore his empty belly, but too wary to come entirely to heel over a slab of cooked meat, Morgan left his study, his eyes narrowed in suspicion.

What the hell was that little miscreant up to?

He made his way down the main hallway, his nose guiding him on a leash of savory smells, his ears pricked by the clatter of someone laying out dishes.

He hung back in the doorway of the breakfast room. It was also the luncheon room and the supper room in a house the size of his, and the only room on the bottom floor open to the back garden.

Morgan saw that the draperies had been flung wide to frame a majestic moon now flooding the overgrowth with light. The three large windows that claimed an entire wall were perhaps the only grand touches in the simple dwelling. Morgan had always liked them, for they reminded him of the captains' cabins aboard the largest sailing ships of the White Rose fleet.

But the magical view did not hold his attention long. He found his gaze drawn to the apron-wrapped, kerchief-topped figure who moved about briskly. She smoothed out a length of clean linen she must have found tucked away in storage. She set out two place settings and laid the silver.

Brass candlesticks that had belonged to Morgan's mother held fat candle stubs that cast a welcoming glow over a platter of sliced meat and cheese. A bread basket covered in a kitchen towel steamed lightly. Squat pottery goblets declared themselves as good as any crystal in their perfect placement in relation to the chipped plates and silverware.

Supper at the palace.

Morgan shook his head. He was hungry. That was why

he'd become prone to such uncharacteristically fanciful thoughts.

The question remained—where had all this bounty come from? He knew he could not have been brooding in his study for more than half an hour.

Morgan recalled how his mother used to tell him folk stories of the ellyll, a household spirit who could either ease the occupant's life with ready hearths and good repair or disrupt it with pranks and sabotage. The ellyll required homage in the form of saucers of beer or bowls of cream, Rose Pryce had told him, as well as giving the warning that one must never, ever try to catch the ellyll by peeking around corners or setting boyish traps for it.

Good Welshman that he was, he very nearly drew back from the door for fear that his luck would turn worse than it already was.

But that was mere superstition. What was real was the woman who had arranged the late supper before him. She glowed. With her golden hair and ivory skin, her eyes of sky and her lips of perfect rosebud pink—she was like a dream caught between an angel and a siren.

A bit too earthy to fully personify a heavenly being. A bit too innocent to fully portray a man-devouring temptress. That is, unless one knew for a fact that she had set out to snare a wedding ring from the poor, defenseless Duke of Camberton.

Morgan sent a mental apology winging Neville's way. How quick he'd been to agree with Oliver that Neville was hood-winked because he was foolish and naive. Morgan was beginning to suspect his half brother's only crime was that he was a man . . . and breathing. Perhaps any man would have been caught in this creature's honey-baited trap.

Bliss Worthington was that spectacular.

Even as Morgan watched, she reached behind her back to untie the yards of canvas apron. It dropped away from her to uncover the figure he'd tried so hard to ignore in the carriage. Then she slipped the kerchief from her hair. Nimble fingers quickly repaired the few disobedient golden strands. Before she took her hands away, she gave a last smoothing gesture and a little pat. Her lips formed a faint curve of approval as she looked down at the table and surveyed her handiwork.

Morgan felt his breath catch at the sight of Bliss Worthington—Pryce!—in the candle glow. She spotted him lurking in the shadows of the doorway. As she turned toward him, he saw her smooth her dress down one last time and inhale deeply. The resulting motion was nearly as diverting as the jiggling caused by the carriage! Morgan suspected that she was perfectly aware of the effect of that particular maneuver, and that she'd done it most intentionally. That sent his hackles up. He was no green boy, to be gobsmacked by a nice pair of breasts.

And dear God, what a pair . . .

"I thought perhaps we should have a bit of late supper," she said softly. Her voice was pleasing, Morgan realized distantly. Clear and musical, if a touch breathy. Or perhaps she was nervous after all?

Any discomfort she felt was at her own hand. If she had been outmaneuvered, it was her own fault. He refused to be played like a shuttlecock by her racquet.

"I am hungry," he said shortly.

Morgan strode to the table and sat at the head of it, even though she had laid the settings to the right and left of that chair. Her setting implied a discussion between equals. Morgan meant to disabuse her of any such notion at once.

He was captain of this ship—er, house! He waited while she silently reset his place. She kept hers at his right hand, the seat of the honored guest. It would do for now, because Morgan would certainly not be shifting dishes about like a servant.

She dealt him a generous plate of food before seating

herself. Morgan felt his point had been satisfactorily made, so he fell to without a word.

The simple fare was astonishingly delicious. Of course, he'd had little but hardtack and fried fish for the past three weeks at sea. His own boot leather would taste good by now, no doubt. Still, he could not quite quell the low noises of appreciation as he dug in to the rich seared pork belly stuffed into the lightest crumpets he'd ever tasted outside Camberton House.

He hadn't expected a lady to cook. Then again, hadn't her actions already established that she was no lady?

AWARE THAT CAPTAIN Pryce was predisposed to dislike, Bliss ate daintily and pretended not to be fascinated by the way the captain enjoyed her simple cooking. She had no need to feign a petite and feminine appetite. She was too appalled by the situation in which she had propelled herself to be hungry.

Bliss had done this to herself. She could not deny it. Rarely did Worthingtons find themselves outfoxed, but it had happened tonight. She had been careless, obviously. Someone in her chain of trusted delivery persons had been more afraid of this man than they were of her.

She blamed her face and bosom for that failure. While it was often useful to be underestimated, she imagined that it was even more useful to be intimidating.

After all, no one would dare defy her cousin Elektra so! Or even frighteningly precocious thirteen-year-old Atalanta!

However annoying it was for Bliss to learn that she'd been netted so neatly, it was doubly so to realize she'd knotted the net with her very own hands.

Her head seemed overly filled with oceangoing metaphors. It must be the salty scent of wild sea air that lingered on the captain's skin.

"Have you only just arrived back in London?" she asked.

She took a tiny bite of her food and gazed at him expectantly. Men found her eyes pretty. Bliss appreciated her excellent vision and used her long lashes to good effect, but she was not vain. Old Dally would never stand for vanity.

"Beauty is a gift," she had told Bliss firmly. "You didn't earn it. And it's only borrowed. Some keep it longer than others, but it's borrowed all the same. Better to develop a kindly soul and a sensible manner. Those are forever yours to keep."

Dear old soul.

Tearing her thoughts from the past, she noticed that Captain Pryce was intentionally avoiding her gaze. She could see the struggle between his anger and his obviously gentleman-like manners. Someone had raised him well, despite his rough appearance.

She knew very little about Captain Pryce's mother because Neville knew almost nothing. "I think he misses her still," was the only thing Neville knew to tell Bliss. She'd perhaps been overly curious about this mysterious brother, this welcomed bastard.

Neville had been only too happy to oblige her interest. Tales of Morgan's adventures clearly fascinated him far more than crop reports and tenant complaints. From his stories, Bliss had pictured an older, harder, more adventure-worn version of Neville. She hadn't been far wrong in her imaginings—but nothing could have prepared her for the man in the flesh.

He was a large man, but with a catlike ease of movement. He reminded her of a beautiful panther she'd seen in the Prince Regent's menagerie. He didn't lumber. His footfalls didn't thud upon the bare wooden floors.

Yes, there was something of the hunter about him. He had a wary slant to his dark eyebrows that perhaps spoke of a lifetime of knowing himself to be a bastard. It made him seem fierce, yet she sensed it was a vulnerable area.

Even the way he tried so hard not to notice her, along with the way he had abandoned her in the hall earlier, made her think perhaps he was not altogether sure of his own actions in tricking her.

Abruptly, she gave up any attempt at casual conversation. Pushing back the plate she'd scarcely touched, she lifted her chin and regarded him evenly. "It isn't a lawful marriage. You know it isn't."

He pushed his fork through the bacon drippings on his plate. "It is, actually. You spoke your vows. You signed the contract."

"Under false pretenses," she reminded him.

He still would not look at her. "There were witnesses." His tone was gruff and definitive. "Even your aunt will be officially compelled to speak the truth about it."

Bliss didn't smile. "Aunt Iris's truth depends upon the direction of the wind and how long it is until tea time. I wish you good fortune in deriving actual fact from her truth." She folded her hands in her lap, prepared to debate all night if necessary. Worthingtons excelled at debate—or better yet, confabulation.

His lips quirked slightly. "Your fate is quite inextricably tied to mine now, Mrs. Pryce. Please, let go of your ambitions of duchesshood and proudly claim your place as the bride of a bastard ship captain!"

Bliss shook her head. "You try to sound cruel, yet I know that you are not. Neville admires you so. He speaks of you often. You don't wish to destroy that, do you? Why will you not agree to annul this mistaken marriage and release me?"

He shifted in his seat. "I imagine that it is quite a disappointment, being wedded to a man like me when you had designs upon a much grander station in life. Yet here we are. Till death us do part."

Captain Pryce's words came hard upon Bliss's hopes, but it was the intensity in his gaze and the dark resolve in his voice that shook her deeply.

She had always known precisely who she was and what she wanted. Marriage had always been a sensible option for her and she'd meant to choose a husband for sensible reasons. Neville matched her list perfectly, and was sweet and gentle, which she'd always known she wanted in a mate.

Neville had never made her feel unsteady. He made her feel admired and sure of herself.

This man, this not-Neville, had the opposite effect. Her belly trembled at the depth of his voice. Her knees weakened at the banked fires in his dark eyes. Even his sneering dislike shook her expectations, for she had always found herself universally liked.

Now she found herself wishing that Captain Pryce liked her. The very notion tore her free of his predatory gaze and gave her the impetus for a counterattack. "How could you have done such a thing to Neville?"

She'd kept her tone soft, yet he visibly flinched from her question. Then the banked coals inside his expression roared to life.

"To save him from a temptress like you! To that end, I would throw myself on half a dozen sacrificial matrimonial altars!"

She stared at him for a long moment. Then she shut her mouth and regarded him primly. "Six brides? How very untoward of you."

He didn't laugh, not quite. However, she rather thought the choked noise that rose from his throat counted as a point in her favor.

Encouraged, she continued. "Lord Oliver doesn't regard me highly, but that is only because he doesn't know me. I am an utterly likable person. And I am not after Neville's gold—"

"No? Then it is his tasty title? What in the world makes an ordinary woman think she ought to be a duchess?"

"Worthingtons are not ordinary. And besides, if only I could explain to Lord Oliver—"

At his uncle's name, Captain Pryce growled. "I don't know why you insist on arguing the point. It is done. We are wed!"

Bliss focused her considerable will. "I wish an annulment."

"And I wish a gooseberry pie. That doesn't mean I'm going to get one."

"I can see that you are not yet prepared to listen to me at this time," she replied patiently. "Perhaps you should take me home to Worthington House. Spending the night here will only confuse matters."

He leaned back in his chair and stretched out his long legs. "Yes. That is the general idea."

She frowned at him. "I know you care about Neville. You are trying to be a good brother, but I fear you have acted without the proper information. If you only knew how he feels about me."

"Oh, I know. He went on at some length."

She was astonished. "Then how could you do such a thing to your own brother?"

He regarded her sourly. "You are strange, indeed. Not how could I do such a thing to an innocent girl? Odd how that never comes up. Very odd, considering that you purport to be exactly that, don't you think?"

Bliss stood, as if rising to her full height would prove her point. "I am a very respectable person . . . except that, well, there is one thing that I never did have time to explain to Neville—"

"I'll wager you have many such secrets. There is only one thing you need to understand, Mrs. Pryce."

She wished he wouldn't call her that. "And what is that?"

"One thing you should not do is mistake me for a gentleman. I am a bastard. I do what I must, for my family, for my men, for myself." He leaned forward then and raised his blazing blue gaze to meet hers. "I will never set you free."

With those words, he wrapped one long arm around her waist and tugged her down into his lap. His other hand swept to the back of her neck and brought her mouth to his.

Chapter 7

BLISS considered herself a well-brought-up young lady, but she was a country girl for all that. One could not observe the seasonal cycles of sheep and horses without gathering a few practical notions of reproduction. These notions sometimes gave way to curiosity, so it was a rare country lass who made it to the vast age of twenty without at least one kiss.

However, getting a peck on the lips from the butcher's boy behind the springhouse was poor preparation for having one's mouth ravaged by the likes of Morgan Pryce.

He wasn't harsh. He was overwhelming. In an instant, his skill and masculine dominance had opened her lips and even captured her tongue before she knew it. He tasted of whiskey and the sea and scorching, aroused male. His hot mouth covered—no, conquered, invaded—hers, while she was still catching her breath at the feel of his firm arm around her waist.

Hot tremors traveled through her and for a moment, the merest moment, she forgot everything. Neville didn't exist.

Propriety didn't exist. The entire world consisted of this room, Morgan Pryce, and Morgan Pryce's hot, hungry mouth.

And then there was Morgan Pryce's hot, hard body beneath hers.

At first, she had pressed her hands against his wide chest in objection. Now she found her fingers digging urgently into the rigid muscles there. Her bottom had landed squarely on his lap. She squirmed on him and she would swear upon her life that she fought for her freedom, and it was mostly true. It was also somewhat accurate to say that a deep hidden portion of her mind had become very focused on the aforementioned lap.

Sheep and horses. Or, to be more exact . . .

Rams and stallions.

Something tugged at her attention. An unexpected sensation of icy chill on bare skin—

Her perfectly appropriate, demurely bridal, happiest-night-of-her-life gown slid right off her shoulders!

With a gasp of shock, Bliss tried valiantly to pull away from the man who had disrobed her with such practiced ease. It was no use. His hands were searing and hard on the bare skin of her back, pressing her close to him, sliding down beneath the unbuttoned gown to wrap themselves urgently over her daintily clad buttocks to press her closer still to his hardening groin.

The act instantly cleared Bliss's fogging senses.

This Morgan Pryce fellow needed a gentle reminder that, legally wedded wife or not, a woman was no man's property! Especially not when she was a Worthington!

Therefore it made perfect sense for her to kiss him back with all her might—as she slipped his dagger from its hiding place within his boot.

Bliss knew she had made her point when his large body went quite still beneath hers. She pressed the dagger the tiniest bit more firmly to his throat. His big hands slid slowly off her bottom and out from under her dress. If they lingered ever so slightly upon her flesh, she pretended not to notice, just as she pretended not to notice her own shiver as her skin felt the cold once more.

When his hands were raised to either side of his wide shoulders in evident surrender, Bliss allowed herself to straighten and pull her gown back up to a somewhat more decent altitude. The way his gaze fixed upon the brief exposure of her barely clad bosom told her that while he might be calmed, he was by no means cowed by her defensive maneuver.

This was her explanation for why she remained seated on his lap. It would be easier to apply the dagger as needed from this short distance, and if distraction techniques proved more effective, her bottom on his rigid lap ought to do quite nicely.

That was her reason and she would adhere to it for all of eternity.

Morgan Pryce's gaze rose to meet hers. She raised her eyebrows in sad disappointment. He narrowed his eyes at her.

"Is that my own boot dagger?"

Bliss still had the point of the knife pressed to the hollow just beneath Mr. Pryce's sculpted jaw. She gently removed it and held it into the light. "It is. I withdrew it from your hidden sheath while your attention was diverted. Why ever else would I kiss you back?"

"You should be more careful. That is a very dangerous spot to put a blade."

Bliss regarded him gravely. "Yes. One nick of your carotid artery and there would be no saving you. However, I needed you to take me very seriously."

His expression was grim. "I see. You now have my undivided—"

Bliss's unbuttoned bodice suddenly fell prey to the pull of gravity. She grabbed it quickly with her free hand and drew the little sleeves up over her shoulders once more.

"—attention."

Morgan kept his tone very flat, but he knew that she must have felt the surge of lust from the vicinity of his lap.

She focused that mesmerizing blue gaze upon him. "Now, Captain, while you seem like a perfectly serviceable husband for some, you simply won't do for me. I fear I have set my sights on my dear Neville, and no other man will do. If you do not intend to behave like a gentleman, I will be forced to take drastic measures."

Bliss pressed the tip of the dagger to his neck once more. "I believe that you are under a misapprehension, Captain. Unfortunately, you have proven yourself unwilling to listen to the truth. I believe that I should return to Worthington House, and we should take up this discussion tomorrow."

"No. You will remain here."

"Captain, that would be most inappropriate."

"Truly? You are my wife." He smirked. "Furthermore, you are sitting on my lap."

"It was easier to reach the dagger that way."

Morgan held very still. Laughing with a dagger at one's neck was not the best way to end an evening. *Do not laugh.*

He should be furious. Morgan licked the taste of her off his lips. Strangely, his righteous anger seemed in short supply after that kiss. His head still swam with lust.

He should lift her into his arms right now and carry her up to that single usable bedroom. The thought of her spread naked upon his covers, with that shimmering golden hair spread upon his pillow, did nothing to clear his lust-muddled mind.

She shook her head in disappointment. "You fail to understand me, Captain Pryce. This dagger is by no means a toy in my hands."

"I could take that from you in a breath."

Her lips curved in a saintly smile. "You might try."

Oh, she was delicious. It was too bad that she was a conniving, lying, ruthless fortune hunter. Yet he now found himself rather intrigued by his odd bride. "What manner of woman are you, to be so calm at this moment?"

She lifted her chin. "Why, sir, I am a Worthington!"

That reminder helped to quell his simmering desire—at least for the moment. "A notorious family, known for shady scandals and disregard for propriety."

"Nevertheless, you are quite wrong about me."

His eyebrows went up. "I have a dagger at my throat. How wrong could I be?"

Her prim expression did not falter. "I'm sorry. Were those *not* your hands inside my gown?"

She had him there. He grimaced and made a go-on motion with his hands still in the air.

The painfully delectable creature on his lap shifted her bottom slightly. Morgan fought the urge to moan in pleasure.

"If you knew more than mere gossip about my family's reputation, you would understand that I am not who you think I am. Worthingtons do nothing for financial gain—"

"Didn't your cousin kidnap a wealthy earl to force him into wedding her?"

She pursed her lips. "Do not interrupt. It is rude." She waggled the dagger at him reprovingly. The irony made Morgan's blood pound in his head.

"At any rate," she continued earnestly, "that particular fellow—an earl's heir, not an actual earl, by the way—couldn't be happier with the way matters turned out."

From the last few moments of his own life, Morgan could understand the poor fellow's deadly bewitchment. Worthington women must be like opium, a dark and fatal road to travel, but what a way to go! No wonder Neville was so in her thrall.

However, this Worthington female would not find him as easy to manipulate as a pampered son of the ton!

She went on. "I understand that I cannot wrest an annulment from you at knifepoint. You would only withdraw it later. What I require is time to convince you entirely that you are wrong about me. I am perfect for Neville. Neville is perfect for me."

Time. Morgan had plenty of time. The repairs to the ship would not be complete for at least ten days. Plenty of time to turn the attentions of one wayward Society wench. He had seduced foreign princesses in less time than that!

He needed a plan to keep her here with him. The bargain with Lord Oliver had included actual consummation, in order to keep her away from Neville forever. If he offered his bride no hope of winning her case, she would flee the house—which would end any chance he had of securing that all-important wedding night.

His mind began to move more quickly as his lust ebbed to bearable levels. To be truthful, this was not his first bargain at knifepoint. He had survived many a dockside wrangle and come out on top to boot! He narrowed his eyes at her, prepared to negotiate her into a losing position.

First, challenge her claim. "You say you want only Neville, that you have no concern for the luxury and status he can offer. Prove it."

He knew he'd snagged her attention. She tilted her head. A wisp of shimmering hair slipped to curl along her cheekbone. Morgan forced himself to focus on her words.

"And if I do?" There was hint of canny sharpness to her blue gaze. "If I prove to you that my affection for Neville is real? That I would never do anything to hurt him?"

Bait the hook. "I care nothing for you, but I would never stand in the way of true happiness for my brother." She would hear truth enough in that. "That is, *if* you can convince me." Which would be impossible, of course, so he had no qualms about promising her the moon and all the stars. "Not only will I grant you an immediate and uncontested annulment, but I will intervene with Lord Oliver on your behalf and convince him of your worth as well."

Her lids fluttered slightly. Ah yes. *Come here, little fish.* Or mermaid. He'd always wanted to catch a mermaid.

She wanted not only Neville and all his status, but respectability as well. Morgan tossed out more bait. "Oliver garners enormous respect in Society. His approval would turn Society's opinion indelibly in your favor. No more clandestine midnight arrangements. All would be properly done, open and aboveboard. You could have the wedding of your dreams and the unquestioned status of Lady Danton, without a whisper of scandal following you."

He smiled sourly. "Do not underestimate the hold His Lordship has over my half brother. Neville is entirely dominated by him. If Oliver continues to reject you, Neville will never defy his decree."

That was plain truth, and he could see that she knew it as well.

Biting her lower lip, she regarded him seriously for a long moment. "You believe you can sway Lord Oliver's opinion?"

"Entirely." Morgan put on his best arrogant captain face. It had allowed him to swagger unmolested through more foreign ports than he could recall. "*I* am not Neville."

She regarded him seriously for a long moment. Then she nodded. "Very well. Call upon me tomorrow at Worthington House. You must meet my aunt and uncle, and my cousins."

Morgan shook his head with a smile. "Absolutely not. Neville won't be wedding your cousins. It is you I must learn to understand." Time for the final bait, hook and all. "Do not forget that my ship is leaving in just a few days. If you cannot convince me by then, a year or more may pass before I am back in London again. I doubt that even the most generous bribe to the Bishop of Canterbury would undo our vows after a year."

She drew back slightly, although her dainty grip on the blade did not waver. "I cannot reside here with you alone! What will Neville think of that?"

Morgan narrowed his gaze. "He will kiss your cheek and call you 'sister,' for if you cannot tolerate a few days in my lowly company, I will remained unconvinced of your devotion. If Neville is indeed your heart's passion, should you not do anything you must to make this right so you can wed him?"

The advantage of her prim perch on his lap was that he knew the precise moment when defeat softened her spine. During their conversation, Morgan had lowered his hands from their position of surrender. Now he slipped one palm up the silken calf dangling from his lap.

He felt the prick of the dagger at his throat. He did not flinch, but he did stop. The dagger withdrew. He felt a single warm drop of his own blood run down into his collar. Damn. He didn't own very many shirts.

He raised his hands once again. "Point taken."

"I have some conditions of my own, Captain."

"You have the dagger." He raised an eyebrow. "State your demands."

"Captain Pryce, I require your word."

Morgan's gut went cold. How could she possibly know what his word meant to him?

He forced himself to grin fiercely. "You can have as many words as you like, love. But you should know you can never trust a bastard."

"You play the brigand, but you forget." She continued to fix him with her angelic blue eyes. "I know how much Neville respects you. My Neville would never trust a bounder. So I require your word. You will not make advances on me again. Do you agree?"

He didn't smile. He didn't laugh. Morgan showed no sign of his vast relief. He could keep his hands to himself easily enough. That didn't make her safe from him.

This conniving female had no idea what she was up against. "You have my word that I will not make advances on you again."

In reply, she merely slid off his lap, then handed him his dagger, hilt first. With a regal nod, she turned, picked up her sagging skirts with one hand, and floated serenely from the room.

Morgan had to swallow hard at the sight of her undone gown dropping to reveal the delicate curve of her spine. She seemed so vulnerable in her mussed dignity.

Which was no doubt precisely her intention. God, he was going to have to be on his toes against her connivances!

No matter the lady's manipulation, he would abide by his own code. Then again, there was nothing stopping him from turning on the old sailor swagger, which had never yet let him down.

By the time he was done with Bliss Worthington Pryce, she would be making all the advances needed.

Chapter 8

IN her hijacked bedchamber, Bliss shut the door behind her with a sigh. Need she lock it as well?

Captain Pryce had given his word. Either he would abide by it, or she wasn't safe in his house, even in the middle of the day. She decided to put her faith in his honor and left the key unturned.

The room was icy and dark. She had the benefit of predawn light coming through the window draperies. It was enough to find the edge of the sheet protectively draped over the bed and pull it off. Waving one hand against the dust rising, she allowed her other hand to release the sagging bodice of her wedding gown at last.

The beautifully worked beading made the bodice heavy. It slipped down at once. Bliss removed the gown carefully, shivering as she lost the warmth of the heavy satin skirts. Although the calendar might claim summer, London was cold when it rained.

No matter. She would warm quickly enough in the bed.

After draping her lovely bridal gown over the single chair

next to the cold, blackened hearth, she lifted the covers and slid between them. Captain Pryce wasn't one for luxury, as evidenced by the rest of his furnishings, but to her surprise the sheets were silken and fine, probably the best India cotton she had ever experienced.

Morgan Pryce seemed like a reasonable man, as much as men could be expected to be reasonable. Bliss tried very hard not to think about the astonishing, heart-pounding kiss. After all, she was sure that Neville kissed very nicely, too, even though he had never actually made any move to do so.

Morgan Pryce was an odd man, certainly. The monastic condition of his home notwithstanding, as the recognized bastard of the former duke, Morgan should be a wealthy man.

He was certainly a confusing one. So much like dear Neville—yet so opposite. He was hard where Neville was gentle. He was sharp where Neville was gracious. He was altogether more difficult to influence than Neville would be. Not that she would ever try to persuade Neville to do something that was bad for him. It was just that men never seemed to know what was good for them!

This might take more time than she thought.

Then again, Neville had lived his life as the treasured heir. Morgan had been pushed to the edges, always without, looking in. Bliss knew a bit about that as well.

I like him. I shouldn't like him, but I do.

That and the dire need for a good sweeping for the entire house were her last thoughts before she succumbed to the exhaustion of her rather trying wedding night.

DOWNSTAIRS, MORGAN TOSSED uncomfortably on the sofa, trying to ignore the taste of a woman on his lips, his first taste in months.

As much as he scorned that Worthington wench, he had to admit that she'd been brave to hold him off with a knife.

It was no coy maneuver, either. He was quite certain that if he had pursued the matter, there would have been some bloodshed—considerably more than one drop.

He reminded himself that she guarded her virtue because she hoped for an annulment. He wondered what would happen if she decided that seducing Morgan would get her what she wanted. Not that it would work, of course. Still, he'd be happy to let her try.

Now, wouldn't that be interesting? All that fair silken skin revealed to his curiosity? All that tender, rounded flesh pressed to his? She looked like a milk-fed angel, but she kissed like a starving siren. What else would she do if she was aroused enough?

Wearily, he sank into a restless sleep, dreaming of his fingers twining in imaginary golden hair.

Chapter 9

Go on. Better sooner than later.

It was only a few hours past dawn, but Morgan had found he could sleep no longer. Not that one could consider tossing and turning on a too-short sofa actual sleep.

Now he was fully dressed and dawdling over his grooming, dreading what came next. Yet how could he rest easy when matters between himself and Neville were so awry?

"I knew I could count on you, my brother."

Morgan gave a last impatient yank to the knot in his cravat and regarded his image in the speckled mirror over the parlor mantel. *I did my best.*

The face in the mirror only scowled. A ship's captain didn't allow his emotions to show on his face. When the tropical winds threatened to snap the masts, when the waves towered over the deck, the crew needed him to stand like a rock at the wheel without a shadow of apprehension on his brow.

Neville was just going to have to understand. Or not. Either way, the Duke of Camberton had been saved from his own youthful poor judgment. Family duty had been done.

God, he hoped Neville would understand. His place as captain left him with no ability to be a friend to his crew. His place as bastard did not allow him to truly join with the ton. Lord Oliver was family in name only. Morgan knew that his uncle tolerated him merely as long as he produced for the fleet and as long as he remembered his place.

Neville was the only person on earth who called him Morgan, who smiled in greeting when he arrived, and who embraced him unashamedly when he left. But that was before Bliss Worthington ruined everything.

I did the right thing.

As soon as he actually believed it, he would stop saying it to himself.

As he left the quiet house, he could not help glancing up at the window of "his" bedchamber. He'd not expected to be so attracted to Neville's little gold digger. No matter what Morgan might wish, last night's kiss had changed matters. And while Bliss had not screamed or fainted at his rough advances, neither had she reacted like a skilled seductress.

Oddly, that had made him like it all the more.

And if he was not mistaken, she had liked it as well. There remained the fact that he needed to secure her virtue before she could wrangle her way out of the marriage while adhering to his vow to remain a gentleman.

Damn, he wished he hadn't made that promise. He would have to wear her down through other means.

At that thought, his lips quirked and his step lightened on the walk to Camberton House.

Women liked rogues. Women loved ship captains. But what every woman truly wanted, Morgan had long ago realized, was a pirate of her very own!

BLISS OPENED HER eyes. The aged but pretty canopy that should be over her bed in Worthington House was missing. She rolled her head to one side to frown at the simple dressing table and row of rustic pegs on one wall. Pegs for clothing. She hadn't seen that since Old Dally's farmhouse—but Dally would never allow dust to build up so!

Then Bliss peered closer to see that from one peg hung a pair of gentleman's drawers. Old Dally wouldn't have those, either.

But Captain Pryce would. Her husband.

"Husband," Bliss said out loud, trying it out. No. The only husband she wanted was her dearest Neville. Her plan had gone awry. Obstacles had been laid in her path. But, as she well knew, obstacles could be overcome.

No one was going to make that happen but her. As usual.

With fresh determination, she threw back her covers to swing her feet over the side of the bed. It seemed as though she'd only slept for a few minutes. In her chemise, she walked to the window to take a surreptitious peek at the day through the heavy draperies.

Captain Pryce passed directly beneath her window. Bliss did not draw back, although she did tilt her head out of the light as she watched him walk. He looked very fine in his gold-buttoned sea captain's coat and his black boots. Dashing, even.

Then his deep blue eyes flicked upward to her window. He could not see her. It was impossible, for her room was dark against the bright light of day and she peered through the narrow gap in the draperies—yet his gaze lanced into her, making her gasp.

This time she did involuntarily duck away. After a breath or two, with her hand pressed to her middle to soothe her leaping stomach, she stepped back to the window. The captain was long gone, of course.

She saw by the place of the sun that it must have been only a few hours since she fell into bed so exhausted. That explained why she didn't feel well rested, but it was no excuse for dallying about in her underthings.

When she'd risen, a very practical portion of her mind

noted that dust rose from the coverlet. The floor of the chamber was like ice on her bare feet.

As she had noticed the night before, Captain Pryce was not one to keep servants about. Very well. Bliss didn't need anyone to help her dress.

Except that the only thing she had to wear was her wedding gown. With her hands full of satin and the taste of disappointed hopes in her mouth, she set it aside. Instead, she rummaged in the drawers of the chest and found a dark blue silk gentleman's dressing gown. The fabric was frail with age, but it had once been fine.

She wrapped herself in the stiffened silk and slipped her shoes upon her feet. Upon exploration of the empty house, she found more than the kitchen, dining room, and bedchamber she had already seen. There was a parlor with faded wallpaper, its furnishings draped in canvas. There was a gentleman's study, somewhat more recently used, but still worn and outdated.

Someone who cared had once lived here, it was plain. A lady, Bliss thought. There was a refinement to the choice of little things, though they were not expensive things. Strange birds stood arranged on the mantel, not silver or even china, but beautifully carved of some exotic wood. Drapes and rather plain carpets of complementary hues, if not the finest weave.

Bliss continued to wander about, dragging her finger through the dust that had collected on every surface—every molding, every table, every mantel.

Eventually, she found herself in an attic. It was mostly empty and dim, lit only by a bit of sunlight filtered through a single soot-covered window. There, in the far corner, was a wardrobe.

Bliss opened it and pulled out a bundle of muslin that turned out to be two outdated workaday gowns. Holding them up, she could tell they would be a bit too long on her frame and definitely too small in the bodice, but they would be better suited to housekeeping than either a silk wedding dress or a man's dressing gown.

Bliss dressed, deciding that if fate had brought her to this place, there was no point in tolerating unpleasant surroundings. While not entirely filthy, the house was an example of what Bliss privately called "man-clean," and in dire need of a female's sense of order and balance.

Because Worthingtons always remained prepared for anything, she was not without resources. With a bit of effort, she could do much with what she had.

With her mission clear in her mind, Bliss put on her white cloak and left the little house in search of a few amenities. Perhaps if Captain Pryce saw what a good, practical wife she could be, he would reconsider his opinion of her intentions toward Neville. And, while he ate her excellent cooking and slept on clean sheets, she would bat her eyes and inhale deeply and convince him that he was absolutely wrong about her.

Not the most worthy of methods, perhaps, but she was a Worthington and she intended to do whatever was necessary to undo this horrible mistake of a marriage.

Furthermore, she liked a clean house and a full larder. So, for as long as this rather unpleasant situation continued, there would be one person she was determined to please.

Herself.

THE VISIT TO Camberton House wasn't as bad as Morgan had expected. It was far, far worse.

First of all, he was shown into a very formal parlor that he'd never before spent much time in. Lord Oliver used it to impress certain advantageous people, but Neville had always preferred the overstuffed family parlor that, while still exquisitely tasteful, didn't make one feel as though one shouldn't actually sit on the furniture.

This forest green and mahogany room cried out *wealth*

and *status* in every end table and ornament. Even the crystal decanters on the side table shimmered like diamonds. Morgan had never before been called up on this particular carpet by his uncle, and at first he thought Regis, the stout, stone-faced Camberton butler, had put him here by mistake.

But Regis didn't make mistakes. Ever.

Then Morgan waited for more than an hour. It didn't take that entire period of time for him to realize that someone, either Oliver or Neville, wished he would just leave.

With a small, grim smile, he parked his rear on the priceless velvet and gilt settee and stretched his boots out across the imported Chinese carpet as if he were the king of this particular castle. If they wanted him gone, they would have to throw him out personally.

When the door finally opened, it was Neville who appeared. But it was a Neville Morgan had never before encountered. Neville was drunk. And not companionably steamed as he'd been the night before, tossing down a few extra whiskeys after dinner, but ghastly, angry drunk.

"Out!" Neville turned and barked the dismissal at Regis with the snarling abandon of a man who'd lost everything.

Oh hell.

It looked as though this wasn't going to go well at all.

Neville fixed his reddened gaze on Morgan. "Why are you here?"

"Good morning to you, too, Your Grace."

At this point, Neville would normally laugh off his title and remind Morgan that he preferred Morgan's boyhood nickname for him, Nev. "Not Neville. I hate Neville," he'd say. "It sounds like 'snivel,' don't you think?"

Since Neville had been their father's name, Morgan had no real fondness for it. But young Neville had adored the old duke with all the passionate longing only a barely acknowledged child can feel for a distant parent. Yet Neville hated their father's name . . .

That was something Morgan would have to ponder at a

later date. Right now there was a younger, slighter duke before him who seemingly wanted to tear his throat out.

Over that scheming, golden-haired seductress?

Women!

"Uncle Oliver told me what you did. Why? How—" For an instant Neville's rage faltered and the heartbroken young man shone through. "How could you do such a thing . . . to me?"

"I did it *for* you." Morgan kept his tone low, but not cajoling. One wrong move and Neville might break apart right in front of him. "You were about to make a terrible mistake."

Neville drew back, his expression closing against his heartbreak. "Mistake? I didn't even know about this elopement you trapped Bliss into!"

"And if you had? What would you have done? You would have been standing in that bloody freezing church at midnight instead of me, endangering yourself and Camberton for the rest of your life!"

"I would not!" He halted, then shook his head like a dog shaking off water. "No—I mean, yes, I would have wedded Bliss Worthington in a heartbeat, had I known she was willing—God, to think that she wanted me so badly that she was willing to sneak our wedding past Uncle Oliver—"

"That's hardly the point," Morgan said drily. "Every unmarried woman in England would line up at your door in a quick second, if you even mentioned you were in want of a wife. You're the bloody duke!"

"That's not—I didn't mean that—it's just that she's so independent, so sure of herself—I didn't think she really wanted someone like—"

His befuddlement faded abruptly. He turned on Morgan once more. "She *did* want me—and I wanted *her*! Oliver said he thought you were jealous of me. What, you couldn't stand me getting one more thing you couldn't have?"

Morgan nodded. He'd wondered if Oliver would blame him in order to keep the peace in Camberton House. It was something the old duke used to do now and then, putting his own unpopular decisions on Morgan when it was really Neville he was trying to curtail.

It had worked, to some degree. The old duke had been remotely fond of his good son, more so than he was of the son he'd had with a passionate, headstrong Welsh woman. Although Morgan knew that his father had come to respect his prowess at sea, he'd not lived to see Morgan make captain. Beyond a small twinge of regret for a relationship he'd never had, Morgan had not mourned the old fellow.

Neville had been devastated by their father's death. Of course, he'd only been sixteen to Morgan's twenty-two, so perhaps that was why. Morgan had gone back to sea and Neville had turned to Oliver to help him step into his new role as Duke of Camberton.

Oliver had readily obliged. Morgan knew his uncle was competitive in business and was driven to win, and he'd admired Oliver for his willingness to sully his noble hands with actual effort. But it was Oliver's devotion to Neville's welfare that had won Morgan's loyalty. Yes, His Lordship was a snob, as was usual for his rank, and he could be calculating and ambitious, but it was always for the good of Camberton and, by extension, for Neville.

Try explaining that to Neville now.

"If you can bring yourself to understand, I believe that in time—"

"In time? The way you arrived home just in time to help me?" Neville took a swig of the amber liquid in his glass. He shuddered slightly and wiped the back of his hand over his lips, then turned his burning gaze back on Morgan. "I cannot believe you have the gall to face me at this moment. And when I think that I was so relieved when you came home in time to help me—that I sat there last night and begged—" He passed a shaking hand over his pale face.

Morgan wasn't sure if it was thwarted love or if it was the morning after a drinking binge that had taken the gentle, playful light from his younger brother's eyes. Instead, they blazed like twin blue fires of fury in reddened whites.

Morgan had predicted that Neville would be upset, but he hadn't truly believed that this act of sacrifice on his part would sever their brotherhood entirely.

He didn't want to believe it. He wanted to believe Uncle Oliver's claim that Neville would come round, that he might even be relieved to be free of the temptress. Morgan wanted to believe it so he could take Oliver up on his offer of the *Selkie Maid.*

I betrayed my only family for a ship.

No. He had to believe that ruining Neville's little infatuation was the right thing to do. And, truly, so far the incandescent beauty had failed to prove anything to Morgan other than she was rather handy with a blade. Not exactly a recommendation of demure maidenhood!

He tried once more. "Neville, she isn't who she seems to be—"

This time, Neville didn't hesitate to fling his glass into the fire. It erupted violently into a thousand shards that hissed and popped on the coals, the remaining gloss of whiskey burning off with a brilliant blue hue.

Neville turned on Morgan. "Get out of my house. In fact, stay out of Camberton entire. I do not wish to see you ever again, do you hear me?"

Morgan stared at his half brother's face. Then he turned and left. His last thought as he quietly shut the door on Neville's misery was that his sibling had never looked more like him than at that very moment.

He'll see me every time he looks in the mirror. I did that. I broke my half brother's gentle heart.

Morgan strode past Regis and passed through the grand entry hall, his gaze intent on the door, ignoring the gilded spiraling stair and the priceless statuary. Faster. His boot heels rang on the marble. Without waiting for the butler to catch up to him, he yanked the front door open and fled the house.

"Morgan! Blast it, boy! Wait!"

Morgan slowed at Lord Oliver's preemptory tones. Only a lifetime of respect kept him on those gracious steps as he waited for his uncle to catch up to him.

"Stay out of Camberton entire."

Morgan's vision blurred slightly as he gazed down at the marble doorsteps. He had never been much impressed by the grandeur of his father's holdings—at least, he'd never allowed himself to be. In fact, he'd played with an India rubber ball on these very steps as a boy. They were wide and high, surely intended to be imposing and to make it difficult for callers to climb—as if to imply that an audience with a man of the duke's stature must be earned.

As a child, Morgan had used them for a playground. One day they might have formed a tropical volcano, another day a frozen slope, and of course, most days a grand sailing vessel, like the stories told to him by his great-grand-da, his mother's grandfather, the original Captain Pryce.

He'd never wanted Camberton. He'd never envied the weight of responsibility Neville had to bear. He liked his freedom. He loved the sea. The threat of banishment from Camberton should mean little or nothing to him.

Yet it did.

Lord Oliver came even with Morgan. He ignored Morgan's icy expression and clapped him on the shoulder as if they were enjoying a jaunt in the park.

"Well done, lad! I must express my appreciation for your heroic salvation of the duke. At least you understand how important family is. Women come and go, but the family is forever."

Morgan looked at Lord Oliver in disbelief, but his uncle only gazed into the distance with a slight smile on his narrow features, as if passing acerbic approval upon the beautiful day. Then he slid his gaze sideways to look Morgan in the eye. "And how is your bride? Did you bed her properly?"

Not much in the world could render Morgan speechless, but this blunt question from his uncle did. He could only blink at the man for a moment.

Lord Oliver smirked. "What an unsavory creature, that female. She probably wasn't even a virgin, was she?"

Morgan narrowed his eyes. What was Oliver up to? "I wouldn't know. I hardly expected her to succumb to my charms when she'd only known me an hour."

Lord Oliver snorted in disappointment. "Really? I'd expected better of you. You know you cannot give that woman the slightest opportunity to obtain an annulment. You must bed her, and soon!" He turned fully to Morgan and raised an eyebrow. "That is, if you still wish to win the *Selkie Maid* for your own."

"I am not a rapist, my lord."

Oliver lifted a lip in a supercilious derision. "You're a bastard, not a gentleman. No one cares what you do."

Cold fury swept Morgan. He could not take a swing at his own uncle. The very urge shocked him. So he merely growled something noncommittal and left, taking the steps two at a time and leaving his uncle and his half brother—and Camberton—behind him.

Morgan could only pray that someday Bliss would prove herself so entirely unworthy that Neville would see the truth.

Morgan had not betrayed him. He had saved him.

LORD OLIVER NOTED the rigid set of Morgan's shoulders as he descended the steps and marched off toward the hired cab. Once seated, he slammed the door.

Aha. Oliver smiled to himself. Had the evil little vixen managed to get her claws into Pryce? No matter. The boy's personal affairs were of no interest to him. Oliver's sole concern was whether the bastard captain held up his end of their bargain, and thus far, Morgan had done so with aplomb.

The hack kicked up a cloud of dust as it raced down the circular drive. Oliver turned toward the doorway, stopped, then spun back around, stunned by a completely unexpected sight. Another hired cab was making its way up the drive just as Morgan's exited. What was the meaning of this sudden rush of carriage traffic? Had Camberton House become the new Rotten Row?

He blinked in disbelief as yet another hired cab followed, this one weighed down with teetering stacks of travel trunks and boot lockers!

Who the devil . . . ?

Anger constricted Oliver's throat. This kind of intrusion was utterly unacceptable. He waited until the hacks neared the front steps, then waved them on.

"Turn around and be quick about it! This is the home of Lord Neville Danton, fourteenth Duke of Camberton. Clearly, you have the wrong—"

A woman's pale countenance appeared, framed in the carriage window. She offered him a weak nod by way of greeting. Then a second woman's face popped into view, younger and plainer, but equally wan.

Slowly, Lord Oliver's thoughts began to find purchase. Before him was a weary pair, likely a mother and daughter, who had brought with them enough travel chests to outfit a small army. He felt his shoulders sag with the burden of acquiescence.

Oh hell. The Beckhams had arrived from Barbados.

He had houseguests, whether he wanted them or not. And he did not. However, it was the price he had agreed to pay, and a gentlemen made good on his promises.

Oliver pasted a pleasant smile on his countenance, reminding himself that the Beckhams' arrival was more of an investment than inconvenience. In exchange for hosting the sugar plantation widow and her backward daughter for the London Season, the White Rose Line would be awarded an exclusive contract to ship Sunbury Plantation sugar to every corner of the English Empire.

And that would be only the beginning. He was certain of it. The pieces would fall into place easily. First, Lord Oliver would provide the Beckham girl an introduction to the ton, single-handedly saving the unfortunate child from social obscurity. Second, Mrs. Beckham would undoubtedly feel indebted to him for his kindness. Therefore, she would accept Oliver's offer to take the plantation off her hands, even at a greatly reduced price.

Simply brilliant, if he did not say so himself.

The cabdriver opened the carriage door and a dainty shoe set down upon the footboard. Being sure to keep his polite smile frozen in place, Lord Oliver took a step toward his guests. He only hoped he could wrap up the terms of the plantation sale early in the Season so he could pawn off this pair of useless females to someone else.

Surely he could find another host. Any other host.

He bowed graciously. "Mrs. Beckham. What a pleasure it is to finally—"

"Oh, Ollie!" Paulette Beckham clutched her breast and nearly tumbled from the carriage. "Those awful, horrid sailors had no sympathy for my severe discomfort! Can you imagine the insensitivity! Barbarians! All of them!"

Mrs. Beckham staggered, leaning on the driver's arm as she took a wobbly step onto solid ground. "I am utterly exhausted, darling Ollie! I hope you don't mind me calling you that, but I feel we have become the dearest of friends during these many months of correspondence. Don't you agree?"

Lord Oliver felt his jaw unhinge. Darling Ollie? He tried to recall the last time anyone had addressed him in such a thoroughly inappropriate fashion, let alone a woman known only through an exchange of letters. He drew a blank. "I . . . er . . ."

"Oh, my dearest, darling Ollie, every mile was unbearable! Every day aboard that ship seemed an eternity!"

"Mummy, please." The girl dipped her bonneted head and alighted from the carriage. She was a thin and drab little bird, as weak and worn-looking as her mother but devoid of the older woman's charms. The girl gazed directly into Lord Oliver's eyes, her mouth pulled in a tight line. "Forgive us, Your Lordship, but my mother is correct. These past weeks have been exhausting. Perhaps your staff can show us to our rooms?"

If Oliver recalled correctly, this unattractive waif with the rather arid manner was called Katarina. The name seemed far too regal for one with dull brown hair, a bony figure, and sharp and humorless eyes. He had heard the young Miss Beckham was no beauty, but Oliver was certain he had never met such an unpleasant girl in his life.

He looked her up and down, noting her plain dress. Clearly, a childhood in the wilds of Barbados had left her woefully unprepared for the social intricacies of the London Season. This inconsequential person would be eaten alive!

The girl began to herd her mother toward the entrance of the house. "You need to lie down, Mummy."

"Oh my, yes!" Paulette patted Oliver's coat sleeve as she passed by him on her way toward the steps. "I am positively swooning with fatigue, Ollie, my pet. 'Tis a wonder I am able to walk at all!"

A series of loud grunts made Lord Oliver turn toward the carriages. He saw that both drivers had already begun unloading the bulky trunks. He watched helplessly as one man attempted to drag a particularly cumbersome boot locker backward up the marble steps, the impact of each stair echoing like a cannon blast in his ears.

"I say!" Oliver looked about, horrified. The entire situation had slipped from his control. Somehow the arrival of two petite ladies had turned his sedate household into a grunting, chaotic, "darling Ollie" madhouse!

"Your Lordship."

Oliver spun around, nearly sighing with relief at the appearance of his butler, Regis.

"I assume you wish our esteemed guests to have the Lilac and Hyacinth suites, my lord?"

"Er . . . of course. Quite right."

With a subtle wave of his hand, Regis contained the hullabaloo. He dispatched two footmen to escort the ladies inside while a parade of under footmen took the trunks from the drivers, commencing an efficient and orderly unloading distinctly free of cannon fire.

Lord Oliver raised his chin, pleased that the women were now on their way to their rooms and that calm had returned to Camberton House.

Unfortunately, he realized that the two hired drivers lingered nearby, waiting. For something.

He turned toward them, perplexed. "Be off with you, then."

One man removed his hat and pressed it to the lapel of his grimy coat. "There be the matter of the fare, sir."

The second driver rolled his eyes. "Aye, and there's extra for all the bloody . . . all the ladies' trunks, guv'nor."

A fare? These men expected Lord Oliver to carry coin in his pockets like a commoner? He glanced toward Regis in disgust.

"I shall arrange payment, Your Lordship."

"I should expect so."

Oliver cleared his throat and straightened his spine, then began to climb the steps. He waved away a fawning footman he encountered in the great hall, then made his way to his study. Once ensconced, he took refuge in his favorite chair by the hearth, where he set about quieting a lingering sense of unease. It must be the ruckus. Oh, how he hated chaos and clatter!

A respectful tap on the library door was enough to drive Oliver to distraction. "What the bloody hell is it?"

Regis poked his unflappable countenance into the room. "Does Your Lordship require anything?"

"Yes! I require to be left alone! Is that too much to ask?"

"Very good, sir."

"And pour me a brandy before you go."

Regis nodded and entered with footfalls as soft as a cat's.

Oliver stared at the butler's back with distrust as the man poured brandy into a crystal goblet. Regis was far too composed. Lord Oliver didn't trust a man who revealed nothing in his expression.

With brandy in hand and Regis gone, Oliver stretched out his legs. The first sip delivered a rush of heat that managed to relax his shoulders and settle his worry, and it was not long before he felt a smile spread on his face.

His plans were progressing quite nicely, despite the commotion. All was going according to plan. He had Sunbury Plantation in his sights. He had gotten rid of Bliss Worthington and the accompanying threat of a Camberton heir. And he had managed to insinuate doubt and distrust between Neville and Morgan, leaving little chance the two would confide in each other enough to ever band together against him.

It was obvious that Paulette Beckham was just another frivolous and empty-headed female, weakened further by the rigors of travel.

Extracting the Sunbury Plantation from Lady Beckham's flitting female hands would be almost too easy, like stealing sweets from an innocent babe or taking advantage of a simpleton. The truth was, the silly woman was no match for Lord Oliver's savvy business strategy. The whole affair would be embarrassingly simple.

His smile began to fade. The nagging unease returned, settling heavy upon his chest. He straightened in the chair.

That woman had just stiffed him for cab fare!

Chapter 10

BLISS had to admit that, even though a certain un-named ship captain seemed intent upon ruining her life, she found roaming London's shopping districts as a married woman incredibly liberating.

She had not brought her reticule along to her wedding, for it didn't match her gown. Therefore, all she had in the world was the penny in her shoe. All her life, the women she knew—Mama, Old Dally, and even impractical Auntie Iris—had repeated the same lesson. "A woman should never leave the house without a penny in her shoe."

In Bliss's case, since Papa had also taught her that there was no reason to do if one can overdo, that meant a guinea in her shoe. Worth hundreds of pence, the large gold coin was much heavier than a penny, and she'd had to get used to the feeling of it riding along just under her instep, but she'd never been happier about her decision than she was today.

After an unfortunate incident the previous year with a wide pony cart on a narrow bridge, where she'd taken a brisk dunking and her shoe had been lost entirely, Bliss had begun to carry that guinea inside her stocking. This morning, she had shaken out that stocking and gazed at the gleaming golden coin with great satisfaction.

Further rummaging in the second bedchamber had unearthed a small leather pouch that would do for a reticule. With her fine white cloak over her outdated and unseemly tight gown and, of course, flawless hair, Bliss felt absolutely ready to face the world.

A brisk walk took her to the nearest well-traveled road and her piercing country whistle got the attention of a bitter-looking hack driver. He pulled his horse to a stop and looked sourly down upon her.

Some people were not good conversationalists. Bliss forgave him and bestowed a serene smile upon him. "I'd like to be taken to Bond Street, if you please?"

It was a fair distance from Captain Pryce's Shadwell neighborhood. The driver's expression curdled further. "Ye got fare?"

Bliss held up her little purse in reply. The driver merely regarded her with suspicion. "Let's see it, then."

With great patience, Bliss withdrew the gold coin and showed it to him, letting it gleam in the light of the cloudy day like a piece of the sun itself. Impressed in spite of himself, the man looked at her with new respect. "But I canna change a guinea."

Bliss nodded regretfully. "I understand." She tucked the coin away slowly, making a tedious show of it. The man held out longer than she'd expected him to. Finally, of course, he caved.

"What of yer 'usband, eh? Can 'e pay?"

Bliss blinked. Did she look married already? Then she realized that it was a reasonable assumption, for a woman to roam unaccompanied would be either married or a person of unfortunate repute.

The husband was going to come in handy after all. She

beamed an angelic smile up at the driver. "Of course! You may come to the door this evening and he will pay you—and tip you handsomely for your trouble."

The man's perpetual gloom did not lift, but he did give a shrug and a grunt, then heaved himself off the seat to open the door for her. When he gave her a hand in with awkward courtesy, Bliss warmed to him entirely. "Pray, what is your name, good sir?"

He looked at her in surprise, as if no one ever recognized his existence, much less inquired about him. "Cant."

Bliss tilted her head. "Why not?"

He snorted. "Ephraim Cant. But folks mostly call me Eff."

"Well, I shall not. Imagine shortening such a noble name as 'Ephraim'! I shall call you Mr. Cant until we are better acquainted, at which time I should like to call you Ephraim. You may call me Miss—Mrs. Pryce. Is that agreeable to you, sir?"

His expression now drifted somewhere between bewitched and befuddled, which was precisely where Bliss preferred the gentlemen of her acquaintance to exist. She smiled at him gently. "Shall we drive on to Bond Street now, Mr. Cant?"

Ephraim Cant, former official grouch, now a prince of gallantry, pulled his cap from his head, pressed it to his breast, and bobbed a rusty bow. "Yes, m'um. I'll 'ave ye there in the twitch of a cat's tail!"

IT WAS A delightful day in all, Bliss decided. Mr. Cant had driven her everywhere she desired and, at the promise of yet more liberal tipping by her generous husband, began to accompany her into the shops to carry her purchases. A lady with a manservant, no matter how rough, immediately attracted the benevolent attention of the proprietor and further calmed said proprietor's distress at not being able to "make change."

The guinea popped out of Bliss's little pouch, which was soon replaced by a proper beaded silk reticule, and always went back in. Bliss ended the day no poorer than she'd started it, although her carriage was piled with paper-wrapped parcels and even a number of boxes.

Other than the reticule, she'd indulged in no clothing. She had some very pretty things at Worthington House, all packed and ready for her new life as Duchess of Camberton. She only needed to send a message to her cousins to carry them to Captain Pryce's residence. She wouldn't need them for long, but she might as well be comfortable while she waged her campaign for the annulment. Fashion had ever been a woman's armor, so she would need her battle gear.

It was the house that needed attention if she meant to spend even another hour within it. It lacked even the basic necessities, so Bliss industriously set about rectifying the fault. Inspired by the deceptively simple loveliness of the items in Captain Pryce's house, Bliss had purchased things of the same ilk. A lovingly embroidered tablecloth from Spain. A set of earthenware dishes from a county up north, painted with a delicate nosegay of wildflowers that reminded Bliss of her cousin Callie's artwork. A comfortingly round blue-glazed teapot that recalled Old Dally's morning cuppa to her mind. She reminded herself that she might as well indulge her taste for modest beauty now. These sorts of things would never be allowed in a grand place like Camberton House.

That was not all she purchased, however. She put in orders at the butcher's, the grocer's, the chandler's, and the collier's for foodstuff, fine beeswax candles, and a good month's worth of coal. She didn't wish to be self-centered, so there were stops at the tobacconist's, the brewer's, and the vintner's. All, of course, to be delivered at great speed and billed to the now legendary heavy tipper, Captain Pryce.

Yes, all in all, it was an excellent day.

* * *

WITH MUMMY FINALLY settled and resting in the Hyacinth Room, cocooned in the vast and luxurious bed with a cool cloth for her brow and a steaming pot of tea at her side, Katarina made her escape. She simply could not wait to explore the grounds of Camberton House and get her first taste of England. The carriage ride from the harbor had been enough to show her that all the things she'd heard about London were true, only more so. The architecture was more spectacular. The air more filthy. The streets busier, and the elite more elegant.

Though Katarina was an English lady through and through, she'd learned her English-ness secondhand by reading books and hearing the recollections of Mummy and her friends during visits to Bridgetown. Barbados was the only home Katarina had ever known, but as Mummy often reminded her, England was in her blood.

It was time to discover what she was made of.

Katarina walked the halls of the east wing, careful to avoid any members of the household staff. She was in no mood for another of Mummy's lectures about propriety and the importance of a chaperone, a sermon Katarina knew by heart.

Fear of a scolding was not the only reason for her caution, however. Though the Beckhams were invited guests at Camberton, Katarina could not help feeling a bit like a trespasser. She sensed immediately that Lord Oliver Danton was not a friendly sort of man. His welcome had seemed calculated, and his face not particularly trustworthy. Of course, her mother had not tolerated these observations when Katarina later shared them. Mummy was quick to point out that Katarina's entire future was in Lord Oliver's hands.

"Your dear father, God rest his soul, wanted this for you," her mother had said. "Don't forget that you are the daughter of a long line of English gentry, and a place in London Society is your birthright, your destiny! Lord Oliver will arrange for us to attend only the top-tier balls of the Season—earls, barons, and viscounts everywhere we look!"

Katarina hadn't bothered to remind her mother that she cared nothing for balls and viscounts and neither had Papa. Her father had long promised Katarina that he would never force her into a marriage not of her choosing. Now that he was gone, Mummy seemed to have other designs.

As a widow, Paulette Beckham had more wealth than she would ever know what to do with. What she lacked— and was intent on obtaining for her only child—was a title. And Katarina knew that once her mother set her sights on something, she would find a way to get it.

Katarina continued down the hallway, past the endless display of framed portraits and landscapes, certain she would eventually find the grand staircase. Camberton was extravagant, certainly, but a structure could not go on forever!

She rounded a corner to find herself beneath a towering ceiling and within steps of the ornate, gold-leafed stair railing that would guide her to the main floor. Unfortunately, a chambermaid emerged from the opposite wing, forcing Katarina to backtrack. She molded herself to the wall and waited until she no longer heard the maid's footfalls, then took her chances.

Katarina whipped around the corner and raced down the white marble monstrosity of a staircase, right out in the open for anyone to see. She made it to the great hall and hurried toward the back of the house, looking for a way into the walled gardens she'd seen from her bedchamber windows.

How intriguing they'd been! With their precise design and—

"Whoa!"

Katarina skidded to a stop and braced her arms, but slid directly into the stranger's embrace.

Chapter 11

O H horrors!

Katarina pulled away, a flush heating her cheeks.

"Please forgive me, sir. I—" The man standing before her raised one eyebrow in curiosity while his mouth curled in amusement. He was terribly handsome, a slim and tall gentleman, just a little older than she, with dark hair and deeply intelligent blue eyes. He was . . .

Oh dear! He was the young Duke of Camberton!

She dropped into a deep curtsey. "Your Grace, pardon me. I am deeply sorry for my carelessness. It is inexcusable." This was a disaster. If Mummy heard about this . . .

"The error is mine, I fear."

Katarina straightened at the kindly voice, daring to look up.

The duke bowed most elegantly. "I am Neville Danton. You must be—"

"Katarina Beckham, Your Grace. I am . . ." Caught—that

was what she was, and now there was nothing to do but return to her room and await the lecture.

"Is there some way I may be of assistance, Miss Beckham?" The duke's voice was friendly, if a bit detached. "My uncle informed me that you and your mother were to be our guests for the Season. Is your mother with you now?" He peered over her shoulder.

"Of course! Yes, Your Grace, but she is resting at the moment. I was looking for a way to the gardens." Katarina gestured straight ahead, then doubted her sense of direction and motioned to her right.

The duke smiled and pointed to her left. "I shall accompany you, Miss Beckham."

"I couldn't possibly ask you to—"

"It shall be my honor, Miss Beckham."

That was how Katarina came to spend a thoroughly enjoyable—and improper—half hour in the company of Lord Neville Danton, fourteenth Duke of Camberton. As it turned out, they shared a common interest in botany, and the duke was quite knowledgeable. He showed her around the gardens and their immaculately groomed boxwoods, lush flower beds, fountains, and tidy gravel walkways. To her great surprise, the duke seemed unconcerned that she was out and about without a chaperone.

"I suspect the gardens in Barbados are quite beautiful as well," he said.

Katarina kept her hands clasped daintily in front of her as they walked, fighting back the desire to caress each leaf between her fingers and pull each bloom to her nose. "Indeed, Your Grace, but even with constant attention they are never this orderly. The tropical flora always manage to dominate the designs of civilization, I'm afraid."

He nodded and even smiled a bit, but did not reply. Katarina could imagine that it was a chore for the duke to engage in meaningless chitchat with a bothersome houseguest. His crinkled brow and stiff shoulders revealed he was troubled. Well, of course he was! A duke had many responsibilities, and entertaining a silly girl was no doubt adding to his melancholy.

Katarina was preparing to excuse herself when a rather large butterfly landed on the duke's coat sleeve. From its shape and black and royal blue markings, she recognized it as a member of the Machaon species.

"It seems we've company, Your Grace." Katarina nodded toward the duke's sleeve.

He ceased walking, careful not to jar the beautiful creature. "Ah yes. These fellows are frequent guests to our gardens. I believe he is a—"

"*Papilio machaon*, a swallowtail, and a she. There are no claspers on her wings."

As if that were her cue to go, the visitor flapped her wings and ascended into the breeze.

Oh drat. She had just interrupted—and corrected—a duke in his own gardens. He must have been horrified by her manners, as he stared at her with his lips parted in disbelief.

My, he was handsome, even when perplexed.

And she had ruined his opinion of her already. Mummy was always reminding her that men preferred to know more than women—or at least, to believe they did. Katarina could never seem to keep her sharp mind to herself.

"A female, you say?"

Oh dear. "Yes, Your Grace."

"What was the species, again?"

Katarina pursed her lips, hesitant to answer. Few people enjoyed her references to binomial nomenclature, as Mummy often pointed out. However, the duke had asked her a direct question.

"*Papilio machaon*, Your Grace."

He nodded seriously, then looked away. Suspecting she had offended him beyond repair, Katarina curtsied and prepared to take her leave. "I fear I have taken too much of your time. Thank you for showing me the gardens, but I should return to my room."

"Wait, Miss Beckham."

She glanced up.

"You have spent time observing butterflies in Barbados?"

"Oh yes! Frequently." She straightened. "I have long studied Lepidoptera. My island contains a vast array of plant and animal life."

The duke's eyes flashed. "You don't say?"

Their visit continued on for another quarter hour. Katarina learned that butterflies were one of the duke's interests, and they spent an enjoyable ten minutes debating the purpose of the complex pattern and color palette of a butterfly wing.

"Many might just say the wing is brown," the duke explained with charming seriousness, "but upon closer inspection, a whole world of texture and design is revealed. What looks drab at first opens up to an entire landscape of texture, hues, and flashes of brilliance. But I have found few people are patient enough to see past the brown."

Since Katarina occasionally mourned her own rather lackluster looks, this made her like the young aristocrat even more.

He liked to listen as well as talk. The duke peppered Katarina with questions about species common to both the West Indies and England, particularly their migration patterns. Their conversation had been so riveting that Katarina was shocked when she looked up to see the sun dip behind the garden walls. "I must return to my mother, Your Grace. No doubt she will be waking soon."

He nodded. "Of course, Miss Beckham. I have greatly enjoyed our conversation. It was a welcome . . ." The duke paused, shaking his head, deciding not to continue with the thought.

It was plain to see that something weighed heavily on Lord Neville Danton's mind.

He straightened and put on a smile. "I hope you and your mother will dine with my uncle and me tonight. Is she well enough, do you think?"

"Of course, Your Grace. We would be delighted."

But oh dear. There was one problem—how could Katarina have obtained such an invitation if she had not left her room?

She began to say something, then stopped herself. She glanced around the garden, unsure how to worm her way out of this fix.

"Are you quite well, Miss Beckham?"

She sighed. "In truth, Your Grace, I'm afraid I left my room without permission and without a chaperone. If I accept your invitation, my mother will learn of my transgression."

"Ah." The duke's eyes crinkled up in amusement. "Then I shall send an invitation to your mother directly, and our most pleasant afternoon in the garden never even happened."

Oh, she liked this man. Katarina gave a rare smile. "Wonderful! Then I shall look forward to making your acquaintance tonight, Your Grace. Rumor has it that you are a very interesting conversationalist."

THE DINING ROOM in Sunbury Plantation's great house was extravagant by Barbados standards, but quite plain compared to the one in which she now sat. The scale and opulence of the dining room in Camberton House made Katarina feel insignificant, which was surely the intention. The dining table itself was the largest single piece of furniture she had ever seen, and the idea that the duke and his cold-water fish of an uncle took their daily meals here, alone, waited on by a virtual army of staff, was almost comical.

She imagined one servant per piece of silverware. The Servant of the Salver. The High Footman of the Fork.

She wasn't far wrong. The party of four now dined at one far edge of the table, dwarfed by the vast, gilded ceilings.

Despite the thick carpets, magnificent tapestries, and velvet draperies, their voices echoed in the emptiness. The tinkling of silver and china glanced off the paneled walls.

No wonder the young Duke of Camberton was melancholy. Katarina would be, too, if she were expected to sit in this glittering cavern with the sour Lord Oliver as her only company.

"I feel ever so much better after resting, darling Ollie." Mummy had been attempting to engage the old man in conversation, with only mild success. "Our rooms are so luxurious! I'm certain Katarina and I will be most comfortable here during the course of our lovely, long visit."

Oliver accidentally clanked his spoon against his soup bowl. "Wonderful to hear."

Katarina dared to peek across the table at the duke. Neville Danton was already looking her way, one eyebrow askew, clearly entertained by her mother's audacious conversation style. Katarina stifled a giggle.

Mummy had been aquiver with joy upon receiving the duke's dinner invitation, which made Katarina curious.

"We are their houseguests," she told her mother. "We require regular nourishment. Where else would we eat?"

After Mummy finished laughing, she called for their new ladies' maid, who had promptly been hired by the efficient Regis, to assist them with dressing. Then she patted the sofa and pulled Katarina down alongside. "Oh, little Kat! You've so much to learn." Mummy had kissed her forehead. "Don't you see? The duke himself invited us, which means he is aware of our presence. He will be an excellent social connection for you, my dear. One can never have too many dukes in one's circle."

As she had met the Duke of Camberton only briefly, Katarina was curious to see how he would carry out their harmless deceit at dinner. As it turned out, he was masterful. Mummy never suspected that any prior meeting had taken place.

The duke did not speak much, reaffirming Katarina's suspicion that he was troubled. Then again, perhaps he did not have the opportunity to slip a word in over Mummy's enthusiastic chatter.

The meat course was served, which provided a respite from Mummy's talking, but she soon regained her rhythm. She described in detail the rigors of their ocean crossing, the weather patterns of the West Indies, and some of her favorite memories of her girlhood in England. It was only when she began to talk about the sugar business that Lord Oliver perked up. He put down his knife and fork to put all his attention on her.

"Mrs. Beckham, I am quite curious about something."

"Yes?"

"I do not expect you to have a grasp of the figures, of course, but do you know if Sunbury's production has increased in this last year?"

With a bite of roast beef in her mouth, Katarina nearly bit down on her tongue. Lord Oliver had no way of knowing that Mummy had been at the helm of plantation operations before Papa's illness, and was running the business single-handedly since his death six months prior.

"Oh, dearest Ollie. You are so correct—numbers do vex me so! My head simply swims when I look at a column of figures!" Paulette smiled prettily at Lord Oliver. "But if I am not mistaken, I've heard talk that business has been good. But surely the late Mr. Beckham shared some of those details with you? You have been doing business with him for quite a while now."

Katarina stiffened. Her mother was up to something.

"Of course. Of course." Lord Oliver raised his wine goblet and smiled as if Mummy were the most fascinating woman in the world. "To Sunbury Plantation!"

Katarina glanced at Neville Danton. Not only had he not said much that evening; he had barely touched his meal. It was if a dark cloud hung over him. Just then the duke held up his crystal goblet and waited until it was filled with wine. He drank it down without stopping for breath.

Mummy did not seem to notice. "Katarina and I are most certainly looking forward to receiving our invitation to the Fletchers' ball, Lord Oliver. Do you know when we might expect it?"

"Er . . . no, but, Neville, do you know the date for the Fletchers' ball?"

The duke glanced up and shook his head, an utterly lost expression in his eyes. "Who?"

"Fletcher. Their ball. When is it?"

He shook his head. "I am afraid I do not know, ladies. My sincere apologies. But I shall find out and share the information with you promptly."

"Well, now, isn't this lovely, Neville?" Lord Oliver leaned back in his dining chair, looking particularly pleased with himself. "Here we are, enjoying a pleasant meal with our refined visitors—such perfectly respectable ladies. It has been a while since you've been in the company of respectable ladies, has it not?"

Neville's face went scarlet. His upper lip curled and his eyes shot daggers at his uncle. The hatred in his expression made Katarina flinch.

The duke grabbed his goblet and held it aloft once more. No one said a word as the server poured. When the crystal was filled to the brim, he stood. "Excuse me, ladies." He kicked his dining chair with such force that it toppled over behind him. "I fear I have another appointment."

With a sloshing wine goblet clutched in his hand, he stomped out.

After several long seconds of silence, Mummy tried to smooth things over. "How unfortunate that the duke is not feeling well."

A sinister smile flickered over Lord Oliver's face. Then

it was gone. "'Tis naught but a temporary ailment, I assure you. He shall make a quick recovery. Men always do."

"Excellent news," Mummy said.

Katarina folded her hands in her lap and stared up at the gilded ceiling. For a dinner conversation about nothing at all, a great many details had been revealed.

Chapter 12

AFTER the joy of acquisition came the bother of putting it all in order. Bliss stood before Captain Pryce's unassuming little row house, at the top of a short flight steps that led from the walk down to the kitchen service entrance, and allowed herself a small sigh of weariness. Simply because she was very good at making things just so did not mean that she found anything but the driest satisfaction in it.

The deliveries of staples and foodstuffs were quickly filling the larder and cupboards, so she remained above, serenely directing the traffic from the various purveyors. The butcher had come and gone, leaving a variety of beef and pork, both fresh and salted. Men liked beef and pork, didn't they? And the dairyman had delivered a nice selection of cheeses and butter.

She was directing the final delivery of fresh produce down the stairs when a familiar rattletrap carriage pulled up. The two elderly horses in harness came to a grateful stop.

One whiffed a greeting in Bliss's direction. Bliss plucked two apples from a bushel being carried down the steps to the kitchen and moved to reward Constantine and Pie for their valiant expedition through London's chaotic streets. She was happy to see that they seemed none the worse for their stormy outing the night before.

As the white-muzzled gelding and mare gently took the treat between yellowed teeth, an assortment of Worthingtons tumbled from the carriage.

Bliss could not help smiling. It seemed like a month since she'd seen them, yet it had only been the day before that she sat at dinner, dreamily planning the last details of her secret wedding.

Great lot of good that had done her.

"Bliss! A midnight wedding? You sneaky vixen!"

"Is this the house? I thought it would look more sea-captain-ish."

"Has anyone told poor Neville yet?"

"Cousin, are you sure you don't mind?" or perhaps it was "Cousin, are you out of your mind?"

That last was Daedalus, who was Bliss's favorite cousin, if she had to pick one. Although sometimes she thought it was primarily because Dade rarely caused a ruckus, got into a brawl, or blew something up—things that could not be said for any other cousin.

Dade made it much easier to maintain one's calm.

Now, however, he looked like a summer storm about to strike. His fair hair was untidy, as if he'd run his fingers through it a few times too many. His blue eyes, grayer than her own, were dark with simmering fury.

Bliss blinked. "Heavens, Dade! There is no need to come to my rescue. I am quite well, I assure you." His concern was rather warming after her night of frustrated hopes. Still, men were touchy about family honor and all that rot, prone to getting themselves into pickles over it, so Bliss kept her tone firm and her expression unworried.

"But for Pryce to pull such a foul trick on you?"

"He had good reason, I suppose." Bliss blinked at finding herself defending the man. After all, it was a nasty bit of work, was it not?

Normally, she was so very sure of things. Now she carried a niggling doubt that perhaps she *had* tried to manipulate Neville, just the tiniest bit. Even if her intentions were pure, it wasn't a very good start to a life of trust and happiness with dearest Neville . . .

Fie on Captain Pryce for his self-righteousness! He'd confused everything! However, she could allow her cousins to see nothing of her uncertainty. As Dade, Cas, and dear, war-darkened Lysander carried her trunks into the house, Attie followed alongside Bliss, peering up into her face.

Not peering that far, Bliss realized. Attie, though not quite fourteen, was already almost as tall as she. And still dressing like a mad escapee from a costume trunk! Today's ensemble consisted of a cast-off pink silk party dress that must have been Elektra's, for it was too short and too roomy in the bosom. This was worn over a pair of boy's breeches that were pegged halfway down her shins and baggy men's stockings, one green and one blue, that ended in shabby boys' boots. At least Attie's brilliant ginger hair now lay in two more or less neat braids instead of the multistrand, spiderlike arrangement she'd once preferred.

Bliss wondered, as she had so many times before, if Attie had any idea of the sort of stellar beauty she had yet to grow into. If so, was this daft wardrobe some sort of final childish protest against that future?

Plenty of time to worry about Attie's future when it arrived. At the moment, Bliss was still left a bit unsure of her own present.

"You don't want to stay here," Attie said flatly, as if she expected argument. "You want to come home to Worthington House."

I want to go home to Camberton House, with my sweet,

quiet Neville and my sweet, quiet future. Instead, Bliss smiled at Attie with all the serenity she could muster. "If I want Captain Pryce to grant me an annulment, I must convince him that I am not what he thinks I am. I cannot do that from a distance."

"Lysander thinks we should just kill him."

Bliss sighed. "That's sweet. But killing him won't solve the problem. The law bars a woman from wedding the brother of her dead husband."

"Half brother."

That forgotten fact arrested Bliss's attention for a moment. Then she shook her head, as if ridding herself of homicidal thoughts. "I foresee a long, sticky courtroom debate there. No, my way is the best way, I fear. I must act quickly, however. If I do not gain that annulment soon, Captain Pryce will sail away and my opportunity will be lost."

Attie looked askance at the bounty still being carried into the kitchens. "So you're going to feed him into submission?"

Bliss smiled conspiratorially at her young cousin. "Indeed."

When they reached the bedchamber where the boys had carried her things, Bliss thanked them sweetly, obdurately resisted their urgings to come home, deflected more than one murderous offering, and patted Lysander on the arm, gazing into his shadowed eyes.

"I'm fine," she assured him. "Completely in control of the situation. Everything is *just fine.*"

The shadows did not disperse—they never did—but they did recede somewhat. Lysander gave a short nod of assent, then turned and strode from the room and from the house itself.

Cas looked alarmed. "I'd better chase him down," he said hurriedly. "You know, just in case . . ."

Then he, too, was gone.

Dade looked no happier than when he'd arrived. "This house is so far away from us. And—" He looked about, concern darkening his handsome brow. "—I know Worthington House isn't grand, but this? Is the man a monk?"

Bliss took his hand in hers. "Dade, you're very kind to be so concerned for me, but trust me, I do have matters under control here."

He began to protest again, but she held up one finger to stop his words.

"Daedalus Worthington, have you ever—ever!—seen anyone get the best of me?"

He thought about that for a long moment. She could see how reluctant he was to let his worry ease, but in the end, he nearly smiled. "No, Cousin, indeed I have not."

"Then you must trust that I know what I am doing."

Dade nodded, but then his expression hardened once more. "If he so much as touches—"

"Then—and only then!—may you wipe the floor with his mighty captain hat."

Dade nodded shortly, then pulled her close. Surprised, she embraced him back. Although they treated her as a sister, with teasing affection and random thoughtfulness, she had not realized how much her cousins truly cared for her until today.

Then Dade was gone, with Attie bouncing at his heels, and Bliss was left alone with her master plan . . . and her doubts.

"I FEEL AS IF I'VE failed Bliss." Dade Worthington sat next to Attie in the family's carriage, looking so forlorn that she reached over and squeezed his hand.

"It's not your fault."

"Quite to the contrary, I'm afraid." He smiled sadly at Attie. "As Bliss's oldest male cousin, I must ensure her welfare. I should have done something to stop all this."

"Rubbish." Castor Worthington sat across from Attie and Dade, with Lysander at his side. "How were you supposed to know she was running off in the middle of the night to be married?"

"Iris knew, and our mother could not keep a secret if you chained it to her wrist. She probably mentioned it at some point," Dade answered. "I should have paid closer attention."

Cas chuckled. "Paying closer attention to Iris is rarely the path to enlightenment."

The carriage had gone no more than two blocks when Attie's attention was drawn to a large, masculine figure making his way along the street. He reminded her of someone. The shape of his jaw, perhaps, or the tilt of his dark head. Aside from the arrogant way he carried himself, he looked very much like . . .

Neville. She jumped from the bench and smacked her palm against the ceiling of the carriage. "It's him! Let's get him! Stop the horses!"

"Attie, sit down."

"But, Dade, it's Captain Pryce, right there! Let's make sure he understands that he's trifled with the wrong family."

"Really?" Cas moved aside the curtain to take a look. "Well, you're right. It must be Pryce. But Bliss was very clear with us just now—she wishes to handle the matter in her own fashion."

Attie fell back on the seat, exasperated by her brothers' lack of fervor. Sometimes she felt that she was the only Worthington willing to fight for justice.

Cas closed the velvet curtain. "Besides, she told us explicitly not to do anything."

Attie saw her opportunity. "No, that's not at all what Bliss said. She only told us not to kill him." She looked to her perpetually silent brother for confirmation. "Isn't that right, Lysander? Didn't she say not to kill him? See? Lysander agrees with me!"

"By God, you're right." Dade banged his palm against the roof of the carriage and ordered the driver to pull over.

While her three brothers exited the carriage, Attie remained inside, nearly hanging out the open door to get a sufficient view of the action. Cas, Dade, and Lysander surrounded a bewildered-looking Captain Pryce and swept him into the carriage, Dade giving instructions to the driver along the way.

The captain was corralled on the bench opposite Attie, Lysander situating himself between their captive and the door. Cas and Dade squeezed in next to Attie, nearly crushing her in the process. It worried her that the Worthingtons' old carriage and even older horses were not up to the task of pulling this many large men, but the concern soon vanished in the drama of the moment.

Attie braced herself in the corner and narrowed her gaze at their new travel companion. He did not look a bit guilty. Nor did he look frightened or even puzzled by the notion of being kidnapped by a group of strangers. Perhaps it was not entirely unexpected in his line of work.

Because the truth was, Morgan Pryce did not look so much like a sea captain as he did a pirate.

Cas introduced everyone by name and the captain nodded in response.

"I assume you know who I am, as you've just snatched me off the street. But might I inquire our destination?"

His tone was assured and commanding, the voice of an educated man. He even sounded a little like Neville, except older and deeper. If Attie was not mistaken, there was even a hint of amusement in his question. Not what she had expected, on either count.

Soon, Attie came to comprehend her brothers' strategy. Dade had asked the driver to pull toward the center of the street, and they now moved at a snail's pace, blocked in by milk wagons and fish carts and any number of horses and people. The captain could not get far even if he threw himself out the window.

Attie didn't bother to hide her grin of satisfaction.

Dade answered their captive. "We thought you might enjoy a leisurely trip around the block."

"I see." Pryce nodded, then slowly fixed his eyes on Attie. She coiled her long legs as if ready to spring, imagining herself a furious tigress, giving him her famous stare. She had often been told her green gaze was bloody frightening.

"You must be Attie." A smile curled the captain's mouth. "Neville has mentioned you."

She was no fool. Attie figured most females would be ensnared by the dashing pirate's handsome smile and rich voice. But she was not most females. "That's Miss Atalanta to you."

"Yes, of course. My sincere apologies, madam."

She sat forward. "And you are about to learn that when you harm one Worthington, you risk vengeance from us all!"

Dade patted Attie's arm. It seemed she was always being denied the opportunity to complete particularly riveting speeches. Her brother's approach turned out to be a bit more restrained.

"Captain Pryce, we need to talk to you about our cousin Bliss. Your trickery has inflicted grave distress upon her, distress she did not deserve."

Morgan Pryce's jaw tightened, but he said nothing.

"What is the purpose of your deceit?" That was Cas, leaning forward to rest his elbows on his knees. Attie approved of the hint of aggression.

Pryce shrugged. "Bliss Worthington wanted a secret wedding. She sent many secret messages to Camberton House and made all the arrangements. She got what she desired."

Cas growled. "But the man she hoped to marry was not you—it was your brother!"

"My half brother." The captain's tone had chilled. Attie watched his whole body stiffen. "Is that what this is about, gentlemen—my being a bastard?"

All the Worthingtons looked to each other for clarification. Dade frowned. "Of course not. We hadn't even thought of that, Pryce. Who your mother happened to be is none of our concern."

"We have a question for you." Cas took over the interrogation. "Bliss wants an annulment. It is a straightforward and justified desire on her part, so why do you resist?"

Morgan Pryce laced his fingers together on his lap and leaned back in the bench. Attie thought he looked like a man settling in for a long conversation. "I'm afraid it is not as simple as all that."

Dade smirked. Attie had heard that smirking worked quite well in inquests. "Well, then, how is this for simple, Captain Pryce? You lied to a lady. You pretended to be someone you weren't. There is nothing complicated about that."

Their prisoner sighed and then slowly shook his head. "You do not know the entire story, Daedalus. Let me ask you a question."

Dade nodded for him to proceed.

"If you believed your dear cousin Bliss was in danger—about to be irrevocably harmed—would you step in to save her?"

Dade reared his head back in surprise, then let go with a loud guffaw. "I believe we've already established that."

"Good. Then it is only natural that Neville's family would wish to do the same for him."

Cas and Dade looked sideways at each other.

"Come, now, Pryce," Cas said. "You claim you lied to protect Neville? Protect him from what, pray tell? Neville was never in any danger, unless you consider love a danger. Bliss adores him. He adores her."

"So you say."

Attie could bear no more of this nonsense. "He's up to something!"

One of Pryce's dark eyebrows arched, but Attie noticed that he did not dare deny it.

Cas narrowed his gaze at Pryce. "And we should know. Up-to-something is a daily occurrence at Worthington House!"

The carriage suddenly lurched to a stop, shooting Attie back to the bench. It was a rather undignified end to her speech, but she was satisfied. She had made her point.

Cas leaned back in his seat, his arms crossed. "We will be watching you, Pryce."

Attie threw in a significant glare of her own. She was fairly sure she saw Captain Pryce flinch slightly.

Lysander reached over and popped open the carriage door. The captain peered outside. "So I am free to go?"

Cas shrugged. "We need to head home. It's my turn to watch the baby."

Attie perked up. "I'll do it!"

"No. Absolutely not. The last time we let you watch the baby, you locked him in a box!"

Attie huffed in offense. "It wasn't a box, Cas. It was a trunk and it wasn't even locked. And perhaps you've forgotten, but I did drill air holes."

The captain rose and tried to squeeze past everyone to escape.

"Just to clarify . . ." Dade grabbed his arm. "You're doing all this for Neville?"

Pryce paused and looked over his shoulder at Dade. "He deserves happiness." The captain then jumped to the street in front of his house.

Dade leaned out the open door and called after him, "And did you succeed? Is Neville now a happy man?"

Chapter 13

"SIR? Sir, if I may be so bold . . . be you Captain Pryce?"

What now? Morgan kept his hand stretched toward his own front door and turned.

The young man before him looked like an ordinary enough fellow, not a Worthington at any rate, not another harbinger of doom riding in a moth-eaten carriage. "And if I am?"

The man bobbed a quick bow and gave Morgan an apologetic smile. "I'm sorry to bother you, sir. I work for the old butcher on Echroy Street. He sent me to collect, he did."

Morgan frowned. "I did not make an order."

"No, sir . . . I mean, Captain Pryce, I mean . . . it were the lady of the house what done it."

Morgan stiffened. "The lady done . . . did what, exactly?"

The messenger held up both hands and smiled again. "Oh, sir! 'Twere wondrous, how she floated in like an angel—even the beastly old man couldna help smiling at her! And she ordered all the best cuts—near cleaned the butcher out, she did."

Morgan supposed he had only himself to blame. He recalled, most reasonably, that he'd chosen to leave his bride to her own devices. Furthermore, he'd left her in a house without more than a scrap of food in it.

But . . . the best cuts? Cleaned the butcher out? He regarded the fellow narrowly. "What does she owe you?"

"Oh, sir, 'tisn't much at all. The butcher was that charmed, he was! And he gave her a discount as well, seein' as how she cleaned—"

"Cleaned him out. Yes, I believe we've covered that fascinating detail already." Morgan gave the man his best Captain Maims-A-Lot glare. "How? Much?"

The messenger gulped and told him the amount.

Morgan took a moment to remind himself that he was a rational man. Strangling this poor fellow wouldn't resolve the situation. The act might be temporarily satisfying, but then he would owe the butcher for a shop full of prime cuts and one relatively polite errand boy as well.

So instead, he reached into his weskit pocket and pulled forth more shillings than he cared to part with. He dropped the coins in the young man's palm and narrowed his eyes in warning when the fellow had the gall to wiggle his fingertips slightly, hinting for a tip. "I'll be needing a receipt."

"Oh, aye, here it is, sir. I mean, Captain Pryce, sir!" He pulled a stub of charcoal pencil from behind his ear. "And here's me mark on it, sayin' as how you paid up right and tidy." The man bobbed another bow and backed away. Before he had taken more than three steps back, he'd turned and run off.

"That's right. You'd better run," Morgan growled, and reached for his door latch again.

"Oh, sir!"

Morgan flinched. *Oh no.*

"My apologies, sir, but are you by any chance Captain Pryce?"

He turned to see not one but three fellows hurrying toward him, waving bills. All the improvements he wished to make to his ship began to sink under the waves along with his drowning solvency.

WHEN MORGAN FINALLY made it safely into his own house, he strode through the door prepared to do battle. He would break down his stolen bride's resistance and claim his reward so he could quit this bloody city and get back to the sea before she beggared him any further!

He shut the door behind him with vigor. The slam should have echoed through his empty house like thunder through a cavern. Instead, the harsh sound was muffled.

Morgan gazed at his front hall. Something was wrong. It was a tiny entry, hardly more than a short hallway, with the stairs to the first floor on the left and an opening to the doorway to the front parlor on the right. Well, the only parlor, to be truthful.

The entry hadn't changed much. There was the little spindle table that his mother had brought from her family home in Wales. There was a vase on it that he'd brought back for her from one of his longer journeys. It wasn't a valuable piece, but she'd claimed that she loved the delicate brushwork that decorated it.

He blinked. There was a new carpet runner on the floor of the hall. It wasn't ornately woven, just a simple blue and gold pattern, but it shone in the candlelight like a jewel. In fact, everything gleamed, from the candlesticks to the woodwork. He'd forgotten how attractive the mitered paneling was, like the milling of a fine ship. He walked closer to the wall and peered at the wooden detail. It appeared to have been oiled and polished. The sheen had returned and he could smell the faintest hint of linseed.

Even the marble herringbone pattern of the floor, pleasing even though it was pieced in smaller tiles than the ostentatious entry of Camberton, was absolutely spotless.

Then he noticed that the door to the parlor was open. Enough light leaked into the room from the entry that he could see that instead of a few sheet-covered furnishings, the room had been fitted out in full feminine comfort. As he entered the room, he felt another thick, soft carpet underfoot. There were new man-sized chairs on either side of the fireplace, and the short, never-intended-for-sleeping settee had been replaced by a long, deep barge of a sofa that shimmered in the dimness as only fine velvet could do.

On the mantelpiece stood an appealing arrangement of fresh flowers, bracketed by a few of the possessions that had belonged to Morgan's mother. A pair of painted porcelain vases that he'd brought home from his first voyage to China. A set of brass candlesticks that had come from her own mother in Swansea. A dainty gilt ormolu clock that she'd treasured more than anything. Morgan peered closer at it. The ornate case was bracketed by a pair of leaping dolphins. Yes, it was the same one he remembered from his boyhood, but he'd not seen it since then.

It was alarming to think that his reluctant bride had so thoroughly investigated his house that she had found belongings he'd forgotten existed! Yet, for all the changes, everything was much as it had been. All was now spotless, with just enough touches of luxury, rugs, flowers, and jewel-toned cushions on the settee to turn monkish and severe into comfortable and welcoming. No grand elegance, no outlandish display, nothing to overshadow the small treasures he'd kept to remember his mother by.

Just enough to turn a house into a home.

Then he smelled food. His stomach growled. The tempting aroma of a roast . . . and baking bread . . . and the bubbling sweetness of gooseberries in a pie . . .

God, that woman was evil.

Morgan stuffed the handful of debt notes into his pocket and followed his nose into the kitchen.

With all the changes in his house, he'd expected to find an army of overpaid servants lurking around corners. He found no one but his blushing bride. She stood at the stovetop, clad neck to ankles in the same old apron, her blush no doubt due to the steaming pot she stirred.

It didn't matter. Even with only her face and fair hair visible, her beauty was still like a punch to the gut for a man who had been at sea for such a long time.

She must have heard him enter, because she turned to regard him with those wide, innocent blue eyes. Ha! He knew her measure and he would not be fooled! She was a thief, and a manipulator, and a—a—

A wife.

He looked down at the wad of notes crumpled in his hand. A grocer. A furniture maker. A butcher—whom he no doubt had to thank for the astonishing aroma coming from the oven.

It remained to be seen just how far he was going to have to allow this miscreant to beggar him before he won his own ship out of the deal!

As she untied her apron, she offered him a small, serene smile, tinged with a bit of hopeful expectation. His throat tightened. She was so very pretty.

So very evil and manipulative.

But pretty.

Doubt twanged again. Could he be wrong about her? Could she truly be the woman Neville believed her to be?

No. He would not fall for the same tricks that Neville had fallen for. Beyond the loveliness he saw the truth. Hell beckoned. Satan had fair hair, blue eyes, and pink cheeks. And, beneath that damned apron, the beast possessed a figure that would rouse a dead man.

Though Morgan realized his musings might be a tad dramatic, he'd had a rotten day. He'd been on land for only thirty hours, not even long enough for his legs to stop aching.

He'd barely had time to grow accustomed to the static hardness of the street beneath his boots instead of the springy give of the ship deck.

But in that time he'd gotten himself married. Before him stood his new bride, cheerfully embracing her new circumstances, as if all was right with the world.

For an instant, Morgan envied her adaptability.

Last night, Bliss Worthington had worn a priceless silk satin wedding dress. Her hair, despite the weather, had been perfectly done. Even the fashionably tiny silken slippers she'd worn had probably cost more than a new sail.

She'd looked every inch a duchess-in-the-making.

Now, flushed and bright-eyed, she wore a gown made of flowered muslin more suited to a country parson's daughter. It fit superbly, of course, as almost anything would on her figure, but it lacked the ruthless style Morgan had come to associate with ladies of the ton. Her shimmering blond hair was relaxed into a thick braid that was knotted up at the back of her neck, allowing soft, steam-curled tendrils to fall to each cheekbone.

At his silent examination, her chin lifted. A gleam of something almost like defiance sharpened the serenity of her expression. Did she think he would criticize her informal appearance? Let her think it. Even if she might think she looked a mutinous mess, he was not about to inform her that he much preferred her this way!

"Mew."

The sound startled Morgan, pulling his attention from the sky blue snare of the siren's gaze.

"Mew."

A kitten.

He blinked, but the mirage did not fade. There was a real, live kitten on his mother's chair, the old wooden one where she'd sat peeling potatoes and stripping peas.

It was the orange tabby variety of cat creature. The scrawny little beast regarded Morgan with eerily familiar green eyes, and he shuddered at the notion that the bizarre little girl from the carriage had transformed into an animal and planted herself in his house. *"Pwca,"* he muttered. The Welsh shape-shifting animal spirit.

"Attie."

Morgan flinched. "What?"

"The cat. Her name is Attie, not Pooka."

Morgan was an educated man. He had seen the world. He knew a thing or two about the silliness of superstition. But Rose Pryce's son had been raised on a wealth of folk-tales from her Welsh homeland. The chill raised the hairs on the back of his neck. "Where did it come from?" *And when is it going back?*

"My cousin Attie gave her to me. Actually, she claims the kitten stowed away in one of my hatboxes of its own volition and arrived here with my things, but I don't know if I believe that. I think Attie wanted to ensure that I had protection."

"Protection? From me? By a two-ounce puff of fur?" Just to prove he didn't believe in superstitious twaddle, he picked up the kitten. With one hand under its birdlike rib cage, he held it up to examine it. "What is it going to do, adorable me to death?"

"I wouldn't do that if I were you." Bliss held up her hand. "Do not attract the vengeance of Atalanta Worthington. Not even in jest. Actually, especially not in jest."

Before he could scoff, the little rodent took an open-clawed swing at his nose. He clutched it to his chest in self-defense. In an obvious attempt at diplomatic distraction, Bliss dipped a spoon into her pot and stepped close in order to hold it to his lips. "Taste this."

He was a man standing in the female domain of a bubbling, sizzling, delicious-smelling kitchen with his hands full of homicidal feline. As if in a trance, he obeyed and opened his mouth. Too late he thought of the thinly veiled threats upon his life and manhood tossed about by the

Worthington intimidation committee. But alas, he'd already hungrily swallowed the most heavenly bite of stewed beets that he'd ever had in life. And he hated beets.

Evil. No, worse than evil. She was a witch. A sorceress.

"Mew."

A witch with a fluffy, green-eyed familiar! Look at him. He'd been in her presence for less than five minutes and he was cuddling kittens and eating beets!

Clearly, something was amiss here.

Then he saw it. The last straw. A heavy copper tub sat in the corner of the kitchen, near a smaller stove that held two pails of steaming water. A fine bathing tub, the likes of which might rest in the chambers of Camberton House itself.

"Bloody hell." He returned the kitten to her throne with only a bit of bloodshed. "How much did that thing cost?"

Having gone back to her pot, Bliss twisted her head around to contemplate the tub with a satisfied smile as she continued to stir. "Oh, I drove a hard bargain there. It only cost half a pound."

Morgan breathed a little easier.

"Although the immediate delivery did come a little bit dear . . ."

Morgan closed his eyes. "How? Much?"

"Ohh . . . I don't know . . . eighteen shillings?"

Eighteen? By God, he only paid his first mate thirty shillings a year, plus a small piece of the profits. "Eighteen shillings to have some lout carry that thing into the house and set it on the floor?"

"Well, it is a very sturdy tub. I got the largest one, in case you wished to use it occasionally."

Morgan stared at her.

"I shan't mind at all," she added in patently generous tones.

Morgan fought the insane, helpless laughter that bubbled up from the depths of his exasperation. Well, as long as she had invited him to share his own blasted tub . . .

"I'll just carry it upstairs, shall I?" He hefted the damned thing over his head and began to maneuver it right out of the kitchen.

"Oh . . . wait . . . but I was going to . . ."

He turned his head to flash a fierce grin over his shoulder. "I'll be wanting that water brought up as well. For I'm in the mood for a nice, hot soak!"

He began his journey down the hallway and up the narrow staircase, immediately regretting his decision to establish his household dominance with a display of brute strength. This bloody hunk of ore weighed nearly as much as a small ship anchor.

He listened as Bliss sighed in resignation and moved the pot from the flame. She began to follow him up the narrow stairway, staying a few stairs behind, as if she wished to avoid being crushed should he drop the tub. It was a wise decision, as his back and shoulders had begun to tremble with fatigue.

If Morgan had been capable of turning around on the stairway, he was certain he'd find her cute little nose crinkled up in agitation. Turning around was out of the question, however. Remaining upright was trick enough. "Are you already complaining, wife?"

"Of course I am not complaining, husband."

"Good." Morgan tried to hide the fact that he was breathing hard. "Because if you insist . . ." Another step. "That I be a proper gentleman, which you clearly do . . ." Another step. "Then you must be a proper gentleman's wife."

"Hmm. I have noticed you enjoy using that word."

Morgan reached the top of the landing and turned toward his bedchamber, silently counting the seconds that remained before he could drop his burden. "And being a wife means you . . . must agree to a variety of wifely duties . . ." He was panting now.

"How about the wifely duty of hiring a few servants?"

"What need have I—for—servants?" *Dear God, this thing is heavy!*

"No, I can see you have matters well in hand, all by yourself. Except that you don't clean, you can't cook, your house is in the middle of an appalling pigeon crisis—"

His vision began to swim slightly. The outrageous cost of delivery had begun to make more sense.

I am going to drop this thing. I will die beneath it, but at least this brutal climb will be over.

To be truthful, the only reason he did not give up and leave the bloody thing halfway up the stairs was that he would have to tolerate the faintly mocking twitch of one of those perfect eyebrows. For someone who maintained a perfectly placid exterior, she seemed to leak a great many opinions.

"And you are stubborn enough to kill yourself with that tub."

Morgan reached the landing to the floor with the two bedchambers. For a moment, he swayed on the top step. Then with one last mighty heft, he managed to turn the great copper beast and stagger the final few feet to the single usable bedchamber.

When at last he lowered the tub to rest before the fire, he remained there, leaning on the thing with his hands braced on either side and his legs trembling somewhat. Thank God it was too dim in the room for her to see—

A candle flared to life on the mantel. Then another.

Morgan drew himself upright in a hurry and gave a disdainful grunt to cover his breathlessness. He had no excuse for this charade except that he was a man and she was a pretty woman and that was how things were done. Men pretended to be towers of boundless strength and women pretended to be impressed.

Who was he to break with tradition? It had worked for humankind so far. He turned.

Bliss stood in front of the fire, a steaming pail of water to each side. Her adorable bare feet were planted on the gleaming hardwood, and her hands were folded before her. It appeared that she, too, was slightly out of breath.

Morgan widened his stance and settled his fists upon his hips, hoping he appeared authoritative even while he gulped the air. "As I was saying, this is my house and you are my wife, and I have decided that your role as such shall encompass a myriad of duties."

"Myriad?"

"Yes, including massaging my shoulders and neck, and perhaps trimming my hair and shaving my face should I so desire."

Bliss's eyes widened. "Like . . . a barber?"

"Like a wife. After all, I've been a good husband to you, have I not? I paid all the bills you rang up today. I praised your cooking last evening."

"You wolfed my cooking."

He suppressed a smile. "Wolfing is a form of praise."

"And then you belched, sir."

Morgan unleashed a severe glare in her direction. It was the only way he could combat his desire to laugh. "Further praise. Now." His legs began to give with exhaustion, so he lowered himself to the edge of the tub. "Have I not kept my word to behave with gentlemanly restraint?"

A single eyebrow arched on Bliss's forehead. "I suppose, but please allow me to ask for some clarification on that matter."

He waved his hand in permission.

"You wish me to bathe you whilst you are without . . . accoutrements?"

"Is that a fancy word for drawers?"

Bliss lifted her chin. It was obvious she fought to keep her brow unfurrowed, but Morgan saw that she blushed in earnest now. How did she do that? he wondered. How did one blush at will? Perhaps it was something they taught in the school for manipulative females.

He knew they had reached the moment of truth: Either Bliss Worthington would give in to his ridiculous list of demands, or her veneer of virginal righteousness would crack and she would tell him to go to hell, revealing the shameless gold digger she truly was. Either way, his evening looked to be improving rather soon.

But what Morgan would not admit, not even to himself, was that the very thought of this pretty, blushing woman kneeling beside him, washing his back . . . among other things . . . had abruptly become a forceful private fantasy.

Except that she looked so very . . . vulnerable. He relented just a bit. "I will cover the tub with a sheet, if you like. But—" Perhaps now would be a good moment to go somewhat helpless male. He ran a hand through his overlong, shaggy hair, still stiff with salt from his last sea bath. "I truly could use your help looking more presentable."

Bliss considered him for a wary moment, then lowered her gaze and gave him a nod so soft that it was barely noticeable. "Shall I bring up your meal before I fill the bath?"

Chapter 14

BLISS stood at the stovetop, trying to remember what she'd been doing. Her task was a simple one: ladle the stewed beets next to the sliced roast. But her mind was a churning storm of complications, her peace shattered.

She had blushed! And for good reason. Bliss had spent several moments directly behind Captain Pryce on the stairs. The view had been stupendous. He was just as good-looking from the back as he was from the front!

She'd still been in awe of his powerful form when he requested that she shave him sans clothing. Her head now spun with imaginings of his naked, glistening manliness.

Oh! He had balanced that tub in midair as if it were papier-mâché. His muscled rear had flexed impressively with every step he climbed. It had been an effort not to stare at the shoulder and torso strength that bulged beneath the captain's coat. Truly, his vigor was astounding!

The sound of silver crashing to the floorboards roused

Bliss to attention. She retrieved the dropped utensil and fetched another, then made her way up the steps once more.

She ought to be thinking of Neville, for it was he who wanted and needed her, not Captain Pryce. The man in her room might be impressive, but he was not the man for her.

What would she see when she entered the bedchamber? Would he already be disrobed? Would he dare dine in such a bacchanalian fashion?

Bliss felt the corner of her mouth lift. Captain Pryce had turned the bargain on her. The man was clever. *I like clever. I like it very much.*

Alas, he was clothed as he sat on a chair near the hearth. He had already pulled a side table near, ready for his meal. His deep-sea eyes flashed as she appeared in the doorway with his food and drink. He straightened. Bliss could not tell if he was aroused by her, the savories, or both.

It took a great deal of determination to keep her countenance serene, but she could not let him see her smile.

"Will you be dining with me, wife?"

She set the plate, utensils, and wine goblet upon the table with pleasant efficiency. "I shall dine later, after you have had your bath."

Up and down she went, lugging one pail of hot water after the next and pouring the contents into the tub. All the while, the captain ate and drank without comment in the light of the candles she had lit for his comfort. Despite the silence, the rapid rate at which the food disappeared was proof enough that he relished his meal.

With each trip between floors, Bliss contemplated the matter at hand.

Theirs was an unusual bargain, to be sure. Because the captain had been quite understanding about the little matter of consummation, she found herself in a position where she could not refuse his other requests. Fortunately, none of these additional duties would necessarily negate her options for an annulment . . . as long as no one ever knew about them.

Bliss reminded herself that she was, indeed, a proper young lady. But she was a Worthington, and as she had learned long ago, the rules, when applied to Worthingtons, were rules only in the most general sense.

So that was a promise she could make to herself—she would remain *generally* proper. She was sure Neville would understand, in the end.

"I am quite ready for my bath, wife." The captain had devoured every scrap of food and had pushed the table aside. He lounged in the chair now, his long legs stretched out before him. "Would you be so kind as to remove my boots?"

"Of course." With an air of cheerful obedience, Bliss knelt before him. She tugged the heel of his black leather boot with one hand and cradled the shaft with the other. Just the leather itself. No true contact whatsoever. She pulled off the other boot in the same manner.

She rose, produced a tranquil smile, then set his boots aside. It seemed the captain took that as his cue to stand and immediately begin to unbutton his breeches. Bliss grabbed the tray of empty dishes and scurried toward the door.

"Where are you rushing off to, wife?"

"I . . . I must retrieve more water."

His low chuckle rumbled behind her back. She heard the sound of his breeches slipping to the floor.

"SIR, YOU ARE naked."

Morgan tried not to smirk, but was not entirely successful. He gestured for her to enter the bedchamber. "It is time for you to fulfill your other wifely duties."

She blinked at him slowly. Her composure was remarkable—unless she was far more experienced than she professed. For she was correct. He was naked, entirely. Soaking wet and sudsy, too.

The bath sheet draped over the more . . . *informative*

portions of the tub but did nothing to hide his chest and shoulders.

As his flustered bride placed another full water pail by the tub, Morgan leaned back in the vast copper tub and sighed with contentment. The thing was a monster and worth every shilling, though he would never tell her so. When he moved, the sheet shifted and slipped down to touch the water, revealing more of his torso.

His bride's blue gaze jerked away and fixed upon the fire glowing beyond him. Morgan grinned openly and stretched his long legs in the warm water. "I put my shaving kit on the dressing table, and I have stropped the razor for you."

She stood absolutely still. By the candlelight, he thought he saw her swallow hard. Her fingers twined before her. Her betraying signs were subtle, but Morgan was accustomed to reading the sea itself by no more than the color of its waves.

No matter how understated her manner, he was beginning to read his bride the same way.

"Wife? I have requested your assistance in the bath. Do you mean to deny me this husbandly right as well?"

She stared at the fire, obviously not looking at him with all her might. "You gave me your word that I shall remain un . . . unfrittered with."

He laughed out loud. Did she even realize that her cheeks were aglow with the heat rushing through her? Or was it all artifice? Yet again, the question plagued him. Who was this woman? Was she evil or innocent? He had to admit that her mystery fascinated him.

If he hadn't been feeling the pressure from Lord Oliver to consummate their union, it might have been fun to take his time revealing her game. To peel back each layer of her deception as he peeled back her resistance . . .

As he peeled off her ridiculously demure clothing. He felt himself harden further. His throat tightened.

Was he positively mad? How could he have forgotten that only two days ago this woman had claimed to be madly in

love with his brother? How could he have forgotten Lord
Oliver's warnings?

"I have not 'frittered' with you whatsoever. What is this,
wife? You choose to not hold to our bargain? Fine! Then I
am entitled to—"

"Oh, for pity's sake!" Bliss shook her head in exasperation, and a few more blond tendrils fell loose upon her cheek.
"I will shave you if I must."

"And cut my hair."

"And cut your hair."

"You should remove your gown as well. I feel in the mood
to splash."

She finally met his gaze. There was a bright blaze of
warning in her wide eyes. It faded instantly, giving way to
her usual bland imperturbability. "Yes," she said thought-
fully. "Perhaps I should."

She turned and left the bedchamber. The moments ticked
by. Just when Morgan had decided to start bellowing her
name, she reappeared. He stared at her with his jaw practically hanging into the bathwater.

She had indeed removed her gown.

And donned that damned gigantic apron she'd found in
his kitchen!

She looked like a mermaid wrapped in a fisherman's tarp!
Hardly an inch of her was visible but for her face, tiny muslin sleeves on the arms holding two pails of water, and the
lacy edge of her shift and her bare toes emerging below the
crumpled hem. She placed the pails upon the hearth.

Morgan lifted an eye brow. "Off to do a spot of blacksmithing, are we?"

She was utterly adorable. It occurred to him that there
seemed to be two Bliss Worthingtons—one innocent and
endearing and the other cunning and dangerous. He just
wished he could be sure that the engaging one, the one who
stood before him at that moment, was the real Bliss.

Suddenly, a fascination for those naked pink toes overtook him. Of course it did. A fellow had to take what he could get.

"You look ridiculous, you know."

She seemed unperturbed by his opinion. "And yet I feel entirely comfortable, for I am in my own bedchamber, am I not? I may wear what I like in my own room, I should think. Or is that against your arbitrary marital rules as well? If so, you ought to have brought it up in negotiations."

Damn. He wished he had. He tore his hungry gaze from her toes. *One body part at a time, lad.*

He indicated the dish of soap once more. "If you please."

She shuffled forward and knelt by the side of the tub. He could hear the thick canvas crunch with her every movement.

Then, when she leaned over him to reach the soap, he caught a whiff of something sweet and light—it made him hungry. She smelled like . . .

"Vanilla!"

She retreated at once, sitting back on her heels with the soap in her hand. After giving him a reproachful glance, she dipped his shaving brush into the water next to his side and began to create a lather, using it against the soap. Morgan found his attention snagged by the twist of her graceful wrists and the sensual movements of her fingers as they intertwined, sliding, soaping—

He caught himself short and used one arm to sweep her thick cover of suds from the surface of the water onto the floor. When she ducked backward, he laughed. "I told you I was in the mood to splash."

Not a grumble. Not even a glare. She simply set down the soap and lifted the lathered brush.

Being shaved was much more enjoyable than shaving oneself, usually. Then again, even the gruffest barber actually laid hands on his clients occasionally. Morgan waited in vain for a feminine caress, even an accidental one, but none came. She was very diligent—and entirely removed.

Snick! He opened his eyes to see her with his razor in

one hand, her head tilted as she examined it closely. The candlelight shimmered on the six-inch blade as she tilted it to and fro. She reached a finger of her other hand to test the edge.

"Don't!" Morgan shook his head in warning. "It's very sharp, trust me."

She pulled her hand back and fixed him with her unreadable gaze. "Good."

Ah. "Perhaps I should just take that—"

She rose to her knees by his side and waved the blade before his nose, forcing him back against the back of the tub. "Nonsense. Shropshire shears a great deal of wool. I know precisely what to do."

This was both reassuring and alarming. He would likely not get his throat cut, but he might emerge looking like a freshly shorn ram!

She bent to her task and began to shave him with sure, adroit strokes. Morgan relaxed somewhat. Again, she did not touch him once.

When she set the razor aside he lifted a hand to stroke over his cheeks. "Well, that's a fine job of it. Better than I could do for myself."

She regarded him without expression. "I'm so happy you're pleased."

He was going to get her hands on him if it was the last thing he ever did. He didn't stop to question whether his motivation still had anything to do with gaining a ship. "Do you ever shear a sheep and leave a bit of the wool on?"

She merely rose to take his scissors and comb from his kit. "I am entirely capable of cutting your hair. Do you prefer it short or—"

"I do not care for the girlish poet style that is currently in fashion. Quite short, if you please."

Now standing next to the tub, she looked down at him. Her pretty face was close, for he was tall and she was not. Yet there was nothing in her expression but the coolest assessment. "Girlish, no, but I do believe you could manage the poet charade, now that I can see your face."

He gave her a slow grin. "Mrs. Pryce, was that a compliment?"

"Heavens no," she said briskly as she moved to stand behind him. "I cannot bear poets. Too much overwrought theatrics. I see that enough at Worthington House."

Morgan snorted. "I have met your cousins. They accosted me outside my own front door earlier. Scoundrels and assassins. There is not a poet amongst them."

She began to comb, pulling quite gently. He noticed that she touched only his hair, not him.

"Oh, they've never actually killed anyone. Not even Attie, although there have been a few close calls. Although . . ." She began to snip with the scissors.

"Although?"

"Well, Lysander did go to war. I expect someone might have died at his hands."

Recalling the silent, lethal-seeming fellow in the carriage, Morgan expected that more than one French soldier had met an early end because of him. Not that Morgan held that against him. Things were different in battle.

"And I was speaking of the incorporeal denizens of Worthington House."

Morgan blinked. "Ghosts?"

She made an impatient sound. "Worse. Writers. I love a good book as much as anyone, but I would just as soon not run into King Lear in the halls on my way to the privy in the night."

Morgan set his jaw. "I don't believe in ghosts." He resolutely didn't, not even when he felt his mother's disappointment at the state of her beloved house.

"I told you, not ghosts. My uncle Archie likes to live out the great plays." *Snip, snip.* "He believes that they can only be truly appreciated aloud. Repeatedly. Trust me, Shakespeare is alive and well at Worthington House."

She was becoming quite relaxed, he realized. The tasks he'd set her had all been done quickly and efficiently, yet she seemed rather energized by them all.

Her serene stillness might not be her natural state after all. Perhaps Bliss was more of an achiever than an observer. Morgan could sympathize with that.

"There." Her tone sounded quite satisfied. "That should do it. But your hair needs washing the sea out of it, or it will poke out like a hedgehog."

Morgan smiled. *Let's see you get out of this one.* "If you will do the honors?"

Chapter 15

BLISS fought the rather overwhelming desire to splash sudsy water into the captain's knowing eyes. But she could not. This man held her future in his hands. She must not antagonize him, no matter how he vexed her.

He gazed at her innocently. "I need my hair washed. It's not easy to pour the pitcher over one's own head, you know."

Patience. Calm. It was a reasonable request. Even she usually asked her young cousin Attie to do that for her. She stood up and wiped her wet hands down her stiff apron front. "Very well. After you soap your hair, I will pour the pitcher."

"I don't think I can." He gestured to his right shoulder, pointing her attention to a bulging line of scar tissue that followed the curve of his deltoid from the outside of his arm to the interior of his triceps.

"A souvenir from a Saracen's sword. We became acquainted in a Trinidad marketplace, where he, for no apparent reason, made it clear he didn't much care for the cut of my jib."

Bliss blinked at the mark. She'd not even noticed it in her first sight of his naked body. Of course, in her defense, she had been mightily distracted by the very matter of his nakedness. Now she drew her eyebrows together in pity. "It looks a terrible wound. Does it still pain you?"

His dark gaze was most sincere. "Only when I soap my hair."

With that, Bliss reached behind her to grab a pail of hot water and sluiced the contents over his head. While he sputtered and laughed, she pondered how she would fulfill her duties without actually touching her husband.

Her wifely duties.

She had washed Old Dally's hair for her, near the end. There wasn't that much difference between a man's head and an old woman's, was there?

A few minutes later, standing over Captain Pryce with her fingers digging into his soapy scalp, Bliss had to admit that there was a great deal of difference.

His hair was so thick, and the black strands slid through her fingers so temptingly that she took rather a long time about the job. But she could feel the heat of his big body, even through her sturdy apron, and she could feel every rumble of pleasure that sounded from his throat. The vibrations traveled through her fingertips and ricocheted through her body.

Bliss had never thought of herself as starved for anything, but she had never felt as intimately connected to another person as she did washing Captain Pryce's thick dark hair. She suddenly became very aware of the empty house and of the silence, broken only by the dripping of the suds into the bathwater and by Morgan's throaty sighs of pleasure.

She decided to listen to the snap of the coals on the hearth instead. She would focus on her own breathing—although it was strangely shallow. She would pay attention only to her own pulse—although she thought it was a bit faster than usual. Bliss took a moment to remind herself that as handsome as Morgan was, as fascinating, as appealing, he would not do at all.

It was Neville she desired. She longed for Neville and the life of constant companionship she envisioned with him.

No more waiting.

Captain Pryce shifted his body. He leaned back in the tub with his eyes closed, as if making it easier for her to transfer her attentions to the front of his hair. With his eyes closed against the soap, Bliss had an opportunity to do something she'd not realized she greatly desired. She could study his handsome face to her fill.

It was not disloyal to Neville to find Morgan handsome. The brothers were so very much alike that any compliment to Morgan naturally applied to Neville as well.

Did it not?

Except, perhaps, for the small crinkles that sun and sea had carved around Morgan's eyes. That was very different. And there was something altogether implacable about his square jaw that she had never seen in Neville's pleasant countenance.

He looked so rough and wary with his unshaven cheeks and shaggy hair. Rougher and warier because of it, but it was certainly understandable. He'd only docked his ship the day before after a long journey, after all. Bliss found herself bristling slightly at the thought that someone might criticize Morgan for his lack of perfect grooming—someone stupid, who had no idea how hard a man like Captain Morgan had to work to make his own way in the world, unsupported by high rank and obscene wealth!

"Ow," Morgan said with a wince. "You're pulling a bit hard."

Bliss bit her lip and eased her grip on his hair. "My apologies, Captain. I—this is—I am unaccustomed—" *I'm babbling. I never babble.*

Ever.

Morgan settled farther into the tub. His movement caused a wave to pull the soaked sheet entirely down into the water. From her vantage point, looking down over him, she found her gaze riveted by the great surging erection that threatened to break the surface of the bathwater.

Oh. My. Heavens.

She froze, shutting her eyes tightly. Her hands went utterly still in his hair. That was . . . *oh goodness . . . oh my . . .*

Bliss understood what that daunting erection implied. Morgan wanted a woman. More specifically, Morgan wanted her. And, if the sheer rigidity of his member signified anything, he wanted her . . . right now.

She began to tremble deep inside. The shiver traveled from somewhere highly personal and raced through her entire body. Her knees became unsteady. Her belly quivered.

Her hands began to shake.

She jerked her fingers from Captain Pryce's very well washed hair with a tiny gasp.

"Ouch!" He sat up straight, lifting one forearm to his face to wipe away the soap over his eyes.

Bliss scrambled backward, closer to the fire. When her foot came into contact with something, she looked down to see the water-filled pail she'd forgotten to put next to the hearth.

Rinse. Rinse and be done. Be done and leave this room!

Without a thought, she grabbed up the heavy pail and took two steps back to the tub. Lifting her hands high, she dumped the chilly water over Captain Pryce's soapy head.

"Arghh!" He slapped both hands on the sides of the tub and leaped to his feet. "Bloody hell! That's cold!"

Oh heavens. He was magnificent. And naked. Really, very naked.

"All done!" The words squeaked from her panic-tightened throat.

"Whaaa?"

"I suddenly find myself famished, sir! I shall dine down-stairs!"

Before Morgan could clear his face of soap, she fled the room.

Chapter 16

THE next morning, Morgan was more determined than ever to settle matters with his reluctant bride.

The atmosphere over breakfast was surprisingly unruffled. Morgan had decided that the best revenge was no revenge. He'd pushed Bliss too far last night, obviously. He'd meant to shake her damned imperturbability, and challenge her claims of innocence, but he had been the one left shivering and shaken.

He'd not been prepared for the way her tentative touch had stirred him. And if he was truthful, he would have to admit that hesitation had left him a bit unsure of his opinion.

There had been no sexual knowledge in her hands, no jaded assurance.

On the other hand, neither had she shied from her assigned tasks, nor gone into a faint or some other silliness that would be typical of a young maiden of the ton.

And she'd turned the tables on him, quite neatly, too. He'd meant to test her, to shock her, to cow her—but she'd left the fray with a decided upper hand.

One had to admire a woman who could manage that with a man like him.

So which woman was she, seductress with nerves of steel, or vulnerable virgin? Looking over his breakfast plate at his bride, Morgan honestly couldn't tell.

And what a breakfast it was! Last night's hurried meal was this morning's tender beef roast, floating in a delicious gravy that nearly made Morgan close his eyes and moan, served alongside perfectly prepared eggs.

What pampered lady of the ton could cook like this?

Then again, that Worthington family was an odd bunch. Word had it that the mother was some sort of obsessive painter and that the father had been drummed out of a literary society—the Fiddlesome Society for the Study of Romantic Drivel, or some such thing—for making unseemly insinuations about Shakespeare.

Even with his life at sea, Morgan had heard of the Double Devils, the Worthington twins Castor and Pollux. Yesterday, Cas had seemed settled enough, and there'd been no sign of the other Devil, but that dark brother, the one who didn't speak—now, there was a dangerous man!

Morgan had been in many a tight and lethal fight, protecting his ship from those who took cargo and lives with equal enjoyment. He knew what a man on the edge looked like, recognized that depth of isolation, that withdrawal from life, until life itself did not seem terribly valuable—and therefore easily taken.

Lysander Worthington was such a man.

Morgan's thoughts skirted away from considering the other odd passenger in the carriage yesterday, but not before his gaze turned to the third occupant of the breakfast table.

Attie Cat crouched at the end of the table on a lacy mat, her fuzzy face deep into a bowl of cream. As if she sensed his attention, she raised her head and gazed back at him with those eerie green eyes.

The witch's familiar. But which witch? Was it Bliss, who

seemed a practical, brisk sort of sorceress, or was it that odd little person who had stared at him from the darkened corner seat as if calculating how long it would take to dismember and conceal his freshly dropped corpse?

Morgan shook off a shudder and turned the full force of his limited charm upon the woman opposite him. He had business to attend to and could not afford to waste any opportunity to secure milady's affections.

He smiled at her. "I take back everything I said about the bills yesterday. This breakfast alone is worth every penny."

She regarded him for a long moment with her fork poised in midair. Then she put it down, the bite of roast on it still uneaten. "Thank you, Captain Pryce. That is very kind of you to say."

Morgan could honestly refute that. "No kindness involved. You are an excellent cook. Your relatives must miss your talent in the kitchen."

She only blinked at him. "My relatives most assuredly miss me, but I have never cooked at Worthington House. Mrs. Philpott would be aghast at having to share her domain."

"Ah." Morgan smiled encouragingly. "Did you learn from this Mrs. Philpott?"

"Mrs. Philpott is an abominable cook. Her specialty is tea. All sorts of tea." Bliss tilted her head slightly. "I learned from my guardian, Mrs. Dalyrymple. She did not keep a cook, so she had me in the kitchen when I was of an age to stir a pot whilst standing on a chair."

Morgan felt his smile slip from his face. "I'm sorry. I did not know you are an orphan."

She folded her hands in her lap and regarded him without expression of any kind. "Whatever gave you that idea? Forgive me, Captain Pryce, but you are quite mistaken. Both of my parents are alive and well."

"Yet you were raised by a guardian?"

"Yes, in Shropshire."

Morgan couldn't imagine anything worse. He found London an utter bore. "Shropshire seems one step from the end of the earth to me."

Bliss remained silent for a moment. Then, as she picked her fork up once more, "Shropshire is most essential," she told him gravely. "Britain itself would falter if not for the wool of Shropshire sheep."

Morgan couldn't help it. He laughed and lifted his dainty new coffee cup high. "Then here's to the fluffy denizens of Shropshire. Long may they wool."

With her bite of breakfast almost to her open lips, she froze. Those blue eyes locked on his for a long moment. He was just beginning to fear that he'd offended her again when a short, strangled sound emerged from her parted lips.

Morgan crinkled his brow. "Was that a laugh?"

Bliss popped her bite of cold eggs into her mouth and chewed it most thoroughly while she poked her fork about her plate for a time.

Perfectly comfortable with silence, Morgan leaned back in his chair and let it grow. He'd made her laugh. That in itself was nothing new to him. He'd made many a lady giggle over the years. There was no better way to warm a woman's nethers than to bring on a belly laugh.

Yet he didn't think he'd ever been more proud of a jest in his life. This woman with her wide blue gaze and guileless face was a deep, cool pool of control.

He'd just made a ripple on that glassy surface.

Then Bliss swallowed her bite of everlasting eggs and turned the tables on him again. "And what of your childhood, Captain?"

Morgan didn't talk about his life as the bastard son of the Great Man, the prominent and respected Duke of Camberton.

However, in the spirit of fair play, he owed Bliss something. "This was my mother's house. We moved here to London after the new duchess moved into Camberton."

Bliss nodded. "Neville's mother."

Morgan did not speak of the Lady Nessa. Ever.

He picked up his own fork and began to trail the tines through the sheen of butter on his plate, all that remained of Bliss's astonishing meal. "My mother loved this house. Living at the lodge on the estate was too much like being a member of His Grace's staff. I had enjoyed the woods and hills of Camberton Park, but after one look at the ships at the East India Docks, I wanted nothing more of life than to sail."

"So you were both content here."

Morgan smiled slightly, remembering. His mother had begun every day in the house singing, as she puttered about in a kitchen of her very own, even as she smacked the rugs in the small walled garden behind the house. "She was more than content. This was her nest, she used to say. Finally a nest of her own."

Bliss nodded. "This was a cozy home once. I saw that when I tidied yesterday."

Morgan shook his head. "You didn't tidy. You scoured. I know what shipshape looks like, remember?"

"I'm happy you think so." Bliss looked down at her hands in a proper lady's acceptance of praise. Her perfect manners made Morgan want to growl. One day, he'd like to see a woman grin and say, "Thanks, mate!" like a person and not a paper doll.

Bliss persisted. "And you?"

He shrugged. "I was restless, as young men are. As soon as I cleared six feet in height, I was down at the ships, begging for a place. I was only fourteen, but I looked older. I might have made it, had my mother not worried I would fall into bad company. So she asked the duke for a boon, which she'd sworn she'd never do."

"A ship for you to captain?"

"Hardly." Morgan laughed. "No, a job. Swabbing decks and peeling potatoes on one of His Grace's four-mast clippers. The *Pegasus*. We called her the *Pigeon*. She was a fat, wallowing barge of a ship, but I adored her with all the passion of first love."

"And you fell in love with the sea as well?"

Morgan tossed down his napkin and stood. Some things were too large and powerful for offhand breakfast conversation. "I fear I cannot delay here any longer today. I have a great deal of business to see to on the *Selkie Maid*."

Bliss stood as well. "I hope I have not said something to offend you, Captain Pryce?"

Morgan shot her a look, but she was entirely serious. She was cool as a cucumber about avariciously tricking his half brother into an elopement, but concerned enough to crack a frown over whether she'd said a wrong word over eggs.

"What manner of woman are you?" He hadn't meant to say that, for it brought back pulse-pounding memories of that kiss while she writhed on his lap—

"I am a Worthington," she said again, just as she had on that night.

"Not anymore," Morgan growled.

It was clear that the détente had reached its end. Her spine stiffened, perfecting her already exquisite posture.

God, that figure! She made him want to run raging into the street before he flung himself upon her!

"Yes, thank you for reminding me," she said crisply. "I remember now that I have a boon to ask of you, husband."

Morgan did not react in any way. He made certain of it. "No more bills, I hope."

BLISS CAREFULLY DID not flinch at his question. Nothing further would slip unwarily from her lips. She could not afford to betray herself to this man. "It is a simple request. I require your escort this afternoon. I have an appointment, and my driver of yesterday is unlikely to be available. As you keep no staff, you must accompany me yourself." She fixed him with her best stare. "As an appropriate husband should."

He strode past her and left the room. She picked up her

hem and sailed after him. She'd long ago mastered the art of racing along while looking as if she took a relaxing stroll.

As he shrugged on his topcoat, for a thin drizzle fell outside, he slid his gaze sideways to regard her with suspicion. Really! The captain's refusal to believe a single word she said was beginning to grate.

Actually, it threatened to erode her calm most severely.

She lifted her chin slightly. "I assure you, Captain, that I have no nefarious agenda. I have an errand I must run—a rendezvous that would be most unkind to miss. A dear friend is awaiting me and I should not like to disappoint him."

He turned on her, his dark blue gaze sharp. "Him? Your dear friend is a man? You are a married woman now. Do you think friendships with other men is entirely appropriate?"

Now he was just being obstinate. Spare her from the whims and whiffles of male moods! "Well, you will meet him shortly," she pressed on. "Why don't you see for yourself that he is no threat to any husband I may have? He is a dressmaker, and we shall be there for my dress fitting."

He tilted his head back slightly and surveyed her from head to toe. Bliss endured his examination, for she knew perfectly well that she was most appropriately and demurely attired for an afternoon errand. Just so, as always.

Yet still he grumbled. "I do not see any reason why you cannot simply—"

"We." She corrected him gently. "Yesterday I was forced to hire a stranger to pose as my escort. You are my husband. A wife has a right to expect a minimum of husbandly assistance, does she not?"

She didn't smile at his startled befuddlement. She did not laugh when his gaze shot about the room in his desperate attempt to think of a reason, any reason, why she was not entirely correct. It was a very nice moment, but Bliss cherished it in an inward fashion only. Men did not deal well with glee at their expense. Such tender feelings.

It was rather exhausting, all told. She longed for her

tough-skinned cousins, who were so used to Elektra's abrasive temper and Attie's lethal revenge that they jumped to do as Bliss bade them, simply because she asked politely.

"It is a dress fitting, you say?"

"Yes."

"You cannot possibly need another dress. Your cousins brought a cartload yesterday."

"No, I need another ball gown."

He was probably not aware of the way he covered his weskit pocket with a protective palm. She should mention that it would not cost him a farthing, but why make matters easy for him?

"Why do you need another ball gown?" he asked.

Bliss forced herself to patience. "Why, to go to the Fletchers' ball in two days. The invitations came out simply ages ago. I must go, for I have already accepted. Oh, and I shall need an escort for that as well. *Husband*."

She had him, fair and square, and she knew he knew it.

He gave a horsey snort, a sound both annoyed and acquiescent. "Fine. I'll take you this afternoon, after I have checked on my ship."

"That is agreeable." Bliss nodded serenely. "I have much to do myself."

Morgan gave her a short nod, then turned and left the house. He was nearly running.

Bliss allowed a small smile to cross her lips. He likely wanted to get out before she found something else emasculating for him to do. This wasn't going to take as long as she thought.

Sooner or later, Captain Pryce would remember that he wasn't the marrying kind.

Chapter 17

LORD Oliver found Neville slouched in a library chair with legs askew. The younger man was still attired in last night's dinner ensemble, though the cravat was untied and weskit unbuttoned. A half-emptied bottle of their finest Madeira teetered on a century-old Turkish carpet. And though one of Neville's ridiculous insect books was open upon his lap, his eyes were closed.

Oliver made a *tsking* sound as he shook his head. The boy had just experienced his first heartbreak. It would not be his last. Who knew the boy would turn out to be such a sensitive sot?

"Neville!" Lord Oliver kicked at one of the duke's boots. "Wake up!"

Neville started, gripping the chair arms like a drowning man clinging to a lifeboat. He blinked at Oliver in confusion. "Erph?"

"At this rate you'll deplete our wine cellar by the fall."

Neville straightened and cleared his throat. He tried to

button his weskit but gave up when the task of slipping buttons into holes proved too challenging. "What time is it, Uncle?"

"It's time for you to regain your dignity, boy! That Worthington girl does not warrant this kind of collapse. Think of all the people who depend upon you."

Neville rubbed his palms over his face and looked up with red-rimmed eyes. "I love Bliss. I hate Morgan. I just don't understand how my own brother could he have done this to me."

"Oh, nonsense. He's not your brother—he's a bastard, your father's regrettable by-blow." Oliver sat in a chair opposite Neville, crossing his legs to get comfortable.

"I shall never speak to him again."

Lord Oliver hid his twitch of a smile behind a cupped hand. Oh, but this was too rich! His attempt to turn the brothers on each other was working, and since they had chosen not to rely on each other, they would have to turn to their dear old uncle instead.

Such an arrangement would make it so much easier for him to shape Camberton's future.

Neville dropped his elbows upon his knees and hung his head, staring at the carpet. Oliver knew that before him was a thoroughly defeated man.

"Morgan knew how I feel about Bliss." Neville's voice was now nothing but a moan of despair. "He stole her! It's . . . it's . . . a knife in my belly. I shall never trust my brother again."

Oliver grew weary of all the blubbering. He fiddled with an arrangement of lilies on the side table, wondering how long he needed to remain here before the boy was convinced he had his dear uncle's heartfelt sympathy.

He sighed in boredom. "Well, I told Pryce it was a bad idea. He doesn't listen."

Neville's neck tightened. His head perked up. His eyes—

now wide and fiercely alert—locked onto Oliver's. *Oh no . . .*

"You knew, Uncle?"

OLIVER KNEW?

Neville felt his jaw unhinge. His mind was so fogged by drink that he could not be sure he had heard Lord Oliver correctly.

Uncle Oliver drew back. "Well, I—"

Neville jumped to his feet. Too quickly. He nearly toppled over. "You knew what Morgan was up to, yet you did not warn me? You just let it all unfold?"

"It's not as simple as that, my boy. Truly. I—"

"Why did you not stop him?"

Uncle Oliver looked flushed. His eyes darted about the library in what looked like panic. Neville heard himself emit a bitter laugh. This was unbelievable! It was bad enough that his brother had betrayed him, but his uncle, too?

It was no secret that Lord Oliver disapproved of the Worthington connection. Yet for him to know that Morgan meant to betray him—and do nothing?

The hollow in Neville's gut grew larger. Truly, he had never felt so alone in all his life. "Why, Uncle? Why did you not stop him?"

Lord Oliver stood. "You're a bit jug-bitten at the moment, my boy. I must advise that you avoid making accusations you will later regret."

"You advise me, Lord Oliver? Still? And yet you do not answer my question!"

"This is ridiculous." Oliver turned to go.

Neville stepped in front of him. He might be unsteady, but he was determined to see this exchange through to a satisfactory end. "Why did you let Morgan steal Bliss from me?"

His uncle looked terribly insulted. "While I agreed with Morgan that the girl was unsuitable, I did not believe Morgan would go through with something so outrageous. I intended to appeal to your better judgment instead, as I always have!"

Neville blinked, trying to marshal his intellect against the fog of drink. "Did you mean to—"

"I assure you, young man, my only fault was thinking too highly of your so-called brother. Now . . ." Oliver looked him up and down, his expression impatient. "Do clean yourself up and arrive promptly for dinner this evening. We have house-guests, as you might recall."

Neville watched his uncle stomp from the library, his back straight with self-righteousness. He stayed there, staring into the empty hall, as he fought for some bit of clarity. It was true that his uncle had always pushed him toward success, and often insisted he do things his way. But until now, Neville had believed his father's brother had only honorable motivations. He believed Lord Oliver only wanted what was best for Neville, the Danton family name, and Camberton Park.

For the first time, Neville wondered if his uncle might be driven by self-seeking motives. Simply wielding the power of Camberton like a borrowed sword might not be as satisfying as having it for his own.

One thing Neville was sure of—his family was family in name only. No one took him seriously. No one cared what he wanted.

And he was the bloody duke!

KATARINA PRESSED HER palms against the large double doors and entered the library of Camberton House quietly, but then again, she did most everything quietly. She had long ago discovered that her mother had ears like a wild dog, though she'd not appreciate being compared to the mongrels roaming the streets of Bridgetown.

Regardless, Katarina knew that if she were to enjoy the pleasures of reading, taking walks in nature, or daydreaming, she had to learn to make her escape with stealth and restraint. Otherwise, Mummy would put her to some sort of "improving" task—usually something of the ladylike variety, such as embroidering cushions or tatting lace.

If she never tatted another lace for the rest of her natural life, it would be too soon for Katarina.

The library might have been hushed and soothing, but it was the most spectacular sight she had ever seen. With seemingly miles of shelves, and many thousands of books, the two-story chamber called to her as no other place in England had. Her heart beat faster at the sight of shelves stacked to the high ceiling!

Katarina closed her eyes in delight and breathed in deeply the scent of fine books, catching a faint hint of oils, too, no doubt from the paintings that covered every inch of wall not reserved for books.

The Dantons certainly loved their books, to house them in such a fine room. With her steps cushioned by rich wool carpets, Katarina made her way silently around the perimeter of the room, appreciating the glow of richly dyed leather spines and the sparkle of gold embossing.

A library this splendid almost made up for leaving behind her beloved island.

Almost.

Within a few moments, a particularly large tome caught Katarina's eye. She gasped, reached down toward a lower shelf, and snatched the volume.

"Oh heavens! Is this possible?" Katarina stared in awe at what lay in her hands—a first printing of Maria Sybilla Merium's *Metamorphosis Insectorum Surinamensium*. The volume was more than a hundred years old and considered the most comprehensive study of butterfly metamorphosis in the world. The German woman's work was legendary, and Katarina had often seen references to it in other books, though she never imagined she would ever have the honor of reading the original work.

Clutching the precious volume to her bosom, Katarina hurried across the room toward a library table, smiling to herself. Why should anyone wish to tat lace when there were thousands upon thousands of books in this world?

NEVILLE HAD MADE a discovery. He now knew that he enjoyed the act of drinking but disliked passing out from drink. He must learn to pace himself. If he had started drinking at a younger age, the way many men did, he would be an expert by now.

Perhaps that was his failure. Perhaps he should have chosen to be a selfish rake instead of a sensible duke. After all, what had sensibility gained him? There he sat, alone, unwashed, and unwed, a decidedly undignified state of affairs for the fourteenth Duke of Camberton.

Neville was a disappointment to himself.

And he missed his Bliss. No. She was no longer *his* anything. She was Mrs. Morgan Pryce!

Neville grabbed the wine bottle and brought it to his lips. Shockingly, it was empty. He would have to ring Regis for another.

At that very moment, the door to the library opened. Yet again, Neville marveled at the preternatural abilities of the butler of Camberton House. Regis was so devoted to his duties that he could read minds!

Alas, it was not Regis with a fresh bottle. A girl, a slip of a thing in a pale blue dress, had just entered. It took a moment for him to realize it was Uncle Oliver's houseguest Miss Beckham. He decided to remain quiet and pretend to be invisible. Perhaps when she realized there was nothing in the library but books, she would move on.

He rather liked her, if he recalled correctly. Katarina was her name. She had an inquisitive mind and knew a thing or two about butterflies, an attribute he had not often encountered in members of the fairer sex.

Neville watched her wander through the library, a look of awe on her face. Clearly, she understood the importance of books. She brushed her fingertips along the bindings. Occasionally, she would reach for a volume, flip through it, smile, and put it back. Never once did she sense that someone else was in the room with her.

How unlike him to spy on a lady. How terribly rude. But then, if he announced his presence, he would lose his chance to watch her unaware.

Miss Katarina Beckham was not actually plain. Neville reminded himself that on their first encounter, she'd still been wan and weary from her journey.

But she was no Bliss Worthington, either. Where Bliss was blond and blue-eyed, Katarina was dark. Where Bliss was lush and full—and oh, dear God, was she was ever so lush and full!—Miss Beckham was slender.

But as Neville continued to observe her, he noted that this slight young woman moved with an exceptional grace, a feminine economy he much admired. He imagined Miss Beckham would be a fine partner for a quadrille.

Katarina now carried a large book in her hands. She was headed for the table, coming in his direction. Neville knew he should announce his presence. He began to stand. More precisely, he positioned himself in preparation to stand, since the act of rising to his feet could prove difficult in his current condition.

The book laid across his lap thudded to the floor.

"Oh!" Katarina clutched the book to her middle, staring at him as if she'd just seen a phantom. "I . . . I did not know anyone was—I had no idea . . ."

"It's juss me." Neville partially rose and bowed, aware that he had managed nothing more than a floppy wave of his arm. "Mizz Beck'im. So verynicetoseeyouagain." He fell back into the chair.

"Hmm." Katarina tipped her head curiously, then walked toward him. She retrieved the fallen book from near his feet and returned it to him. "Reading up on moths?"

"Yes! Yes, I am! Er . . . did you know that moths are vital to pollin"—*hic*—"nation?"

Miss Beckham offered him a patient smile and then sat down in the chair recently vacated by Uncle Oliver.

That bamboozler. That trickster.

"Quite. In fact, moths are the workhorses of nocturnal pollination." Miss Beckham balanced the large book on her knees, then folded her small hands atop it. "One night in Barbados, just a few miles from our plantation, my papa and I observed a moth feeding on a honeysuckle bush—with a six-inch proboscis!"

Neville felt his eyes pop. "No! Thass incredible!"

"I assure you it is true."

Suddenly, he saw that her cocoa brown eyes were not just intelligent. They were animated, flecked with gold and green, and framed in generous dark lashes.

"I can only imagine the wonders of Barbados," Neville said dreamily. "Do you enjoy living there?"

"Enjoy?" Katarina seemed puzzled. Neville hoped he had not offended her. "I reveled in it, Your Grace. I have been gone from my home less than a month and have seen many unusual places and things, but nothing compares to Barbados. The Bajans are the most gracious people on earth, and nothing is more magical than the island of my birth."

"Will you show it to me someday?" Later, Neville would wince at his overly familiar manner, but if his question was too brazen, Miss Beckham did not seem to notice.

"I should be honored, Your Grace. I believe you would find the biological diversity of the West Indies fascinating."

"Please call me Neville."

She nodded. "If you call me Katarina. But, Your Grace . . . Neville . . . may I ask you something?"

"Please do."

"It is obvious that you are very drunk. I might also surmise that you are not accustomed to escaping into drink on a regular basis. What has caused you such terrible sadness?"

Neville froze. He was so stunned by the force of her direct question that he was incapable of answering. But he had just told her to dispense with formalities, had he not?

Katarina frowned, a tiny divot forming between her neat eyebrows. "Forgive me, but it is obvious you are struggling. I saw it last night as well. You seem to be a very nice man in great distress."

When she gestured toward his sloppy appearance and the empty wine bottle, she did so to illustrate her point, not to judge his behavior. He saw no disapproval in her expression, only empathy.

"When my papa died," she went on, "I was heartbroken. Talking about it was the only thing that helped me sort out my sense of loss and find a way to carry on. I recognize such grief in you. Should you ever wish to share your story, I shall keep it in absolute confidence. You have my word."

Neville stared at the remarkable creature in disbelief. Never in his life had anyone offered such a thing, with such matter-of-fact kindness. Obviously, it would be unwise to trust someone he had only just met. And yet . . .

Neville could not contain his bitter laugh. So much for wisdom! He had just been viciously betrayed by his brother and uncle, the two people closest to him in all the world, the two people he trusted most.

Neville shook his head at Miss Beckham. "I must warn you, mine is not a pleasant story."

Katarina laced her fingers together and tilted her head, obviously waiting for him to continue.

Neville caught himself up, pushing himself more upright by the arms of the chair. "I am sorry about your father, Katarina."

She nodded. "Thank you."

"I appreciate your kind offer of sympathy. But my complaints are trivial by comparison."

Katarina narrowed her unusual dark eyes and pondered that for a moment. "If it pains you so, it cannot be trivial. Now, you have made all the appropriate polite noises, so you may go on."

"You are a rather unswerving person, aren't you, Miss Beckham?"

She smiled at him. Her smile changed her entire countenance, and the features he saw as mousy just a day ago he now saw as charming. Neville almost hated to burden this perfectly delightful young woman with his story of woe.

"And you are an observant person, even in your condition." Katarina's voice was as soothing as it was sweet. "So, tell me, or send me on my way. I can leave you to your privacy and never speak of this again."

"I had the perfect woman." Neville was surprised how he'd just blurted it out like that. "At least I believed she was mine. We were to marry. My only brother stole her from me."

Katarina's lips parted in surprise. "Oh."

"He tricked her. My brother—my half brother impersonated me at my own wedding, and Bliss had no idea she was marrying the wrong man! My uncle knew of my brother's deception yet did nothing to warn me or put a stop to it."

Katarina pressed her fingertips together and drew back slightly. Her large eyes widened in sympathy.

"Bliss . . ." Neville dropped his head to his hands for a moment, trying to compose himself. Eventually, he looked up again to find Miss Beckham gazing at him, her brow etched with compassion.

"Bliss is so lovely, you see. Perfect in every way. She is all I ever wanted—so regal, so sure of herself, well organized, practical. She always knew the perfect thing to wear, to do, to say at the perfect time. I never know what to say." He ran drink-numbed fingers through his unruly hair. "She is a goddess, truly! And . . . she was the perfect woman for me!"

Katarina blinked a few times. "My goodness. She sounds . . . perfect."

"Yes! Exactly! You can see the cause of my suffering!"

"Indeed."

"The truth is, I sometimes feel overwhelmed with my responsibilities, and Bliss always knew how to step in and help me with my burdens. She would have made a perfect duchess, Katarina. I could picture it."

She nodded slowly. "The perfect picture."

"Yes! You understand!"

"Perfectly."

Surprisingly, Neville felt somewhat better. He smiled blearily at his new friend. "You are a wonderful listener, Katarina. Your companionship seems to relax me. I feel as if I could tell you anything."

She smiled again. Really, such a charming smile. "Do you love Bliss?"

Neville started. "What? Why, yes. Of course I do."

Katarina gave a tiny shrug. "I ask because you never said the words. You listed her many outstanding attributes, but you never mentioned love."

The *Atlas of English Moths* slipped from Neville's lap and thudded to the floor again. Embarrassed, he retrieved it, wondering if Katarina could be mistaken. Had he not said he loved Bliss? How could that be?

"My papa was always reading, too. You are like him in that regard."

Neville straightened up, his mind still snagged on that truth: He forgot to declare his love. But he had to find his way back to the conversation at hand. "Perhaps you inherited your love of reading from your father."

"Oh, most assuredly! My mother would scold Papa, saying, 'You've always got your nose in a book!' But that was where he was happiest."

Neville smiled at her. "It is true I enjoy books, but I doubt I could ever build a sugar empire as your father did. I fear I lack that kind of untiring drive, especially when it comes to business."

Katarina said nothing, but that tiny divot returned to her brow.

Suddenly, Neville felt a twinge of guilt. He suspected these poor Beckham women had not been invited to Camberton House out of the kindness of Lord Oliver's heart. Because, he now realized, his uncle had no kindness, or even a heart. "May I tell you a secret, Katarina?"

Her eyes flashed with humor and she leaned forward in the chair. "Of course. But I thought you already did that."

Neville laughed. "No, this is different. I feel I should warn you about something. It has to do with why my uncle invited you and your mother to London. It concerns business. Our family's White Rose Line will receive an exclusive shipping contract for Sunbury sugar once my uncle has introduced you to Society."

Though one of Katarina's eyebrows arched high on her forehead, Neville did not see any surprise in her expression. "Yes, I am well aware of that arrangement," she said.

"Oh, good. That's very . . . practical of you. But there's something else."

"Pray, go on."

"My uncle wishes to push your mother out of the plantation. I believe he seeks to take advantage of your widowed mother's lack of business acumen to acquire the entire line of production."

He watched for Katarina's reaction. When she bit down on her lower lip and began to glance uncertainly about the library, Neville feared the worst. When her shoulders began to shake, he braced himself for a flood of tears. But it did not take long for him to realize his mistake.

Katarina Beckham was trying desperately not to laugh.

She returned her attention to him, her eyes sparkling with amusement. "And now I'd like to tell you a secret. May I?"

"Oh, most certainly."

Katarina leaned closer still. "Mummy worked by my father's side from the beginning, but it was she who built the empire. Papa would have been happy with a simple farm and his bees and his books. Mummy has a nickname in Barbados. Would you like to hear it?"

Neville felt himself collapse against the back of the chair, stunned. "I cannot wait."

"They call her Lady *Perai*."

Neville shook his head. "I fear I don't follow."

"That's the Bajan word for piranha. They call my mother Lady Piranha."

Neville's mouth opened in delighted disbelief. That silly, shallow creature—was the mastermind of a sugar operation that had shrewd Oliver panting with longing?

Katarina smiled with tranquil satisfaction. "So you see, Lord Neville, your uncle has cast his line for the wrong fish."

Chapter 18

WITH Morgan safely off to his ship and her dress appointment still hours away, Bliss made a decision. She must go to Neville. It was true that her last name was now Pryce, but Bliss would forever be a Worthington, and Worthingtons did not sit about wringing their hands and complaining that the world had done them wrong.

Worthingtons were people of action.

"Camberton House, please, Mr. Cant."

Dear Ephraim Cant had been waiting for her on the street, just as he had done the day before. She'd not actually expected him to appear, but Captain Pryce must have tipped very well indeed the previous evening. She blithely assured her new personal driver that her generous husband would continue to do so, but that she would prefer that Mr. Cant simply run a tab for the rest of the week. And it would be best if he waited just out of sight unless he saw her emerge from the house alone.

The fact that she'd hired her own personal driver was a fact that Captain Pryce did not need to know. She hoped he wasn't going to continue to be so miserly. After all, he'd been rather ungrateful for all her hard work bringing his home back to a "shipshape" condition, as he'd called it.

Once settled in the hired hack, Bliss reviewed the disordered state of her life. She had wedded the wrong man. She was a married woman sneaking—well, riding in full daylight—off to see the man she had intended to wed in the first place. That man, however, had ignored her many messages. Bliss found it astonishing how quickly something so pure and certain had become so muddled. In fact, she found herself more confused by the hour.

It was Neville she loved. It was Neville she desired to wed. So why, then, did his brother now occupy her thoughts, send her pulse racing, and . . .

No! Bliss would pursue only positive thoughts. A few moments in Neville's company would surely return him to his rightful place in her heart. A few moments with Neville would banish this inappropriate fascination with Morgan Pryce, forever.

Bliss was certain Neville would listen to reason and assist her in bringing order to chaos. Neville adored her as much as she adored him, and that bond was more powerful than deception and misunderstanding. She was sure of it.

Therefore it came as a shock to Bliss when she was greeted at the door like a beggar. The Camberton butler, Regis, a man who had always extended a reserved but sincere welcome, now examined her as if she were a stranger.

"Good morning, Regis. I have come to see Neville. It is imperative that I speak with him."

Regis looked her up and down. "Does Madam have an appointment?"

Bliss was too stunned to speak for an instant, but recovered nicely. "No, I do not. You must assist me, Regis. There's been a terrible mistake and I need Neville's help. I need . . ." Bliss was surprised to feel her eyes grow hot, as if tears gathered there. As a rule, she did not blubber, and through all the recent disarray she had not shed a single tear or lost hope. Yet standing on the stoop of Camberton House like an outcast, pleading for an audience with the man she wanted above all others . . . that was almost too much to bear.

It was too much like the old, familiar loneliness that had plagued her, always. Watching as her parents drove merrily away, with no notion of when they might return. Left behind. Waiting.

"Please, Regis. Pray tell him I'm here. I would forever be in your debt."

The butler's inscrutable expression left her wondering whether she would be thrown into the street or offered tea and cakes. One could never tell with Regis.

"This way, madam."

Bliss followed, at first greatly relieved. But she felt confused when Regis led her to the formal parlor. In her many visits with Neville here at Camberton, they had always enjoyed each other's company in the family's private parlor, a cozy retreat fitted with comfortable seating and filled with the Danton family's simple delights: well-loved books, casual portraits of family members, and the treasured possessions of Danton ancestors. Every item in the family parlor helped create an atmosphere of ease and familiarity, reminding Neville of the unbroken history of the duchy and his heritage.

Bliss now sat perched on a stiff and overly ornate settee, designed to intimidate, not relax. The room lacked warmth, feeling more like a museum than a retreat. All around her were items that reflected the Dantons' power and wealth—priceless collectibles, art from renowned painters, plush carpets, and extravagant floral arrangements.

The parlor was grand indeed, though, in all honesty, she found herself rather unimpressed with the display.

She waited. And waited. The ticktock of the heavily gilded mantel clock caused her head to throb. Bliss was forced to consider that Neville was punishing her by making her wait or, worse yet, never intended to receive her at all.

"Oh, *Oll-lieee-eee*!"

Bliss jolted in alarm. What a hideous sound! It took her an instant to identify its origin, and wonder when, and why, the Dantons had acquired a monkey.

The screech repeated itself a moment later, farther away and fainter. Bliss felt relieved. At least she would not be assaulted by a wild creature while trapped in this gilded cage. Bliss straightened her skirts until they were just so. She waited . . . and waited . . . until she sensed someone's presence. Her gaze went to the parlor doorway. Her heart sang with the knowledge that her Neville had finally come!

How very unexpected.

It was not Neville, but a young woman, someone she did not know. She was petite and slim, with glossy dark curls and wide-set, intelligent eyes. She seemed to be as startled by Bliss as Bliss was by her.

"Hello." The woman in the doorway smiled tentatively and arched her eyebrows, a sign she was not entirely displeased by their meeting. "By any chance, is your name Bliss?"

Bliss perked to attention. "Why, yes! It is!"

The woman gazed upward toward the ceiling and mumbled one word: "Perfect."

Such an odd reaction, Bliss thought. "And you are . . . ?"

The woman shook her head as if to scold herself. "Forgive me. My name is Katarina Beckham. My mother and I have traveled from Barbados to be Lord Oliver's guests for the London Season."

Neville had mentioned that someone was to join the household for a time, but he'd not said anything about a young lady in the party. "Oh! How lovely! Would you care to join me?"

Before she answered, Miss Beckham checked the hall behind her, to the left and then the right, much like a thief hiding from the Bow Street Runners, Bliss thought. Once assured of her safety, she turned to Bliss with a rather charming smile. "Thank you. I should like that very much."

The women sat opposite each other on equally stiff chintz settees. They politely evaluated each other. It was, indeed, an awkward meeting, and Bliss could not help feeling an unexpected twinge of envy regarding Miss Beckham. It took a moment for her to comprehend the cause.

As a guest in Neville's home, the young lady from Barbados had every right to be at Camberton House, while Bliss had none. Bliss was married to someone else. She did not have an appointment.

She felt her spine stiffen at a strange thought. Was the reason for Neville's sudden disinterest in Bliss seated right in front of her? Had his attentions shifted? Was Neville already smitten with his pretty houseguest?

"Would you care for tea? I shall ask Regis to . . ."

As if waiting for his cue, Regis appeared in the doorway with a lavish tray. He poured for the ladies and asked if they needed anything else. His query was directed to Miss Beckham, not Bliss.

Though her chest burned with the hurt of dismissal, Bliss was determined not show it. "Are you enjoying your stay here at Camberton House, Miss Beckham?"

"Oh yes." She took a dainty sip from her fine china cup. "Though we have only been here two days, Lord Oliver and Neville have made us feel quite welcome."

Neville. She had just referred to the Duke of Camberton as Neville, and a mere two days after making his acquaintance! Bliss took a sip from her cup as well, reminding herself that in addition to being people of action, the Worthingtons also were people of active imagination. Perhaps that was to blame for her discomfort.

Bliss looked toward the hall. "And is Neville on his way?"

Miss Beckham shook her head. "I'm afraid His Grace is rather indisposed at the moment."

His Grace is rather indisposed . . . such intimacy that statement implied! It almost seemed as if the young lady from Barbados was protecting Neville . . . from her!

"Pardon me, but is Neville aware that I am here, waiting to see him?"

Miss Beckham placed her cup and saucer on the tea table, then folded her hands neatly in the skirts of her morning dress. A rather outdated morning dress, truth be told, of simple cut and plain blue muslin, accessorized with an equally plain bandeau around her hair. Perhaps fashion was not of much import in the West Indies. "I can't really say, Miss . . . ?"

Bliss smiled. How clever she was, forcing Bliss to say her name aloud, thereby emphasizing the crux of the matter— Bliss was married to someone else. "My name is Mrs. Pryce."

Miss Beckham smiled sweetly. "Neville did mention that congratulations were in order."

Bliss tilted her head and studied the industrious Miss Beckham. In just two days she had become Neville's protector and confidante, the knowledge of which sent an odd sorrow washing over Bliss. It was then that she fully understood that Neville did not wish to see her.

This meant that when Bliss finally did win her annulment, Neville might not be waiting.

"Oh, Ol-lieee-eee!"

There it was again! Bliss flinched as before, but now questioned whether even a monkey could be responsible for that singsong screeching. "Has Regis taken up yodeling?"

Miss Beckham's eyes widened, and then she laughed aloud. It was such a pure-hearted sound that Bliss found herself smiling, too.

"I fear that was my mother."

Bliss did not know what to make of that confession.

Should she comfort Miss Beckham? Express pity? Press her for what would surely be fascinating details?

But she said nothing, and the conversation faded. It was obvious to Bliss that Neville was not coming.

She stood. "I apologize for the brevity of my visit, Miss Beckham, but I must be going. I have a dress appointment."

She escorted herself from the parlor, through the hall, and out the front door.

She knew the way.

PERFECT . . .

Katarina laughed at herself. As much as she would prefer to think Neville had exaggerated the charms of his stolen bride, he had not. And her visiting gown! Good gracious! Katarina had never seen such fine fabric and skilled construction . . . so impeccably fitted . . . on such a lavish female form.

Katarina collapsed into the settee in a most unladylike position, allowing her thoughts equal freedom. Bliss Pryce was everything Katarina was not, and if that level of elegance and natural endowments was expected of young women during the London Season, she was woefully unsuited for the task ahead.

She sighed in exasperation. "How I wish I knew the name of her dressmaker!"

Not that a new dress could perform miracles, if Bliss Pryce was the sort of woman Neville preferred. The same could be said for all men, everywhere, she supposed, but that meant her friendship with Neville would remain just that—a friendship built on common scholarly interests and a few shared secrets.

Not attraction.

At least such an admission would save her from future disappointment.

"His name is Lementeur, miss."

Katarina scrambled at the sound of the butler's voice, straightening herself into a presentable position and gripping the edge of the settee for balance.

"What?" She adjusted the bandeau now sagging over one eye. "What did you say, Regis?"

He handed her a card embossed with nothing but a London address. "Pardon me for intruding, Miss Beckham. The name of Mrs. Pryce's dressmaker is Lementeur. He runs the most exclusive ladies' shop in London."

Katarina realized that her mouth had fallen open in shock. She snapped it closed and smiled at Regis. "Do you think it is possible to—"

"I'll have the carriage brought round, miss, and I'll summon your maid to accompany you."

With a bow, Regis was gone.

Katarina stared at the card in her hand, blinking in disbelief. What an exciting day this had been—and it was not yet noon!

Chapter 19

"**O**H, *Ollieeee!*"

Not for the first time, Lord Oliver found himself flinching. On paper, it had seemed a simple enough proposition: Invite the beleaguered widow to London, introduce one insignificant girl to the ton, and win an exclusive shipping contract that would fatten the Danton coffers for decades to come.

In practice, however, the daily proximity of Paulette Beckham had transformed his peaceful home into the bowels of hell. Not coincidentally, he now suffered from an aching head, a tensed jaw, a painful tooth, and an overarching sense of doom.

Not exactly the bargain he had planned.

"Where are you, *Ollieeee?*"

He ducked into to the butler's pantry, an untried first-floor hiding place. So far, his private rooms had proven the only safe haven in the entire grand house, as even Paulette Beckham was not brazen enough to enter a lord's bedchamber. But he couldn't very well stay locked away like a recluse.

Lord Oliver Danton absolutely refused to be a prisoner in his own home!

He shut the pantry door, leaned against the cabinets, and sighed with relief. Almost immediately, the door was flung wide upon its hinges.

"Oh, there you are, dear Ollie! I was looking absolutely all over the house for you, darling! Why, you're not trying to hide from me, are you?"

Bloody hell.

Lord Oliver straightened to a stand in the most nonchalant way possible, then extended his hand to snatch whatever item might happen to be within reach. "Of course not, dear lady. I simply came in here to find a—" When he glanced down to determine what, exactly, he now held in his hand, his mind went blank. "This lovely silver . . . bauble."

Paulette Beckham pursed her lips, seeing right through his ruse. She gave him a pitying smile, as if she believed him daft. "It is called a napkin ring, Ollie dear. Will you be assisting Regis with today's lunch service?"

Lord Oliver tossed the silver knickknack to the shelf and tugged mightily upon his cravat. This woman was positively maddening! "Exactly how may I be of service to you this time, Mrs. Beckham?"

"Well, I thought you should be aware that an invitation to the Fletchers' ball for Katarina and me did not arrive this morning, as you assured me it would. And the event is a mere two days away! *Two days!* What are we to do, Ollie? How are we to prepare for a ball to which we have not been invited? I think I shall weep from the distress of it all. And my poor, sweet Katarina! She has allowed herself to have such high hopes of securing a suitable . . ."

Lord Oliver felt his eyes glaze over. He stopped listening. Bloody hell, what had he gotten himself into?

". . . and then I shall have to find some way to console her broken feminine heart."

Lord Oliver cleared his throat, committed to ending this

excruciating encounter, regardless of the cost. "Do not fret, dear lady. You and your daughter shall accompany the duke and me to the Fletchers' as our personal guests."

"Oh! Joy!" Mrs. Beckham clapped her hands together, then pressed them to her smiling cheeks. "How terribly sweet and thoughtful of you, Ollie! I am deeply touched by your kindness. I cannot tell you how pleased this makes me!"

Then, please don't.

By this juncture, Lord Oliver was dizzy from the effort required to remain civil, and desired nothing more than to flee the swirling madness induced by her shrill voice and never-ending demands. But he also knew that now was an opportune time to bargain with Mrs. Beckham regarding the future of Sunbury Plantation. After all, he had just given her something she desperately wanted. She surely would be softened by his generosity.

"Dear Mrs. Beckham, I have been thinking . . ."

Her eyes widened. "Oh dear. You have?"

Lord Oliver cleared his throat. Had she just insulted him? With this woman he found it most difficult to determine insult from inanity. "Yes, and I've been thinking how terrible the burden must be for you now that your husband is gone. All the details of managing Sunbury—labor, production, harvest, shipping, income, accounting—it must be too much for a gentlewoman of your breeding to manage."

She folded her hands demurely before her and sighed deeply. "I thank you for your concern."

"Oh, it is more than concern, I assure you, Mrs. Beckham! Your husband and I corresponded often, as you know. He was a brilliant businessman. And in the course of our discussions, I learned quite a lot about the sugar business."

"Oh?"

"Indeed, madam. And I would like to propose that, in addition to granting White Rose the exclusive shipping rights to Sunbury exports, you might consider selling the entire operation to—"

"Please! No more!" Mrs. Beckham rubbed her fingertips into her temples, shaking her head as if in agony. "Oh, Ollie! You know all this business nonsense makes my head swim. You know I've come to London to find Katarina a suitable match, not engage in endless talk of balance sheets and shipping costs. Her happiness is my primary concern now."

Dear God! Oliver saw the handwriting on the wall, and it was a eulogy. No tasty marriage prospect for that insipid chit, no business dealings. Furthermore, if he didn't secure Sunbury soon, this brainless bit of female fluff would run the plantation to the ground! "Of course, my dear Mrs. Beckham. But think on this. If you sold the business, then you would be free of all those boring, distressing details! You would have unlimited time to dedicate to your lovely daughter's future happiness."

She blinked at him, as if she did not understand a word he said. It was all Oliver could do not to shake the stupid cow.

Pressing the back of one hand to her powdered brow, she sighed gustily. "Might we talk about this later? My head is simply pounding now."

"Fine." He sighed, thoroughly exhausted by this futile discussion. "Then please excuse me. I must—"

She stepped directly in front of him! "What time shall we depart on Thursday?"

Lord Oliver ground his teeth—Paulette Beckham had just blocked his exit—with her body! She had him quite literally cornered.

She batted her lashes at him. "You see, my lord, I must manage our time carefully in order to have Katarina's hair styled and her gown freshened in time. And oh! The weather! Will she require a wrap in the evening, do you think? Silk? Or wool? I daresay, London is even chillier than I recalled."

Lord Oliver knew that if he did not immediately escape the confines of this butler's pantry—and the hellish inanity of this conversation—he would go utterly and completely mad.

"I shall send Regis to you to discuss all matters of scheduling and vagaries of climate." Lord Oliver pushed past Mrs. Beckham with the desperation of a fleeing convict. "Good day to you, madam."

"Shall we see you at luncheon, Your Lordship?" Her piercing trill followed him down the hall.

Oliver pressed on, pretending not to hear her inquiry. He would rather dine in his rooms. Alone. Like a hermit. Not at all like a prisoner.

BLISS WAS MERE steps away from escaping Camberton House when she nearly collided with Lord Oliver Danton, who approached from the opposite direction. It appeared he had been rushing toward the grand staircase.

The two froze in place, an arm's length from each other, in the center of the main hall. They stared in silence. It occurred to Bliss that Lord Oliver Danton was perhaps the last person on earth she wished to see at that moment.

As a wave of revulsion spread across Lord Oliver's face, Bliss learned he was of a similar opinion.

"Why, Miss Worthington—or should I say Mrs. Pryce? What an unexpected . . . visit this is."

Bliss stood her ground. She might suspect that the bitter old man had a hand in ruining her happiness, but she was incapable of being rude. At least not until thoroughly provoked.

She curtsied to the appropriate depth. "Lord Oliver."

"May I ask what brings you here to Camberton?"

Bliss considered her words carefully. She did not know what games Lord Oliver played or the rules by which he played them, which left her but one option. She would answer him in the only manner that had ever served her—she would speak the truth. "I came to speak to Neville, my lord."

"Oh?" He cocked his head, examining her from head to toe, a barely contained smirk snarling his lip. "And did you have a nice visit?"

"On the contrary, my lord. I waited for him in the formal parlor, but he did not come."

"'Tis a pity. Yes, indeed."

Lord Oliver rested his elbow on the staircase newel post, almost as if staking his claim on the structure, or perhaps the entire house. Bliss thought the pose looked rather ridiculous.

"And how are you finding the wedded life, Mrs. Pryce? I daresay it was quite a shock to hear of the mix-up at the chapel, but surely the unique pleasures of matrimony have made up for any inconvenience you may have experienced."

Bliss blinked at him in disbelief. Though she felt perfectly calm at her core, her fingers tightened their grip on her reticule and began to tremble with tension. "Does this sort of thing usually work with people, my lord?"

He straightened up from the newel post, clearly offended. "I beg your pardon?"

"The backhanded concern. The spiteful innuendo. Do you find that most people cower before you when you belittle them in such a fashion?"

His lips parted in disbelief.

Bliss pressed on. "You see, my lord, I much prefer to speak plainly. I find there are fewer opportunities for misunderstanding between parties."

Lord Oliver stared. She watched his expression move from faint surprise to pure loathing, and when he spoke, his words were delivered in a low hiss of rage. "You stupid, greedy little tart. Did you think I would allow you to ruin Neville's life, to siphon off the Danton fortune?"

Oh dear. Plain speaking indeed.

Bliss sighed. How unfortunate that Lord Oliver had betrayed his nephew out of a miserly fear. Knowing the truth was painful, but Bliss did possess a sense of clarity now. It was always best to know the motivations of those who wished one ill, and now she knew Lord Oliver acted out of greed. "I take it you arranged for Morgan to replace Neville at the chapel."

Lord Oliver laughed bitterly. "Of course I did."

"Has Neville received any of my messages? Did he even know I was here today?"

He shrugged. "I highly doubt it."

"You kept my correspondence from him, then. You lied to your own nephew."

His sneer deepened, if that were possible. "I find this whole discussion tedious."

Bliss realized that the worst part—the source of the sudden and unbearable sadness she now felt—was knowing how Morgan and Neville trusted their uncle. They loved him and welcomed his guidance, believing he had their best interests at heart.

The old man had betrayed them both.

Lord Oliver had convinced Morgan that Bliss was out for Neville's fortune. It was Lord Oliver's accusations that made Morgan step in to protect his brother. Morgan's intentions had been noble. Morgan had acted out of love and concern for Neville.

Which explained why Morgan accused Bliss of being a common fortune hunter. He was repeating his uncle's words.

Bliss had to wonder . . . if Lord Oliver lied to Morgan, did he lie to Neville as well? What horrible things did Neville now believe to be true about his own brother? What evil lies had Lord Oliver told Neville about Bliss?

Her heart ached for Neville. He must be suffering so, believing those he cared for most had betrayed him. If there was any man who did not deserve to be the victim of such manipulation, to experience such unjust anguish, it was Lord Neville Danton, Duke of Camberton.

Bliss decided she would return to the formal parlor, to Miss Beckham. Perhaps Katarina could pass a message to Neville. Bliss turned . . .

"Where do you think you're going?"

Agony laced through her. She looked down at the old man's clawlike hand wrapped around her upper arm. His bony fingers dug so deep into her flesh that she knew she would bruise.

She would not cry out, not in front of this despicable man. She met his vicious gaze without flinching. "I insist you release me, my lord."

He smiled. "Oh, Regis?"

"Yes, my lord." The butler instantly appeared, as if he had been waiting around a corner.

Lord Oliver loosened his grip on Bliss's arm, then dismissed her with an exhausted wave of his hand. "Remove Mrs. Pryce from the premises. Immediately. And do not allow her entry again."

"Of course, my lord." Regis gestured toward the door with a slight bow. At least he was respectful enough not to put his hands on a lady.

"I can see myself out, Regis."

As Bliss stepped over the threshold, she thought she saw a flash of apology—perhaps even concern—in the butler's eyes. But he slammed the door behind her before she could be certain.

Chapter 20

TRUE to his word, Morgan returned to the house that afternoon in plenty of time to accompany his bride to her damned appointment with her damned dressmaker to be fitted for the damned ball. Although matters were proceeding steadily in the hands of his trusted first mate, Morgan chafed at being pulled away from the repairs. Instead of using his time to see to very necessary preparations for his ship's next journey, he was forced to run womanish errands all day.

This was not what he wanted. The time for action was now. If he desired his freedom, if he desired to return to his old life, he must consummate this marriage in the next thirty-six hours. Once the deed was done, he could pack his things and head to the *Selkie Maid*, putting this whole unpleasant interlude behind him.

But if Morgan hesitated, if he continued to abide by Bliss's ridiculous rules, he would be doomed. He would be prancing about at the aforementioned ball in coat and tails, stumbling over the slick marble floors like a goat on the ice!

Dressing up and going to balls was not something Morgan had ever enjoyed, nor had it been something to which the "Bastard of Camberton" had been regularly welcomed.

At least he wouldn't need any fine new clothes. He could wear his "proxy groom" suit.

No! Morgan opened his front door. He would end this charade now. He would bed Bliss Worthington and he would enjoy it, and then he would be gone. Damn his oath!

Morgan's resolve evaporated the instant he entered his parlor. Though he had been determined to snarl his way through the afternoon, his heart made an odd sort of flip at the scene before him.

There sat a lovely woman, in a comfortable, welcoming room, with steaming tea and sandwiches ready on a tray on the table. And not dainty, wouldn't-tempt-a-street-cur sandwiches, either. Succulent ham was piled deep between slices of bread so thick that they alone would fill a plowman to repletion.

What more could a man ask for?

Morgan was so stunned at the thought that he forgot to greet his bride. As he sat down next to her, she said something and began to pour tea, yet all he could hear was a roaring in his ears.

He'd fled any such domestication for so many years. He'd scorned the very thought of keeping a comfortable house or taking a wife. Why bother? He returned from sea so infrequently that maintaining a home filled with warmth and pleasure would be a waste.

Morgan knew he should feel stifled by the notion, as he always had before. Yet, when Bliss handed him a cup of tea, which he loathed, he nodded his thanks and took an absent-minded sip.

She'd had the wisdom to lace it with plenty of milk and sugar, just as he took his coffee. So she had taken note this morning, had counted the lumps he'd added to his cup, had recalled the amount of milk he'd used—and then served it to him piping hot after a drizzly morning on the docks.

I could get used to this. But I shall not.

He set the cup and saucer down on the table and turned to his bride—a beauty by any terms, the perfect woman, the wife of any man's dreams—except for the heartless ambition and manipulation that filled her soul.

She gazed back at him expectantly, her stunning eyes of sky fixed on him with her full attention.

Damn, she was pretty. Why did she have to be so damned pretty?

"We should go," he heard himself say. "I cannot spare the entire day for this nonsense."

If we don't leave this instant, you would be tumbling naked in my bed, begging me for more.

Morgan shook off the confusion, the desire, the regret. She was getting to him, that was all. Her machinations were effective, to be sure. His estimation of Neville's backbone rose a bit when he realized that his half brother had known her for months and had not yet flung all his worldly possessions at her feet.

She said something. He tore his gaze away from her plump, soft pink lips and looked into her questioning blue eyes. "I beg your pardon?"

"I said, I have something I wish to discuss with you. I think—that is, I am concerned that—"

She was stammering a little, which was a strange break in her usual flawless self-possession. There was a tiny frown between her perfect eyebrows. This human crack in her marble facade hit him in the gut like a blow.

I must get out of this house before I roll her upon the floor and break my oath.

He stood abruptly. "We can discuss this on the way. I already told you I haven't much time to spare."

He helped her into her spencer and had her through the front door in mere moments. The cool air outside helped a bit, as did the sooty smell of the coal fires in the surrounding houses and the tang of tar and fish from the docks just a mile away.

Morgan reminded himself that the clean wash of sea air would strip her from his memory. And that air would taste all the sweeter from the deck of his own ship.

It was not always easy to hail a hack in this neighborhood. The few that ran past carried people and baggage to and from the passenger ships along the Thames. Morgan didn't keep a carriage, or a horse, for what would be the point of that for his few weeks a year in the city?

They walked north and west, zigzagging up and across toward London's finest shopping district. Morgan set a bruising pace, for hadn't he told her he had no time to spare?

Surprisingly, his elegant bride kept up very well, though his legs were longer than hers. She somehow managed to execute a ground-swallowing stride while appearing to merely stroll. Then he recalled that she was a sturdy country girl at heart, raised by her no-nonsense guardian in the vast emptiness of Shropshire.

As a man who had made his own way in the world, Morgan admired vigor and ability, and esteemed those who did what was necessary without complaint.

His new bride looked like a highborn lady, worked like a washerwoman, never gave in to temper or melancholy, seemed as fearless as a pirate and as patient as a hunting cat.

He didn't want to admire this woman. He didn't want to enjoy her tenacity and her strong will and her skill at seemingly everything she did.

Yet he couldn't force himself to be a complete ass. "My apologies," he said gruffly. He slowed his pace. "I am forcing too great a march upon you."

She cast him a serene glance from beneath her bonnet. "No need for regrets, Captain. I enjoy a brisk walk. I have been too much indoors since I came to London. Fresh air is good for one's health."

"Is that so?" They were passing an appalling heap of horse apples in the road, not two feet from the sidewalk. Even Morgan wrinkled his nose at the stench. "Then I suspect we shall live forever."

Her lips pursed. "Droppings don't bother me," she said. Then she clapped her hands over the lower half of her face. "But what is *that?*"

Rank-smelling yellow steam poured out from the doorway just before them. "Tannery!" Morgan gasped. Then he gulped a lungful of air, wrapped one long arm around her waist, and pulled her into a run.

Shropshire girls could really make haste when they had to. She grabbed up her skirts with one hand, pinched her nose shut with the other, and shot past the reeking doorway like an arrow from a bow.

Twenty yards later, she slowed once more to her deceivingly quick stroll and, without seeming hurried about it, stepped to her right, which removed her neatly from his half embrace.

Morgan felt a bit colder without her resilient form pressed to his side.

"Oh no." She stopped suddenly and peered at her reflection in a window. "This will not do." She turned her head both ways, obviously looking for something. Then she made for an alley that angled off the street just ahead of them. "Come along, Captain."

Morgan found himself obeying her brisk command by pure reflex. His mother had used that no-nonsense tone often during his troublemaking boyhood. He smiled slightly as they turned into the alley.

She paused only a few strides in and turned to him.

"I fear I have come all undone," she said, her tone a confiding whisper.

Morgan blinked. Did she know what those words, voiced in that husky, breathy tone, did to a man who hadn't dipped his wick in nearly eighteen months?

No doubt she did know.

Which confirmed his belief that she was an entirely artificial creation born of greed and connivance. No real woman could be so resilient, so resourceful and yet so refined. No doubt she had summed him up quickly, as confidence artists were wont to do, and had sculpted herself into a woman perfectly molded to meet his deepest desires.

Desires he'd not even known he had.

Who had she made herself out to be for Neville's benefit? A delicate blossom, breathlessly hanging on to his every discourse on butterflies and integrated natural systems and what really lies under stones in the fields?

Had Neville ever kissed her, when she stood close to him, gazing up at him with her damned blue eyes and heaving that damned fine bosom?

Morgan swallowed, recalling the kiss. The Kiss. The only time he'd touched his bride, the single taste he'd had of her hot, sweet mouth, the brief moment of sliding his hands over skin as smooth and hot as fire-warmed silk . . .

"You must be my mirror," she said then in a brisker tone. "My bonnet is askew and I'm certain my hair is a shambles."

She began to adjust the straw confection of flowers and ribbon she wore, tucking in a few strands of hair that had come loose in their dash.

Bemused by this endearing show of feminine insecurity, just when he'd thought she'd intended seduction, Morgan silently pointed out a flaxen lock that threatened to fall to one faintly flushed cheekbone.

"Where? Here?" Her seeking fingers missed it.

He hadn't meant to. His hand rose all by itself and tenderly stroked the silky threads. His fingertips brushed her cheek. Fire-warmed silk indeed.

She froze at his touch.

Waiting?

Waiting for him to set upon her? To break his oath, like the bastard he was?

He hung on the edge of doing just that, in truth. With all the will he could muster, he pulled his hand away.

She swiftly went back to her repairs, tucking that tempting strand away, settling her bonnet and retying the ribbon beneath her chin.

"Goodness," she muttered. "I can still smell the stench." Then her wide blue gaze shot to meet his. "Is it me? Do I reek?"

God help him. Clasping his hands tightly behind his back, Morgan leaned forward and took a deep breath through his nose. She smelled of soap and flowers and something that made his pulse quicken, something he suspected was simply Bliss.

"I want to kiss you," he heard himself say.

What the hell? Why had he said that?

Because he did want to, in the worst way.

She drew back and met his gaze, a tiny furrow appearing between her eyebrows. "You promised you would not."

"I know. Not without your permission." He took a step closer. "Mrs. Pryce," he said, his voice tight and low. "I beg permission . . . for I really, truly want to kiss you." To Morgan's shock, he found himself entirely lacking in motivation to trick or defeat her in any way. What he wanted, all he wanted, was her sweet, soft mouth under his.

He saw her swallow, hard. She did not say yes.

She did not say no, either.

"Captain, I . . ." She inhaled deeply. He saw something in her eyes he'd never before witnessed.

Indecision.

For once, it seemed that Bliss Worthington Pryce did not know exactly what to do.

Then she lifted her chin and he saw the warm glow of almost-invitation leave her expression. With one step back, she put crucial distance between them.

Damn. She was stronger than he.

She turned away slightly, folding her hands before her with her silly little tasseled reticule dangling from her wrist. "Captain Pryce, I believe that I should warn you . . ."

"I'll be havin' that pretty li'l purse now, milady."

Morgan didn't bother to look over his shoulder at the rough words coming from the mouth of the alley. In a single swift motion, he pushed Bliss against the wall and pressed his back to her, covering her entirely with his larger form.

Morgan had survived many a brawl over land and sea—but his heart sank when he saw the size of the three brutes blocking their escape.

Silhouetted against the brighter street, they loomed like dark towers, sentinels of doom blocking safe haven behind their backs. All were Morgan's height or nearly so, and all were thickly muscled. Worse, there was an air of accomplished violence about two of them, as if brutality was their profession and they deeply enjoyed their work. The third man was the largest, but he blinked stupidly at Morgan with a nearsighted squint.

Then the first, the man who had spoken, reached behind his back and pulled a long skinning knife from his belt.

The tannery. Morgan thrashed himself inwardly. What had he been thinking, walking this route with a lady? How could he be so foolish?

Because you never walk with ladies.

He might have had a chance to strike back and escape on his own, for he was probably faster than the footpads, but with Bliss to protect? His gut roiled at the very thought of these swine laying one finger on her faultless skin.

Morgan knew that if he bent to reach for his dagger they would be on him too soon. He'd had no idea errand day could be dangerous!

Poor Bliss was obviously terrified. She cowered behind him, slipping down his back to press her body to the back of his legs, on her knees in fear.

From some other area of his mind came the random thought that he had finally found something that broke through her perfect facade.

Then he felt something long and cool being pressed into his hand from behind and he closed his fist around the hilt of his boot dagger.

Unshakable Bliss.

Armed, he took the offensive and attacked. If he could get them on the run—

The leader, quicker than he looked, spun aside at Morgan's rush, so Morgan used his momentum to strike down the larger, second man behind. A single blow to the man's temple with his fist wrapped around the weighted hilt of his dagger sent the brute to the slimy cobbles without a sound.

Then Morgan turned on the chief. Like most leaders, he was smarter than his followers. The man backed away from Morgan, crouching slightly, with his knife hand making loose circles in the air. A professional, keeping his arm warm and ready.

Morgan realized that he'd allowed the thief to get between him and Bliss, who still crouched on the ground, pale and wide-eyed, her reticule clutched to her bosom. The man grinned a broken, yellowed smile.

"Now I'll be takin' the lady as well as 'er purse," he informed Morgan. "Nick, get 'er."

Morgan was aware that the third man began to work his way toward Bliss, sidling carefully around the imminent battle between Morgan and the leader.

Despite his gut-twisting fear for Bliss, Morgan kept his eyes not on the flashing blade itself, but on the leader's knife arm—specifically his shoulder, where every move began.

The fellow was bigger, and possibly stronger, and his knife was longer than Morgan's. Morgan flung himself forward anyway.

This is almost certainly going to hurt.

* * *

IT DID HURT. A bit.

Morgan was swifter than his opponent. He charged, getting so close that he no longer offered an easy target. The man swung his knife. With his left arm Morgan deflected the weapon. With his right he drove his dagger deep into the man's shoulder joint. He felt the blade stick, the shock of hitting bone traveling up Morgan's arm.

The attacker screamed in agony and rolled away, clutching his shoulder, his blade skidding to the edge of the alley. As Morgan lunged for the knife, he heard a series of breathless cries—feminine cries—followed by a sob of agony.

Morgan whirled, wild with rage, ready to rip that that yellow-toothed degenerate to pieces with his bare hands . . .

The cries were not from Bliss. Her attacker was doubled over as she flogged him with her beaded reticule, swinging it repeatedly into the man's crotch and belly.

Her attacker fell to the cobblestones in a harmless heap, pleading for mercy. He crawled away from her and scrambled to his feet. With one fearful glance back at the mistress of his doom, he lurched down the alley, howling the whole way.

Morgan stood in astonished silence as Bliss, seemingly without a care in the world, opened her reticule and dumped out a jagged brick she'd shoved inside, probably when she'd been "cowering" in fear.

Astounding.

"Did he touch you?"

She looked terrible. Her bonnet was a crumpled ruin, her gown was filthy from knees to hem, and her hair, well! Then she flashed him a brilliant grin of triumph that stopped Morgan in his tracks. "He did not have the opportunity." Then the smile was gone and he doubted his own memory at once.

Morgan helped her to stand, watching as she straightened

her bonnet and tucked in her hair. The attempt to repair her appearance was futile this time, however.

His mind reeled from what he had witnessed. This dainty woman had just flogged a ruffian until he begged for mercy! He could barely comprehend it. He had no idea what to say. Unfortunately, he made what was perhaps the most ridiculous of all possible observations.

"Well, it's a damned good thing I carry a dagger in my boot."

Bliss looked up at him. "Oh, it would have been fine either way. I have one, too." From the sleeve of her spencer she retrieved a gleaming stiletto, lethally sharp and set with pink and white pearls in the handle.

Morgan blinked at it, stunned. "Uh . . . that's very, um, pretty."

"Yes. Mama selected it for me. She has very good taste." Bliss raised the skirt of her gown and tucked the stiletto back into the thigh sheath she wore beneath her gown.

Morgan's throat went dry as he let the facts settle. His wife wore a stiletto blade on her succulent thigh. His wife could fight off an attacker twice her size. His wife had a smile that could banish rational thought.

There was more to this woman than he would ever have guessed.

"Who are you?"

Morgan realized he had posed the question aloud when Bliss startled him with that deviously charming grin once more.

"I told you. I am a Worthington!"

Morgan shook his head in pure admiration. "No," he assured her. "You're a Pryce!"

There in that grimy alleyway, they smiled at each other, and then broke into exhilarated laughter.

"I daresay, we are both quite undone now, Captain Pryce."

He extended his arm to her. "Let me take you home, then, Mrs. Pryce."

Chapter 21

THE presence of the living souls around him seemed to press upon Lysander Worthington. The urge to walk away was sometimes overwhelming. It didn't get any better when Lysander left his family home to take to the streets of London, walking for hours. Night or day, people seemed to instinctively shun his striding darkness as they would evade an unknown animal who approached them. That circle of threat that surrounded him at those times at least granted him a sort of strangely comforting silence.

However, Lysander had elected to stay close to Worthington House for the past few days, in case the family believed it necessary to kill that Pryce fellow on Bliss's behalf.

"Are you going to eat those peas?"

Lysander looked down upon Attie's pointy little face next to him at the luncheon table. He loved her, as he loved all his family, with a burning ache of helpless wordlessness. He nodded and she helped herself, and when his plate was empty she placed her small hand on the sleeve of his coat.

He adored his little sister. He looked away, unable to sustain the contact.

Now, what had he been contemplating? Oh yes—Morgan Pryce's murder. The notion of it did not disturb him particularly. Life was fragile. Death was easy. The end was a mere bullet hole away, every man equal in his susceptibility to death, if not in his deserving of it. Lysander had seen too many of his fellow soldiers, some very fine men, die while flinging themselves against Bonaparte's horses and cannons. If good men died so easily and well, what difference did it make if a bad one died under questionable circumstances?

Lysander briefly checked his moral register. It was a basic scale, simple and fundamental, but it was all he had left to work with.

He weighed the facts as he understood them. A man had tricked a woman, a member of the family, into a marriage she did not want. Women were to be protected. He believed that much. Therefore, a man who committed such an act against a woman was a wicked man.

Yes, he could kill that man. What was one more corpse when the fields of Waterloo still leached blood when shovels broke the soil?

To keep the shine of worry from his little sister's eyes, he served himself more leeks and roast, aware that laughter had suddenly risen around the table. He saw Cas tug Attie's braid with pride. His sister must have said something entertaining.

From the shadowy recesses of Lysander's mind came a faint whisper of protest. He knew who spoke, for that dim corner was the home of the man he had once been, a man of reason, and occasionally that man would sigh his disapproval. The voice had been his own before the war, powerful and clear. It had begun to fade his first day on the battlefield, the first time his bayonet had pierced human flesh. He was mostly silent these days, stirring only when he'd judged Lysander's thoughts to be utterly heartless. Lysander wondered if the day would come when the voice went forever silent.

He did not attempt to fool himself. He knew that as a Worthington, he had always been somewhat slapdash in his efforts to be a law-abiding man, even when he had been his old self. Such uprightness did not seem to come naturally to any of them, except perhaps for Dade.

Lysander examined his eldest brother from across the dinner table. Dim memory told him that even when he'd been the real Lysander, he never truly understood Daedalus Worthington.

Mrs. Philpott dished a bit of blood pudding on the plate before Lysander. He turned his gaze down at it slowly. Although meals had improved around Worthington House since Elektra had married so well, Lysander remained unmoved by the savory aromas surrounding him.

Yet he tried to sit down to at least one meal a day with his family. Although he had little interest in food, he still felt the sting when tearful worry filled his mother's eyes. His father, normally oblivious of anything other than his own scholarly musings, was razor sharp when it came to Iris. Archie's bushy eyebrows would climb and his forehead would wrinkle with concern, his vague blue eyes sharpening as he gazed at Lysander. So there they would be, both his dreamy, dotty parents, gazing at him intensely as they counted the forkfuls he put into his mouth. Lysander had little choice but to chew and swallow until they were reassured he was eating, whether the food interested him or not.

It seemed their watchfulness was paying off, for he did feel a bit better after a meal. Easier, more relaxed, as if a bit of the tumult in his mind was silenced for a time, giving him a tiny measure of peace. So he ate, though even the finest food tasted like sawdust. He tried to answer sensibly when someone spoke to him. His responses often came out in short blurts. He had trouble finding the proper words. For the most part, his family let him be, accepting him for who he had become.

Lysander felt a dusty gratitude for that, even as he dimly mourned the loss of how things had once been.

Of all his family, Elektra had been the easiest for him to spend time alone with. Her absorption in her mission to save the family from its poverty had reminded him of a rather military dedication. It made sense to him. They were like soldiers together, and she was his commanding officer. She gave him clear instructions but did not seek to comfort or change or distract him in any way.

Of course, she had worried over him, but her way of imparting that worry had been to involve him in her quest, to give him some direction in which to march. His relief had been so great that he had not questioned a single order. And they hadn't done anything too terribly deplorable. It ended well. The wealthy man they had kidnapped fell in love with his captor and made her his bride.

But Elektra's mission parameters had changed when she married Aaron. She and her husband left Worthington House in London to rebuild the family's rotting estate in Shropshire. Lysander had regretted that he could not accompany her on her new venture, but he was not a builder, nor would he have been of use at running any sort of restoration effort on her behalf. After all, that would likely have involved speaking to strangers. As Elektra well knew, Lysander did not—could not—speak to those outside the family.

So he stayed behind, and as he looked around the Worthington table now, he knew he was seeing a family in flux. In addition to Elektra, Lysander had watched Callie and Ellie marry and leave. Castor won Miranda and stayed, adding a baby to the family. Orion and Francesca traveled in their biologist pursuits. Poll took his broken heart and left the family home to his twin, Cas, and the woman they had both loved. Lysander had felt sympathy for his brother, but, when the opportunity came to comfort Poll, Lysander had not found the words. As usual.

Life went on. Lysander got up each day and he dressed and he ate and he sometimes pretended to read, although the words swam upon the page, even words he recalled that he used to love. It was easier to pretend, to go on as if all was well. And if sometimes he woke in the night with icy terrors and shattering nightmares, he usually managed to keep his shaking, sweating recovery to himself.

Lysander studied his brother Daedalus. He sat across the table, pushing peas about the plate, pretending to eat. Lysander knew he had not taken a bite in half an hour. He was thinking of Bliss. It was obvious. Dade and Bliss had a special bond, one that Lysander had watched develop over the months. They were not like the rest of the madcap Worthingtons. They even resembled each other more than the others and were far fairer than the rest of the family, especially when compared to Lysander's own darkness. But what bonded them most were their temperaments. Both Bliss and Dade were more steadfast and less impulsive than the others. More placid and analytical.

Lysander took a sip of wine, questioning his own reasoning. Hadn't Bliss just run away to marry someone she'd known only a few months?

Perhaps she was more of a Worthington than he gave her credit for.

"ARE YOU QUITE well, Dade?"

"Of course, Archie. I'm fine."

Apparently, Dade had been so distracted that even his vague and dreamy father had taken notice. He shoved a forkful of blood pudding into his mouth, smiling reassuringly at the rest of his clan, though his own thoughts were anything but calm.

He could not stop thinking about Bliss. How could he

have allowed her to make such an awful mistake? How could he have let her roam so freely that she could arrange a secret marriage?

It was true that Iris had been an accessory to the crime, but she was not at fault. Bliss knew perfectly well that Iris was a useless chaperone and that was why she had chosen her to accompany her to a secret midnight wedding.

To the wrong man, as it turned out. It was a development that Iris found delightful, better than a play, she had said!

And then there was Neville. Dade had come to know and trust the younger man, though, blast it, he had not thought Bliss a good match for him. Worthingtons had a tendency to plow right over people who did not possess spines of granite. Neville was as upright and decent a man as Dade had ever known, but his decency meant he sometimes compromised his own interests.

Dade's concern had been that Bliss—and her relentless practicality—would have flattened the young duke.

So whom had she married instead?

Neville had previously shown a tendency to wax admiring on the topic of his half brother, extolling his integrity, hard work, and loyalty, among other characteristics. Dade had listened to such high praise on many occasions. For that reason alone, he tried to believe that Pryce would not actually harm Bliss.

Dade had always assumed that Worthington women could look after themselves. Elektra was fiercely self-reliant and Attie—well, Attie was downright bloodthirsty. Even gentle Callie was handy with a sword. And only a month ago at a family picnic on the estate in Shropshire, Dade had watched Bliss shoot clay pigeons from the sky like a champion.

So it wasn't Pryce's character that bothered Dade. It wasn't fear for Bliss's safety. It was that Dade should have known.

This was his fault. In the face of Bliss's unruffled calm, and her seeming lack of ambition, he'd failed to notice the steely determination that would drive a young woman to make such an awful bargain.

And what of poor Neville? What must he be thinking? Neville, however, was not Dade's problem. Bliss was a Worthington, and all the Worthingtons were Dade's problem.

Bloody hell—he'd taken his eye off Bliss, assuming she was the least of his worries for the time being. Instead, he'd been preoccupied with the two most troubling of his siblings. Lysander was still a silent dark shadow of a man. Attie was poised to bloom into a beautiful young woman who was far too brilliant and far too undisciplined to be let out of the house without an army of keepers.

And what about Poll? The family hadn't heard from him in a month. The family had considered running out after him. Castor couldn't do it, however, not with the new baby and a wife who never had any rest. It was certain that Archie was useless in such an endeavor. Lysander was quite willing but too unstable. And so it was left to Dade.

It seemed that it was always left to Dade. He had been playing shepherd to this flock of wayward sheep for so long. Orion had been a steadying influence for some time, but he was gone now, too.

Finding a way out of Bliss's predicament was up to him.

Thoughts of legal annulments and possible charges of fraud swam in Dade's mind. There must be a socially acceptable—i.e., legal—means to free Bliss from her midnight error. A non-Worthington method.

He let his head fall to his hand. God, he was tired. Thirty-one years old and he felt as if the weight of the world—or at least, of Worthington House—rested on his shoulders. Dotty parents, madcap siblings, a crumbling house. Those were his inheritance. Being the eldest son was supposed to be a good thing, wasn't it?

He had failed. He had been so busy trying to manage Attie's wildness, monitoring Lysander's slow recovery, and worrying about Poll's wandering, that he neglected the one person he had relied on. Bliss had been his confidante and helper. She had been the only other sane and stable person in this house!

Bliss. He'd thought she was just like him. He'd thought she could always be counted on to choose wisely. She'd always seemed so calm!

Apparently, Bliss was a true Worthington after all.

Chapter 22

IN a severely stylish shop in the finest shopping district in London, a man known to his friends as Button, but to the rest of the world as the great Lementeur, caressed the fine cornflower blue silk and stared at the clock. He was becoming truly worried about Bliss Worthington—er, Pryce. Yes, that was right. Her ball gown fitting had been scheduled for a quarter hour ago, yet she had not arrived or sent word of delay.

It was terribly unlike Bliss Worthington—er, Pryce—to be late for an appointment. In fact, she had been precisely on time for each of their prior fittings. Bliss was perhaps the most punctual of all his clients.

Button's assistant, Cabot, peered through a crack in the dress shop's thick velvet drapes to scout the street outside. "Are you sure she said three o'clock?" Cabot glanced over his shoulder and regarded Button. "I fear there is no sign of the rather distinctive Worthington carriage."

Button could not help laughing at Cabot's choice of words. The Worthingtons were indeed an unusual clan. They lived in a ramshackle mansion. They traveled in a moldy hack pulled by decrepit horses. And yet they moved blithely through the most elite circles. Bliss, a cousin to the London Worthingtons, had never once inquired about the cost of her many custom gowns.

Yet seeing one of his creations draped on her arresting frame was one of Button's greatest satisfactions.

The question remained: Where could she be? It was no small source of irritation to Button when appointments were not honored. As everyone who was anyone knew, Lementeur's personal services were in such demand that when girls were born into Society, their mothers rushed to put their names on the dress shop's waiting list. A missed appointment not only meant lost profit for Button—it meant a lost opportunity for a deserving new customer.

"A carriage has arrived," Cabot announced. "But it carries the crest of the Duke of Camberton, so I doubt it is our Bliss—unless the duke is a particularly forgiving chap."

Button raced to the window to join Cabot, curious indeed. News that Bliss Worthington had run off to wed the duke's bastard brother instead of Lord Neville Danton himself had become the talk of London. Today's gossip pages had been atwitter with news of Bliss and her dashing sea captain.

Button felt a wave of forgiveness for Bliss. Captain Pryce was reported to be a charismatic fellow. She was a newlywed, after all, and likely distracted. Button spared a sigh of envy.

The carriage door opened and out stepped a lady's maid.

Cabot glanced at Button. "Do we know her?"

"I don't believe we do."

Behind the maid appeared a woman. Smallish, slender, with dark hair, and attired in a gown of rather drab pastel gray muslin. Button saw through the unattractive dress to the young lady beneath. She possessed a graceful way of moving. Almost as if she danced each motion. How intriguing! "I am certain I don't know her."

"Hmm." Cabot tipped his chin. "Graceful. Lovely eyes. Whoever she is, someone absolutely must tell her to avoid that tired shade of gray."

Button smiled. "I know just the man for the job."

The young lady was apologetic upon entering, and glanced about the shop with quick, unsure turns of her head. She became flustered while admitting she did not have an appointment, and hoped she had not interrupted other customers.

Button thought her concern for others charming, and despite the simple cut of her dress, he suspected this unplanned visit would be fortunate for all involved. There were two reasons for his optimism. One, the girl had arrived in the Duke of Camberton's carriage. And two, she positively reeked of wealth.

It was not an overt display. On the contrary. Button sensed none of the condescension that sometimes oozed from ladies of privilege. Nor did she boast of a familiarity with fashion. The young woman simply had impeccable manners, kind eyes, and the carriage of someone who had never doubted her position for one moment of her life.

With a sincere curtsy, she introduced herself as Katarina Beckham, houseguest of Lord Oliver Danton and his nephew, the duke. In the next breathless sentence, she conveyed an urgent need for a ball gown to wear to the Fletchers' event a mere two days away.

Cabot shot him a sideways glance accompanied by a lift of one eyebrow. Button knew it was the look of a man who appreciated the intersection of commerce and art as much as he himself did. With his assistant's agreement, Button graciously accepted the challenge. "I do have a few sample designs made up that could be fitted to you quite quickly. Mere thoughts on paper tried out in silk—but you may find something to your taste." Oh, this was going to be such fun! His fingers twitched.

"Oh! I am ever so grateful, sir. I brought dresses with me from home, but I have discovered they simply will not do here in London! But—" The young lady's cocoa brown eyelashes lowered with something akin to shame. "You see, I met someone today, a lovely woman, one of your customers, and she was so stunning, so naturally beautiful and so exquisitely dressed, that I worry I could never do one of your gowns justice."

Yet again, Button and Cabot found each other's gaze. Button felt the corner of his mouth twitch. "I am thinking . . ."

Cabot nodded emphatically. "By all means, yes. The plum violet."

While Cabot retreated to the workroom, Button insisted that Miss Beckham and her maid relax on the velvet settee near the rear window of the shop. Button served the tea he had prepared for Bliss, and sat about getting to know his new customer.

Unfortunately, Cabot had not returned in time to hear the young lady say, with an almost humble shyness, that she happened to be an heiress to a Barbados sugar fortune. "My mother sees this as my one chance to make a suitable match."

"Oh, how perfectly splendid!" Button rose from his chair. "Would you pardon me for a moment, ladies?" He walked calmly toward the back of the shop, then poked his head through the workroom door. Though he didn't see Cabot upon first glance, he whispered his request. "Bring seed pearls, oh, and the opals!"

Cabot's head popped out from behind a storage shelf. The surprise on his face nearly caused Button to laugh. "The opals? And seed pearls? And the plum violet?"

Button nodded. He understood his assistant's disbelief, for such a combination of materials would create a gown worth a small fortune. They had been saving the rather precious bolt of fine imported satin for a special commission, as not every woman could wear such a bold, intense color—or afford the first-rate quality. The slender, dark-haired Miss Beckham had provided them with the perfect canvas.

"But the opals?" Cabot whispered back. "Are you quite certain?"

"Two words. Sugar. Heiress."

The corner of Cabot's mouth twitched. "I shall bring every opal in the shop."

Six months prior, he had purchased a strand of hundreds of small Turkish opals from a London importer. They were exceptional in their gloss and iridescence, sending off subtle sparks of purple, blue, orange, and red. At the time, Button had worried about the dear price, but as of today, he was certain his assistant had made a wise purchase.

Button returned to the front of the shop. He asked Katarina to come stand with him before the huge mirror, noticing that she did not allow her gaze to connect with her own reflection. It occurred to him that he should ask which of his exquisitely dressed customers Miss Beckham had encountered earlier that day. He needed to know what motivated this spontaneous trip to his shop.

"Her name was Mrs. Bliss Pryce." Miss Beckham's gaze flashed at him in the mirror.

"Ahhh."

"And I thought perhaps with one of your gowns I might . . . Oh, I must be mad! Never mind all this. I shall return to Camberton House immediately." She turned away from the mirror but managed only one step before Button corralled her. He guided her back to her position before the mirror, once more face-to-face with her reflection.

"There, there, my dear."

Button patted her shoulders reassuringly and gave her a smile. Meeting Bliss Worthington would give any lady a moment of self-doubt. Yet, though the encounter might explain the lack of confidence, it did not justify it.

"Now—"

Miss Beckham shook her head, interrupting Button before he could continue. "I apologize, Mr. Lementeur. 'Tis a terrible vanity of mine, to worry so over being plain, and I wish that it did not matter to me."

Button's heart twisted for this young lady. She truly did not know how spectacular she was—or could be. In the right hands. His hands.

Fortunate, indeed.

"Do you know what can be found in the shadows, Miss Beckham?"

She shook her head.

"Mystery, my dear. Things unknown and unexpected. You say you are from Barbados?"

She shrugged in response, a scowl forming between her eyebrows.

"I can see it. Yours is an exotic beauty, an unusual elegance, and we shall capitalize upon it! You shall turn every head at the Fletchers' ball."

Miss Beckham erupted in a bark of incredulous laughter. The ladies' maid, who had just placed another scone in her mouth, appeared startled. Crumbs rained down into her lap.

"I am quite serious, Miss Beckham. Let me tell you what I see when I look at you."

She pursed her lips.

"Your eyes are large, wide-set, and the color of rich chocolate—all very uncommon, indeed. Your skin is flawless, perhaps a benefit of the West Indies climate, and we shall play it to great advantage. Your cheekbones are striking. Your nose and mouth delicate. And the overall effect is a subtle beauty that draws one in."

Katarina narrowed one eye at him in the mirror, obviously in doubt of his earnestness.

"And your shape—"

"What shape would that be, Mr. Lementeur?" She swished her hands down her sides as if to emphasize her lack of curves.

"Oh, but there are many types of beauty, my dear, and your slender elegance is a quality many women covet. Believe me. Ladies confide in me every day, standing right here in this very spot, begging me to make them appear slim."

Cabot returned to the front room then, his arms weighted down with fabric and accessories. He placed everything on the table, unrolled several yards of the imported silk satin, and held the bolt alongside Miss Beckham's face.

Button smiled. "Ah."

"You were absolutely correct about the plum violet," Cabot said.

Button smiled to himself. Of course he was correct. He was Lementeur.

For the next hour, Cabot set to work with Miss Beckham, doing what he did best. He draped the fabric this way and that, pulled it snug about her slight frame, made pinnings and marks, all frowning in concentration. Button smiled at her as if she were the most exquisite creature who had ever stepped foot in their shop.

Which, with Cabot's attention to detail, was proving to be not much of an exaggeration.

After a great deal of consultation, Button and Cabot decided on a classic and restrained cut for Miss Beckham, almost severe by ball standards. Pure elegance that would make anything less look tawdry.

They would construct cap sleeves without ruffle or ribbon, create a crisscross design of opals along the bodice that would pick up the shimmer of the satin, and fashion a straight neckline just a bit daring for a young lady on her coming-out.

Her hairstyle would be austere, pulled up and back without the added curl she now struggled to attain, sleek and straight, accented with exotic feathers. Miss Beckham was kind enough to tell them the names of the birds from which the plumes were plucked, though Button got lost after she rattled off the Latin names for the great Argus and South Asian peafowl.

Regardless of where the plumes originated, they looked as if they belonged on the plum violet–draped Miss Beckham, who had been transformed into an exotically beautiful creature of mystery.

"Delicate girls have such incredible bone structure," Cabot pointed out.

"Indeed," Button said. "Her long neck implies importance and refinement. She will be utterly striking, the rarest of rich tropical flowers in sea of pastel blooms."

"Oh dear. Oh no." Miss Beckham's eyes widened in concern when the men debated her décolletage. "I . . . well, Mummy will not approve of something this revealing. She will not think it appropriate."

Cabot flashed a rather devilish smile in the mirror. "Mummy will think whatever Lementeur tells her to think."

Miss Beckham smiled back. "I suspect you are right about that."

"And perhaps Mummy would like a ball gown as well?"

She grinned at Button's question. "I believe I am beginning to understand why your shop has a reputation for genius."

Button laughed, utterly bewitched by their new friend.

Cabot spent a quarter hour with the lady's maid, instructing the awed young woman on how to style Miss Beckham's hair. They found a pair of amethyst earrings that perfectly accented the rich hue of the fabric, and a pair of slippers that complemented both the color and style of the dress.

When the appointment ended, Button and Cabot saw Miss Beckham and her maid to the carriage.

Cabot sighed as they drove off. "We should get to work. We've not a moment to spare."

Button agreed. "This will be a long two days, even with the added seamstresses."

"But we are up to the task, of course."

Button grinned at his assistant. "'Tis a good thing we are geniuses."

Chapter 23

BY the time Bliss and Morgan returned to the house, she found that she had lost some of the giddy sense of invincibility brought on by the battle. When he closed the door behind them, shutting off the sounds of the street and the world outside, she found herself overcome by a strange and sudden shyness.

Morgan grinned at her, his pirate smile a slash of white in the shuttered dimness of the house. "I'll see to heating up some water for your bath," he told her. "A warrior's welcome home."

He reached out for her hand and gave it a small squeeze, then strode away whistling down the hall.

Bliss closed her fist around the warmth his fingers had left behind. Her breath would not slow. Her pulse refused to return to normal.

In a burst of alarm, she picked up her skirts and ran for her room.

Oh, she wanted the touch of his hand again! With her belly shivering, she pressed her back against the door of her bedchamber. Even the heavy oak could not barricade her from the man's powerful allure.

Magnificent. Valiant. Bloody amazing.

Nonsense, she assured herself. *It is some sort of a reaction to danger. It must be. He's just a man, like any other.*

She closed her eyes, trying to convince herself of just that. Instead, the image of him leaping forward with only a boot dagger, alone against three vicious ruffians—

Her knees went weak.

With one hand, she reached out blindly for the chair before her vanity and sank into it before her lust-weakened knees could drop her to the floor. Heavens, what a man!

Your husband.

No. No. That was a mistake, soon to be corrected. She would win her annulment, she was sure of it. She always got what she wanted, in the end, with enough patience and dedication.

She didn't feel patient. She felt like the sea in a storm, all surging waves and frothing whitecaps. It had been so exciting! She'd felt so breathlessly alive.

I want more.

Which was ridiculous, of course. No one wanted danger. Certainly no one in their right mind. A quiet life, a life of predictability and safety, where she would always know what would come next, day after day after bloody boring day . . .

No, she was simply overexcited. Still, a warning bell clanged within her. Unexpected longings boded ill for her future contentment and serenity. If this was her reaction to danger, she had best avoid it at all costs—for she surely had a weakness for it!

A brisk knock sounded on her door. Bliss stood up straight, locked her knees against the trembling, and opened the chamber door for her husband.

He carried four pails of steaming water, two in each hand. "Milady's bath?"

She stepped back and allowed him in, for above all else,

she longed to be free of the confining reek of alley muck and *eau de* tannery.

He carried the pails in and set them before her fire. Seeing that she'd done nothing to the morning's coals, he sent an inquiring glance over his shoulder.

She must have looked strange somehow, for he frowned at her in concern. Then he moved quickly to the hearth and dug a few hot, glowing nuggets from the ash and piled fresh coals atop them. Dusting off his hands, he stood and regarded her with that same furrow between his eyebrows.

"Did you take injury during our adventures?"

She shook her head quickly. "No, the brutes never touched me."

Morgan drew back. "But I did. Damn, I was too rough, wasn't I, tossing you against the wall?"

Bliss could not help a small smile as she quickly shook her head. "Captain, I am very well, I assure you."

Then she spied a dark drop falling from his left arm. "But you are injured!" With a gasp, she forgot all about her misgivings and stepped forward to wrap her fingers gently around his wrist. When she lifted his arm, he twisted his neck to see the back of his forearm between wrist and elbow.

"Ah. So he did nick me. I wondered."

Bliss met his gaze with furious concern. "Nick? This gash is at least four inches long!"

He shrugged. "But it's shallow. I am cross about the coat, though. I haven't many things here at the house."

Bliss pursed her lips and shoved at his chest with one hand. "Take that off at once. Your shirt as well. I won't have you bleeding away while you carry hot water for me!"

She flew from the room and pattered quickly down the stairs to the kitchen. The next two buckets were steaming away on the stove. She pumped two more to warm, grabbed up some clean toweling and a small pot of honey. There was nowhere to put them but in the bodice of her gown, so she stuffed the honey between her breasts and the toweling anywhere it could fit. That left two hands free for the heavy pails of hot water.

Country living had left Bliss in fit condition, but as she ran back up the stairs, she did note that small houses had their advantages, as in having the bedchambers only two short flights from the kitchens.

When she arrived back in her bedchamber, she was only puffing a little. She could not blame her sudden breathlessness on anything but the sight of Captain Pryce naked from the waist up.

Last night the soapy water had hidden everything but his upper chest and shoulders. Excellent as those were, his trim waist and rippling, muscled stomach truly set the stage for manly magnificence!

I appear to have a weakness for excellent muscular development as well. And the way a man's chest hair arrows down into his trousers in just that way . . .

She learned something new every day on this adventure.

Swallowing hard, she moved past him. He caught at her hands, covering her fingers on the handles of the pails. Her heart flipped somewhat sideways in her chest.

"I'll take those." His deep voice seemed to vibrate inside her.

She allowed it, even though she worried for his injury. He poured most of the water into the bath before she stopped him, putting her hand over his in the same way. "I need to clean your wound."

He went very still. His deep blue eyes fixed on hers. As she watched, they seemed to turn quite black, a hot and hungry sort of color that made her belly twist and something alarming happen a bit lower down.

She'd always thought people were a bit silly about love. She'd always shaken her head at the notion of being "swept away" by someone's touch, of being lost to sense, of making uncharacteristic decisions based on someone's face, or form, or words . . .

I want to touch him. I want him to touch me. I want him to kiss me. I want to press myself to his hot, hard body.

He is your husband. He wants you as well. It is entirely fitting.

No, it wasn't. He didn't care for her as his wife. He'd wedded her in a terrible trick.

But he did it out of loyalty to his brother. He was mistaken, that is all. He protected you today. Perhaps he is beginning to believe in you.

The temptation rolled through her in caressing waves. She could give in to it so easily.

She looked down at their joined hands, unable to gaze into his hungry eyes any longer. Then she blinked to see his blood had smeared into her sleeve where their arms aligned.

Practicality returned in a snap. She straightened, tugging the pail from his grip. Only a small amount of steaming water sloshed in the bottom. It would have to do. She turned away, bustling toward the chair. "Sit here, by the fire." Without thinking, she reached into her bodice to tug her supplies free.

It was his grunt of surprise that made her halt with her honey and her bandages in her hands and turn to see him staring at her like a wolf gazing at a plump rabbit.

She drew back slightly. "You must sit down. I have to tend to your arm."

He moved slowly toward her, his gaze roaming from her disheveled neckline to her face. She had to fight the impulse to step back. To flee the hunter coming for her.

He sat down in the chair slowly, as if ready to spring up at any moment. Bliss nerved her hands to be more steady and stepped forward. He leaned back until she was forced to move between his spread knees to reach him.

He reached out with one hand and dipped his finger into the honey. "Warm," he said, his voice low and husky. Then he put his finger in his mouth and licked it clean, never taking his eyes from hers.

She tore her gaze from his and shook out her makeshift bandaging, making him duck slightly. "Behave, Captain." Then she dipped a corner of the cloth into the hot water and began to clean the slice on his arm.

Even though she could feel his gaze on her, she did not look up from her task until she had wrapped his arm snugly and tucked the last end of the bandage into the folds of cloth.

"That was neatly done," he commented. "I thank you."

She stood and brushed her hands down her skirts. "Well, you did save my life today."

"No."

She looked at him and was surprised to see true regret in his expression.

"I should never have forced that walk on you, and I definitely should not have taken such a lowly route with a lady in my company."

Lady. Not gold digger. Not conniving manipulator.

Bliss shook her head. "Do not forget that I was the one to drag you into that alley. Were you alone, I'm sure you could stroll down any street in the world and remain undamaged."

He grinned, a fierce, sideways smile. "Well, perhaps not entirely undamaged, but certainly less so than my opponents."

Bliss recalled the image of the three large men limping and moaning, fleeing the alley, and grinned back at him.

The captain's face went blank with shock. Bliss recollected herself at once, smoothing her expression into her usual tranquil composure. "Now for that bath you so desire, sir. I shall fetch the rest of the hot water."

He came with her and carried the lion's share back up the stairs for her. All the while she felt his curious gaze on her.

When she had poured the last of the water into the tub, she turned to him. "I must dispose of this gown, I fear, and don my apron before your bath. If you do not mind stepping from the room?"

He stood for a long moment, staring down at her with piercing inquiry. "And if I do mind?"

She lifted her chin and met his dark gaze without flinching. "I know the events of today have stirred your"—she faltered and swallowed hard—"your mettle, sir, but I beg you to recall your oath to me."

He stepped closer. "Have I touched you inappropriately, Mrs. Pryce?"

She shook her head and fought the urge to step away . . . or step forward . . .

Her feelings swirled within her, pulling her this way and that, confusing her. And she was never, ever confused. Ever.

"Have I made scandalous suggestions to you, Mrs. Pryce?"

Her curiosity tingled at the very thought of such "scandalous suggestions." And the way he said "Mrs. Pryce" tightened her throat . . . and her nipples.

Except that she didn't want to be Mrs. Pryce. At all. She must remember that.

Somehow she managed to step backward once, then once more. "No, Captain, you have not. And yet still you stand here when I have asked you to leave my bedchamber for a moment. And while you are out, you might want to fetch the last of the water heating in the kitchen."

He nodded a short bow and smiled genially, but his eyes still gleamed with a hungry light. "As you wish, Mrs. Pryce."

After he left and closed the door with facetious care, Bliss let out a long, slow breath. She was allowing him to get too close. She had to remain in control of this odd negotiation.

A few moments later, she stood wearing her chemise and her "blacksmithing" apron. The day was beginning to catch up to her. Her arm ached where Lord Oliver had gripped it as he berated her. Her knees were skinned from the gritty cobbles of the alley. Anger and peril, piled on with temptation, had sapped her usual vigor.

She used the last of the warm water in the pail to daub

the filth of the alley from her skin. Her bonnet, gown, stockings, shoes, and gloves were in a pile, fit only for the rubbish. She had more gowns, but the bonnet had been a particular favorite of hers. She picked sadly at the broken straw as she waited for the captain to return.

As MORGAN TRUDGED up the steps with pails of steaming water in both hands, he found himself admiring his new bride even more. She had such spirit! He found himself laughing again at the memory of her swinging her prissy little reticule like a battle hammer at the giant thug—and the man's high shrieks of pain and alarm.

She was beautiful. She was strong. She was clever enough to keep him confused about her motives—and he prided himself on being an excellent judge of character. For all of Oliver's warnings, Morgan could not rid himself of the notion that from within her seamless composure, he might someday see the true woman emerge. A sea goddess rising from the shimmering waves.

He wanted to be there for that unveiling. That was a woman he deeply wished to meet.

When he knocked at the bedchamber—his own bedchamber, at that!—she opened the door to grant him entry. He held up the pails and grinned at her. "You had to buy the largest tub in London, didn't you?" he teased.

She didn't smile back. In fact, he thought he saw a flicker of sadness beneath the veil of her usual poise.

Well, he would just have to see about that. After pouring the last of the water into his tub, he turned to grin at her. "I'll be needing a bit of help tugging my boots off, wife." He held up his bandaged arm. "Wounded in battle as I am."

His words did not bring a spark of defiance to those blue eyes or even cause her to lift her chin. Still, she indicated the chair and when he sat, she knelt quite unselfconsciously before him to remove his boots.

Who was this new Bliss? And how could he bring back the one with the fire in her eyes and the brick in her purse?

When she rose once more and turned her back to him, he quickly stripped out of the rest of his clothing. Moments later, he sat immersed in the hot water to his pectoral muscles.

He cleared his throat, and when she turned, he waggled the washing cloth at her. "Wounded, remember?"

Her eyes narrowed. Morgan celebrated inwardly. He could admit to himself, even if he would never admit it to her, that he was enjoying their ongoing battle of wills. Never had a woman struggled so against his charm, not when he'd truly put his mind to seduction.

But didn't he normally go for widows and jaded wives? Wasn't that low-hanging fruit?

Those were fine-looking fruit, who had their pick of men swarming to their sides! Nothing easy about it!

And yet none of them had resisted him as Bliss did—and none of them had so intrigued him, either.

Who was she, really? Greedy seductress? Virginal maiden? Or something in between, both fascinating and indefinable? Getting to know her was like mining diamonds—hard work, but with the promise of immense reward.

When she knelt at the side of the tub and took the cloth without objection, Morgan began to worry. Had he done something wrong, on the way home? Said something to offend between the alley and his own front door?

Then her warm hands began to stroke the soapy cloth over his shoulders and he forgot everything but her touch.

BLISS TOOK THE cloth and began to soap it thoroughly. Then she took a deep breath and reached over to slide it across the broad, muscled back now exposed to her.

His skin was browned, as if he went shirtless at sea. Perhaps he did. In her mind's eye she pictured him standing in his tight breeches under a canopy of billowing white sails, his dark curls tossed by the wind.

Her fingertips came in contact with his skin. How smooth it felt to her touch! Like satin, satin over iron, for his back was plated with those powerful strapping muscles she had spied beneath his coat. The man beneath her fingers was incredibly strong.

Suddenly, Bliss felt small and frail in comparison, a sensation she had never experienced in the company of a man before. Not Neville, certainly. Yet she knew she was not afraid of the captain.

Her own thoughts were to blame for that.

As her hands sluiced water over Captain Pryce's bare back, Bliss found her mind slipping a bit sideways. Her usual patient focus gave way to an odd dreamlike state. Her thoughts swirled strangely in her mind—thoughts of smooth warm skin, of hard sculpted muscle, of the difference between men and women, the difference between this man and herself, of the way the genders met and danced and flickered, like the firelight reflecting in the wet, rippling back of the man she touched.

Then her thoughts began to slow. He was so hard. Strong. Beautiful. Dangerous.

Touching his body felt so good. She passed her wet hands over his wide back slowly, feeling every bulge and hollow. Up. His shoulders were so broad, so strapped with muscle, so dark with sun that her own hands looked small and pale and soft against him.

Lost in that slow, absentminded place, she stroked her hands down his bowed spine, feeling the tension in his back. Down, into the water, stroking the small of his back, spreading her fingers wide and pressing her palms into the hollow there.

He moaned, a low, animal noise of pleasure. The noise traveled into her through her hands, shooting deep into her belly—and other places—

She snatched her hands away, pushing against the edge of the tub and scooting backward.

By the time he turned his head to look at her through heavy-lidded eyes, she sat primly with her wet hands clasped in her lap and no expression whatsoever on her face. She was sure of that, just as she knew that her cheeks were aflame and that she'd been biting her lower lip for some reason, for it was now plump and wet.

The water was very hot. Anyone would have pink cheeks bending over a steaming tub.

Her practical nature offered no explanation for the warm, melting sensation she felt between her thighs. Thank goodness Captain Pryce had no idea about that!

Except that his dark blue eyes held a gleam of secret knowledge, along with a smoky hunger of his own.

Bliss cleared her throat slightly. "I am finished."

"Oh, I don't know," he said mildly. He turned in the tub to lean his forearms on the edge as he gazed at her. "I'm a big bloke. There's a lot of me left to wash."

"You can reach everything else yourself," Bliss pointed out.

Morgan held up his bandaged arm in reply. She hesitated, and he knew he had her.

"Then I must wash the alley off you, I suppose. It is only your due for saving me."

Was it his imagination, or had her voice gone husky with something like longing? When she tilted his head back and poured warm water through his hair, he only had thoughts of her fingers tugging gently at his temples, stroking the soap away . . . and the tenderness of her touch made him ache.

He'd planned to seduce, to tease, to upend her damned equilibrium as he had done the night before. Yet he could not bring himself to break the spell of her gentle ministrations. There was no sound in the room but the spitting of the coals and the streaming water rinsing back into the tub.

Except for the thudding of his heart. Could she hear it? It seemed as loud as surf pounding on a cliff to him—but she only carried on, bathing him carefully.

He'd tried to tell himself that it was only his long deprivation that made him ache for her. That and her obviously desirable figure. And her beautiful hair. And her eyes of sky . . .

His past was strewn with beautiful women, but none of them had ever dug her slim fingers into his soul. None had ever filled his head with dreams of home and warmth and sleeping side by side until they were old and gray.

He couldn't bear it any longer. He reached up and caught at her fingers. She went still when he grasped her hands, but allowed him to pull her to kneel next to him.

Pushing back his wet hair with one hand, he gazed at her lovely face. "Who are you?"

She gazed back but did not answer. Was it because she did not know, or because she thought he already did?

He tugged her closer, until the tub rim pressed to her ribs. Still she only gazed back at him. There was only a single candle flame to see her by. They were nearly nose-to-nose, yet he saw nothing in her wide blue gaze but calm and distance.

Kiss her.

I cannot. I gave my word.

You are a bastard. No one expects you to keep your word.

I do.

He could not kiss her. She would not kiss him. The gulf of this simple contradiction yawned between them, keeping them apart.

"Why?" He barely recognized his own voice, so rife with need and desperation. "Why will you not concede?"

Why will you not be mine?

Her response came from a distance. Her gaze was blank. "Because I am meant to marry Neville."

His grip tightened on her fingers, but she did not flinch away. "Neville. Does the title mean so much to you?"

She gazed back at him calmly, with neither defiance nor apology. "Neville will give me what I need."

You feeble ass! It is your own fault. You let her in!

With a snarl of self-loathing, he released her fingers and stood. The water streamed down over his skin, washing back into the tub. He only wished he could shed his need for her so easily.

She did not flee his nakedness this time. She did not even look away but only sat back on her heels and met his furious gaze.

"Neville would bore you to death," he snarled. "And you bloody well know it!"

Still dripping, he stepped from the tub and stalked from the room. Better to freeze to death in the dark parlor than spend one more moment in the same room as that conniving witch!

BLISS WATCHED HIM go.

Morgan Pryce's magnificence took her breath away, but his anger crushed her. And though there was no point in denying that he had turned her world upon its head, she could not go to him.

If she chose to stay in this marriage, she would spend a lifetime watching him leave. Captain Pryce would forever be walking out her door and sailing away.

He would leave her. Alone. Time and time again.

Waiting. Just as she had done all her life.

With this man, it was all she would ever do.

Chapter 24

THE following morning, nothing went well. Breakfast had been a farce.

As Bliss prepared and served the meal, she attempted to keep the conversation cheerfully bland. She spoke of the upcoming ball. She discussed the weather. She inquired from Morgan which of the butcher's finest meats he might enjoy for his evening meal.

And though he commented here and there, the life was gone from his voice. He was aloof, visibly angry.

Bliss understood Morgan's discomfort. Her blathering was no more than an attempt to dispel a specter from the room—last evening's bath. She failed in this effort, as her fingertips still sizzled from contact with Morgan's hot, slippery skin. Her mind's eye was seared with the sight of his chiseled torso, his muscled buttocks, the aching beauty of his head-to-toe nakedness. Bliss had slept little the night before, her body on fire with the miracle that was Morgan, her mind swirling with a thousand unanswered questions.

Perhaps Morgan suffered from the same torturous malady this morning.

Bliss had the power to heal him. She could easily reach out and touch him now if she so chose. She wanted to. But that was impossible, as such brazen physical affection would only muddy the annulment process.

She could not remain married to him. Even if she had lost every chance to wed Neville, she refused to condemn herself be alone for the rest of her days.

How odd that she needed to remind herself of this simple fact. How strange that this facade of a marriage had become so . . . complicated.

Morgan thanked her for the food and prepared to depart for his ship. It was as if he could not take leave of her company fast enough.

She followed him to the front door. Once again she was left gazing at his back.

"Morgan?" She had not meant to speak.

He stopped and turned, caution in his eyes. He waited.

"I should very much like to visit the ship today."

His eyes narrowed. "You wish to come aboard the *Selkie Maid*?"

"I shall not make a nuisance of myself, if that is your worry. But it was your demand that I remain with you in order to prove myself. So I wish to remain with you."

Morgan pondered her request for a moment and shrugged with obvious reluctance. "If you must."

An hour or so later, Bliss found herself with an unexpected visitor. Cousin Attie sat on a stool by the hearth, engaged in some kind of whittling, her namesake kitten curled up at her feet.

"You're not supposed to have a knife," Bliss pointed out. "You're not even allowed scissors. What on earth are you making?"

"It's a pasta fork." Attie looked up from her work, a

long strand of hair falling across an eye. "I'm making it for Francesca."

Attie was lonely, and the thought softened Bliss. "You miss Orion, don't you?"

Attie shrugged, focusing once more on her whittling. "And Callie. And Elektra. And Poll . . . and now you. It's like I've been left behind."

Though Bliss was dressed and ready to call upon the ship, she could not simply toss Attie aside. Bliss understood loneliness too well to ever contribute to anyone else's. "You can come with me to the docks, if you like. But I have one requirement."

Attie dropped her whittling project and closed her knife, shoving it in the pocket of a particularly ratty pair of breeches. The rest of her attire was equally dismal. "What request is that?"

"That you put on a dress, Attie. A real dress that is becoming of a young lady of your age. Do you have a real dress?"

Attie rolled her eyes in exasperation. "I have that yellow thing Mr. Button made me wear to Orion and Francesca's wedding."

Bliss clapped her hands together. "How lovely that dress was, and how pretty you were in it!" She reached for her bonnet and reticule. "Come along, then. Let's stop by Worthington House so that you can change."

"But why would anyone wear a dress to a ship?" Attie followed at Bliss's heels as they left the house and climbed up into Mr. Cant's waiting carriage.

Attie and Mr. Cant bonded instantly, surly companions of the soul. Like cats forced into alliance against a world of dogs, they kept their distance with utter mutual understanding.

Bliss thought it was most appropriate.

Finally, they were both seated within, after lengthy debate over whether Attie should be allowed to ride up top and learn to drive a hack, "just in case I should need a profession, a legal one."

Bliss answered Attie's question as if none of the querulous protest had just occurred. "You should wear a dress because you are a young lady, who happens to be visiting a ship."

Attie groaned as if she were in agony.

"I shall not force you, Atalanta. Perhaps you should remain at home instead."

"No! I'll do it! Ugh!" She slouched against the carriage bench in defeat. "But only for you, Bliss."

MORGAN LOOKED PARTICULARLY handsome—if not exactly welcoming—when he greeted them at the bottom of the gangway. After helping them aboard, he excused himself for a moment. As he turned away from them to call instructions to the men repairing some rigging on the center mast, he leapt upward and caught himself on the ropy ladder by one hand and one foot, poised in the air like a circus performer. Bliss realized this was the first opportunity she'd had to see him in his world, thoroughly at home. His hair was tousled by the wind, and his careless garb, which looked rather rough in the civilized setting of a drawing room, seemed suddenly practical and easy to move in. It was as if half of him had been left behind when he stepped off that gangplank and she was only now seeing the whole man.

He had never been more attractive to her.

When he dropped down to land lightly on the deck, Bliss turned her head away to hide the sudden hunger she felt.

"Now I can take a moment to give you that tour, ladies."

Attie replied with a decidedly unladylike snort.

Bliss ignored her cousin's lack of manners, since Morgan seemed not to notice. He responded with a bow. "Miss Atalanta Worthington. This is quite an honor."

"Captain."

Bliss was confused. She looked from Morgan to her young cousin, and to Morgan again. "You two have met?"

"Indeed." Morgan stifled a smile. "Miss Atalanta and her brothers recently offered me a ride in the Worthington carriage."

Attie grunted. "Yes. The captain was in danger of being trampled by a milk wagon."

"Oh?" Bliss waited for further details of their encounter, but no one seemed willing to provide them.

Attie crossed her arms over the yellow bodice of her gown and smirked at Morgan. "We had a lovely chat about the importance of family loyalty, did we not?"

Morgan regarded her young cousin with a flat gaze. "Indeed." Then he turned to Bliss. "Shall we, ladies?" Morgan gestured for Attie to walk ahead, and extended his arm to Bliss. She gave him a sideways glance, hoping he might provide insight into that odd exchange. Instead, he changed the subject entirely.

"Here she is, the *Selkie Maid*. Over the years she's carried a variety of commodities, from coffee, tea, and sugar, to silk and precious metals. She requires a crew of forty, but we've just six men aboard while we're docked. The others are taking leave with their families."

A young seaman ran up to their group and bowed gallantly to the ladies. Bliss guessed he was no more than fifteen, just a bit older than Attie, and clearly interested in the pretty visitor.

Bliss could not blame the young man, for Attie looked lovely. All it took to bring her beauty to the fore was a good hair brushing, a splash of water upon her face, and the dress. It was clear that one day soon Attie would take Society by storm.

Poor Society.

Morgan introduced Attie to the seaman and then ordered him to show her about the main deck. "Meet us back here in a quarter hour, Tommy."

"Aye, Captain."

* * *

THE SHIP WAS fascinating, and Attie had to wonder why she hadn't managed to board one sooner.

"Have you ever met a real pirate?" she asked.

Tommy thought about it for a moment. "Probably, but real pirates don't go about bragging that they're pirates. That only happens in storybooks and legends."

"Have you ever engaged in hand-to-hand combat with one?"

He frowned, almost as if he thought that an odd question. "No."

"How many times have you been attacked by pirates while at sea?"

Tommy stopped the tour, glancing at Attie as if she were some sort of strange creature. "Most girls are not so very interested in pirates."

Attie sighed. It was tiresome having to repeat herself on such a regular basis. "I'm not a girl. I'm a genius. And a Worthington."

"All right." Thomas smiled a bit and gestured for her to walk ahead. "Then perhaps you might want to see these."

Attie's jaw nearly fell to the deck. The entire side of the ship was lined with cannons. She had never been this close to so much firepower before! She reached her fingers toward the weapon's brass neck but stopped herself. "May I touch it?"

"As long as you don't accidentally fire it."

Attie smirked at that. She went from cannon to cannon while Tommy talked of swivel mounts and oversize muskets, and then showed her the largest cannon on board the *Selkie Maid*.

"It takes five men to fire her."

Attie could only imagine the thrill of combat at sea, the smell of smoke, the crashing waves, the frantic rushing about of sailors. "What other weapons do you keep on board?"

Tommy laughed then, turning to face Attie. She noticed

he had shiny brown eyes and an easy smile. Perhaps he would grow up to be as dashing as Captain Morgan!

And he looked at her so admiringly.

There might be something to this dress question. An equation began to roll through Attie's mind. If dress style was as "X" and bodice measurement was as "Y"— "Oh, guns!" She darted forward to peer at the racks of weapons.

Tommy followed more leisurely. "We've got everything the crew might need in case we are boarded—cutlasses and short swords, carbines, pistols, and even a blunderbuss or two. Why? Are you organizing a mutiny?"

Attie wished she could come up with a clever reply, but she was too busy imagining the vast array of armaments in her immediate surroundings. "I wish I could live on a ship!" She glanced about her. "My family has taken away all my weapons. It's just not fair. Honestly! You shoot *one* sister and all of a sudden you're a danger to society! All I have left is a secret penknife and my slingshot."

When Attie returned her attention to her companion, she noticed that he stared at her in shock. Attie shrugged. "Like I said, I'm not a girl."

The young sailor shuffled his feet awkwardly. "Beg to differ, miss, but you're a girl," he blurted. "A lady, too, like the captain's new wife. But you aren't like other ladies, that's sure enough. Most ladies wouldn't talk to the likes of me, nor know aught about weapons. Maybe it's that genius thing, like you said. Maybe genius ladies are better than the other sort. Pretty genius ladies . . ."

Attie was shocked. She turned away so he did not see her cheeks flare. She liked him, and she didn't like anyone, usually. How confusing. Sometimes Attie suspected that life would be so much simpler if she was not required to grow up.

While she was still blushing from his outburst, Tommy had diffidently moved on to the next attraction. "Over here is ammunition storage. We keep it locked up most of the time." He pointed to a large lean-to covered with an iron grate and battened down with thick chains. Just inside the hatch were two wooden barrels. One was shut tight, but Attie could see black dust had sifted to fall in a faint ring around the base of it. Gunpowder, probably sealed against the damp. The lid of the other barrel sat askew. Attie saw that it was filled with rounded lead pellets the size of raspberries. That would be ball shot for the muskets.

Attie waited for Tommy to turn his attention toward the rigging, then dug her hand into a barrel. Such perfect ammunition for her slingshot! She shoved a large handful into the left pocket of her gown. Unfortunately, this caused her dress to list to port, so she quickly filled the other pocket until she was balanced.

After the munitions closet, Attie lost interest in the tour until they returned to the deck. Her attention was somewhat arrested by Tommy's description of things such as gaff-rigging and foremasts. "The physics are fascinating," she said, shading her eyes with her hand as she gazed up at the long rope ladder that swept from the deck to the upper mast. "I could climb that if I weren't wearing this blasted—I mean, very nice dress."

Tommy turned to her, his expression mischievous. He reached up and tugged at his forelock. "The ratlines? O' course you could, milady. It only takes a few months of practice. Shall I show you how?"

BLISS COULD NOT tolerate the torture another second. Morgan walked by her side and recited facts about his ship with the utmost politeness, but they kept a careful distance away from each other. They did look each other in the eye. She knew the only cure for this awkward discomfort was to speak the truth.

"I do not give a fig about ongoing repairs aboard this ship, Morgan."

His broad shoulders stiffened. He stared blankly out to the Thames as a breeze lifted a bit of his dark hair. "Then why insist upon this visit? It is a waste of my time."

When Bliss touched his coat sleeve, he pulled away. She swallowed hard, forcing herself to speak her mind. "You left this morning in a foul temper. You couldn't wait to be rid of me. I came here to resolve what transpired between us last night."

Morgan laughed. It was not the warm and husky laugh she had come to enjoy, but a quick and hard bark that stung her like a slap.

He despised her. He did not trust her. And last evening's clumsy and vague conversation had only intensified his loathing.

"I believe you misunderstood me last evening, Morgan."

"I doubt that."

She pressed on. "When I said that only Neville could give me what I needed—"

"Enough." He whipped around to face her, his blue eyes flashing with anger. "There was no misunderstanding, I assure you."

"You must hear me out! I do not care about Neville's title or his fortune. I have no interest in being a duchess. It is simply—"

"No more of this game, Bliss. I have been true to my word but at a terrible price. And you will not yield—you will not consent to be my wife despite our obvious . . ." He stopped himself.

"And you will not grant me an annulment, even though I have done all that you asked."

"I cannot."

"Why not? Why must you be so stubborn?"

Morgan dragged his eyes away from hers and gripped the brass railing. "I cannot say."

Bliss barely suppressed her cry of frustration. They were both stubbornly hiding their secrets, and they would never break free from this impasse until someone dared to reveal the truth.

She would begin with the things she had not told him. "I have sent several messages to Neville. I went to Camberton House to see him yesterday."

Morgan shot her a sideways glare, his lips drawn into a smirk. "You do still want him. See? No misunderstanding."

"He never responded and he would not see me. I believe Lord Oliver has kept him in the dark about my desire to speak with him."

One of Morgan's eyebrows arched. "As he should. He's protecting Neville."

"I do not think so." Bliss attempted to squeeze herself between Morgan and the railing, forcing him to look at her. She wanted him to see her face, to see that she spoke with integrity. "I encountered your uncle on my way out. He is not an honorable man, Morgan. He as much as admitted that he has manipulated you and your brother. He—"

"Enough." Morgan straightened and backed away. Bliss saw a furious streak of red flush his neck. "How dare you, woman? Will you stop at nothing?"

"It is the truth, Morgan. Lord Oliver wants you and Neville to be enemies. He has used me as a wedge between brothers!"

Morgan's dark blue eyes flared, but she saw something in his expression that gave her cause for hope. Was he finally seeing his uncle for who he was? Morgan had opened his mouth to speak when a piercing shriek cut through the air.

Bliss's blood turned to ice.

It was Attie.

THEY FOUND HER with one hand covering her mouth and the other pointing skyward.

Morgan didn't hide his anger. He tilted back his head and

bellowed upward, "What the bloody hell are you doing up there, Tommy?"

The reply was faint—and frightened. "S-sorry, Cap'n!"

The young seaman hung helpless, tangled upside down like a fly in a spider's web. One of his ankles was snarled in a section of rope while his opposite hand held a tenuous grip on the edge of a tiny wooden platform. The boy was at least forty feet above the deck, plenty high enough to break his neck should he fall.

As he swung there, the rope around his ankle slipped, dropping him another few inches. Bliss put her arms around Attie and pulled her a safe distance from the rigging.

Attie's face was red and furious—which Bliss knew meant that she was very frightened indeed.

"Blasted stupid fool," Morgan hissed. He whipped off his coat, weskit, and cravat, tossing everything into a pile on the decking. He jumped to grab a section of rope and easily swung himself up. "Don't move, Tommy."

"I'll try not to, Cap'n!"

"The ratline is about to break." Morgan pulled himself higher. "Keep as much of your weight on your hand as possible."

"I'm trying!"

Bliss watched Morgan continue up at a steady pace, agile and graceful as he climbed the ropes. She was stunned by his confidence and strength, and could not help admiring the power in his muscular thighs and calves, the might of his upper arms and shoulders. He did not rush or lose his composure—he was focused and steady, not revealing the slightest bit of fear as he climbed higher and higher from the safety of the deck. Bliss supposed she was terrified enough for all of them.

"Boys are stupid." Attie clutched at Bliss as she whispered miserably in her ear. "I never asked him to show off for me. Why did he do it?"

"Oh dear. Men can be a bit brainless when they're around a pretty woman."

Tommy's body began to sway to and fro in response to Morgan's shifting weight. The rope slipped again. Tommy gasped.

Morgan rebuked him once more. "You knew the rigging was under repair—what the bloody hell were you thinking?"

"Sorry, Cap'n!"

Morgan reached the larger of the two wooden landings, about ten feet below where Tommy dangled. Just as Morgan began to pull up to stand, Tommy's rope broke entirely.

The boy's ankle slipped free. He flailed his arms, trying to find something to grab, but his fists clutched at nothing but air.

"No!" Attie cried.

Bliss could scarcely believe it, but Morgan managed to leap upward just in time. He snagged Tommy with one brawny arm and pulled him in. They both crashed back onto the platform and began to roll.

Bliss gasped—it looked as if they would continue right off the edge! But Morgan's fingers found a taut line of rope and he held on.

Only then did she notice that Attie had her eyes closed tight and her fists clenched just as tightly. "It's all right, Attie. They are not injured."

They watched Morgan send his young sailor down the rigging and then follow behind him. Sweat had soaked through the back of Morgan's white cotton shirt.

Tommy limped off on the shoulder of the first mate, clearly humiliated and thankful to be alive, and Attie followed them to a quiet corner of the ship. As soon as Morgan's boots hit the deck, he reached for his discarded clothing and then turned his back to Bliss.

"Morgan."

"No." When he glanced over his shoulder, Bliss saw that

his expression was one of pure torment. He was breathing hard. "No more lies, Bliss. I cannot bear any more of your lies. Not today—not ever." He pulled his weskit on but let it hang unbuttoned. "I think it's time you left my ship."

Chapter 25

SOMETHING was terribly wrong when a man could not find refuge in his own home after a day's work. But that was Morgan's predicament later that evening, for if he dared go home for a hot meal, a warm bath, and some rest, he would place himself in close proximity to the greedy, scheming harpy he had married.

There was no denying it. Bliss Worthington had not only driven him to a lust-induced madness; she'd driven him from his own bloody house!

Why had he agreed to perform in this absurd circus? Why had he ever listened to Lord Oliver?

Because he told me precisely what I wished to hear. Because he dangled the Selkie Maid *before me like a carrot before a mule.*

He needed to relieve his desire for his exquisite, devious bride so that he could retake the upper hand. She had power over him as long as his deprived libido obsessed over her sweet body and her breathy voice and her—

Damn it! He was doing it again!

Morgan left the docks and hailed a hack. When he told the driver his destination, the fellow raised an eyebrow, which was laughable. The man would likely pay a month's wage just to be allowed in the front door of such an establishment.

It occurred to Morgan that only one truth was at the core of all his current troubles. He had long ago promised himself that his word would be his most valuable asset. Yet his life would be so much easier if oaths mattered little to him. He would be free.

He could lie to Oliver, claim the marriage had been consummated, and gain title to the *Selkie Maid* without further ado. Lying to his uncle would damage his last ties to anything resembling family, and he was not yet prepared to do that.

He could force Bliss into marital congress despite his promise to the contrary. She would have no recourse to gainsay him. She was his wife, his property, and he had every right to demand a consummation.

But blast it all, he could not force her. Her proven ability to defend herself aside, he would rather die an honorably impoverished man than a rich bastard lacking in self-respect. Perhaps such a stubborn stance was his mother's doing, as she'd desired her son to be more than a bastard. She wanted Morgan to soar far above Society's expectations of the position he'd been born into.

It struck Morgan that he might be more like Neville than he'd ever admitted.

Morgan arrived, paid the driver, and climbed up the stairs to the door of Mrs. Blythe's House of Pleasure. Famous for opulent parties and eager, sensational women, and according to rumor, men as well, Blythe's was a place where a man could relax with good food, fine tobacco, excellent drink, and cheerfully lascivious company.

A lovely creature answered the door clad in artfully arranged scraps of a maid's livery. There was perhaps enough fabric in her costume to cover a sofa cushion.

She greeted him with sultry welcome, handed him a whiskey, and gestured for him to relax in the front parlor. She sauntered away, clearly aware that Morgan could not tear his gaze away from her revealed flesh.

It was very nice flesh. It was simply not the right flesh. Morgan leaned back in his chair and closed his eyes. It didn't matter. He was here for a right rogering to relieve the strain of battling Bliss at every turn.

Yet the expected relaxation did not overtake him. He was afraid he knew why.

He was a married man, for God's sake. He had sworn his fidelity to Bliss and signed his name to the commitment. Of all the oaths he had taken, this was perhaps the most solemn of them all.

He had not yet taken a sip before he straightened in the chair and barked a bitter laugh at himself. *Till death do part us.*

Morgan set the whiskey glass on the side table and stood. He had no business being here. His business was to go home, charm his bride into his bed for once and all, and get his ship.

He was met at the door by none other than Mrs. Blythe herself. She was a buxom woman with silver-streaked blond hair and light blue eyes. Though on the far side of her forties, she was still a comely woman. Her smile had an unruffled quality about it that reminded him of someone . . .

"Going home, Captain Pryce?"

How amusing that she would try to convince him and his coin purse to stay. "I'm sorry, but I really must go."

Her eyes crinkled in amusement. She stepped aside, granting him access to the door. "Oh, I absolutely agree. You really must go home—to your *wife*."

She wanted him out? Morgan's frown relaxed into a smirk of comprehension. "So Lord Oliver has told you to refuse me, eh? I wonder when the old man will release his grip on my life."

Mrs. Blythe placed a hand on his shoulder. "I assure you, Captain, it is I who wishes you gone."

With that, four of her burly footmen politely escorted him to the street.

Thrown out of a brothel . . . for being married? Morgan shook his head at his own ridiculousness. Self-respect was indeed a virtue, but it would not assuage the simmering lust he felt for his wicked bride.

He hailed another hack and, unhappily, headed home.

BLISS TOOK A turn before the large bedchamber mirror, attempting to examine the back of the gown.

"Hold still, Bliss. Do you have any idea how hard it is to alter a moving target?"

She laughed. "Forgive me, Button. It's just so beautiful and it fits so perfectly."

"And a good thing, too, since there's no time for any but the most minor adjustments." Cabot held the pincushion for him as he tacked down a side seam.

"I am so sorry for missing that appointment."

"Oh my goodness! After all you've been through!" He waved off her apology. "It sounds like such a horrible ordeal. I'm only relieved no one got hurt."

"Well, *someone* was badly injured. It simply wasn't the captain or myself." Bliss turned again, admiring the cornflower blue satin and the elaborate snowy white embroidery of the bodice. She looked again and frowned.

"Is there a problem?"

Bliss did not know how to say it. She would never want to criticize Button's work, and there was truly nothing to criticize. She merely had an observation. "There is no problem, exactly. It is simply that this gown is . . . well, it is far more mature than the one I originally ordered. It is so . . ." Bliss turned to the side and brushed her hands down the bodice. "It's quite revealing."

Button laughed. "Well, you are a married woman now, dear. That spectacular bosom was always meant to be shown off, not hidden away like before. As a dressmaker I find it quite liberating—think of all the fun we'll have with future gowns!"

She bit her bottom lip, still not convinced.

Button brought his face near to hers. "My lovely Bliss, you are no longer a virgin. There is no need to dress like one!"

She felt herself go still. She stared at Button in the mirror, her eyes wide in surprise and her lips parted. It was true— the world would assume she had already consummated her marriage. The world would no longer see her as an innocent.

None of which was true.

She could barely breathe.

"Bliss? Are you quite certain the robbers didn't hurt you?"

It was Cabot. His whisper jolted her from her private worry. His gaze locked with hers in the mirror, and then he glanced at the back of her arm, and back again. Button hurried to stand with him near Bliss's left elbow and began clucking in concern.

"Whoever did this to you, Bliss?"

"What—?" She raised her arm and craned her neck to find what had disturbed them so. That was when she saw it—a bruise in the shape of a man's hand, just below the dainty cap sleeve of her ball gown. "Oh heavens!"

On the inside was a black and blue thumbprint. The back featured four distinct fingerprints in a similar dark hue.

Lord Oliver!

"You stupid, greedy little tart. Did you think I would allow you to ruin Neville's life, to siphon off the Danton fortune?"

Bliss was so disturbed by the memory that she did not know what to say.

"Oh, now, do not worry so much, Bliss dear." Button stood behind her and patted both her shoulders. "I brought the most darling little shawl to complement your gown, so perfectly stylish. It will cover it right up! Let me fetch it from downstairs."

Bliss nodded, watching Button scurry from the room. When she caught Cabot's eye again, he gave her a worried look.

The last thing she needed was interference. "Cabot, please say nothing to my family about this."

His handsome jaw worked for a moment. "Was it the captain, Bliss?"

Her eyes widened. "Heavens no! Why, he would never!" She met Cabot's concerned gaze in the mirror with deep intent. "Morgan would *never* harm a woman."

He narrowed his eyes and gazed searchingly into hers for a long moment. Then he nodded once. "Very well, then. I shall say nothing to your cousins."

She could never tell her friends or family that her injury was the handiwork of a respected member of the aristocracy, Lord Oliver Danton, the uncle of the Duke of Camberton. It would mean war.

And Neville would end up on the opposite side.

"Oн!"

Button nearly ran into the man stepping through the front door into the foyer. Button knew exactly who he was—Captain Morgan Pryce, Bliss's husband and owner of this house. The captain, however, had no such knowledge of Button.

"Who on earth are you?"

"Oh! I do apologize, Captain Pryce, but we are here to fit Bliss's ball gown, as she did not appear for her appointment yesterday."

Captain Pryce's face relaxed. "Of course. You are the dressmaker friend?" His eyes flashed toward the stairwell leading to the upper floor. "Is she upstairs?"

"Yes, Captain. We are almost finished."

"No hurry. I'll be down in the kitchen so as not to disturb you."

"Very good, sir."

Button grabbed the shawl from the various spare accessories spread out on the parlor sofa and was about to return to the bedchamber when the captain stopped him. Button could not help noticing the startling blue of the man's eyes and the rugged handsomeness of his face.

My goodness. What a delicious plateful. Every bit of gossip he'd heard about Morgan Pryce had been correct, if not too modest.

"Mr. Button, might I trouble you for a moment or two?"

Button let the shawl drape over his forearm and nodded. "Of course."

"Is Mrs. Pryce still determined to attend that bloody ridiculous ball? Are you quite certain? Because I can scarcely believe she would want to expose herself to ridicule like that, considering the scandalous nature of our . . . our marital situation."

Button coughed politely to cover his surprise. He was the direct sort, wasn't he? "Captain, all I can tell you is that we have delivered her gown. What she intends to do with it is another matter."

The captain shook his head as if to clear his thoughts. "I do apologize, Mr. Button. Forgive me. It's just . . . I don't know how familiar you are with the details . . ."

"I am not privy to my clients' personal lives, Captain." Completely untrue, of course, but it would have to do for the moment. "Forgive me, but I must return to Miss Worthing— er, Mrs. Pryce."

"Of course."

The captain turned on his boot heel and glanced about the foyer. It looked to Button as if the man were lost, as if he were puzzled by the interior of his own house. Button felt a pang of sympathy for him, but he had to get back to work if Bliss's dress were to be ready for tomorrow's ball.

"One more thing, Mr. Button."

He nodded but took a backward step toward the stairway.

"How long have you known Bliss? How well do you know her?"

"My acquaintance with the family goes back many years." That was enough of that, however. Button could not continue this line of questioning. "Captain, I do beg your pardon, but you are her husband. If you wish to know her better, I suggest you speak with her directly. Now if you'll excuse me."

Button left the clearly perplexed sea captain alone in his foyer. He had been witness to many unusual marital pairings in his line of work, but this one was perhaps the most curious of them all.

KATARINA KNOCKED ON the door to her mother's bedchamber, hoping she was still awake.

"Come in."

She peeked into the candlelit room and smiled at her mother nervously.

"Good heavens, daughter! Up so late?" Mummy began frantically waving her inside. "And parading about the halls of Camberton House in your dressing gown—hurry in here and close the door!"

Katarina did as she was told. Her mother patted the edge of her bed and motioned for her to climb in. Once snuggled next to her, Katarina was unsure how to begin the conversation. Perhaps it would be best to slowly work her way to the crux of the matter. "How did your appointment go today, Mummy?"

"Oh, Katarina! What a thrill for me, after all those years of settling for our dressmakers back home. That Lementeur is a true *artiste*! A visionary! But I shall hold my praise until both our gowns are finished and delivered in time for the ball tomorrow, for although everyone claims he is a magician, I have no idea how they can meet such a deadline."

Katarina stared at the flames in the fireplace, still debating how to broach the subject. In the past, the only discussions of love included her mother's reminders to stand up straight, memorize the rules of Society, and keep up with her piano, French, and lace work—and, of course, her knowledge of accounts.

But love? Never had Katarina been the one to bring up the topic.

She felt her mother's warm hand cover hers. It was a protective gesture, one she had enjoyed all her life. It was true that Mummy could be trying at times, but Katarina never once doubted Paulette Beckham's devotion to, and deepest love for, her family.

"Speak, child. There is clearly something troubling you."

Katarina turned to her mother. "What do you think of Neville?"

Mummy tipped her head back and laughed. "Oh, my darling girl, I am honored you would come to me for approval, but the question is—what do *you* think of Neville?"

Katarina found herself without words. Though she had not known how her mother would react, she had never envisioned this . . . camaraderie. It was almost as if her mother considered her a woman.

Mummy smiled warmly. "I trust you, dearest Kat. You have a fine mind. I have taught you well. And you are quite perceptive for a young lady of nineteen."

Katarina nodded, her throat tight.

"That said, perhaps it is time I speak plainly."

Katarina tried not to wince, but she feared the worst.

"As you know, your father and I met at a ball in London, when he was here to negotiate additional business for Sunbury. The plantation was owned by your grandfather Beckham at the time."

Katarina scooted back a bit so that she could better observe her mother. Obviously, she was enjoying her reminiscence.

"But when it was time for him to return to Barbados, I could not bear the idea of never seeing him again. So we married. I know he was quite wealthy and had very good connections, but we married for love, my dearest Katarina. A love so deep that I was willing to move to the edge of the earth for it. I wish that kind of love for you."

Katarina's eyes went wide.

"I was from a respectable family, though not highborn. You, however, are an heiress, my dear—a beautiful heiress of the gentry—which puts you in a position of power. Please take advantage of it."

Another silent nod.

"But for heaven's sake, do not separate love from reason. Be sure that the object of your affection is a good man with a station in Society, of excellent reputation. He does not have to be a duke, but if he is I will not complain."

Mummy patted her hand again. "So, do you think Neville is a good man?"

"Oh, I do!"

"As do I." She placed a kiss on Katarina's temple. "All I ask is that you do not rush the process. We are here for the entire Season. Enjoy the attention you are about to receive and choose carefully. Do you promise me that?"

"Of course, Mummy."

"Now, as for Neville's fondness for the bottle—"

"But he has a very good reason!" Immediately embarrassed by her outburst, Katarina took care to lower her voice. "His brother stole his fiancée!"

Mummy waved her hand through the air. "I know all about it, dear. It's all the servants can talk about, and I have

a niggling suspicion Lord Oliver is behind the entire debacle. He is an unpleasant soul, that one."

"But, Mummy!" Katarina was shocked. "I tried to tell
you as much only yesterday—"

"Shh. It takes more than one conversation to be sure of
a man's character, my dear."

Katarina shrugged. She was not of the same opinion but
chose not to argue the point.

"And that is why I endured several conversations with
'darling Ollie' before I knew with certainty—Lord Oliver
Danton is a faradiddling weasel!"

Chapter 26

NEVILLE was sober at last—shockingly, disturbingly so. As he stood, waiting, in the main hall of Camberton House, he calculated that he had gone without a drop of strong drink for well over twelve hours, a period of time during which he had been as miserable as a man could be.

Perhaps he had already come to prefer the hazy detachment of alcohol over the sting of reality, for all he could think about was how a shot or two of whiskey would have made this upcoming event more bearable.

For the moment, he only had to bear the minor wait for Miss Beckham to finish dressing. His uncle and Mrs. Beckham waited with him.

He found he could not control his thoughts—they kept returning to what this evening should be. If not for Morgan's interference, Neville would be attending the Fletchers' ball with his gorgeous bride, Bliss, and not his uncle and houseguests. The happy couple should be making their social debut as the Duke and Duchess of Camberton.

His Bliss, his lady, his wife . . .

Mrs. Pryce.

Neville tugged at his cravat, glancing at the hall clock. It was past nine, and though a duke's late arrival to a private ball was practically de rigueur, Neville wanted to get the evening over with as quickly as possible. He had no desire to be the object of whispers and pitying smiles tonight. Indeed, he had no desire to be with people at all.

His mind veered to the contents of the wine cellar, the half-empty whiskey bottle he'd set on the mantel, and the refuge of his corner library chair. All so very tempting . . .

At least one thing about the evening was cause for gratitude: Bliss and Morgan would not dare make an appearance at the Fletchers'. At least he would not have to come face-to-face with the traitors. He would not have believed it of Bliss, but she had not called upon Camberton House, nor sent him a single message—

"I do apologize for my daughter's delay." Mrs. Beckham tapped her gloved fingertips to her cheeks, a way to induce a blush, Neville supposed. "I believe there was a complication with Katarina's hairstyle, and, as you might know, a lady's hair must be perfect if she is to feel beautiful. I do so want my Katarina to feel beautiful tonight. This is her first London ball, you know!"

"Yes, you have repeatedly informed us."

Neville glared at his grumbling uncle, stuffed into his formal ball attire and obviously tiring of the wait. Lord Oliver did not enjoy the company of Paulette Beckham—he had made that abundantly clear. In fact, Neville had never seen his uncle treat a lady with such sharp impatience. He found it disgraceful, really, as he expected more gallantry from his father's brother.

But then, Uncle Oliver's conduct of late had been dreadful all around. He had betrayed Neville's trust in the most hurtful fashion, had he not? Neville felt no fondness for the old man at that moment, and knew it might take quite some time before trust was restored and forgiveness could take hold. If it ever did.

Neville turned his attention to Mrs. Beckham. She might seem to be nothing more than a flittering matron in a satin ball gown, but thanks to Katarina, Neville knew better. While Uncle Oliver considered Mrs. Beckham's comments no more than insipid prattle, Neville realized they were part of her long-term strategy to distract—even fool—Lord Oliver. Certainly, Mrs. Beckham had already convinced him that she was a vapid Society mother, devoid of business aptitude. It was an assumption the old man would surely come to regret.

Served him right.

Neville smiled at Mrs. Beckham, deciding he would quite enjoy a game of chess with the Lady Pirhana. He was about to suggest a match when he heard the rustling of fabric from the floor above. All eyes moved to the top of the grand staircase.

At first, Neville's mind could not make sense of what he saw. Who was this woman? Were they not waiting for Katarina? And then it dawned on him . . . the woman was Katarina.

He heard himself gasp.

"Here she is! Isn't she absolutely stunning?" He was aware that Mrs. Beckham was practically jumping up and down in delight. "Just look at her hair!"

Neville was already looking . . . at her hair, certainly, as it had been pulled back close to her head and adorned with a spray of magnificent feathers. But he was also looking at her, at Katarina. Neville had not noticed her height before. He had observed her slenderness, of course, but somehow he had missed the fact that she was elegantly tall.

And why had he not noticed the graceful length of her neck before? Or the dramatic line of her cheekbones? Or the gentle rhythm of her shoulders as she walked?

Katarina made her way down the stairs. That dress. It had to be the dress that had so altered the appearance of their bookish houseguest. The color was nothing he had ever seen before, a saturated shade of purple, snugly fitted to her bosom, the bodice alive with tiny iridescent jewels. A great deal of her faultless skin had been exposed from throat to bosom.

Was she stunning? Absolutely. Indeed, Neville had to admit that at some point in the last two days, little Katarina Beckham, princess of a sugar kingdom, had become a queen.

Moments later, on their way to Fletcher House, Neville found himself overly aware of his proximity to his houseguest. She sat across from him, her gown catching every hint of light, her face composed.

Why was he finding it difficult not to stare? He had seen his share of beautiful women in beautiful ball gowns. Was it guilt he was feeling? Was he wrong to notice the allure of one woman when he was supposed to love another? Katarina caught his eye and smiled at him. It appeared she was thoroughly unaffected by his nearness.

Neville envied her composure. It reminded him of Bliss.

He stared out the window to the London streets, wondering where she might be this evening. Was she with Morgan, sharing his table, his home . . . his bed? Or had she returned to Worthington House?

How could she have done this to him?

Such was Neville's distracted state when they arrived at Fletcher House and ascended the grand staircase to the ballroom.

Despite his love of fine architecture, Neville barely noticed the fanciful details for which the home was famous. He detected only a monotonous blur of mirrors, gilded ceilings, crystal chandeliers, and floor-to-ceiling windows.

Oh, how he wished this evening was done.

Chapter 27

THE members of Duke of Camberton's party were introduced immediately upon entering the ballroom. Neville heard his name and title announced and that of the lady he escorted, Mrs. Paulette Beckham, of Barbados. Right behind them came Uncle Oliver and Katarina.

A hush fell over the grand hall. The sudden silence tugged Neville from his dour introspection, and he noticed the wide-eyed stares, the parted lips, and the frozen gestures of the ball guests.

Katarina was their focus. She stood alone at the edge of the ballroom, a shining beacon of violet elegance in a frilly sea of white and pink. Neville then noticed that his uncle had simply walked off, leaving Katarina alone in a room of social vipers!

Was Oliver mad? When had he become such an ill-mannered boor?

Neville was furious. He excused himself from Mrs. Beckham and went to Katarina's side.

"Thank you," she said, attempting a smile as she slipped her arm into his. "Clearly, I have made a terrible mistake in my choice of gown. I fear I am a spectacle."

When Neville looked at her, he felt an unexpected lightness spread though his chest. For a moment he did not know what to say. "You are an original, Katarina, never doubt it. You are a monarch among the moths. I am honored to stand by your side."

When her gaze met his, Neville saw the sparkle of moisture in her brown eyes. She lowered her thick black eyelashes and whispered, "The honor is mine, Neville."

Paulette Beckham wasted no time in setting the stage for her daughter's debut. She sidled up to Neville and asked for his assistance. "Your Grace, would you be so kind as to introduce me to the most wealthy and powerful woman in the room?"

Neville found himself smiling. "I believe I am speaking to her now."

Paulette laughed none too daintily and gave him a friendly pat on the shoulder. "Indeed, Your Grace. I shall settle for the second-most wealthy and powerful, then. Please lead the way."

He introduced the Beckhams to their hostess, Edna Fletcher, who welcomed them with a restrained enthusiasm and a blatant appraisal of their attire. "Wherever did you get those gowns?"

Paulette stroked her blue satin skirts. "Oh, a humble little London dress shop. We happened to stumble upon it, didn't we, Katarina? Perhaps you have heard of it?"

Mrs. Fletcher raised a doubtful eyebrow, then exchanged glances with several of her associates in the business of Society. "Surely not."

"Oh! Well, the dressmaker's name was 'Lemon' something. What was it again, dear?"

"Lementeur, Mummy."

"Quite." Paulette pretended not to notice the stunned

expressions of the women before her. "He claims to be terribly busy, but perhaps I can offer you an introduction."

Neville asked Katarina if she would like some punch, and they left the ladies to their negotiations. They had not gone far when Neville heard Paulette managing to include "sugar plantation," "widowed," and "heiress" in the same sentence.

Katarina sighed. "I shall be terribly relieved when this night is over."

"You do not care for balls?"

She shrugged "I would not know. This is my first true ball. There were cotillions in Barbados, certainly, but nothing as grand as this."

A wave of whispers rushed through the room. Neville glanced about, knowing he had never witnessed anything quite like it. It was as if he were seeing and hearing a great wind sweep across the wheat fields . . . "That girl is a sugar plantation heiress."

They never made it to the refreshment table.

For the next half hour, Neville held the line against an advancing horde of potential suitors. Poor Katarina was wide-eyed and flustered at first, overwhelmed with all the attention and invitations to dance. She proved to be a quick study, however, and in short order was an expert in the mating rites of a minor but bothersome local subspecies: the poor-but-titled English aristocracy.

Neville fended off the most egregiously unsuitable ones, whispering in Katarina's ear as each fellow made his approach. "That one lost the family estate in a poker game," he told her. And "that one fathered three illegitimate children before the age of twenty" or "that one drank away his fortune."

Mrs. Beckham returned to her daughter's side, her satisfied smile indicating she was pleased with the evening's progress.

Neville was surprised to realize he was enjoying himself as well. Although new to the game, Katarina was no fool. Soon, she could guess a prospective suitor's suitability before Neville even spoke a word. "This one looks like a handful," she murmured to Neville on the approach of one aging dandy. "I cannot drum up interest in anyone who wears his breeches so tight."

It was clear that the lovely Katarina would have her choice of suitors, and Neville knew he should be happy for her. Therefore he was dismayed to admit that he felt somewhat territorial. He told himself it was a brotherly kind of protectiveness. After all, she was a guest in his home.

Even as he laughed quietly at one of Katarina's acerbic assessments, his gaze was suddenly drawn to the opposite end of the ballroom. He would later wonder what had snared his attention so absolutely. Was it the way she moved? The shiny brightness of her hair? The overflowing charms of her figure, perfectly framed in a flawless pale blue gown?

Or was it her demeanor? For as Neville stared at Bliss he saw she seemed distressed. Her shoulders drooped ever so slightly. There was a shadow in her expression, a sadness, perhaps.

It was so unlike his tranquil, imperturbable Bliss.

Neville knew he must go to her. None of this was her doing. He believed that now. They would find a way to move beyond all this confusion. He took a step in her direction.

BLISS FOUND HERSELF in a most unexpected circumstance. She stood alone at the edges of the ballroom, observing the ebb and flow of the elegantly attired crowd. Every now and again she would overhear snippets of conversations or recognize a laugh. Bliss smiled and nodded when an acquaintance strolled past. Those so-called friends met her greeting with frozen expressions and twitchy unease.

If it were all not so terribly awkward, she might have been amused. She imagined she presented them with quite the poser. After all, as Bliss Worthington, she had been legitimately invited to the event. Here she stood, in one of the finest gowns in the room. She was not vain to recognize that she was also one of the most conventionally attractive females present.

Her Worthington family might be considered odd, but they had long been accepted because of various high connections.

Yet—her recent marriage was still a white-hot scandal. The groom was a lowly sea captain, a bastard.

But he was a duke's bastard.

Really, she must be such an unsettling dish for Society to stomach!

She reminded herself that being alone at one of London's most fashionable balls was not a hardship. Increasing her social status had never been one of her goals.

And, in the strictest sense, she was not alone. Bliss had sent a message to Worthington House the moment she realized Morgan would not be accompanying her.

Her male cousins had been suitably protective when they arrived at Morgan's small house in their rickety carriage. Apparently, Bliss had been so successful in her assurances that she much preferred to go alone that once they had escorted her inside the ballroom, they wandered off to visit with friends, raise a glass or two, and dance.

As they should. Bliss was now a married woman. She no longer required constant chaperonage. In fact, she found the independence rather novel.

Her gaze was drawn to the opposite end of the grand hall. Neville had attended after all. There he stood, tall and boyishly handsome in his evening attire. But who was that stunning creature on his arm? It took a moment for her to realize it was a nearly unrecognizable Katarina Beckham!

Miss Beckham must be a girl of great resourcefulness, for Bliss had no doubt that the regal violet gown was Lementeur's handiwork. Who else but Button and Cabot could create a style so perfectly flattering to Katarina's slim figure?

The real mystery was how Katarina managed to get an appointment just days after arriving from the West Indies.

Bliss gazed at Neville with new eyes. As always, he was sweetly handsome when he smiled, something he seemed to do often in Miss Beckham's presence. Bliss noticed how he inclined his head to speak with her, how his face lit up at her words.

This is your chance. Go now and speak to him. Tell him about Lord Oliver's interference! Tell him how badly you wish to be free of Captain Pryce!

The very thought of being free of Morgan sent a jolt through her, and it was not relief she felt. It was loss.

There was Neville, mere steps away. Neville, who was the man she'd always wanted.

I don't know what I want any longer. Bliss tore her gaze away from Neville. She had no right to stare. She was married to another.

Yes, to a man who does not believe a word you say!

Bliss pulled her shawl tighter over her shoulders and forced her expression into one of stately geniality. She could not allow her face to hint at the unhappiness now threatening to overwhelm her.

Morgan had not said a word to her since he'd lost his temper on the *Selkie Maid*. Bliss missed him more than she could ever have anticipated.

He was clearly avoiding her now. He spent nearly every hour since their disagreement on his ship, and when he returned home he was careful not to enter any room where Bliss might be. He did not dine with her. He left without saying when he planned to return.

This pushing and pulling had left Bliss utterly exhausted. How could a man want to kiss her one day and then refuse to listen to her the next? Bliss had merely wished to tell him of her encounter with Lord Oliver. But he refused to hear the truth. He did not believe in her.

Yet only a day earlier he had asked Bliss for permission to kiss her, and she had been dangerously close to granting it. What if they had chosen another alley and had never met those ruffians? Would she have submitted to Morgan? Would she have thrown away all her resolute plans for another taste of his lips on hers?

Bliss knew that if she had, she would be standing here this evening a married woman in truth, a woman in full, for she would not have left Morgan in that big copper tub. She would have joined him and become his wife once and for all.

Bliss suddenly felt her skin tingle. She turned this way, then that, in search of the source.

There, striding toward her.

Morgan.

DAMN IT, HE had not wanted to come, but Morgan supposed it was the curse of being an honorable bastard. He had promised to accompany Bliss to this silly event, and he kept his promises. Always.

Even to a woman he could not fully trust, a woman who tried to malign his uncle, a woman who drove him mad with her beauty, her bravery, her bloody unwavering capability!

Blast! The Worthingtons! Morgan slipped behind a large potted palm, pausing until he could be certain Daedalus and Castor Worthington hadn't spotted him. The last thing he wanted was to be forced to defend himself to that crowd again, not until he himself stopped questioning the wisdom of his own actions. At this juncture, Morgan was no longer entirely certain his masquerade had been a righteous one.

Assured the Worthingtons had not spied him, Morgan straightened to his full height and continued through the ballroom.

Damn it! Neville!

Morgan made a dash to the next strategically located palm. He hoped there were enough potted plants in the place to get him through the night.

He peeked through the fronds, and was pleased to see

Neville looking so well—and so sober. The duke strolled arm in arm with a striking young woman draped in a column of purple silk. Neville seemed to like her very much.

As much as the pairing intrigued him, Morgan knew he had to get as far away from this side of the room as possible. He stood once more, turned, and stopped in midstride.

Bliss.

God, that woman is beautiful.

Morgan could not deny it—the first thing he noticed was the cut of her ball gown. He could not help himself, for the gown was a bloody declaration.

The neckline did more than accent Bliss's bounty—it proclaimed it with the fanfare of angels and trumpets. She was glorious. Alluring. Tempting. She was a ripe, bounteous miracle of femininity and grace.

He was clearly not alone in his admiration of her. Every man in the vicinity still drawing breath had difficulty keeping his attention focused elsewhere—anywhere—but on Bliss.

Heat simmered in his gut. Morgan's shoulders stiffened. He itched to shout out to all of them that this woman waited for him.

Mine.

Oh hell. I think I'm jealous.

The concept shocked him.

Morgan denied it, squelching the very thought. Yet he kept walking, his eyes never leaving Bliss. She tipped her head to glance at the ceiling. Jeweled bobs flashed in her ears.

Then Morgan realized what he should have seen sooner: Bliss Worthington was from a different world than he. She was from this world, the realm of wealth and manners and grand ballroom and fine jewels. Bliss belonged here.

Morgan did not.

Bliss had no need to marry Neville to gain station in Society. She *was* Society.

Morgan felt heat spread up his neck. Could it be possible that Bliss and Neville had shared a true affection, despite what Uncle Oliver claimed?

She glanced down at the marble floor. Morgan was not fooled by her halfhearted, feigned interest in the comings and goings. He saw melancholy in Bliss's eyes.

Was he responsible for it?

Morgan strode toward her. Faster. Bliss turned his way. He could barely breathe.

Their eyes met, and he watched Bliss come to life. Her face lit up with delight, her eyes flashed, and her smile widened. Morgan had always found her appealing, of course, but at that moment, when she approached him in that delicious confection of pale blue silk, he saw more than just an appealing woman. He saw his goddess of the sea, his mermaid, his Bliss.

Could she truly be as good as she looked?

"You came."

Morgan wanted to wrap her in his arms. He wanted to kiss her, rejoice in the knowledge that she was his wife. Morgan wanted to trust her—oh God, how he wished he could trust her.

"I always keep my word, Mrs. Pryce." He reached for her hand and took a step back. "You are absolutely stunning this evening."

"Thank you, Captain Pryce." Her cheeks flushed prettily, but there was a question in her eyes. "I had little hope you would join me this evening. You were so terribly—"

"I apologize." Morgan bowed to her gallantly, hoping to end the topic of conversation. Not now. He merely wished to make good on his promise and leave as soon as possible. He had not come to continue their disagreement.

He straightened and smiled politely at Bliss. "Would you like to take a turn around the floor, Mrs. Pryce?" He already began to spin her, and the flickering chandeliers shone in her hair and the blue silk glimmered about her ankles.

Bliss's light scent carried on the air and into his brain. It was enough to make him dizzy with longing.

To trust or not to trust?

Morgan had not intended to dance, but he had to do something other than stand there and gape at her while doing battle with himself. One turn around the ballroom and he would have met his obligation.

It was a waltz. Morgan boldly pulled her close to the front of his body, which caused Bliss to gasp. They were married. Such proximity was perfectly acceptable. And it was no violation of his promise—he was quite certain that dancing did not count.

Dancing never counted.

NEVILLE HAD NOT realized that Morgan was as at ease in a ballroom as he was on the deck of a ship. Or perhaps it was merely the obvious suitability of the pair on the dance floor.

Gone was Bliss's air of sadness. She glowed in Morgan's arms. Moreover, that smile—

Never did I make her smile so.

The truth thudded to the pit of Neville's belly. Morgan and Bliss were together by choice. They were a married couple, a loving couple. However it had begun, with trickery or conspiracy, it was now something much more. When Morgan dipped his head to kiss her cheek, Neville had to look away.

No! Bliss should have been *his* lovely wife! She should have been the Duchess of Camberton!

To hell with it. Sobriety was overvalued. Neville stalked off toward the gentlemen's card room, forgetting all about defending Katarina from her mob of suitors, determined to find relief in the first bottle of whiskey he could get his hands on.

He would not look at the blissful dancers. He would never look upon them again.

* * *

AFTER A FEW turns about the floor with Bliss in his arms, Morgan found himself fatally entranced. The heat of her body, the satin of her skin, and the glorious music had lulled him into a reverie. His thoughts wandered to the memory of her stirring a pot in the kitchen, to the look of sweet welcome in her eyes a moment ago, to the fantasy of waking in her arms every morning. It was jarring when Bliss tugged him to a sudden stop.

"Oh heavens!" Bliss stared over Morgan's shoulder, her eyes wide with wonder. Then she mumbled, more to herself than Morgan. "The Prince Regent is here?"

"Prince—?" Morgan turned in time to be swept aside by a host of royal guards. Bliss had not been mistaken. The Prince Regent approached, clearly as taken with Bliss as every other man in the room.

Prince George reached for Bliss's hand and bowed over it.

"Hello, my pretty creature!" The prince kissed her hand and kept it in his, pulling her a bit closer.

Morgan straightened in protest, but he could not reach her. The Prince Regent hired the largest and the most devoted men in England. Though the guards did not put their hands on him, they kept him at bay.

Morgan was stunned and furious—the Prince Regent was flirting with Bliss! Trust the old goat to seek out the prettiest woman in the room. Even at his age, he was always on the lookout for a new mistress, it was rumored!

"Well, now, don't you look splendid!" Prinny gushed. "What a prize! Much too good for the common man!" The prince shot a sideways glance Morgan's way. "Couldn't you leave this oaf and come pass the Season in my palace? Hmm?"

The entire ballroom was watching the exchange. The Prince Regent sought out the wife of the Bastard of Camberton! It was all too delicious for Society to refuse.

"No, I could not!" Bliss laughed as she playfully slapped away the prince's arm. "I would only get lost among all your other 'pretty creatures' at court!"

Any other man in the room would realize that he had to step aside when his monarch crooked his finger at his wife.

Morgan was not any other man. His mind began to fill with the reddish haze of possessive rage. He broke free of the guards and pressed himself between Bliss and the prince. He managed to hiss out a warning before the guards pulled him ungently back again. "My wife. *Mine*."

The prince waved away the guards and wiggled his eyebrows at Bliss, as if he were amused by Morgan. Aghast, Bliss snatched Morgan's forearm and quite literally hauled him away.

Once Morgan and his bride were out of the Prince Regent's immediate proximity, the primitive fog faded from his brain, clearing his mind.

What had she done?

Bliss had just laughed off a prince. He was now more befuddled than before. If Bliss were the gold digger his uncle described, wouldn't she jump at such an offer?

And suddenly, it became painfully clear to him. The truth lodged itself in his gut like a stone. He had been wrong about Bliss.

God, what an ass he was! He had stolen her from the man she really wanted and ruined her chance for true happiness. The way he had treated her was beyond unforgivable.

Morgan had accepted his uncle's bribe—marry Bliss and get his own ship. Who was the gold digger in this scenario?

Morgan was distracted by his growing sense of shame, but in the back of his mind he could not help being impressed by Bliss's country-girl strength. She had already tugged him many yards away from the royal guards.

"Morgan!" Bliss's voice chided him, but when she spun around to face him, he saw the mirth in her eyes. "You . . ."

She began laughing. "You could have been thrown into the Tower for that!"

Her little shawl had slipped down her shoulders in the commotion. Morgan froze. The music went shrill and tinny in his ears.

There, on her upper arm, was a discoloration, a black-and-blue bruise the exact shape and size of a man's thumb. He tugged her hand gently, turning her slightly as she frowned at him. On the underside of her arm were four fingerprints.

Morgan feared he would be ill. How could he have been so careless? He brushed his fingertip along her bruised skin, and his words came out in a rasp. "I hurt you, Bliss. Forgive me. I did not realize that when I pulled you behind me in the alley—"

She looked away. "It was not you who left those."

Every trace of mirth was gone from her face. Bliss drew the shawl about her shoulders again.

"But you said the footpads did not lay a finger on you."

Bliss gazed over the ballroom, as if she could not bear to see him. "It did not happen then."

Morgan was perplexed. "But when—"

Bliss shook her head, now staring at the tops of her shoes. "I tried to tell you, Morgan." Her voice dropped to a barely audible stammer. "You did not believe that what I said was true."

She glanced up and looked over his shoulder, and all the color drained from her face.

Morgan turned to see Lord Oliver Danton joining them. And he knew.

His accusation erupted in a furious hiss. "You dared put your hands on my wife."

Oliver smirked, glancing toward Bliss and back to Morgan. "Spare me the attempt at chivalry, Pryce. The greedy creature was causing trouble at Camberton House. I merely . . ."

Oliver's words faded when Morgan took a menacing step his way. Morgan felt Bliss's light touch on his back, but he would not stop. He would say what had to be said.

"You injured her, you spineless coward. You lied to me. To Neville. To everyone." Morgan was now just inches from Oliver's face. He saw the old man's cheek twitch with alarm.

"I may be the bastard," Morgan snarled, "but I am more of a gentleman than you will ever be!" Morgan cocked back his arm and was about to lay Oliver out flat when he felt Bliss's grip on his elbow.

"No! Please!"

There was such desperation in Bliss's whisper that Morgan relaxed his arm. Oliver scurried off into the crowd like a frightened schoolgirl. Morgan would deal with him later.

The Shropshire farm girl hauled him away yet again. That made two near fisticuffs in one evening—perhaps Morgan was wise to avoid dress balls.

He allowed himself to be tugged off the floor and into a curtained alcove, the sort of antechamber where ladies went to loosen their corsets. Clearly, she wanted privacy.

Morgan prepared himself to receive a tart tongue-lashing from Bliss. He supposed he deserved it.

But she spun him around and grabbed the back of his head, her bosom trembling and her eyes flashing. Indeed, Bliss was mightily aroused, but not with anger.

She went up on her toes, pulled his mouth down to hers, and kissed him to within an inch of his life.

Chapter 28

ENOUGH light shone beneath the curtain to reveal that the anteroom held only a fainting couch and a small side table. A servant could bring a candle in, or a vinaigrette, if a lady actually did faint.

Bliss had no intention of calling in a servant. Everything she needed in the world was right before her.

She'd found it secretly adorable that Morgan had waxed territorial when the Prince Regent teased her. How many men in the world would dare raise a hand to a prince?

But when Morgan faced down his own uncle, defending her—believing in her!—Bliss had realized that no other man in the world would do for her.

Neville would never have done that. Neville had never even dared to hold her hand, much less fight for her. How could she have been so blind?

When she thought about whom she wanted to touch, whom she wanted to be touching her, it was Morgan's hands she imagined on her skin. When she slept and woke in tangled sheets and fading visions of hot, wild kisses, it was Morgan's mouth she'd tasted in her dreams.

And now, when she thought of the rest of her days, there was only one man she thought about spending them with, even if it meant that she would only have him part of the time. Love would manage—somehow. After all, she was no ordinary woman. She was a Worthington!

I choose you, my captain.

And the best part—the very best part!—was that the pesky obstacle of marriage was already out of the way. If she wanted to push her very own husband down onto that fainting couch and tug at his cravat while she straddled his thighs, she had every right to. So she did just that.

So very convenient.

Then all thought melted away when her husband pulled her down onto his hard chest and began to kiss her back in earnest.

Oh yes. Yes, please. More.

She gave up on his knotted cravat and slid her fingers into his hair. All she could think to do was to hold him, to keep him, to get as close to him as she could. Morgan, always a man of action, didn't waste precious time on words. She did so admire decisiveness in a man. He cradled her head in his palms and drove his tongue between her lips, claiming her even as she claimed him.

My husband. Mine.

The taste of his mouth became addictive. The scent of his skin, the silky curl of his hair, the rough need in his hands as they roamed over her—now at her jaw, holding her still for his kiss, now sliding across her bared shoulders, pushing down the nonsensical little sleeves of her gown, lifting her breasts free of her bodice.

He tore his lips from hers to wrap them around first one rigid and aroused nipple, then the other.

Bliss dug her teeth into her bottom lip, a scream of pleasure fighting to rise in her throat. How could she not have known he was the only one for her? His hot, hungry mouth ruined her, slaughtered her, saved her.

She was barely aware of his hands moving again, now gripping her waist so he could grind himself up between her spread thighs.

Her skirts twisted between them. Blinded and driven by the pleasure he gave her, Bliss yanked at the costly silk with no regard. All she could think was to remove the obstacles— her gown, his suit—

In the end, it wasn't so complicated.

Morgan slid one hand between their bodies. Then with a tug, he ripped her skirt up the side and pulled it free. Another swift yank and her filmy drawers slipped torn and ruined down to her bent knees.

Brilliant.

"Easy—" he gasped. But Bliss was in no mood for easy. When she felt his thick cock pressing upward to her pleasure-slickened labia, she acted on instinct.

Inside me. Inside. I need him inside me.

He felt her urgency and trapped her into stillness with his large, hard hands wrapped tightly around her waist. She keened her frustration at him, trying to twist away so she could drive her hungry body down upon his rigid spear—

He held her there, poised and writhing, while he used his mouth on her breasts—teasing, nipping, sucking until she couldn't breathe for the aching need ripping through her body. She was empty. She was lost and alone and pining to be filled with his body, his soul, his love . . .

He began to move her slightly, thrusting his hips upward, sliding the thick length of his cock against her wet center, against the throbbing, rigid point of her clitoris even as he suckled her relentlessly.

She fought him, beating his shoulders with her fists, panting and twisting in his ruthless grasp, desperate, so very desperate to be filled by him—

She ached, she throbbed, she shivered and moaned—and then she exploded like a Chinese rocket in his hands.

Oh. Her last thought was swept away almost before she formed it.

How unexpected.

Then she threw back her head and howled soundlessly into the darkened anteroom as her body bucked and pulsated and rang like a clear crystal bell on a winter night.

She dropped her head, resting her forehead against his.

"We—we should stop," he gasped. "You are—this isn't—"

"Do you want to be inside me, my captain?"

His answer was a low, wordless moan. At that moment, he shifted her slightly upward and began to enter her.

"I want to kiss you," he moaned. "I want you to kiss me back. Forever."

She tightened her hands in his hair and lowered her mouth down to his. She gave everything with that kiss, all her secret dreams of being truly loved, of being wanted, and needed. She banished fear and hesitation, for she had made her decision.

Morgan. It was only Morgan for her, for the rest of her life.

Trusting him entirely, she allowed him to press her down upon the blunt tip of him. When his rigid organ began to penetrate her, her eyes closed. There was no need to flinch from the pain. She was country-raised. She knew that it would pass soon enough, and then it would be good for them both.

Instead, she narrowed her thoughts to welcoming him inside her, aching for him to possess her body as he had already taken possession of her heart. His erection pierced her slowly until she couldn't bear the tender care he took.

Her breath left her in small pants of pleasure-pain. She wanted to drive herself down upon him, to end this sweet agony and move on to the purest pleasure she suspected was waiting on the other side.

The moment seemed everlasting as his length and width stretched her deeply.

To her enormous frustration, he paused, holding her above him, his own breath coming fast as he waited for her.

I need you. I want you inside me. I love you.

She realized that she whispered the words on each short breath. Her gaze met his and she saw something in his eyes she'd never seen before.

Wonder.

Now. While his attention was diverted her words, she seized control. His grip had slacked and she drove herself down upon him. Oh no. Too big. He was—

"Too big," she whimpered as she tried to rise from him. "I can't—I ca—"

Morgan pulled her down to his chest and held her tightly, not releasing her even as she moaned and pushed at him. "Shh. Be patient. Just wait. It will ease, my mermaid. Shh."

His deep voice in her ear distracted her for an instant. He'd never called her anything like that before. She forgot to struggle. Her body forgot to fight the thick invasion of him. A warm easing of the pressure began. Encouraged, she took a deep breath and let her body relax further.

With his arms still about her, he sat up and rolled her beneath him on the fainting couch. When his weight immediately pressed her down again, she sighed in pleasure and slid her hands behind his back.

He dropped his mouth to hers and kissed her deeply, tasting her and letting her taste him. She lost herself in his kiss, barely aware as he began to withdraw. Then he was back, driving into her slowly, powerfully, fully.

She cried out again, this time in pleasure as her body took his slick cock deep with only the slightest twinge, which was washed away in a wave of sweet, hot pleasure.

It seemed she'd taxed the last of his gentle patience, for he groaned into her mouth and he drove helplessly into her again and again. His very loss of self-command thrilled her.

She reveled in her ability to excite him, in being so desirable to him. Each deep, hungry thrust and each slow, reluctant withdrawal swept her away like a fatal tide.

Then her own pleasure began to rise once more. She was so wet and ready that he buried his length with every stroke. She cried out and dug her fingers into his wide shoulders.

"My sweet mermaid." His hoarse whisper filled the small room. He grasped her hips and pierced her again. Again and again, each time plunging as deeply as he could. "I need you!"

She fell apart in earnest then, her orgasm crashing through her so that she had no thought to restrain her cries. There was no ballroom of dancers on the other side of the curtain. There was only Morgan. Her Morgan. Her husband, finally right where he belonged.

With one more wild thrust, he shuddered, deep inside her. In her drifting slide from the breathless peak of pleasure, she quivered as his shaft throbbed inside her, triggering a final burst of ecstasy. A last wavering cry escaped her lips.

With a breathless groan, he slipped down beside her, still half covering her with his big body. Bliss turned her face into his shoulder and shivered into his solidity as the music outside the anteroom rose and the dancers whirled on, still unaware.

"Oh my God," he gasped into her throat.

Bliss could not have agreed more. She planned to say something similar—as soon as she could speak again.

He lifted his head to gaze down into her eyes. She reached trembling fingers to stroke his cheek, smiling past her panting breaths. He shook his head a little.

"Who are you?" There was wonder in his tone this time, flavored with a hint of pride and possessiveness.

I am the woman who loves you, Morgan Pryce. I am your wife.

She would say it. In just a moment, after she'd caught her

breath, when it wouldn't come out all choked and trembling. Her body still shuddered with the glorious pleasure he had given her. She swallowed hard, forcing herself to calm. Then she closed her eyes and parted her lips to say everything in her heart.

"Oh my heavens! How *shocking!*"

BLISS OPENED HER eyes and looked over Morgan's shoulder to see Lord Oliver framed in the doorway. He had lifted the curtain wide to leave a clear view for anyone in the ballroom who might be interested.

Everyone seemed to be interested. Faces crowded close behind His Lordship, eyes wide and mouths gaping in astonishment.

Bliss hurried to cover herself. Bloody meddling Oliver! Yet what could anyone say, really? It was embarrassing, to be sure. Still, they were hardly the first couple to be caught in dishabille late at a raucous ball.

Unlike many of those couples, she and Morgan were married.

And it wasn't as though the Prince Regent himself witnessed anything. She'd seen him being escorted out by his stubborn guardsmen after Morgan's outburst.

Pulling her gown back into place as well as she could, she stepped out of general sight into the shadows at the side of the arched doorway. Quickly, she began to twist her hair back into something presentable. She sent Morgan a quick rueful grin, but his gaze was fixed on his uncle.

Her fingers paused as she noted the strange look on Morgan's face. Then Oliver announced, loudly enough for everyone to hear—

"Well, it's about time, Morgan! I thought you were as shy as Neville, taking so long to consummate your marriage!"

Morgan flushed angrily and, Bliss was surprised to see, seemed deeply ashamed. He still did not look her in the eye.

Well, enough was enough. Oliver could carry on all night if he were allowed to, she was sure. It was naughty of them to make love at someone else's ball, and there would be a bit of resultant gossip, but just look at her handsome husband! She was comfortably sure that it would be chatter of the most envious sort!

She brushed at her torn skirts. Her appearance was restored as well as she could get it without a maid and a team of seamstresses.

No time like the present. Lifting her chin, she stepped from the alcove with aloof dignity. She glared defiantly at Oliver as she passed him, but he retained his cruel smile. Strange.

"I heard the Prince Regent call you a prize." Oliver sneered. "If you only knew the half of it."

"Oliver, shut it," Morgan snarled as he pushed past his uncle, emerging from the darkness with that murderous glower still in place.

A chill began somewhere deep in her belly. Bliss knew a secret when she saw one. She stared at the two of them, Oliver practically crowing with nasty pride, Morgan flushed and angry, looking anywhere but at her.

"My lord, why is it that Morgan is to be congratulated for—for cavorting with his own wife?" She asked the question of Oliver, but it was Morgan she watched.

Was she sure she wanted to know?

This is quite probably going to hurt.

Oliver clapped Morgan on the shoulder. Morgan flinched away from Oliver's touch.

He held out one hand to her. "Bliss, we should go now." Still, he did not meet her gaze.

Bliss stepped back, clasping her hands behind her. She felt something seeping away, something that had filled her soul with light just moments before. Happiness was leaching away and she could not make it stop.

Oliver smiled that awful, smug grin again. "I am not

congratulating Morgan for toppling you onto a sofa, you obvious little tart. I am congratulating him on becoming the proud captain-owner of the *Selkie Maid*."

He held out his arms magnanimously, as if he actually expected Morgan's embrace. "Your own ship, my boy, just as you've always wanted! And all you had to do to get it was save your brother from marrying a gold-digging harpy! You certainly kept up your end of the bargain. And what a performance!" He laughed. "I actually thought you might strike me earlier!"

Oliver turned to regard Bliss with smiling hatred. "Wedded and bedded, for all the world to see. You'll get no annulment now, little thief."

Bargain. Performance. Wedded and bedded.

Oliver's vicious words fell on Bliss like hammer blows, smashing her brand-new, fragile joy like cheap crystal.

She was too shocked to cry out, too stunned by her own stupidity to protest. Morgan still glared thunderously at Oliver. Not once since his uncle began had Morgan looked at her. His dark scowl and averted gaze told her it was true, all of it.

Congratulations, Morgan.

His betrayal made her gut twist. She felt the bile rise in the back of her throat.

Yet what had he done but treat her as he always had done? She had known he scorned her for a manipulator. He had kept his word to leave her alone. She had been the one to drag him into the antechamber. She had been the one to kiss first.

He made me believe.

Or did I simply make myself believe?

In the end, it didn't matter. Either way she was a fool.

Chapter 29

HOT rage and shame coursed through Morgan as Oliver spoke.

He shrank from the truth of what he'd done—what Oliver had manipulated him into doing. Bliss was right to warn him about his uncle!

You can blame Oliver all you like—but you knew what you were doing. You just convinced yourself you were doing it to someone who deserved it.

At last, morbid curiosity overcame his shame and he lifted his gaze to face her.

"I need you. I want you inside me. I love you."

Sadly, Morgan saw that the old Bliss had returned. Straight of spine and unflinching of gaze. Not even her tumbled hair and off-center neckline could shake the expression of supreme unconcern from her face. If she hadn't been so pale, one might have thought he'd not hurt her at all.

He had, though. He'd felt the blow as if he'd taken it himself. The sweet, reckless adventurer she finally shyly revealed to him was as dead as if he'd stabbed her through the heart.

"Bliss, I—" *Damn it, think!* There must be some words he could say, some roguish smile he could flash, some gesture he could make that could bring back the woman he loved!

He stammered to a halt. There was nothing he could say. Her wide blue gaze remained fixed on him, as it had been for all of Oliver's revelations.

"Sir, am I to understand that I could have had my annulment for the mere cost of a ship?" Her tone was cool and distant, almost bored.

She folded her hands before her and regarded him as if they discussed nothing more momentous than the price of tea.

"You should have bargained harder, Captain Pryce." She raised an eyebrow. "If it meant I could have rid myself of you forever," she said, with no more than a hint of mild contempt, "I would have bought you two."

Just then Iris Worthington floated from the crowd and put her arm around her niece. "There you are, dearest. Do come along, now. I find I'm quite fatigued and there is so much to do at Worthington House. We've missed you terribly, you know." The woman looked frail, but she managed to maneuver Bliss away in a cloud of inanities. Morgan watched the crowd close around them. All eyes remained fixed on him.

He'd never cared what these people thought of him. That was what he'd told himself for his entire life. Yet the way they looked at him now . . .

It wasn't condemnation, as it would be for some ungentlemanly behavior. It wasn't anger for the fate of a young woman of good family. To the willfully bored ton, who longed for titillation and grand dramatics, it wasn't even jaded appreciation for a good show.

Their eyes said something else entirely. Their faces held the one impression he'd fought against all his life.

What more could we expect? After all, he's just a bastard.

"YOU BLACKGUARD!"

Morgan turned to see the Duke of Camberton push his way out of the crowd. Neville staggered to the center of the clearing around Morgan and faced him belligerently.

Damn. "Neville . . ." Words seemed so weak at the moment. The agony in Neville's eyes burned a guilt-ridden soul already left scorched by Bliss's devastated anguish.

Neville pulled off his gloves and tried to slap Morgan across the face with them. In his inebriation, he missed. Morgan felt the soft gray kidskin whisk painlessly across his chin.

"I challenge you, in defense of Bliss Worthington's honor!" Neville threw his gloves to the marble floor. They lay there like open, begging hands.

As sorry as he felt for what he'd done, Morgan was beginning to weary of providing entertainment for the ton. He raised an eyebrow at Neville's newly discovered flair for the dramatic. "Bliss Pryce, actually," he drawled.

Neville snarled, "Not for long! I will see you dead at sunrise tomorrow!"

Morgan met his half brother's fury with anger of his own. "Tomorrow? Why not today? It is nearly sunrise now."

Neville blinked drunkenly. "It is?" he asked in more normal tones. He looked vaguely around the ballroom. "I've been up all night?"

A young woman shoved her way through the crowd and moved to Neville's side. Morgan didn't know her, but she blazed hot scorn at him from dark eyes.

"Tomorrow," she said firmly. "Not today. You would take advantage of his state of inebriation? Your own brother?"

"Half brother," Morgan corrected her absently. "And he's the one who wants to see me dead."

Neville roused somewhat. He lifted his head, rage and agony in his eyes. "I will see you in the ground." Then he swayed slightly. "Tomorrow."

He truly loves her. God, I've done nothing but muck this up.

There was just one problem with Neville's plan of righteous gentlemanly justice.

Morgan wasn't a gentleman. Having never been steeped in the social construct that was the peerage, Morgan felt no compulsion to preserve his own honor.

Yet he could not claim total dissociation from that sphere. He was not a gentleman, but his half brother, his friend, his family, Neville, was.

Despite the fact that Morgan could quite literally thumb his nose at Neville's challenge, and stroll back down to the docks where he belonged, he found himself compelled to answer Neville's furious pain with a short bow and a quiet "As you wish, Your Grace."

Two young men stepped forward to take Neville's arms. "Come on, Nev," Castor Worthington urged. "Let's take a stroll out in the air."

Neville blinked blearily at the brothers, first Cas, then Dade. Then his gaze narrowed in fresh anger. "It should have been you," he snarled at Dade. "Cowards, the lot of you! She's your cousin! You should have challenged Pryce the moment you found out what he'd done!" Then he glared directly at Dade. "Have you no honor, sir?"

Dade went pale. He took a step backward. Cas shrugged and looked away.

"But Bliss insisted we weren't to interfere . . . ," Cas mumbled.

Having had more than enough of them all, Morgan turned on his heel and strode from the ballroom. He didn't know where he was going. Perhaps his ship. There would be no point in going home.

She would never grace his humble house again.

It was good that she had gone home with her aunt. He hadn't liked letting her go. He just hadn't felt he had any right to her. Not anymore. How she must hate him now.

He didn't blame her one little bit. He was in total agreement with her, in fact.

He really was a bastard, after all.

Chapter 30

"**H**ow can she still be at it?"

Miranda peered around the door to the kitchen, where Bliss was on her hands and knees, scrubbing the cooking hearth with a wire brush. "Hasn't she scoured that already?"

"She's scoured everything already." Cas shook his head. "I'm afraid to sit down, for fear she'll scour me if I hold still too long!"

"She shelved all my books. By height and topic. I'll never find anything now!" Attie eyed the spotless house around her with an expression of mistrust. "How do we get her to stop?"

Bliss lifted her face from her task, unaware that her cousins were near. As she brushed aside a few strands of hair with her forearm, Dade saw it—a single tear rolling off the dainty tip of her chin.

Attie stared. "She's crying!"

"Oh, Bliss." Dade felt his stomach twist in grief for his cousin. "What a disaster."

Just then Iris joined her children, placing a hand on Dade's shoulder. She clucked her tongue in worry. "The poor dear! The house wasn't in need of much tidying to begin with, yet she's been at it all night and all morning!"

Dade and Cas shared a sideways glance. Iris had always been blissfully unaware of the chaos of their home, but in truth, Worthington House had been in its customary, terminal state of dire disarray when Bliss returned home from the ball with her cousins the previous night.

She immediately asked Iris for an old dress, changed out of her ball gown, and began heating water.

"I shall make this house shipshape!" Bliss had assembled the Worthingtons to make her announcement. "By breakfast time, all shall be sparkling clean. Worthington House will once again be just so!"

That was when everyone scattered to the four corners of the house in an effort to save their treasures from the rubbish bin.

While the others slept, Dade had taken it upon himself to keep a watchful eye on his distressed cousin through the night. She began with the kitchen at the back of the house, then swept and scrubbed and organized her way through the entire main floor, only to return to the kitchen once breakfast was done. She had already informed the family that she planned to conquer the upstairs bedchambers next.

Every time Dade tried to help Bliss carry a pail or lift a table leg, she had refused. Each of his attempts to talk with her was declined.

"Don't be silly," she'd said. "I am not some kind of delicate flower—I am as robust as a person can be! It's only that I enjoy a bit of tidying-up now and then!"

Iris leaned in and whispered in Dade's ear, "Did we manage to rescue Archie's newssheets? And Attie's rodent skull collection?"

He nodded.

"Did you hide the playbills?"

"Yes, Iris."

"Wonderful! They are our only connection to a lifetime in the theater!"

Dade nodded again, then turned to his mother. "I am deeply worried for Bliss. If she doesn't stop soon, she will collapse from exhaustion."

Iris kissed his cheek. "Do not fret, my dear boy. I have a secret weapon."

MORGAN WAITED PATIENTLY on the steps to Camberton House, in the precise spot Regis insisted he remain. He was happy to do so, as he had expected the butler to slam the door in his face.

Instead, Regis had eyed him suspiciously but agreed to carry a message to Neville.

"Let us resolve this matter peacefully, Neville," Morgan had written. "There is much I need to tell you. I wish you no harm."

After a few long moments on the stoop, the butler returned. He cracked the door just enough to slip a note to Morgan and disappeared inside the house without another word.

Morgan glanced down at the single sheet of fine linen paper, folded unsealed. Perhaps Neville did not wish to waste a perfectly good drop of wax on such a terse response. The note consisted of a mere three words, composed in a shaky hand: "Choose your second."

He shoved the paper in his coat pocket, turned, and departed. As he walked toward the street, Morgan began to comprehend the absurdity of his current situation. In a gentlemen's duel, a second was a faithful friend, a man trusted to ensure that the dueling weapons were similarly matched and the "field of honor" provided a fair and equitable stage for the confrontation. Simply put, Morgan's life could depend on the fidelity of his second.

What man would do this for him?

Morgan laughed at the irony. There was no one in his life he would trust to serve him so, save for his half brother, Neville, who happened to be his opponent. Where did that leave Morgan?

It would not be fair to drag any of his crew into this mess. He had no other family, save for his wife's relations—the Worthingtons. And though asking for their help would be an act of desperation, it was his only recourse.

Morgan hailed a hack and gave the driver the address.

"HELLO, SWEETIE. AREN'T you going to let me in?"

Miranda stood in the open doorway of Worthington House staring at their unexpected visitor. And though she knew was being terribly rude, Miranda was left speechless. She bounced the baby on her hip and noted the jewels around the woman's throat and fingers, the heavy silk of her gown, and the pleated capote styling of her bonnet. It took Miranda a moment, but the woman's identity eventually occurred to her.

"You're—"

"I'm—"

"I know!" Miranda gasped. "We have previously met."

"We have?" The woman looked back at her with mild curiosity.

"I believe so." Miranda switched the baby to the opposite hip. "Didn't I burn down your brothel?"

Mrs. Blythe, infamous madam and proprietress of Mrs. Blythe's House of Pleasure, turned a sharp eye on Miranda, then smiled. "You had help from your husband—or was it your brother-in-law? It was so very difficult to tell them apart that night, with all the billowing smoke and flopping Johnsons."

Miranda's mouth fell open in shock.

"Motherhood becomes you, Mrs. Worthington." Mrs.

Blythe stepped past her in a swish of silk and strolled into the foyer. She glanced over her shoulder at Miranda. "Don't worry, pet. I never hold a grudge."

Just then Cas appeared. He froze in obvious alarm. "Ah! Well . . . hello! Ah . . ."

He shot a panicked glance toward Miranda, then the baby. Miranda glared back. *What is she doing here?*

Cas grimaced and shrugged, a tiny movement. *I have absolutely no idea.* He turned to their guest, struggling to remain polite. "Well, then. Mrs. B—I mean, my goodness—"

The notorious madam graciously patted his arm as she swished past him. "Just popping by, Cas dear. No need to fuss."

She swept into the hall, striding through Worthington House as if she knew it very well indeed.

Cas turned to look at Miranda. *Popping by?* he mouthed.

Miranda shrugged helplessly, then handed Cas the baby. "You go put Aurora down for her nap. I'm not missing this for all the world," she whispered to him. She scurried after their visitor.

FROM HER CROUCH at the base of the kitchen stove, Bliss pressed with all her might into the cleaning cloth, rubbing black into the cast iron until it shone. She had nearly finished the endeavor when she heard the sound of a woman clearing her throat. A quick glance to her right revealed a pair of silvery gray shoes adorned with a heavily jeweled buckle and a bit of ostrich feather.

Bliss let her gaze travel up the yards of gray silk, to the fashionable beaded reticule clutched in fine kid gloves, on to the delicately embroidered spencer that contained a rather bountiful bosom.

The visitor gazed down upon her with a gentle smile.

As always, the woman's timing was perfect. Perfectly preposterous.

"Of course you would come now," Bliss muttered. She got to her feet with a sigh, dropping the rag and wiping her hands on Mrs. Philpott's borrowed work apron. "Hello, Mama."

MORGAN'S HIRED HACK arrived at Worthington House, stopping alongside one of the grandest carriages he had ever seen. It was shiny and black, unmarked by crest or decoration. Four perfectly matched black horses were hitched to its front, while a stoic driver in costly silver-trimmed livery sat perched on his bench, the man's posture as straight as iron.

Morgan gave only the barest thought to the identity of the caller, as his mind was on the task at hand. Though he knew he would not be greeted with friendly hospitality, he did pray for basic civility. He only desired to state his case.

Castor answered the door to Worthington House with a pretty, pink-cheeked, carrot-topped baby on his hip.

Before Cas could speak, Dade appeared in the foyer behind him.

"I'll manage this," Dade said.

Morgan moved back as Dade stepped outside and quickly closed the door behind him. It was the second time that day that Morgan had been refused entry. Perhaps he should get used to it.

"I shall only take a moment of your time, Dade."

THE MAN HAD a bloody lot of nerve.

What happened at the ball had been horrifying. Not only had Bliss been publicly shamed; Dade had, too.

And every word Neville said in that ballroom had been true: Dade was a coward. He had not defended his cousin's honor when he should have. Dade had backed down at Bliss's request when he should have challenged Pryce's duplicity without delay.

Dade had failed to protect his family, and when Morgan publicly humiliated Bliss, he had exposed Dade's failure, too—to all of London! Dade would never forgive him.

And yet . . .

The Morgan Pryce who stood before him on the stoop of Worthington House did not possess the air of an unrepentant rogue. He did not appear insolent or haughty. It was clear he had not come for an argument.

In truth, Pryce appeared broken. He raised hollow eyes to meet Dade's gaze. "I most sincerely beg your pardon for any grief I have caused your family. You did not deserve it."

The naked remorse of those words caused Dade to take a step back.

Pryce's face tightened with despair. "Is she . . . is she all right? Tell me she is well."

Dade recalled the long night of frenzied housekeeping, and did not know how to respond. "She's a bit . . . distraught."

"Oh no."

"She's quite miserable, really."

"Oh God." Pryce turned away for a moment, as if to collect himself. When he turned his attention to Dade once more, his jaw was set in determination. "I must speak with her."

"Ah . . ." Dade glanced at the door behind him, imagining the scene unfolding in the kitchen at that very moment. "I'm afraid that's not possible."

"I've made a blasted mess of everything, Worthington, and it is my duty to fix it. Let me speak with her."

"She's—"

"Bliss's happiness matters more to me than anything." He fixed his gaze upon Dade. "I desire most sincerely to do right by her—but to do so, I must survive this damned duel!" Pryce took a deep breath. "Worthington, I have come today to request that you serve as my second. I have no one else to ask."

Dade was stupefied. Never would he have expected Pryce to make such a request of him, and in such a humble and heartfelt fashion. Spotting a gentleman's true character was something at which Dade had always excelled, and at this moment he believed Pryce spoke earnestly.

But this?

Dade heard himself laugh shortly. "Ah . . . given the circumstances, I hardly know how to respond."

"I have no intention of shooting Neville and I do not wish to be shot." Pryce raked a hand through his disheveled hair. "Yet my attempts to find a bloodless resolution have failed. He will not speak with me. He won't see me. I must have someone at my side I can trust to get both of us out of this alive."

Dade rubbed a hand over his face, attempting to clear his thoughts. This was certainly an unexpected complication. "Yes, well, I'm afraid Cas has already agreed to be Neville's second. Neville asked him last night."

Pryce rolled his eyes up to the sky, then closed them for a long moment. "I cannot do this to her." Pryce opened his eyes once more, shaking his head. "I cannot leave Bliss a widow before I even own my own ship! What will she do? How will she live?"

Dade felt his eyes widen. Morgan Pryce had no idea whom he had married. It was an interesting twist.

"She will manage," Dade assured him.

"But she is not the type of woman who should be forced to simply manage," Pryce shot back. "I've come to believe that Bliss is like the sleekest ship in a very fine fleet. She is beautiful and endlessly capable, but shines brightest when she has careful tending. She needs companionship, Dade. Looking after. She needs a man who will constantly check her rigging—"

"Pryce, please!" Dade held up his palm. "You are speaking of my cousin."

"Forgive me." He cleared his throat. "What I mean to say is that Bliss deserves to live in loving security for all her days. If I die she'll—"

"Pryce." Dade simply had to interrupt the poor man. "Bliss is quite well off. I estimate she'll have more than five thousand pounds to help her 'survive' should anything happen to you."

Pryce scowled. It seemed to take him a moment to understand Dade's words. "What?" He appeared stunned. "She has five thousand pounds? I assumed she had resources, but she is that rich?"

Dade tried not to appear pitying. "No, you idiot. That's only the annual interest off her principal. It's her pocket money."

Pryce's jaw unhinged.

"Listen, my man. Bliss is so wealthy that her fortune makes the Duke of Camberton's appear shabby. Now do you understand?"

Dade noticed how Pryce could not help letting his gaze take in the shabby exterior of Worthington House, its peeling paint, its unruly shrubbery.

He knew that some explanation was in order. Regardless of how it happened, Pryce was, indeed, Bliss's husband. "She comes from a different branch of the Worthington family tree—the one that grows the golden apples. Now, that is all I can say. She must be the one to tell you more."

Morgan blinked. He remained silent for a moment, then broke out into a wide smile. "You know what, Worthington? If Bliss did not have a shilling to her name, I would not give a damn. I loved her when I suspected she was a gold-digging fraud. I could do nothing to prevent it. She . . . overwhelmed me. I'll never be able to stop myself from loving her."

Dade's sigh was far louder than he intended. "Look,

Pryce. We greatly admire Neville. He and Cas have been good friends for quite some time. I daresay I have no idea how my brother and I can square off against each other as seconds on the same dueling field."

Pryce laughed bitterly. "I understand your dilemma."

The two men stared at each other for a moment in silence. They broke out into simultaneous smiles.

"Unless . . ."

Dade nodded. "I was thinking the very same thing." He extended his hand. "You've got yourself a second."

BLISS SAT WITH her mother at the kitchen table, a pot of tea between them. Fortunately, it was not Mrs. Philpott's alarmingly relaxing secret blend, for this was a rather important discussion.

Bliss found Mama to be sympathetic, but in a practical sort of way. No one had ever accused the legendary Mrs. Blythe of being overly sentimental.

"Your father wishes he could come as well, but can you imagine the chaos if we were seen together?" She patted Bliss's hand with her jeweled fingers. "Anyway, I come as his emissary as well as on my own account."

Bliss was grateful that her mother did not scold her for the folly of a secret midnight wedding. Neither did she reprimand her for the oh-so-public indiscretion at the Fletchers' ball. "Oh my. Yes, I recall the heat of the moment—very well indeed!"

However, Mama was positively aghast at the mention of Bliss's husband and the upcoming duel.

"It almost sounds as if you fear for his safety," Mama said, her eyes widening in disbelief. "Why should you care what happens to that trickster? That man lied to you!"

Bliss found she had no answer.

Mama continued. "Let the idiots shoot each other, if that

is what they wish. Then you can be a widow. It is ever so much fun to be a widow in London!"

Bliss dropped her gaze to her hands, chapped by housework. It struck her as odd that even after all the scouring and scrubbing, dusting and sweeping, Bliss had failed to establish order in her own heart and mind. As she listened to her mother extoll the benefits of widowhood, Bliss realized she had no idea what she wanted.

Whom she wanted.

One thing was certain. Dearest Neville would never have used her as Morgan had. He would never have traded his honor for a ship! But then, Neville was a duke. He did not need a ship, nor did he need to claw and scrape for a place in the world the way a bastard must.

So what of this superior moral character? What did it matter if she did not love Neville?

And then there was Morgan, a man with so much to prove that he sold his soul for a ship. He was another matter entirely. Did his desperate bargain make him irredeemable? Did the untamed hunger he displayed at the ball make him unworthy of her? What did any of this matter if she loved him?

Bliss suddenly looked up. She stared at her mother as her mind grappled with the truth. Morgan hadn't accosted her at the ball. She had accosted him!

Perhaps she would never see the truth until she was truthful with herself.

"I pushed him down on that settee, Mama."

She raised an eyebrow. "Oh?"

"I ripped off his clothes of my own free will, and it was wild and wonderful. I never imagined I could feel such passion."

And I never, ever would have done such a thing with Neville.

Mama took a hearty sip of tea, but it did not hide her small smile.

So now the question was this: How could Bliss survive the rest of her life without doing such a thing again? The thought of it made her ache.

No more rakish smile that hid a sensitive soul? No more hot, gentle hands? No husky voice calling her name?

Widow?

Bloody hell no. I will not allow that to happen.

Bliss stood up. She pressed both hands to the tabletop and leaned close to her mother. "I love him, Mama. I can't live without him. And I'm going to stop this nonsense right now!"

Mama smiled. "That's the spirit, dearest! You go fetch your man."

Chapter 31

"Did my solicitor call while I was out?" Lord Oliver handed Regis his hat, gloves, and walking stick.

"Yes, my lord. He left the papers on your desk."

"Marvelous news."

Oliver headed to his study, his mind already focused on the particulars he would find in those documents. He had long known that Mr. Christie was a master of legal gibberish, a barrister of balderdash! Oliver was eager to get a taste of his latest legal confection.

Oliver pressed his hands together in delight. How entertaining it would be to see Mrs. Beckham trapped like a fly in Christie's winding web of words!

He almost felt pity for the dim-witted widow.

Almost.

"My lord. Don't forget your correspondence."

Lord Oliver spun around and held out his hand impatiently. He snapped his fingers. "Don't just stand there, Regis. I am a busy man."

"Of course."

Regis placed one thin and uninteresting envelope in his palm, but Oliver's gaze went to the hall table, upon which teetered a five-inch-high stack of invitations.

"What the devil is all this?" He pointed to the pile of social correspondence. "I do not have time for more blasted balls! Nonsense! Decline them all!"

Regis stared blankly at Lord Oliver, which was puzzling, as his butler was usually quite astute.

"Well, what is it, Regis? Just spit it out!"

"As you wish, my lord. Those invitations are not addressed to you. They are for Miss Katarina."

Heat flared beneath Oliver's cravat. He spun around and made way toward his study. Never again! Never again would he allow guests to reside in Camberton House for the Season. By God, this was his home. Not some kind of way station for homely heiresses!

Once at his desk, he began to relax. Reading over Mr. Christie's contract of sale made him chuckle. It was even more brilliant than he'd hoped. The phrasing was so impenetrable, and the word choice so elaborate, that Oliver himself could barely make sense of it.

Sunbury would be his by day's end. All he needed was her signature.

Lord Oliver took a moment to open his sole piece of correspondence. It appeared to be a request for payment, though he did not recognize the address, the handwriting, or the nature of the purchases.

Two ball gowns? Two reticules? Two pairs of slippers? Exotic bird feathers? Two shawls?

Two hundred and forty-seven pounds?

Oliver choked. His coughing fit was so severe that he had to let it run its course before he could call for Regis.

The butler arrived at the first squeak of alarm. "Are you quite well, my lord?"

"Fetch that witch to me right now!"

Regis raised his chin. "Which witch would that be, my lord?"

Oliver poured himself an emergency brandy, grateful for the balm it provided to his distressed throat. "The Beckham woman! I insist she come down here at once!"

"Yes, my lord."

While Regis was gone, Oliver poured himself another, mulling over the absurd waste of money. The woman had no concept of finance. Two hundred and forty-seven pounds! For scraps of silk and assorted froufrous and gewgaws? That could pay the annual salaries of sixteen footmen! He could purchase enough coal to heat Camberton House over the course of three winters!

The nerve of that woman . . . sending him the bill . . . expecting him to pay for their frivolous feathers and—

"Darling Ollie! Has something happened?" Mrs. Beckham appeared in the study doorway, her expression a study in vapid alarm. "Regis said it was urgent."

"Mrs. Beckham, won't you please sit down?" Oliver gestured to one of the room's settees. Now that his temper had begun to cool, he realized he might be able to use this fiasco to his advantage. From his desk he obtained the dress shop bill, the contract of sale, and quill and ink. He found a seat opposite Mrs. Beckham, then laid the items on the coffee table between them. "It appears there has been an unfortunate error."

"An error? Has someone been injured?" Mrs. Beckham's mouth loosened in horror.

"Yes. No. What I mean to say is that I've been injured, mistakenly billed for the services of a rather expensive London dressmaker."

She blinked in complete innocence, as if the words meant nothing to her.

"Two hundred and forty-seven pounds due for the evening dresses you and your daughter wore to last night's debacle of a ball."

Mrs. Beckham's eyes widened, and she brought a dainty hand to her mouth, then her décolletage. "Oh dear. I am ever so sorry this has happened. As you well know, ladies do not carry money on their person. I merely asked that the bills be sent here to Camberton House. I did not intend for *you* to be required to pay them."

"I see."

"Do forgive me, dearest Ollie. Since Mr. Beckham's loss I find managing accounts distressing."

"My dear lady." Oliver leaned forward and produced his most endearing smile. "I do not wish for you to feel distress of any kind. I shall make payment on your behalf."

"Oh, Ollie! You will?"

"Of course, madam. All I ask in return is for you sign this document." He slipped it across the table between them.

"I fear I don't know what this is, Ollie."

"Oh, it's nothing of much import, just a short promissory statement. Please read over it if you wish."

He watched Mrs. Beckham peer at the words, her frown deepening by the second. She pressed her fingertips to a temple. "I . . . I don't understand! It says something about Sunbury. Is this some kind of legal document?"

He shook his head reassuringly. "'Tis simply a manifestation on your part, an expression of intent."

"Intent to do what?" She glanced up at him, her eyes glazed over from the burden of Mr. Christie's obtuse prose.

Most excellent.

"Oh, it's simply a little promise. Intent to consider selling Sunbury to me at some point in the future, for an amount we can determine later. It's really a straightforward little thing."

She tipped her chin. "It is fourteen pages of indecipherable babble."

Oliver was tempted to slam his fist down upon the table. Nothing was ever simple with this woman. She was nothing short of Satan's handmaiden!

He dipped the quill in the inkpot and handed it to her. He tapped his finger impatiently on the bottom of the last page. "All you need do is sign right here—"

The silly hen dropped her face into her hands and began to cry.

Bloody hell.

Her shoulders lurched with each sob. She went on like that for several long moments, nearly howling now and again. Oliver had no choice but to offer her his handkerchief.

"Thank you," she mumbled, snatching the linen from his hand. It took a long moment for her to tamp down her emotions, but eventually she raised her face. Her cheeks were flushed, but she had wiped away any trace of tears.

"I feel a headache coming on. I shall review this later, after I have a bit of lie-down in my chamber." She rose from the settee, the unsigned document gripped in her fingers. "And I do thank you ever so much for taking care of the dressmaker's charges. Good day, Lord Oliver."

He jumped from his seat in alarm. "You can't take the document! Bring it back this instant!" He darted out into the hall but found Regis standing directly in his way.

"Move, you idiot!" He darted to his left.

"Forgive me, my lord." Regis darted to his right.

"Buffoon! Out of my way!" He lunged to his left.

"Ever so sorry." Regis lunged to his right.

By the time Oliver shoved his suddenly useless butler aside, Mrs. Beckham had disappeared at the top of the stairs.

"Bloody hell!" Lord Oliver rested his hands on his knees, trying to catch his breath. He couldn't very well chase her into her bedchamber!

Chaos. His orderly world had crumbled into chaos.

"Do you desire anything else, my lord?"

Oliver did not answer. He returned to his study and slammed the door behind him, and though he was of sound body, on a solid floor in a familiar room, he felt as if the earth were slipping away beneath him.

"Do you desire anything else, my lord?"

He heard himself laugh aloud. The absurdity of that question! *Of course I desire something else.* He'd had just one desire since childhood: to have the title, the power, and the social rank to which he was entitled. He'd desired to be His Grace, Lord Oliver Danton, the fourteenth Duke of Camberton.

Stolen from him.

Damn his firstborn brother! Neville Sr. was ten years older, and Oliver had lived in his brother's shadow his entire life. It was Neville who inherited the title, the property, and the ultimate control of the family holdings. It was Neville who commanded admiration and respect.

Oliver was thrown the scraps. He was put to work as manager of the family holdings, and did a damn fine job of it, too. But Oliver knew the day would come when everything would change, when he would be handed the title.

The day Neville Sr. turned forty, he was unmarried and without an heir. Yes, there was the Welsh bastard, but the housekeeper's issue posed no threat to Oliver's eventual inheritance. To sweeten the pot, Neville's health had begun to fail. Oliver was sure he would not live to see forty-one.

And then the unthinkable happened. Not only did the duke live, but he married and had a son—another bloody Neville—and Oliver's life was destroyed.

Nothing about the turn of events was fair. Nothing about it was right. It was an injustice of the highest order. And sometimes Oliver regretted he had not smothered the infant in his cradle when he'd had the opportunity.

So upon the death of Neville Sr., his milquetoast namesake became duke, instead of Oliver. Oliver's gaze went to the window, toward the midday sunshine. The duel was scheduled to begin in a mere fifteen hours, was it not? If he played his hand with care, there might yet be a way to get what was rightly his.

Instead of trying to control Neville, perhaps it was time to simply get rid of him.

He would finally be Lord Oliver Danton, the fifteenth Duke of Camberton. He liked the sound of it, very much indeed.

Chapter 32

MORGAN refused to remain another minute in the achingly empty row house he had shared with his bride. His ears strained for the sound of Bliss's delicate step. He ached for the savory scents of her cooking. He expected to see her shiny blond head peer around every corner.

And all the while, that blasted, green-eyed sorceress of a cat stared at him, monitoring his every move.

He decided to take a long morning walk, hoping the air and exercise would allow order to prevail in his jumbled mind. It did not work as he'd hoped, so Morgan continued on to the docks. The only place on earth where he'd ever been able to hear himself think had been aboard the *Selkie Maid*.

Or in the arms of his beautiful, good-hearted wife— whom he had lost forever.

He barely spoke two words to Seamus, his first mate, who greeted him on the gangway.

"We didn't expect to see you today, sir. Are ye quite well, Cap'n Pryce?"

He grumbled that he wished to view the outbound cargo manifest, and Seamus, who had accompanied him on dozens of voyages over the last several years, knew better than to inquire further about Morgan's welfare.

The ship was scheduled to depart London for the West Indies in just a fortnight. Morgan had approved the schedule when he returned to London just more than a week before. He'd been sure all his obligations would be met by then, leaving him free to get back to sea. The way Lord Oliver had described it, he would have rescued Neville from his villainous paramour. He would have consummated the sham marriage to a gold digger. And he would have been holding in his hand the title to his ship.

Lord Oliver had made it sound like no more than a simple transaction, and Morgan had been foolish enough to believe him.

He now despised himself for what he'd done. He had broken three hearts—Neville's, Bliss's, and his own. He'd lost the only family he had left in the world. And he'd botched his only chance to own his own vessel.

But worst of all, he'd lost the only woman he had ever loved.

Morgan was astounded by how much devastation he had caused in such a short time.

For many hours, he lost himself in work. Along with his first mate, the ship's carpenter, and the boatswain, Morgan walked the vessel to evaluate her seaworthiness. He examined the hold and found it had been sufficiently reinforced. He checked to ensure that the pitch and tar had been patched. He found that the rigging and sails were still being mended but that repairs to the foremast were complete.

Morgan approved the final purchase orders for supplies needed for the crew, and after, he retreated to his quarters to review the outbound cargo manifest. The document was a listing of all goods being exported from England for use in the West Indies—farming tools and equipment, pig iron, oil, timber, china, silver, and crystal, household furnishings, and fabrics. It would be a fairly typical run for the *Selkie Maid*, and she would bring sugar, molasses, and rum with her when she returned.

With his eyes burning and his head fairly pounding, Morgan sought refuge on the quarterdeck. He stood in his place at the helm as the sun set, letting his hands run over the smooth and highly polished mahogany of the ship's wheel. It was cool to the touch, like silk, like the feel of Bliss's gown in his hands. The wood was sweetly curved, like Bliss's hip as it swelled out from her trim waist.

Morgan lowered his head between his arms as the realization crashed over him like a wave—inescapable now, so powerful he feared he would drown in it.

He would never treat a ship the way he had treated Bliss Worthington. Such a profound mistake, one he would pay for the rest of his days.

He was a bastard. In every sense of the word.

IT WAS LATE when Morgan's hired carriage arrived at his home. All he wished to do was fall into bed—the bed in which Bliss had slept. He prayed he could wrap himself in her sweet scent and disappear into the absolution of sleep, for he would benefit greatly from a few hours of rest before the duel. It was now only hours away.

Morgan opened the door to a most disturbing sight—Lord Oliver Danton, pacing frantically in his candlelit parlor, his hair awry and his eyes wild.

Oliver raised his arms in relief when he saw Morgan. "Ah! My dear boy. I am so glad you've come home!"

His uncle had never set foot in Morgan's house. Morgan had not realized the man even knew his address. But it was clear Lord Oliver did not belong here, and Morgan recoiled at the invasion of his privacy.

He must have been too exhausted to notice the Camberton carriage parked outside. "You had no right to let yourself into my house, Uncle."

"Oh, now, Morgan. Don't be so temperamental. It is of the utmost importance that we speak."

Morgan took a few cautious steps into his parlor.

"Won't you sit down with me for just a moment?" Oliver moved toward the comfortable sofa Bliss had chosen and dropped onto the cushions. He motioned for Morgan to join him.

Morgan shook his head. "I won't be sitting, and I'd prefer that you did not, either. Please remove yourself from my sofa and my home."

Lord Oliver's mouth dropped open. "Well, well." He stood, clearly offended by the lack of respect in Morgan's command. His hands fluttered nervously at his sides.

Morgan began to regret his rudeness. Lord Oliver was an old man after all, and Morgan's habit of respecting his elder uncle had been ingrained. It felt unnatural to address him with anything other than polite deference.

"I shall go momentarily," Oliver went on. "But I have one request, Morgan." Lord Oliver walked closer and clutched at Morgan's coat sleeve. When he looked up at Morgan, there was a crazed desperation in his eyes. "You must tell me what you plan to do tomorrow with Neville. Please! You must tell me!"

Morgan calmly pulled Lord Oliver's grasping fingers from his sleeve. He had never seen his uncle so distraught. Morgan decided to offer him some reassurance before he threw him out.

"You need not worry. I have no intention of doing away with my half brother."

Morgan saw panic—of all things—wash over Lord Oliver's expression. One of his eyelids began to twitch. He spun around on his heel and commenced with the frantic pacing.

"Yes. Oh. I see. Well . . . that's good, that's very good—" Oliver turned and, without another word, left the house. Morgan had never seen anything like it.

Good riddance.

He dimly realized he was hungry. Morgan found the kitchen clean and tidy and the larder stocked with food. But as he tried to decide what to eat, his appetite vanished.

This little house meant nothing good to him anymore. It was just a landlocked structure again, a place to hang his hat when he could not be at sea. It was not his home.

Not without Bliss.

REST WAS IMPOSSIBLE for Bliss. She lay staring at the frayed canopy over her bed at Worthington House, waiting for everyone to fall into deep sleep. She could not make her move until she was certain no one would try to stop her.

"No one" meant Dade, of course.

As she lay in wait, her mother's words went round and round in her mind.

"You go fetch your man."

There had to be a way to keep Morgan from the dueling field, and Bliss believed she had finally settled upon it.

Her plan was a simple one: Not long before the sunrise duel was set to begin, she would go capture her man.

And though Attie was not at all aware of it, she had been the inspiration for Bliss's scheme. Bliss spent the afternoon and evening furtively gathering the supplies she would need to carry out the plan, thinking all the while of how Attie might approach the challenge.

First, Bliss slipped into the Worthingtons' workshop, where she knew she would find the remnants of Attie's trapeze hanging from the rafters. Trapeze arts had been Bliss's young cousin's passion during the prior year, until her interests wandered to something else—as they always did. But Bliss found the ropes still in fine condition. They would perfectly meet her needs once they had been cut into shorter lengths.

Next, Bliss set about finding her wardrobe. She was forced to rummage through her male cousins' things, but she did eventually locate a pair of worn gray breeches that would not fall down, a pair of castaway leather boots only a bit too big for her feet, a white cotton shirt with stains at the collar, and a woolen cloak unraveling at the hem.

The biggest challenge had been locating a weskit that would reach around the circumference of her chest. The one she found was so tight that it pressed her bosom nearly flat.

Bliss decided she would endure the discomfort, for she would need all the flatness she could find in order to pose as a male.

She could wait no longer. Bliss jumped from her bed and began to dress. Within minutes she had donned her cap and cloak and slipped out the front door and into the dark night, her last two coins jingling in her pocket.

Bliss found Mr. Cant and his conveyance waiting a short distance from Worthington House.

"Shadwell, if you please." Then she sat back in the seat. Almost instantly, she was overcome by doubt.

Would this even work?

Bliss gave herself a stern talking-to during the carriage ride, reminding herself that even if she made a fool of herself over a man who cared nothing for her, she could not let him die.

Not before she'd had the chance to slay him herself, at any rate.

When the hack pulled up to Pryce House, Bliss asked Mr. Cant to wait for her. He agreed sourly. She slipped inside the foyer and was immediately greeted by Attie, the kitten.

"Mew."

Bliss put a finger to her lips. "Shh."

She crept up the stairs, careful to avoid the three steps she knew to be a bit squeaky. The door to the bedchamber was ajar, and she silently stole inside and tiptoed to the corner chair, where she plotted out her next moves.

She had to admit that, in truth, there was only one way she would be able to tie the formidable Morgan Pryce to the bedposts without protest. It would require that she be naked.

Without making a sound, she stripped off all her clothing, slinked toward the bed, and after pulling the coverlet away, she straddled his undressed body.

"What the bloody—?"

"It's your wife. I've come home."

MORGAN ASSUMED HE was dreaming, yet every attempt to force himself awake led him to the same unlikely place: A thoroughly and deliciously naked Bliss was astride his bare hips, her lips just inches from his, her breath warm on his face.

Her kiss stifled his cry of surprise, and caused his mind to stop working.

Only when her mouth left his did his questions renew. Why was she here? Had she somehow forgiven the unforgiveable? Were those ropes she was tying to his wrists?

He could not move, and not only because both of his hands were now bound to the bedposts. Morgan had been rendered helpless with arousal.

"Bliss—"

"Hush, now, my captain. I only want you to feel pleasure. This is all for your pleasure, husband."

He heard himself let go with a strangled laugh, which became a moan of lust when her lips began to graze his chest and her tongue tease at his nipples.

Morgan's eyes rolled back in his head when waves of satiny blond hair brushed down his ribs and the hardened tips of her breasts teased his abdomen.

When he felt her nibble along the crest of his hip bones, he could barely contain himself.

She scooted farther down the bed and Morgan was about to wonder what she had in mind when she answered the question for him by sitting on his left foot—while she tied up his right! She went on to tie his left foot to the post and when she was done, she stood by the side of the bed and lit a candle.

She gazed down at him, all golden curves and planes and silky female temptation. The smile on her face, however, was anything but coquettish.

"Are you taking me prisoner?"

She nodded, moving astride him once more. There was enough light now that Morgan could read every nuance in her expression.

"Neville will kill you," she said.

"No, Bliss."

She shook her head, her hair falling over her lovely breasts. Morgan felt himself breaking out in a sweat.

"He might not be much of an athlete, but Neville is a crack shot. When forced to participate in the hunt, he hits his mark with cruel efficiency—he never wants a living thing to suffer."

Morgan sighed, allowing his head to fall back upon the pillow. Being tied to his bed was a bothersome development, but he could not deny that there was a part of him that appreciated her concern for his welfare. "You must untie me, Bliss."

"I will do no such thing unless you agree to my terms."

Oh, hell no. Bliss was not playing fair! She had just stretched her entire naked form on top of him, and Morgan could feel the press of her breasts on his chest, the hot V between her thighs soft against his erection. The woman was ruthless.

"Will you flee the duel?"

"No."

She nibbled on his earlobe and whispered to him, "Will you forfeit the duel, then? For me?"

"No."

Bliss sat up again, her pouty lips in a mischievous smile, her perfect bottom grinding against his rigid cock with torturous slowness. She was teasing him, hinting that she might have mercy on him, change her position just slightly, and allow him to enter her, sink deep into her until . . .

She stopped moving against him. Morgan bit back a helpless groan.

"Will you stand down?"

"No." He panted. There was no point in hiding his desire. His cock was as hard as iron. His skin sported a fine sheen of sweat. His breath came as fast as a racing horse.

But he could not give her what she wanted. "Bliss, I cannot abandon my honorable duty, but you have to believe me when I tell you that no one will be hurt—I won't be. Neville won't be."

He saw tears nearly overflow her eyes. She shook her head and took leave of the bed. He watched her in awe as she dressed in men's clothing and shoved her blond hair into a cap.

"You came dressed like that?"

"How else could I make my way through London in the middle of the night?"

Bliss headed for the bedchamber door.

"Wait! You can't leave me here like this!"

She turned toward him, her eyes sparkling with angry tears. "I can and I will. And now I'm heading out to talk some sense into Neville."

He stared in shock as she left the room. "Bliss? Not in the same way, I hope? Bliss?"

He half expected her to return and unbind him. Then he heard the door open. "Bliss!"

The door closed.

And God help him, but in Morgan's mind all he saw was

a naked Bliss astride Neville. Oh, how he hoped she would resort to some other method of interrogation, and that it be one requiring clothing.

Morgan tugged at the ropes. They would not budge. He pulled harder.

He was going nowhere.

"CAPTAIN PRYCE! YOUR door is wide-open to the street! Captain Pryce, are you here?"

Morgan flinched. *I'm really in the suds now.*

He was thoroughly naked, tied to all four posts of his bed, without ability to cover himself. And the unmistakable voice he had just heard calling from downstairs was that of Bliss's dressmaker.

"We've brought you a new weskit! For the duel!"

If he answered, he would be rescued, but found himself in flagrante delicto—albeit as an innocent victim. If he did not answer he would remain tied up and helpless for an unknowable period of time. There was only one thing to be done. "Up here! I could use some help!"

"Captain Pryce? Are you quite well? We're coming straightaway!"

Morgan heard footsteps on the stairs, then the landing.

"Whatever is the—?"

Button and Cabot came to a sudden halt. They stared. Their mouths fell open. Then they spun about on their heels in perfect unison, eyes toward the hallway.

Morgan cleared his throat. "I do apologize."

"Oh, sweet sugar-covered bonbons! Cover that man before I faint!"

Cabot obeyed Button's desperate plea and managed to run into the bedchamber, grab the dressing gown Morgan had thrown over a chair, and toss it across Morgan's most private attributes—all while staring at the wall.

Morgan grimaced in relief. "I thank you, Cabot."

"No need." Cabot still did not look at him.

At least one thought comforted Morgan. This embarrassing event was not likely to become the hottest bit of gossip in all of London. Dressmakers were akin to physicians in that their clients must trust them absolutely. Surely Button and Cabot would not benefit from speaking of this.

Button dared peek into the bedchamber. In his arms was the oddly ugly weskit. Button dropped it with a thud upon the chair. And set his fists on his hips. "I daresay you do need help."

He and Cabot began untying the ropes that held Morgan's wrists to the bedposts. As soon as his hands were free, he grabbed his dressing gown and covered himself from chin to knee.

"Well, now." Button's voice was overly cheerful as he and Cabot released his feet. "I won't ask how this happened to you, Captain."

"Perhaps that would be best."

Button's laughter exploded from his lips, which was too much for the more serious Cabot, who actually smiled as well.

The instant Morgan's feet were free, he sat on the side of the bed. "May I have a moment to dress?"

"Of course! We'll be right outside."

Good God. Morgan pulled on his shirt and breeches while being serenaded by sounds of chuckling.

"All right." He flung open his door to find Button nearly falling over Cabot in amusement. "You have my most sincere gratitude, but if you will excuse me . . ."

"Oh! But you must try on the weskit." Button pushed past Morgan and retrieved the item from the chair. "A proper fit is of the utmost importance. Cabot, could you assist me?"

"Of course."

It took both men to hoist the weskit upon Morgan's shoulders.

Morgan was stunned. "This thing must weigh five stone!"

"Just a hair over four, actually." Button straightened the seams while Cabot tugged it tight and buttoned it. "Inside the waistcoat we've sewn quite a bit of chain mail from an old suit of armor."

"Seventeenth century," Cabot added.

Morgan stared at them. "Why would you do such a thing for me? Aren't you on the Worthington side?"

"Oh yes, I will be," Button assured him blandly. "As soon as I figure out which side that is."

Cabot nodded. "When it comes to Worthingtons and love, it's always wise to hedge one's bets."

Love? If only. Morgan frowned at his reflection in the dressing table mirror. He'd developed a barrel chest. "I suppose this thing will protect some of my vital organs—if it doesn't cut off my blood supply first."

"At least the vitals above the waist," Cabot said.

The snickering began again, and Morgan insisted his visitors leave. Sunrise was but an hour away. He thanked them again for their kindness and watched as they descended the stairs.

"That was ever so clever, lining the weskit that way," Cabot said.

Button shrugged modestly. "I suppose it's a bit mad, really."

"You aren't mad. You are the most brilliant person I have ever known. It only appears mad to those on the outside."

Button smiled angelically. "I suppose I can live with that."

Morgan looked at himself in the mirror. He was on his way to be shot by Neville. Indeed, madness was in ample supply on this day.

LORD OLIVER NUDGED Neville's shoulder with a cut crystal glass. "Go on, boy. Just a sip or two for courage. You don't want to have the shakes standing in the middle of Sutton Meadow."

Neville shrugged off the glass and then returned to his preferred position before the fireplace mantel, head between extended arms, eyes on the floor.

Katarina could not tell whether the duke was troubled about the approaching duel or on the brink of being ill—or both.

"You know you carry a heavy responsibility, my boy. It is up to you to defend the Danton honor. Your father would expect nothing less from you."

Neville ignored him.

Lord Oliver nudged his arm again with the whiskey glass.

Katarina could remain silent no longer. "Perhaps for his safety Neville should remain as sober as possible, my lord."

Oliver raised an eyebrow at her, clearly irritated by her interference. "And what are you, Miss Beckham? His nursery maid? His physician? His mama?"

"I am his friend."

"Oh? Well, I shouldn't be getting too comfortable in that role if I were you, since you and your idiotic mother will be on a boat bound for the West Indies before—"

"Enough!" Neville straightened, snatched the glass from Lord Oliver's grip, and hurled it across the room. Katarina flinched at the sound of crystal shattering against the far wall.

"My, my." Oliver took a step back. "I shall leave you to your foul temper, then. Allow me to wish you the best of luck."

Neville reeled on him, his face purple with fury. "How dare you wish me anything, Uncle? This duel is your doing. You intentionally exposed Bliss to ridicule! You lied to Morgan about her and bribed him into that criminal marriage. You lied to me! All you've done is spew lies and hate! And now you've cornered me in an impossible position!"

Neville gasped for air. He pointed toward the parlor door, his arm straight and his finger trembling. "Get out of my sight!"

Oliver's eyelids grew drowsy, as if he had only the barest

interest in the conversation. He smirked. "Very well. But mark me, Neville. You may be the duke, but I am still—"

"Leave! Now!"

Oliver exited the room without another word and closed the door behind him. Katarina watched Neville reach out for the parlor chair, then collapse upon it. He cradled his face in his hand.

She approached in silence. She knelt at the side of the chair and waited for a sign—any indication, any hint—of what she could do to help him. She wished she knew all that he struggled with.

Neville groaned. "Why did I challenge Morgan? Why?"

Katarina straightened. "Because you'd had too much to drink. You were angry and you were shocked—everyone was. You felt betrayed and you lashed out from a place of reckless pride."

Neville's fingers parted just enough to expose one blue eye. That eye stared at her, unblinking.

"Well, you asked. I answered truthfully."

"It was a rhetorical question."

Katarina shook her head. "This no time for rhetoric, Neville. This is time for a clear head and a calm demeanor."

"You don't say?" Neville sat upright, propping his elbows upon his knees. His mouth was pulled in a straight line, and his eyes were focused on hers. "Tell me, wise Katarina. How am I to be clearheaded and of calm demeanor when I'm about to shoot my own brother? A man I have always loved, always held in the highest esteem?"

Katarina listened.

"How am I to make Bliss a widow after only a week of marriage? I—I think she has come to love him. I saw it in her eyes. She did nothing to deserve this. What will become of her?"

Katarina said nothing.

"But how can I call it off at this hour? It is simply not done! Gentlemen do not issue a challenge and then retract it. I would rather die than be thought of as a spineless coward, a man who dishonored his family name!"

"You are making a terrible mistake, Neville."

He twitched at the sound of her voice, as if he had forgotten she was there. "What?"

"Calling off this duel would be a mark of strength, not cowardice."

He smiled sadly. "You do not understand, Kat."

"I understand that your uncle has manipulated you and Morgan in equal measure, appealed to the worst in each of you, and thrown you both to the wolves of alleged honor and propriety. Perhaps you should ask yourself why he would do such a thing."

Katarina saw Neville's jaw clench. The tendons in his neck popped.

She had gone too far, perhaps, but it had to be said. "I only wish to help."

Neville shook his head. He stood, turned his back to her, and stalked out the door.

Katarina watched him go. It was true that she'd had precious little experience with the male sex, but she already suspected that the masculine temperament would forever remain a mystery to her.

No more than a few minutes had passed when Katarina heard the front door slam and a carriage depart.

It was too late to stop him.

Chapter 33

BLISS told Mr. Cant to bring the hired hack to a stop well before reaching Camberton House, as she did not want the clatter to attract attention. She pulled her cap low on her head, tucking away a few stray curls, and raced down the street and toward the front steps. The night sky over London was tinged with violet. Sunrise was on its way.

And so, too, the duel.

Neville was her last option. She had to speak to him before he departed for the field of honor. She had to find a way to sway him. Neville was a man of reason, she knew, a man driven more by logic than passion. Surely he would put a stop to this farce once she had laid out all the facts for his consideration.

Neville would be more reasonable than Morgan, she was certain of it.

Bliss's thoughts went to her husband, whom she'd left bound to the bed not half an hour before. She had no illusions. Bliss knew Morgan would find a way to free himself.

At best, the ropes would delay him. They would not deter him.

Not far from Camberton House, Bliss watched a lone carriage speed down the dark street. She ran up the drive and skidded to a stop at the foot of the steps, then froze. She glanced down at herself. What now? Her disguise had been hastily constructed, meant only to give her a few extra seconds of inconspicuousness, in the dark, among those who did not know her. Regis would recognize her instantly, forbid her entrance, and alert Lord Oliver.

Her only hope was to provide a distraction, and pray that fate was with her.

Bliss shoved her hand down into the pocket of her borrowed waistcoat, seeking the coin she'd brought along in case of an emergency. The single guinea shone in her palm. It was her last coin, her last option. It would have to do.

She placed the coin in the loose gravel, centered at the base of the front steps. If someone stood in the doorway, they could not help seeing it. It might just give her the time she needed.

Bliss pounded on the door, then scurried away. She crouched down behind the large boxwood topiary, curling herself into the smallest ball possible. She held her breath.

It did not take long.

"Who's there? Show yerself!"

Bliss almost melted with relief. It was a young under-footman, not the vigilant Regis. But the man shook his head in annoyance and was about to shut the door again.

No!

Bliss reached down next to her shoe and grabbed the nearest pebble, tossing it in front of the steps. The rustle was enough to make the under-footman squint in the dimness.

He saw the coin. He looked around him to be sure he had no witnesses, then scurried down the steps to claim his prize.

It was enough time for Bliss to slip in behind him, enter the house, and make a run for the nearest open doorway. It happened to be the Dantons' informal parlor.

"Oh!" Katarina Beckham pressed her palm to her chest and gasped at Bliss's unexpected arrival. "Who . . . ?" She examined Bliss from head to toe, her face expanding in wonder. "Mrs. Pryce?"

"Shh!"

Bliss shut the doors behind her and rushed to where Katarina stood in the center of the room. Miss Beckham took a few wary steps backward. Bliss couldn't blame her. "I must speak to Neville. He cannot go through with the duel. I have to stop him."

"I have tried. He would not listen."

"Has he already left?"

Katarina nodded. "I believe so."

"Oh no." Bliss shook off her despair. "Did you see him depart?"

"No. I heard a carriage."

Bliss felt a surge of hope. "Then let us be certain. We'll go to his chamber—he might still be here!"

Katarina placed her hand on Bliss's sleeve. "He believes it his duty to uphold the family honor. He has convinced himself this is more than silly male pride."

Bliss began pacing the room, twisting her fingers before her. "Morgan would not listen to me, either."

"There is something else I must tell you, Bliss."

She looked up, startled by the ominous tone of Katarina's voice.

"It's Lord Oliver. He's behind this. I just know it. Bliss, he was practically forcing whiskey on Neville. He wanted him drunk for the duel! What kind of man wants his only nephew, the duke, to stumble about drunk, on a dark field, with a loaded pistol in his hand?"

Bliss blinked, a hot warning buzzing through her veins.

Who, indeed? She knew the answer—a man who did not want the duke to live.

Before Bliss could speak, there was a loud clamor in the great hall. They heard Neville's voice, followed by the slam of the front door. They both ran out into the parlor to catch him, but the carriage was already racing down the drive.

Regis stood tall and unperturbed, despite their sudden appearance before him. He bowed slightly, a wry smile directed to Bliss and her delivery boy attire. "Ladies," he said, and then walked away.

"We must follow him." Bliss's heart dropped at the realization that she'd used her last coin to create a diversion. "But I have no way to pay for a hack! I do not even know where they have gone!"

"I do. Go out front. I shall meet you momentarily."

Bliss did as Katarina asked, wondering how it was that the two of them—who began as rivals—were now conspirators. Katarina burst through the front door with several lovely bonnets grasped in her fist.

"Hurry." She grabbed Bliss's hand and they ran.

They raced down the street until they were able to hail a carriage for hire. Bliss watched in wonder as Katarina attempted to barter one of the fine bonnets for a ride.

"Sutton Meadow?" The driver shook his head. "That's in the middle of bloody nowhere!"

Katarina struck a bargain for two bonnets, and they hopped into the carriage.

As they bumped along the London streets, Bliss turned toward Katarina Beckham, her new friend, a young woman of imagination and tenacity whom she now greatly admired. Miss Beckham was, indeed, an excellent match for the Duke of Camberton.

Bliss reached out for Katarina's hand and squeezed it tightly. As she stared out the window, it occurred to her that if she could just see her two beloved gentlemen through this terrible morning, she had no need to worry about Neville's future without her. He was going to be held in very capable, loving hands.

A MISTY MEADOW appeared in the carriage window, barely discernible in the dim of predawn. The driver had not yet pulled the horses to a full stop, but that did not concern Bliss. She threw open the door and jumped, her boots skidding on the damp grass. Katarina followed immediately after, and they began to run.

In the foggy first light, Bliss could make out two tall, male figures standing back-to-back. It looked as if they had their pistols at the ready.

Her heart took a dive to the pit of her stomach. Such insanity! Such mulishness exhibited by two grown men—brothers, no less!

Bliss ducked her head and ran, grateful for her disguise of breeches and boots. She could barely contain her gasp when she saw that three of her male Worthington cousins were gathered at the edges of the dueling field. They milled about like spectators at a horse race rather than witnesses to senseless bloodshed.

She called out in their direction, "Do something! Put a stop to this!"

All heads turned her way. She continued forward, nearly tripping on the uneven ground. "This is lunacy!" She made eye contact with Morgan as she ran, his gaze widening as she came closer to the field. The next cry she directed at him. "You are brothers! Stop this immedia—!"

Whooomffff! Bliss slammed to a halt. She was now dangling over an outstretched male arm.

"There's no need to fret, dear cousin."

Her head snapped up. She snarled at Dade. "Are you thoroughly mad? They might very well kill each other!"

Cas winked and waved away her concern. "No one will suffer bodily injury here today, Cousin Bliss. You two ladies have nothing to fret about."

Katarina had somehow circumvented the line of Worthingtons and reached Neville's side. "You mustn't go through with this! Please, Neville." She clutched at his arm. "It is senseless."

Bliss's gaze flew to Morgan once more. His intense blue stare was fixed on her, piercing the first light and searing her flesh. She straightened slowly, pulling away from Dade as she tried to catch her breath. It was then she realized she was trembling from head to toe.

In that instant, Bliss imagined she saw everything in Morgan's handsome face. Regret. Anger. Sorrow. She saw love there, too, though he had never been willing to speak the words to her.

And now it might be too late.

Bliss shook her head at him quite slowly, an unspoken plea repeating in her mind. *You cannot do this. I love you. I love you.*

Morgan turned away. He pointed the barrel of his pistol upward and held the weapon at his shoulder. His face went as cold as stone, and his body—the lean and strong body that had brought Bliss so much pleasure—was now tensed in preparation for battle.

"Don't, Morgan!"

He did not flinch.

Neville set his hands upon Katarina's shoulders. "Move to safety."

Katarina ran back to the meadow's edge, her face ashen, tears pooling in her eyes. "What shall we do?" Katarina grabbed Bliss's hand and squeezed it in her own. The women stared at each other in horror.

Dade raised an arm above his head and pointed a finger skyward. "Gentlemen, the dawn has arrived! Take your marks and prepare to fire at twenty paces!"

Dade sliced his arm in a downward arc. "One!"

No. This simply cannot be!

"Two."

Bliss shook her head, lost, sick in her stomach, her thoughts racing as fast as her heart.

"Three."

Bliss and Katarina watched in disbelief as the two men paced away from each other. Yet again it struck Bliss how similar in stature and coloring the brothers were. Even now, as they planned to murder each other in cold blood over a silly matter of pride, their strides were equally long, equally graceful.

"Four."

Yes, Bliss admired both men, and for entirely different reasons. But in that moment she knew she had only given one man her heart and soul—Morgan. It was Morgan who had brought her to life, who had changed her forever.

"Five."

Bliss knew what had to be done. She knew it was up to her to do it. Though such a notion was thoroughly unexpected, and quite possibly dangerous, Bliss steeled herself, took a deep breath, and prepared to put an end to this abomination.

Just then her attention was drawn to the line of trees behind Morgan. The rising sun had just illuminated a patch of unnaturally brilliant yellow shining through a curtain of leaves. Bliss stared in shock—there, dangling over a tree branch about a dozen feet from the ground, were glimmering folds of yellow silk.

"Six."

"Oh my sweet word!" What was Attie doing here?

Bliss slipped behind the line of her male cousins, whose attention was now fixed on the action on the dueling field. Katarina clearly wanted to come along, but Bliss put a finger to her lips and shook her head.

"Seven."

Bliss knew she had but seconds to end this folly, and her only advantage would be the element of surprise.

LORD OLIVER KEPT his head low and took another featherlight step, careful not to snap a twig or rustle a leaf as he made his way through the wood. His tortoiselike progress was horribly frustrating. If he did not reach the meadow's edge before twenty paces were counted out, and take his shot exactly when the other pistols fired, his plan would collapse.

If witnesses heard three shots instead of two, all was lost.

"Six."

Lord Oliver knew one of the brothers had to die today, and since he couldn't trust either of them to carry out the deed, he must ensure that the job was done.

Sometimes it seemed he always had to do everything himself. How tiresome.

"Seven."

Oliver crept on. He clutched his pistol in his right hand and pressed it flat against his right thigh. He noticed his palms were slick. He felt a trickle of sweat beneath his frock coat.

"Eight."

He reminded himself to remain calm and focused, that he had only one chance to take his shot and escape. All must proceed perfectly.

And, when this was done, his grief would need to be extreme, and extremely public. He would insist on an inquiry, demand answers, seek justice for his nephew. Oh, how he would wail and weep over the tragic circumstances! He would tell everyone how that Worthington girl came between two loyal brothers. How she destroyed the Danton family name.

Yes. He knew exactly where to place the blame.

"Nine."

Good Lord, still only on nine! Would that Worthington boy never get to twenty? Lord Oliver fought to remember what he was thinking about . . . ah yes . . . which brother should he shoot?

"Ten."

Neville's demise would bring about the quickest and most direct benefit, of course. With the unmarried duke dead and buried, there could be no risk of an heir usurping what was rightfully Oliver's. But killing Morgan was an equally satisfactory option. Duels were against the law. Even a duke like Neville would surely be hanged for his participation in an illegal duel that resulted in death. Although it would take longer.

"Eleven."

But in the final analysis, either demise would suffice, as either would deliver the Camberton title and fortunes into Oliver's hands, where they had always belonged.

"Twelve."

There was only one mitigating factor. Morgan's death would leave White Rose Shipping without its most reliable and cost-effective captain, forcing Oliver to seek a replacement. What a bother! It would most assuredly cut into profits.

"Thirteen."

He spied a thick chestnut tree at the meadow's edge. Its trunk was wide enough to hide him but unobstructed by other trees, giving him clean a shot.

"Fourteen."

He scurried to his hiding place, sighing with relief as he pressed his back to the solid tree trunk. A quick look about assured him he had not been spotted.

"Fifteen."

Lord Oliver began loading his pistol with shaking hands, suddenly rewarded with an instant of clarity. Finally! He decided which brother would be cut down.

The one who, in the moment of truth, gave him the best target.

"Seventeen."

Lord Oliver hefted the weight of the loaded pistol and turned. He straightened his arm and got into position, smiling at his own cleverness. By leaving the target up to chance, he could never accuse himself of playing favorites.

"Eighteen."

Oliver took aim. He put his finger on the trigger. He waited, his whole body ready to spring into action.

What the bloody—?

Something sharp pelted down upon his bare head, then another, then an entire assault, as painful as the sting of a dozen giant wasps! Was it a sudden fall of chestnuts? He felt it again, this time one sharp and expertly aimed *ping!* to his scalp.

He tried desperately to keep his lit pistol at the ready, but a flash of yellow made him look up into the tree branches above.

THIS WAS ATTIE's first duel, and she had to admit she found all the manly posturing and discussion of "honor" rather boring. She had located the perfect place to observe the action without being seen, and was now perched high in a chestnut tree at the edge of the meadow, the V of two branches providing comfort and shelter. Her brothers would never detect her in this spot and insist she return home.

This time she had managed to outsmart Cas, Lysander, and Dade. They never knew she had stuffed herself in the boot locker at the rear of the carriage. Thinking upon it now, she would have to rank it as one of her more brilliant stowaways. She had even pulled it off while wearing her yellow dress, which she had donned at the last moment just in case any of the captain's crew came to support him during the duel. Not that she was interested in anyone specifically . . .

Suddenly, Attie's attention was drawn to the forest floor

below. She was surprised to see a silver-haired man slinking through the wood, his head ducked down and his back bent.

The old fellow was clearly trying his best to remain undetected, which was rather pitiful, since his footfalls crunched upon the leaves with all the grace of a water buffalo.

The skulking man was up to no good. Attie was certain of this. She had much firsthand experience with such endeavors and could detect all the signs.

Oh bother! Of all the trees in this wood, the old man had just selected her tree to hide behind. He was now directly below her, his head lowered, his hands busy with something.

With one portion of her mind, she kept track of the count. With the rest of her attention, she peered downward, practically hanging from her branch like an ape. Unfortunately, the angle was all wrong for Attie to see what the man was doing. She had chosen this particular nook for its excellent view of the meadow, not its direct sight line to the ground below.

Suddenly, the man spun around and raised his arm.

Attie stifled a gasp. He had a pistol! Absolutely not! She could not allow this man to shoot someone—but it appeared he was about to do just that!

"Seventeen."

Attie took action. She reached into the pocket of her silk gown and grabbed a handful of musket balls, whipping them down upon the top of the man's head. He ducked and grunted in surprise, giving her an opportunity to retrieve her slingshot. Attie loaded it and made a clean shot directly to his balding scalp.

"Eighteen."

The man flinched in pain and looked up into the branches. Their eyes met. He scowled.

Attie screamed as loudly as she could, "Help! Help! He's got a pistol!"

The man snarled, then took aim at the field once more. It was up to her to stop him. She swung around, dangled from the branch, and took flight.

* * *

"SIXTEEN."

Bliss had made her way behind her cousins and was in position, ready to throw her body between Neville and Morgan. She was certain that under no circumstances would gentlemen endanger the life of a lady. It simply was not done.

"Seventeen."

Cas turned to glare at Bliss, suspicion in his eyes. She smiled sadly at him. Satisfied, he turned back to the duel. Bliss prepared to spring into action.

It all happened at once. She hurled her body toward the center of the field and was running as fast as her legs would carry her when she detected a glint of metal near a tree trunk off to her right.

"Eighteen."

It was a pistol. Held by Lord Oliver and aimed directly at Morgan, chest level. There was no time to ponder her actions. What she did next was pure instinct.

Her captain would not be shot down like a dog. Not on her watch.

"Help! Help! He's got a pistol!" It was Attie's voice. Bliss pivoted, crying out, "Get down!" She dove though the air, headfirst, hurling her body against Morgan's. A great explosion cracked her ears. She was hovering, falling, and just as they crashed to the ground together, Bliss thought she saw a pair of bright yellow wings descend upon Lord Oliver.

That was when Bliss felt a terribly odd sensation—a hot, slicing agony, racing across her forehead.

She had been shot.

How unexpected!

Then blackness.

IT WAS A very short flight.

The gun went off. Attie landed on the man's shoulders.

He crumpled beneath her, his lungs emptying when he hit the leaves, his face smashed into the earth.

Attie had plopped sidesaddle upon the old man's back, her legs stretched out before her. Her bones were rattled, to be sure, but she was still in one piece.

She called out, "I got him! I got him!"

Almost instantly, two strong hands reached under her arms and lifted her up and off. Attie turned to see Lysander, his eyes burning like dark coals. He said nothing, of course, but passed her off to Dade and Cas, who came running up behind him. Dade took a quick scan of Attie for injuries. Cas grabbed up the smoking pistol. Lysander reached down, grabbed the old fellow by the coat collar, and dragged him off toward the clearing like a sack of rocks. Attie and her brothers followed right behind.

The old man screamed at Lysander, limbs flailing about. "Get your hands off me! Do you know who I am?" Blood trickled from his crumpled nose. His red face was pasted with mud and leaves. Attie detected a pattern of raised welts on his head, no doubt the result of her musket ball assault.

She knew that now was the perfect time to press her advantage to her brother. "See? This is why it is in everyone's best interests that I remain armed at all times!"

Lysander stared straight ahead. Dade and Cas also remained profoundly serious.

Only then did Attie's attention turn to the meadow. She blinked in disbelief.

Bliss lay unmoving in Captain Pryce's arms. Her head and borrowed surcoat were soaked in blood. The captain barked out a series of orders while his blood-covered hands pressed down onto Bliss's wound.

No! Not Bliss!

Chapter 34

"**O**PEN your eyes, Bliss. Please."

Morgan whispered his plea into her ear as he pressed his fingertips against her blood-slick throat. He moaned with relief when he detected a pulse.

He diverted his attention just long enough to shout out orders. "Bring round the fastest carriage! Someone ride ahead for the doctor! I need bandages!"

Morgan lowered his lips to Bliss's ear once more, wiping away the blood. "Open your eyes and tell me what an ass I am. If you wake up I'll let you go . . . I'll set you free. Please, Bliss."

What had she done? Had Bliss just thrown herself between Morgan and the barrel of a pistol? Foolish girl! Stupid! He should be the one bleeding on the ground, not Bliss. Not his brave, passionate, wonderful Bliss.

"Please, Bliss. Go on and marry Neville if that's what you wish." Morgan heard the agony in his hoarse whisper. When he wiped the blood from her exquisite cheeks, her eyelids flickered. She would live.

She would live.

He brushed his lips against hers. "I'll sail away, Bliss. You'll never have to see me again. All I ask is you open your eyes. Oh God, please wake up!"

Morgan heard a high-pitched cry from the wood. "I got him! I got him! Somebody help me!" The voice belonged to Attie Worthington.

Suddenly, he heard the pounding of hurried footsteps and looked up to see Neville skidding to a stop, his face blanched. Miss Beckham had already hiked up her skirt and was ripping apart her petticoat for bandages. Morgan and Neville locked eyes, saying nothing, until Morgan realized Katarina was trying to pry his fingers from Bliss's wound.

He released his hold. Blood poured out. His coat sleeves were slippery with it. Blood was everywhere.

"I don't think it is very deep." Katarina spoke to Neville and Morgan while he helped applied the bandages. "The cartridge didn't enter her skull. Head wounds often appear much worse than they are."

"Thank God!" Neville dropped to his knees, his breath coming in shuddering gulps. He stared at Morgan with pleading eyes. "I didn't even fire, Morgan! I didn't fire my pistol!"

Morgan focused on his work. It made sense that Neville had not seen their cowardly uncle step out from behind a tree and fire, since he had faced the opposite direction to take his paces.

Neville would be devastated by the truth. But at that moment, Morgan's only concern was Bliss.

He set to dressing the wound, wrapping the strips of muslin about Bliss's head. The sight was shocking—a deep red soaked into her silky blond curls.

Morgan's breath was quick and shallow. Whatever calm he might manage to display was a ruse for the benefit of others. Inside, Morgan was splintering, his heart shattering into a thousand needles of glass. He wanted to howl like a wild thing, let the sobs shake his body.

Bliss had sacrificed herself for him.

He did not deserve her. Only a man as honorable as Neville did.

He glanced up, seeing the pain in Neville's eyes. "You are not responsible for this."

"Then who—"

A commotion broke out about ten yards away. All eyes turned to watch Lysander drag a kicking and screaming Uncle Oliver into the clearing. Lysander then yanked him up by the collar, cocked his arm, and was about to punch him when his brothers interceded. They pulled Lysander off and then sat squarely on top of Oliver, either to restrain him or protect him from Lysander—or both.

His uncle was nothing but a back-biting, bacon-fed pig . . .

Neville shook his head in disbelief, slowly turning to Morgan with a face as white as a block of salt. "Heavens," was all he said.

The carriage came barreling toward the meadow.

"Let's go." Neville helped Morgan lift Bliss from the grass. When Morgan pulled her tight to his chest and insisted on carrying her to the carriage without help, Neville nodded in understanding. Katarina hurried along beside Morgan, keeping pressure on the wound.

Attie Worthington ran up to them, tears in her furious eyes. "Is she . . . Will she . . . ?"

Morgan smiled at her, still moving. "Miss Atalanta."

She nodded, running alongside. The tears began to roll down her cheeks.

"You were quite brave today. Bliss will be fine—I promise you." Morgan did not feel the confidence he heard in his own words. He knew it would be weeks before he could believe that statement.

They neared the carriage. Katarina was doing a fine job halting the bleeding.

Neville remained behind him, resting a hand on Morgan's shoulder and matching him stride for stride.

"Bliss loves you, Morgan."

Morgan did not reply.

"It was you she shielded from harm. Not me."

When Neville moved up next to him, Morgan turned to look at him. "I was merely in the line of fire."

Neville stared at him meaningfully. "We both were. And she picked *you* to save."

The fine carriage displayed the Duke of Camberton's crest. Two startled footmen opened the door for Morgan and helped him get Bliss inside. He laid her down on the white velvet seat, instantly ruined with blood.

Neville poked his head inside. "Nothing matters but her," he said. "You are going to Camberton House where she will be most comfortable. My personal physician will attend to her. You are welcome to remain by her side."

Neville shut the door. "To Camberton!" Morgan heard him bark out a series of orders. "Fetch my horse! Dade, come with me! We're going to find my surgeon. We'll drag him from his bed if we have to!"

And the carriage was off.

NEVILLE STOOD SHOULDER-TO-SHOULDER with Katarina as the carriage pulled away.

"I didn't want anyone to get hurt," he said numbly. "I wasn't going to fire."

"It wouldn't have mattered anyway," Dade assured Neville. "We molded new balls from sand and India rubber. They were guaranteed to break apart on impact."

Cas grunted. "I still think the pistol would just blow up, instead."

The two Worthington brothers went on ahead with Attie, who had gone pale and uncharacteristically silent with worry. Neville hung back, thinking of Bliss stepping in front of Morgan, thinking of Morgan, visibly willing Bliss to be all right.

He didn't intend to say anything aloud, but he did, and he heard a wistfulness in his own voice.

"So that's what love looks like."

Katarina slipped her cool, fine-boned hand into his. "Yes, Neville. That is exactly what love looks like."

Neville turned. What he saw in Katarina's shining eyes took his breath away. Her expression was open, warm, and wise. With that look she was both issuing a challenge and extending an invitation. The dignity and grace of this woman made Neville straighten his spine and raise his chin.

He leaned in toward her. Katarina lifted her lips. The kiss was gentle and tentative, a sweet, light promise of what was to come.

When Neville pulled away, he knew Katarina had gifted him with a smile that might never fade. He wanted another kiss. Or a dozen. But he knew there was something else calling to him.

"My dear Katarina, I know the timing is a bit unfortunate, but please pardon me. Stay right here. I'll be back in a moment."

MORGAN KNELT ON the floor of the carriage. He cradled Bliss, knowing she would be jolted with each rut and rock along the way to Camberton. At least the bleeding had slowed somewhat. Her breathing and pulse were steady as well. All Morgan wished to do was lay his cheek against hers. He wanted to be there when she opened her eyes. He wanted his voice to be the one that urged her awake.

"I love you, Bliss. You are the only woman I've ever loved."

She didn't answer him. Fear threatened to close his throat. She was so very still and pale, not like herself at all. His wife was a woman of grit and indomitable will. If anyone could survive a bullet, it would be his *mor forwyn*, his mermaid.

"Did you hear me, Bliss? I love you. I love you. I love you."

As they neared the edge of the park, Morgan lifted his head to take one last look out the rear window. That was when he witnessed a most extraordinary thing.

Neville punched their dear old Uncle Oliver square in the face. The once haughty Oliver Danton now lay faceup in the grass, his nose bloody, his head covered in strange red welts. Twigs were lodged in his hair. His knee breeches were muddy and his hose had fallen to his shoes.

Morgan felt a twinge of pride. "Good on you, my brother. Good on you."

BLISS KNEW NOT what was real and what was a dream. Faces moved in and out of focus. Voices sounded distorted, as if they traveled up from the depths of the sea to her ears. She had no idea the day.

Who smiled at her now? Iris! And Attie. And Dade and Cas and Lysander and Archie . . . oh, how she tried to smile in return.

It all required so much effort. Too much. Bliss felt herself falling back to the place between sleep and wakefulness. She felt so hot. So confused. So very tired.

But she could not go back to sleep quite yet. There was one more face she needed to see.

"I'm here, sweet Bliss."

Relief flooded her. Emotion caught in her dry throat. It was Morgan. He was still here. He grasped her fingers and put his lips to the back of her hand.

She lay back. Closed her eyes. Concentrated on the cool steadiness of his hand, his solid presence.

All would be well.

When she next woke, Morgan was still there. He brought cool water to her lips and dabbed at her face with a damp flannel. He fed her one spoonful of broth at a time, all day long.

"I love you, Bliss. I love you."

His words sounded so very far away.

And the next time she opened her eyes, he was there. And the next. Until the day she woke to discover she could clearly see his handsome face in the morning light, drawn with worry and exhaustion as it hovered over her. She wanted to tell him she was fine, that he need not worry.

Don't go. Stay with me.

Bliss could not determine if she had spoken the words aloud, or if they had remained trapped in her mind.

I love you, too.

Day after day she felt him near. She heard his deep voice in consultation with the kind physician who had been tending to her. She heard Morgan speak with her family. He read to her often, and one day she heard a familiar passage.

Thou shouldst a husband take by my consent,
As I by thine a wife: this is a match,
And made between's by vows. Thou hast found mine.

Clearly, Iris had stopped by with suggested reading.

"*Winter's Tale*, act five, scene three," Bliss murmured.

She heard Morgan take a quick breath. "Bliss?" he whispered. "Are you awake at last? Bliss?"

But she was already slipping into soft darkness again.

Later, Bliss caught a peek of a maid opening the drapes. She did not recognize the room. Where was she? What had happened?

"Morgan?"

Morgan rushed to her side. "I'm here, Bliss. Right here."

Then the day came that she woke to find the fog had lifted. Her first impulse was to seek out Morgan. She looked down to see his hand resting on her hip and turned to see him lying next to her. He was sound asleep, his body curled around hers atop the coverlet, as if to protect her.

Suddenly, she remembered. The duel! "Morgan?"

Her voice had obviously shocked him, as he bolted to a sitting position and stared down at her in awe. His eyes were red-rimmed with fatigue. "Bliss?"

"I am all right. The duel? What happened? Was anyone harmed?"

Every bit of tension drained from Morgan's rugged face, leaving him at the verge of tears. Instead, he pulled her close, cradled her in his arms, and whispered over and over, "I love you, Bliss. I love you." Morgan deposited kisses upon her nose, her cheeks, and her chin, careful to avoid the throbbing injury on her brow. Eventually he paused, cupped her face in his hands, and gazed deeply into her eyes. "No one else was harmed. I beg your forgiveness, my sweet Bliss. I was wrongheaded about everything."

"Shh." She placed a shaky fingertip on his lips. "There is nothing to forgive." She could see the torture in his eyes, the love, the gratitude.

And it occurred to her . . . How soon would he go back to sea and leave her behind? How would she ever find the strength to let him go?

Chapter 35

THE days passed as Bliss recovered, nestled deep in her luxurious bed in Camberton House. Neville and Katarina came to visit with her, and it was obvious how deeply they cared for each other. Bliss could not have been happier for them.

The parade of Worthingtons was a constant, some arriving while others left. Bliss thanked Attie for her bravery and accepted the smuggled kitten with a wan smile. Regis was kind and helpful, keeping her room tidy and bringing fresh arrangements of garden flowers every day. He delivered a variety of delicious treats to spark her appetite, always with the utmost of efficient politeness. Once he paused on his way out.

"Miss Worthington . . ."

"Yes?"

"I beg your forgiveness for any harm I might have done to you. Lord Oliver . . ."

"I have already forgotten it, Regis. You were doing your duty."

She spent time with Katarina and her mother, Paulette. Bliss found Mrs. Beckham delightful, never once thinking to compare her voice with the screech of a monkey.

Each night, her husband would come to her bed and gently hold her through the night. She would fall asleep in the safety of his arms, and wake to his deep and peaceful breathing. They did not converse much. Bliss had questions, but she was afraid to learn the answers. Did Morgan feel the same way?

How odd it was to feel so much joy—and so much dread—all in the same moment. They had so little time left together. She could not bear to waste a moment of it in truths she did not wish to hear. Bliss knew her fate. She was married to a ship captain, and ships were meant to sail away.

MORGAN NOW KNEW what hell was like. He had spent many days there, not knowing whether Bliss would succumb to the infection that had spread through her wound. He watched her sleep. He paced the floor. He tended to her day and night. He argued with the physician as to her care.

He felt utterly helpless.

Only in the last few days had Bliss felt well enough to leave the confines of her bedchamber, and Morgan had been with her at each step. First came the short walks through the halls of Camberton House, then longer strolls through its gardens. She needed to rest often, but she remained cheerful and pleasant.

Yet Morgan sensed something was wrong. The bullet might have merely grazed her flesh, but somehow it had wounded her spirit. The prim determination he'd encountered that first night at Pryce House was gone, along with the fire he had seen in her eyes. She barely spoke to anyone, even him. Though he had cradled Bliss in his arms each night since the duel, she continued to feel a hundred miles away.

Was it the scar? He knew women could mourn the smallest of imperfections. Bliss insisted she did not mind, though she wore a bonnet to cover the healing line just above her temple where the bullet had glanced hard off her skull. Morgan assured her he would always see the scar as a badge of love and loyalty.

But as his wife got better, she got sadder. Morgan was at a loss.

He hoped beyond hope that the surprise he had in store for her this day would lift the veil. He kept his arm tight around her as they rode together in his brother's carriage. "Would you like to take another guess?"

She smiled faintly. "All right. Is my surprise alive?"

He laughed. "I think Attie is the only living thing we can manage at the moment. I found her trapped atop that painting of the tenth duke in the formal parlor. That kitten becomes more of a daredevil every day."

"Hence the name."

"Indeed." Morgan chuckled as he placed his lips to his wife's hair, breathing her in. She smelled of the rainwater she preferred for washing her blond locks, the flowers that had filled every inch of her recovery room, and the sweet familiarity of her warm, female skin.

He was determined to lift her melancholy. Katarina and Neville had assured him his surprise would do the trick.

God, how he hoped they were right.

Morgan and Bliss soon reached the docks of the Thames, and Bliss lifted her gaze out the window. It took only an instant for her to assess the situation. "I take it we're going aboard the *Selkie Maid*?"

"Not exactly, Mrs. Pryce." He helped her from the carriage and escorted her down the bustling West India wharf and through the tangle of crewmen, lightermen, and dockers. He felt a rush of pride when he first caught a glimpse of the brig's dual masts rising to pierce the sky. It promised to be a fine day to set sail.

He brought Bliss aboard, carefully showing her around the deck. His crew members were gallant—they'd better be—as Morgan had taken great pains to prepare them for Bliss's arrival.

Morgan spoke while they strolled the deck. "She's a hundred-foot schooner-brig, merchant class, with fore-aft-rigged sails. She carries twenty guns for protection, along with a crew of eighty. She's pristine, Bliss, the newest and most superbly made ship in the entire White Rose Line. She was a gift from Neville."

Neville, his brilliant little brother, who had finally taken on the full duties as the Duke of Camberton.

Bliss turned to him, her blue eyes wide with a multitude of questions.

"I earned her. She is my reward for many years of service to White Rose, for my contributions to our great success. And she is mine, free and clear."

Bliss smiled approvingly, the question still lingering in her expression. "That is wonderful, Morgan. Truly. It is well deserved and I am ever so happy for you."

"Come. Let me show you the captain's quarters." As Morgan led Bliss away, he glanced over his shoulder to nod to Seamus, his first mate. He would go forward with his plan.

Morgan prayed he was not making a mistake.

OF COURSE BLISS wished to see the captain's quarters. She supposed it was important, as the wife of a captain, to know where her husband would be living. It might help her imagine the details of his daily routine during his time upon the sea.

Which would be most of his time.

Perhaps eleven months out of twelve.

Three hundred thirty-three days out of each year, according to her calculations.

Bliss felt on the edge of weeping, which was terribly unexpected. She stopped herself. She would not ruin this moment with her selfishness. Morgan was obviously quite proud of his new ship and she could not diminish his delight with her blubbering.

She told herself it was quite simple, really. She was a grown woman. She loved Morgan Pryce and was married to him. Morgan Pryce was a ship captain. And sailing the sea was what brought him joy. So Bliss would accept her fate, and do so happily, because having only a piece of Morgan was far, far better than not having him at all.

But oh! She knew the loneliness would twist her heart every day and every night. Desolation choked her now, so much so that she could not bear another moment on this blasted boat!

Bliss wished to go home—immediately. She opened her mouth to say so.

Morgan cut her off with a devilish smile. "The tour is almost done, I promise."

"It . . . it is a very fine ship."

Morgan lowered his chin and gave her a doubtful glance. "She. And you've not asked me her name."

Bliss forced a small smile, thinking that she did not care to know the name of the lover who would get more of Morgan than she ever would.

Waiting . . . waiting . . . always waiting.

"Her name? Pray introduce me to your beautiful vessel."

They had reached the door to the captain's cabin by then. Morgan placed his fingers on the handle and paused, gazing into her eyes with so much tenderness it took her breath away. "I named her *Mor Forwyn*, Bliss. 'Tis Welsh for mermaid."

"Mermaid?" Bliss felt her lips part in surprise. "You named her—?"

"After my wife, yes."

"There is one thing I must know immediately, Bliss, before we talk of anything else. Please." Morgan lowered his

thick black lashes for an instant, as if gathering his composure. When he looked up again, he locked his intense blue
gaze with hers. "Why me? Why did you step in front of me
and not Neville?"

Oh.

Bliss returned the kitten to the floor and went to Morgan.
She stood before him, not once looking away from those
unguarded blue eyes of his. There was nothing to hide now,
no fear of what she might reveal in her gaze. Morgan was
correct—this was the question that needed to be asked, and
answered.

"Because I do not love Neville. I now realize I never did,
not really." She tilted her head. "I love you, Morgan Pryce."

He reached for her, and immediately she was wrapped
in his strong arms. Morgan tilted his head and then lowered
his mouth to hers, bestowing upon her lips the most gentle
of kisses, the most sincere and loving touch she had ever
felt. It occurred to her that this was the first kiss they had
shared since the ball, the night their passion ignited and
nearly burned down the world.

She had no time to properly respond, for Morgan opened
the door, scooped her off her feet, and carried her across the
threshold. He slowly spun, giving her a chance to see the
grand chamber from every angle. The walls were paneled
in rich wood, and sunlight streamed through the many windows. A large iron balcony jutted from the stern of the ship.
A big bed covered in extravagant silk took center stage.
There were carpets, comfortable seating, and a . . .

"A bathtub?" She stared at the huge copper bath, the very
one from Pryce House. Morgan set her down so that she
could move close enough to touch it. "But I thought you
bathed in the sea."

She turned at the touch of Morgan's fingertips on her
cheek. "I do bathe in the sea, but I prefer my men do not see
you do the same."

At that moment, Bliss noticed the room had two of everything: his and her writing desks, his and her chairs, two inkwells, even two large wardrobes.

"Mew."

Only one kitten.

"Attie?" Bliss raced to the orange tabby, which sat patiently on a hearth rug, and gathered it into her arms. "How did you get here?"

Her head began to spin. "But . . . ?" She went to a wardrobe and opened the door. It was filled with all manner of gowns, slippers and boots, and cloaks and bonnets, too. Bliss spun around to face Morgan, whose face was alight with pleasure at her surprise.

"Your friends Button and Cabot insisted that you lack for nothing on our journey."

Bliss suddenly felt the floor move beneath her. The ship was under way! Ever so slowly, understanding settled into Bliss's mind, and hope filled her heart. She could actually feel it untwist itself within her ribs. "You're taking me prisoner?"

He smiled. "It only seems fair."

"But—"

"Quickly!" Morgan grabbed her hand and clutched it in both of his, his eyes wide with alarm. "Come with me!"

He hurried Bliss from the cabin and back onto the deck of his new ship. Though she did not understand why, Morgan was determined to get her to the port side of the vessel without delay. Whatever his reason, it caused her no worry. Bliss's heart felt as if it were floating, flying high with the knowledge that her husband designed his ship with her in mind—his wife, his partner—and wherever he would go she would go with him.

That included being trundled across the deck, she supposed.

A brisk wind caught her bonnet, tugging it away from her face. By the time they reached the railing, Bliss's hair was flying wildly about her.

Morgan wrapped a comforting arm about her waist and

brushed the curls from her eyes. "I couldn't allow you to leave home without a proper sendoff, now, could I?" He turned her so that she faced the dock.

A small windblown crowd had assembled, a fanciful collection of dancing dresses, askew bonnets, and ruddy faces.

It was the Worthingtons. It was her family.

"Bliss!" Attie jumped up and down in a cloud of yellow silk, her arms flying wildly overhead. "Don't forget to bring me a present! A monkey would be lovely!"

Dear old Archie stood at the center of his clan, beaming proudly. He raised an upturned hand and began to orate, Shakespeare, no doubt, though most of his words faded in the wind.

"Give me thy hand; / Be pilot to me and thy places shall / Still neighbor mine. My ships are ready . . ."

Iris stood at her husband's side, waving her hand in a wide arc, the fringe of her oversize lace handkerchief dancing overhead. "Bon voyage, *ma chérie!*"

Next to Iris was Cas. He stood with a protective arm around Miranda and their baby, and all of them waved enthusiastically. Dade was next to Cas. He smiled, and when his gaze met Bliss's she saw a combination of pride, affection, and longing there. Her dear, sweet Dade—how he had fretted for her, watched over her, tried to keep her safe.

Bliss's heart was full to bursting.

And even the usually dour Lysander bowed at her, and even seemed to smile, though perhaps it was an illusion.

Bliss suddenly stilled. Who was that there, in the shadows behind the Worthingtons? An elegantly dressed woman peered from behind a stack of barrels. Her already tall frame was topped off by a dramatic pleated bonnet as pink as the inside of a seashell, her light curls framing her face. The lady nodded toward Bliss in approval, daintily clapping as she mouthed the word "Bravo!" in Bliss's direction.

Mama!

Never before had Bliss felt so beloved, so treasured. The girl who had feared being left behind was herself embarking on an adventure, with the blessings of those she cared for most.

"We shall miss you, dear!" That was Iris.

"Take care of her, Pryce, or else!"

Morgan laughed at Dade's one last attempt at intimidation. "I shall, my friend!"

They remained at the port side rail for another moment or two, until the faces of her beloved family blurred with distance.

Then Morgan tugged her away from the railing and led her back to the captain's cabin—their cabin!—with his large warm hand cradling hers.

"You truly thought of everything," Bliss said in awe. "Usually, that's my role."

He pulled her close, tucking her head beneath his chin. "I would prefer to be the one taking the bullets from now on."

She felt a shudder move through him.

"So close," he whispered into her hair. "So close to losing you forever."

She lifted her face to tell him that he would never lose her, but he stopped her words with a kiss. It didn't matter. They had all the time in the world now.

They had the world, and a ship to sail her in.

As Morgan continued to move his lips upon hers, she could not be certain which kind of kiss she preferred, or even if she could make such a comparison. In fact, she did not truly know how many types of kisses there might be, though she looked forward to a lifetime of careful study.

They made love in the beautiful bed, with the doors open to the sea, to the rhythm of the waves.

Chapter 36

MORGAN must have fallen asleep, for when he opened his eyes the diffuse evening light filled the cabin, burnishing the wooden paneling and gilding the naked flesh of his remarkable wife. He felt his lips twitch at the memory of that conversation he'd had with Neville, just before Morgan had set off to the chapel. His inebriated brother had used his hands to trace Bliss's shape in the air. Morgan had dismissed Neville's generosity.

As he now knew, his brother had underestimated.

Morgan carefully lifted Bliss from his chest and settled her into the pillows. He propped himself up on an elbow to gaze upon his sleeping wife. To describe Bliss as beautiful and simply leave it at that would be a grave injustice.

Certainly, her obvious loveliness was impossible to miss. Those sky blue eyes, that golden hair, and those outrageous curves had made Morgan a true believer in the bounty of heaven. And yet it was the woman inside who had captured his heart. It had been her determination, her generosity, her willingness, and her unwavering loyalty that had won his devotion.

The fact that she was handy in a back-alley brawl didn't hurt, either.

Morgan knew he was the luckiest bastard to ever walk the face of the earth.

She opened her eyes. Her gaze was guileless and clear, and he watched as a smile curled the edges of her mouth.

He lowered his lips near hers. "Hello, my captive."

She chuckled throatily. Truly, it was the most glorious sound Morgan had ever heard. To make Bliss laugh—to keep her smiling—would be his most sacred duty.

"Hello, my captain."

He lazily traced a finger down the middle of her breastbone, down the satin length of her belly and below. She shuddered with pleasure—another objective to add to his list of husbandly duties.

"I think perhaps this would be a good time to apologize to you, dear husband."

Morgan's fingers lifted from her silken skin. He looked up in surprise. "Apologize for what?"

"For tying you to the bedposts that night. That was wrong of me."

She had no idea how wrong.

"However did you free yourself?"

Morgan looked up to the cabin ceiling and shook his head, trying unsuccessfully to forget that night. "Button and Cabot came by with a gift. They found me in a rather . . . vulnerable state."

He watched his wife's eyes pop wide. Next, the tendons in her neck flexed and her cheeks caught fire. And then she laughed—Bliss guffawed in a way he never had guessed she was capable of—and buried her face into his shaking chest.

"Noooo," she moaned.

"Yes."

"I am so sorry, Morgan."

"You owe me."

"Anything." Bliss raised her face, tears gathered at the corners of her eyes from the force of her laughter.

"All right. I need an answer to a question." He brushed a fingertip across her adorable chin. "Are you quite certain you don't mind being wedded to a bastard?"

Bliss said nothing at first. She sat up, kneeling naked on the bed with an adorable lack of modesty, to address him with matter-of-fact earnestness. "Of course I don't mind. After all, my parents were never wed, at least—not to each other."

Morgan's eyes widened. "Ah. Well, that explains a few things."

She reached over and patted his chest. "My mama never wanted any other man after she fell in love with my papa, but she chose to go on with her life as Mrs. Bly—" Bliss stopped herself and produced a coy smile. "Anyway, I think George loves her still. I think he always will."

Mrs. Bly—?

George?

Morgan shot upright. He stared blankly, his mind buzzing with shock. It all made perfect sense now. The odd self-assurance, even in the face of scandal, the staggering wealth, the strange conversation Bliss had had at the ball with the Prince Regent.

"Wouldn't you rather leave that oaf and come live at the palace with me?"

And Morgan's exchange with Mrs. Blythe . . .

"Go home to your wife, Captain Pryce."

And his conversation with Dade.

"She is from a different branch of the Worthington family tree . . . the one that grows the golden apples."

Morgan blinked. "Oh my God."

His wife was the daughter of London's most notorious madam and the Prince Regent himself.

Bliss sighed.

"But . . . that means you're a princess! How does the world not know of your existence?"

"Mama and Papa never agreed on much, once their grand passion flamed out, but they did agree that I should live my life as an ordinary child in the ordinary world. My mother placed me with family as soon as I was born. I lived with Aunt Iris and Uncle Archie until matters grew too difficult for Iris after Worthington Manor burned down. Mrs. Dalyrymple had been a royal nanny once, but she hated London and had retired to the country. Mama liked her practical sensibilities." Bliss shrugged. "Thinking back, I enjoyed my life for the most part. I was lonely, yes, but Old Dally was very good to me and taught me to be a useful person instead of just an ornament."

Morgan gazed at her in puzzlement. "You scrubbed things and milked things, when you could have lived the pampered life of a princess!"

She gave a demure shake of her head. "No, Morgan. The palace already has a princess in residence. I'm a bastard. Just like you."

He remained in a silent stupor for several long moments. Not only had he been wrong about Bliss; he had been as spectacularly wrong as a man could get!

Morgan felt her soft touch on his shoulder, and when he glanced up he saw Bliss smiling. "You could not have known, my darling Morgan. You were merely protecting your brother."

But something else tugged at his mind. One more thing that didn't quite add up. And Morgan could not wait to hear the explanation for this one. "Then why . . . I don't quite understand . . . how did you get the last name Worthington?"

Bliss's fingers left his shoulder, brushed down the outside of his arm, dragged over his ribs, and snaked along the center of his belly. Then she slipped her warm and silky hand under the duvet and wrapped her fingers around him. "It's really best not to dwell on little things like the facts, my captain. We Worthingtons never do."

Epilogue

THE night had been wild with rough seas, and once again the tossing had caused Bliss to wake from a deep sleep. Her first foggy thoughts were that they were in full sail, heading north and east, on a course for England. Weather permitting, they would return a full month before the wedding.

Bliss reached over to Morgan's side of the bed. Her fingers encountered the cool surface of the bedclothes instead of the warmth of her husband's body.

He was not there.

Bliss sat up, immediately feeling the wind in her hair. A quick glance informed her that the balcony doors were flung wide, and Morgan stood at the railing under the off-and-on moonlight, his fingers gripping the iron.

What a dashing figure he cut, with his too-long dark hair alive in the West Indies wind, the bare muscles of his back and arms, his knee breeches carelessly buttoned low on his hips.

Sometimes when Bliss looked at her husband, she could barely breathe. This was one of those times.

She silently slipped from the bed, reaching for a long shawl that would cover her nakedness from neck to knees. She tiptoed toward him, quietly as she was able, but he turned before she could surprise him.

His smile glowed white in the moonlight. Morgan tugged Bliss to his body and kissed her, hot and tender. This kiss, this man, was all she wanted. It had been ever so wonderful not to be alone anymore. She would never be alone again.

Bliss raised her arms around his neck, offering herself to him, deeper . . . wider . . . hungrier. She melted in the heat of her husband's passion, so familiar to her now, so much a part of the woman she had become.

A gust of wind caught the edges of her shawl, but Bliss did not bother to adjust it. The fabric slipped from her bare shoulders, separated, and pulled open at her breasts. It fell away entirely then, and she felt the cashmere puddle at her feet.

When Morgan chuckled it tickled her lips. He pulled away and looked down at her. "See? Even the sea prefers you this way."

Bliss smiled, so comfortable in the ebb and flow of their love, so certain that the winds had put her on the only course she would ever need. "Do you remember, Captain Pryce, when I claimed you would make a perfectly adequate husband for someone, just not for me?"

He frowned quite dramatically. "Can't say that I recall. Of course, I was traumatized by the dagger at my throat."

Bliss laughed. "Yes, well, that was quite necessary, I'm afraid. I had to wrest my virtue from your greedy hands."

Morgan nodded, pursing his lips. "Of course. And were you successful?"

"I failed miserably, thank goodness. But what I said about you not being adequate . . ."

"Yes?"

"I was correct. You're not adequate."

His dark eyebrows slanted.

"You are perfect, Morgan Pryce. You are the perfect husband for me."

Morgan lowered his mouth to his luscious, loving wife, aware of the irony. He had lived his life believing that all he ever needed was a ship and the sea.

When what he truly needed was Bliss.

How very unexpected.

MEANWHILE, AT CAMBERTON HOUSE . . .

MRS. PAULETTE BECKHAM was born for this. The woman Neville now addressed as "Mummy Beckham" took to planning a Christmas Society wedding the way a shark took to feeding on a school of *Dicentrarchus punctatus.*

The guest list had swelled to more than two hundred, which was fine with Neville. He required only one person at his wedding in order to be deliriously happy, and that was the woman he now fondled with his left hand, Miss Katarina Beckham, soon to be the Duchess of Camberton.

And, of course, his dear brother and sister-in-law, who would be returning home in time for the festivities.

"Have you looked at the seating chart, Katarina? Do you have any changes?"

"It is perfect just the way it is, Mummy. Genius, in fact."

Paulette walked just feet in front of Neville and Katarina through the halls of Camberton. As usual, she was so preoccupied with wedding details that she paid no mind to anything else. Neville began chuckling.

Katarina's eyes shone with mischief when she glanced his way. "Don't you care about the seating arrangements, Neville?"

He shook his head and tightened his grip on her bottom. "This is the only seating I give a fig about," he whispered.

They tried not to laugh, but it was difficult.

Katarina raised her delicious mouth to him and whispered, "Kiss me again, you appalling beast!" Neville obliged, and yanked her against the side of his body, even as they continued their stroll.

"You drive me positively wild," he murmured in her ear.

"I don't think I can wait until the wedding," she gasped.

Neville feared he was on the brink of sporting an obvious erection. He heard the sound of Mummy Beckham's voice, and the concern vanished.

"Well, at least we needn't concern ourselves with where to seat Lord Oliver!" Mummy Beckham tittered, as she often did when mentioning his name. "For he shall be dining with the dockworkers on your wedding day and every day after that for the rest of time!"

Once the duel had ended and Bliss was being cared for by the physician, Morgan and Neville sat down to untangle their so-called uncle's web of lies and manipulations. The brothers decided to give Oliver Danton a choice—life in prison or life as a dockside laborer in Barbados. He chose the latter. Oliver now spent his days in the employ of Sunbury Plantation, loading and stacking sugar barrels onto White Rose Line ships bound for the four corners of the British Empire.

Morgan had written to Neville recently, saying he had spotted Oliver on a run to Barbados. He said their former uncle possessed robust health and the foulest of tempers.

It had been excellent news.

In other excellent news, Mummy Beckham had put Sunbury in Katarina's name, which had always been her intention, and the plantation was to become part of the Camberton holdings after the wedding. Mummy would continue to monitor operations from England, a job for which she would be handsomely rewarded. Though Neville greatly admired Paulette, he was pleased that she had decided to restore a spacious country house in her home county of Buckinghamshire, where she would reside when not in London.

Neville looked forward to some privacy.

A great deal of privacy.

He nuzzled his nose into the curve of Katrina's neck and inhaled the warm, sweet aroma of her skin. Then he cupped one of her perfectly pert breasts in his palm. "If we were wed, I would beg you to meet me in the stables tonight."

She sighed longingly. "Where I should ride you like the stallion you are."

"Whatever are you talking about back there?"

Katarina and Neville separated quickly. By the time Mummy glanced their way, they walked side by side with the utmost decorum, smiling politely at her inquiry.

"Neville invited me for a ride later."

"Oh, how lovely! The weather is a bit unpredictable, so be sure to wear your bonnet." She turned around again.

"And nothing else," Neville whispered.

"What was that?"

"Nothing, Mummy!" Katarina smacked Neville's arm. "What were you saying about the weather?"

"You know, my old bones still haven't quite grown accustomed to this English climate, and I sometimes . . ."

Neville spied a closet between the family parlor and what had been the old duke's private study. He grabbed Katarina's hand and dragged her inside, immediately pressing her back against the bare wall. He held her by the hips and devoured her with his mouth—such sweet heat, such torture! The encounter lasted only seconds and did nothing to slake his desire, but he knew he should not press his luck.

Neville tugged her out into the well-lit hall once more. They scurried to catch up to Mummy, who was still finishing her thought.

". . . but I find it is the combination of cold and damp that is most distressing, and . . ."

Katarina gave Neville a sideways glance. They both had

to stifle their laughter. In that instant, Neville knew he would never grow tired of her lovely face, those fiercely intelligent dark eyes, her kind heart, and her wickedly playful behavior. And to think, this remarkable woman was about to become his wife, his duchess, his lifelong best friend.

Indeed, fortune had smiled upon him. Overcome, he reached for her hand and cradled it in his.

"Now, now, you two! Don't get carried away!" Mummy Beckham had spun around and now wagged a finger in the direction of their handholding. They pulled apart obediently.

"Be patient, my darlings." Paulette faced forward again and resumed walking. "As I was saying, I am still uncertain about the cakes. After all, this shall be the wedding of the year! So should we offer a lemon poppy seed along with a chocolate? Or perhaps the nougat almond cake with . . ."

Neville placed his lips to Katarina's ear. "We're going to have an extraordinary life together, you and I."

She nodded softly, reaching up to caress his cheek. "Indeed, we are."

"I love you, Kat."

"And I you, Neville. Forever."

AND BACK AT WORTHINGTON HOUSE . . .

IRIS DARED NOT to change her rhythm, continuing to brush Atalanta's long ginger hair in repetitive strokes, making a bit more progress on the tangles with each pass.

The youngest—and most combative—of Iris's children had decided that today was the day she would allow her mother to give her long hair a thorough brushing.

Attie fiddled with her slingshot in silence as Iris dragged the boar bristles through the strands. Only a few times had Attie hissed in discomfort. On those occasions, her eyes would flash a warning in the mirror. Iris merely smiled back.

She wondered why Attie had suddenly acquiesced. Since

the day the child was born, everyone in the family had struggled to perform even the most basic grooming on Atalanta's hair. Her screeching refusals were legendary.

Iris wondered if it was her age. She was almost fourteen now. She wore proper dresses regularly, sometimes over hidden breeches, but still it was an important development. Perhaps Attie was aware that she was maturing, approaching the day on which she would become a woman.

Iris concentrated on gathering the thick hair into a single handful. Perhaps, if she could distract Attie long enough, she could even put it up into a chignon atop her head. "Shall we add a bit of satin ribbon?"

Attie looked up and frowned, causing Iris to assume she had asked for too much. Oh well. Tomorrow was another day.

But then Attie nodded. "I don't see why not."

Iris's hands froze. "You don't?"

"I can always remove it if I find it does not suit me. It's not as if a ribbon is permanent."

Iris stifled her smile and went back to brushing.

"So, Iris, I've been wondering about something."

"Mmm-hmm?"

Attie fiddled with a tiny bow on the front of her dress. "Who's next?"

"Who's next for what, darling?"

"You know . . . which Worthington should we match next? So far we've found good homes for Orion, Castor, Calliope, Elektra, and Bliss. Whose turn is it now?"

Iris hummed in thought. "That's a good question, dearest. Who do we have left?"

"Daedalus, Lysander, and Pollux, of course."

Iris pulled up on the thick bundle of hair and began to pin it in place. "Of course. So, do we begin with the easiest match to make? Or the Worthington most in need of companionship? Or perhaps we should start with the one whose match will require the greatest amount of time and effort?"

Attie met her mother's gaze in the mirror. "If you put it that way, I suppose we have quite a decision to make."

"Indeed."

Attie set her slingshot on the dressing table. "Well, if you ask me, Pollux is in most need. He ran away when Miranda chose Cas over him. I think his heart may still be broken."

"You might be right about that, dear." Iris was amazed—somehow Attie had not complained about the position of her chignon. Iris set about placing the last few pins.

"But if Poll's heart is broken, he might not be ready for love," Attie continued. "He might be so afraid of getting hurt again that he would resist even if we found a most excellent match."

"Oh my, yes. That is a very wise observation, dear. Perhaps we should give him more time to heal. So, who will it be?"

"Dade is the obvious choice." Attie absently patted her hair. Still, there was no shrieking. "I should think someone as handsome, brave, and honorable as Dade would be easy to match. I can't see anyone not falling in love with him."

"Ah, that is true, but what will it take for him to fall in love? He holds everyone to the highest of standards, especially himself. Finding a woman who can provoke Dade's admiration might prove to be a challenge."

Attie sighed. "Then that leaves only Lysander." She said nothing more.

Iris stayed quiet as well.

The silence stretched on for a long moment, during which time Iris had begun to tie the ribbon in place. Still no complaining.

In truth, Iris did not know what to say about Lysander. She loved her brave boy dearly, and her heart ached for him. But she worried he might be too damaged to marry, no longer even capable of giving and receiving love from his family. She desperately wished happiness for her taciturn son, but she knew it was almost too much to hope.

Attie broke the silence. "I propose we make Lysander our priority, then. It could take years to find his match, and it will probably be a great deal of bother, and in the meantime Poll might become more amenable. We might even come across someone special enough for Dade in the process."

"Now, that is a fine plan, Atalanta." She tidied up a few stray hairs and patted her on the shoulders. "There we are. Now, don't you look lovely?"

Attie turned her head to and fro, poking at the chignon and fiddling with the ribbon. "It is not terrible, I suppose."

Iris saw her little girl try not to smile at her own reflection. Atalanta Worthington would one day become an exceptionally beautiful woman, perhaps during the time it would take for them to find matches for Lysander, Poll, and Dade.

Iris pressed her cheek to Attie's ear. "Aren't we forgetting someone, my dear?"

Atalanta wrinkled her nose.

"There is one more Worthington—you, Attie."

She dropped eye contact with Iris and stared at herself in the mirror. Attie raised a hand to her cheek. Iris watched her daughter in fascination, noting how her scowl had transformed into a look of speculation.

"Yes," Attie said matter-of-factly. "There is me."